Praise for Iola O

"You'd have to search far and wide to find a voice as distinctive as that of G. M. Monks', a character as unique and appealing as Iola O, or a sense of humor as quirky. This highly original story of a woman's determination to fly planes and break out of the confines of prejudice will leave your own spirits soaring." — Céline Keating, author of *Layla* and *Play for Me*

"Southern storytelling that will totally captivate you. In this page-turner, the interactions of irresistibly flawed yet resilient characters shine through the darkness of prejudice and bias." — Alice Wilson-Fried, author of *Outside Child: A Novel of Murder and New Orleans*

iola O

iola O

a novel

G.M. Monks

Bink Books

Bedazzled Ink Publishing Company • Fairfield, California

978-1-945805-95-0 paperback

Cover Design
by

Sappling
Studio

Bink Books
a division of
Bedazzled Ink Publishing Company
Fairfield, California
http://www.bedazzledink.com

To my husband, John Kiefer,
for his unwavering support and love

Acknowledgements

Many thanks to Anami S., Beth Franks, Mary Jane S., Nicole Simonsen, Patricia D., Sabina Virgo, and Sue for your suggestions, your encouragements, and for your honest appraisals. You were all immensely helpful. To Bedazzled Ink for believing in me. To the person who didn't want his name mentioned here, but spent hours with me sharing his knowledge about planes, piloting planes, and small airports. To my father who probably gave me the writing gene for he tried his hand at it, but never got published. To my mother for encouraging my interest in the arts.

Pilgrim, Tennessee
1931

Iola Boggs

Chapter 1

THE HOUSE WAS calm for no one else was awake. Out the window, the dawn's light had just touched the treetops. But my mind was a mile away where there was a whole different world. Nothing could discourage me. Not if ordered to remove a dead rat from the woodpile, not if berated, not if I got only bread and water for breakfast. Having a need was exciting because I knew I could fill it as soon as I dealt with the obstacles—if I let go of my pride.

When a whippoorwill sang, Ethyl Lou stirred and got herself up. Before long, everyone was. Papa was the last. All morning, I did my chores—sweeping, mopping, rubbing Mama's swollen feet, washing, dumping the garbage in the smelly trash pile, and saying my yes ma'ams. Then I told Ethyl Lou—using my most polite voice—"I'm going neighboring."

But it wasn't cousin Alma Bevil I needed to visit. It was her new blue-glass radio with exotic voices that had captured my imagination several times before. It was President Hoover talking about the Hoover Dam project. It was the mayor of Chicago. The king of England. It all sounded good—their names, their ear-catching stories. I especially liked Amelia Earhart talking about flying planes. I loved her voice. What did she look like? Was she tall? She had to be smart. Was flying like heaven? I imagined flying far away from eensy Pilgrim.

Radio talk was different—the rhythm, accent, the words themselves, words I never heard before. Soon it dawned on me Pilgrim folks often ran words together. And if someone was speaking in tongues, their words ran together like they had melted in rain. Mama was good at it. People claimed she was a saint talking with God in his own private language. But if someone asked me my opinion and said I could be honest, and wouldn't get punished, I would've said, *If Mama's a saint, she's a mean, cruel one.*

Now the radio people—that is, the ones I liked—finished most every one of their words, clear and succinct. It was crisp talk. It said you were going someplace important, having no interest in living your life with a mean saint in a hollow nestled between steep hills, good mostly for hunting wild meat. Except, eating the pawpaws growing by the creeks was fun, and fishing for crawdads with my brother, Buck. Very possibly, if I could learn crisp talk, I might not live my whole life in Pilgrim. So at age fourteen, I made plans.

After doing Saturday chores, I walked, wanted to run, out the old front door, down the two stone steps, turned a bit to the right and took thirty quick steps, past the garden that got a half day of sun, to where the path to town opened up. I headed across the footbridge over Short Creek swollen with rain, past wild azaleas, skunk cabbage, and the woods full of trilliums. In no time, I was on the wide dirt road, avoiding puddles and mud, walking a mile to where the hollow widened and Pilgrim came into view.

It had a feed store that smelled like hay, the one-room schoolhouse with sixty desks, the town square with one bench, where if a boy and a girl sat down together, they had to sit a foot apart. No kissing, except holding hands was okay. There were two magnolia trees, the general store, post office, the church that got noisy Sunday mornings and Wednesday evenings with singing, holy rolling, and talking in tongues, and Reverend Spence preaching like Jesus was present in the holy flesh. The meetinghouse sat off, behind the post office. Buck told me some of the boys would get drunk there on Friday nights. Not that I ever saw them—not being allowed.

I picked up my pace at the road just before town. It went off to the right, where I skipped past the orange daylilies, and on to the Bevils'.

Soon I was sitting down with plump Alma with her thick braid hanging down her back, listening to the magic box. I liked the name *radio*, the knobs that turned the dial that changed the stations, and the glass tubes in the back that lit up and captured voices out of the air. I spent as many afternoons as possible in her kitchen with its big window and pretty blue curtains with ruffles on the bottom. She had soft cushions on every chair. Sometimes I lost myself in her green easy chair that felt like Pilgrim's lap of luxury.

Cousin Alma said, "Iola, you visiting, it's like I have a daughter finally and not just six sons. You're always welcome." What with the friendly words, often a corn fritter, or a pancake with wild blackberry jam, always a glass of sweet-tasting water, I wanted to visit all day. On my way home, I practiced crisp talk one sentence at a time.

One Saturday, I was late getting home. Papa had told me earlier that day to be back before dusk. My big family had already sat down at the supper table. It was mostly potatoes that night. Papa and the older boys each got two slices of meat, and the rest of us got nibbles. The little ones got the last of the milk.

"Late, plus she not do her chores good this morning," Ethyl Lou said.

I knew I had. The first thing come to mind was to use my crisp talk to get back at my bossy big sister. "How was your day today? Mine was definitely fine." I spoke each syllable as clear as my favorite radio folks. Then with tightly closed lips and my tongue pressed against my teeth, I managed a smile.

Friend looked at me cockeyed. Cecil almost fell out of his chair laughing. Ethyl Lou elbowed me and said, "Shush. You loony girl."

"What ailing you, child? The devil get to you?" Mama's molasses tongue wasn't asking a question. It was making an accusation. Everyone knew that.

I coughed, sputtered. Face and neck felt hot. I said, "I was just practicing for a speech I got to give in school. Best way to practice is overtalk. It's what I hear."

"She hearing things," Sledge Jr. said with meat in his mouth.

"Heard it in school." My eyes darted over to him.

"Overtalk?" Mama leaned back in her chair. Shook her head in slow motion.

"It's talking the same thing but not the same way; it's using different words. That way, you won't forget. Gets stuck in your memory good." I had made up the word *overtalk* on the spur of the moment. It was kind of like what I heard in school, so it wasn't really a lie.

"You talking nonsense," Ethyl Lou said. "Never heard that in school." Buck shot me a supportive glance.

"I know what overtalk is. It's talking uppity," Cecil said.

"Problem's her name. Look at Uncle Arvo—no one's as oddball as him. A bad name messes you up," Friend said. "Think about it. I'm the nicest and got the nicest name."

Mama paid no attention to Friend. She narrowed one eye at me. "So you giving a speech about us at the supper table?"

"Just figuring ways you can talk different so I be sure to remember my speech. Like maybe . . . how you might say howdee different."

"Nothing wrong with howdee." Lucine wiped her plate clean and licked her cute little fingers.

"That's not what I mean."

"Well, what you talking about?" Maude didn't even look at me.

"Well, I don't cotton to different ways. You hear me?" Mama narrowed both eyes.

"Yes, Mama."

"She in school too much," Sledge Jr. said.

Papa said nothing. He smelled of liquor.

AFTERWARD, I USED crisp talk only when I was by a side creek in a ravine, a safe mile from the house. It was odd—talking to the trees, so I made a joke out of it. While sitting by a pawpaw tree, I whispered, "Is this where you grew up? . . . (Yes, and I never left home) . . . I hope to leave home . . . (Wish I could)." I laughed so hard at a tree wanting to leave home I keeled over. Then I cried. I knew why, but I couldn't think about it or I'd cry all day. Crying never helped. I'd just get slapped, so I sat up and asked, "Would you like to know about Amelia Earhart? . . . (Love to) . . . Her nickname's Meeley . . . (That's silly) . . . When she was a kid, she made a ramp going from the top of a shed to the ground and she slid down it in a box. She said it felt like flying but she got hurt . . . (Where'd you hear that?) . . . On the radio . . . (Honey, that's interesting, but may I ask why you want to leave home?)" I touched my lips to the pawpaw and whispered, "Because something awful happened, but I can't talk about it or I'll get beaten hard. Sorry for crying . . . (When did it happen?) . . . Three years ago. Can't say no more." I sat there awhile, thinking Amelia Earhart would've approved of my syllables.

When Mama heard a rumor that Cora, Alma Bevil's second cousin by marriage, sang in a nightclub with a colored girl in Chicago, she told all us kids not to neighbor over there. But I had once met Cora and her smile melted stone with joy. She had put her arm around me and said, "You'll go far." Later when I heard her singing, it seemed like the finest thing a human could do. It was obvious I had met perfection, and anything she did had to be good and righteous. Soon after, following my unbridled instincts, on my way home from school and lagging behind my siblings, I popped into the Bevils, and said, "Cousin Alma, I'll do your ironing every Saturday afternoon—for a nickel." She offered me three, a cup of tea with cream and sugar, and called me sweetie.

I told Mama, "Cousin Alma said she'll pay me three nickels to iron for her. I give you the nickels." Next Saturday after doing my chores, I went neighboring again—ironing, planning, dreaming as I listened to the radio, and hoping to hear Amelia Earhart talking about planes and where she flew, how long it took, what it felt like. Was she ever scared? I was pleased I put one over on Mama. From that day forward, I decided I could nudge my life to what I wanted, if I figured out what pieces went together. That might be easy because one time, Buck dragged home a jigsaw puzzle he found in someone's trash. I put it together in no time flat, except for the three missing pieces.

"Anyone can do that," Ethyl Lou had said.

Just to show her, I turned the pieces over to the blank side and finished it almost as quick.

"That be the way the devil put together a puzzle." Mama took it and threw it in the fire.

I GOT GOOD at planning my future. I finished easy ninth grade, did tenth, did my ironing at Alma's, visited Aunt Pleasant and Uncle Dillard the few times possible because they lived in Chattanooga and were awful nice and let me read their newspapers. I saw a picture of Amelia Earhart—she had freckles and modern short hair. Modern was the best. The newspaper said she was the sixteenth woman to get a pilot's license. Sixteenth? Could I ever do that?

Knowing it would never happen in Pilgrim, I helped Buck fix the broken-down car he got for free, because if we got it running he promised me a ride to Chattanooga. I finished eleventh grade, finished twelfth, and then graduated at the head of my five-student class. I said goodbye to Alma, gave her a bag of the best pawpaws as a token of my gratitude. We both said we'd miss each other.

THE NIGHT BEFORE leaving home, under a black sky laden with stars, Papa whispered, "Good luck," and gave me a hug. Then something in me heard the stars, the pawpaws, trilliums, the whippoorwills, crawdads swimming in the creeks, and cousin Alma all calling. Like the air had shimmered them. Some doubt about leaving slipped in.

Back in the house, Mama said, "She's going to lose her soul."

Ethyl Lou hissed between her teeth, then said, "Already has and she better not come back unless she on her knees."

With his sergeant voice, Sledge Jr. said, "She'll be back by year's end, begging forgiveness."

It was hard hearing them talk nasty about me, like I wasn't around. My stomach got knotted up, causing me to not sleep well that night. In the morning, my doubt disappeared. With my anxious, excited head held high and carrying one small suitcase (held together with an old rope, donated by Alma), a letter of recommendation from my schoolteacher, and two dried leaves from the pawpaw tree that wanted to leave home, I got into Buck's old car he finally fixed. He drove me to Chattanooga, dropped me off at Aunt Pleasant and Uncle Dillard's, and hugged me goodbye. He said he was driving on to Florida to stick his feet in the ocean and find a cute girl. I was eighteen.

While hoping my stomach would unknot, I found a job as a secretary because a job was part of my plans. It was nice that Uncle Dillard charged me hardly any rent. First thing was to save my money to buy my own radio. Aunt Pleasant said I could've listened to hers. She didn't understand—I needed my own. Second thing was save for a plane ride. It cost twelve dollars for a twenty-minute ride, which was a lot. When Uncle Dillard realized what I wanted, he said he'd pay for it.

I was beside myself climbing in the four-seater plane, feeling it take off, and seeing the ground fall away as the plane climbed higher. Soon Chattanooga lay before me in one big swoop. It seemed to go on forever. The crisscross of streets, the houses, the roofs, cars, the green hills far away. Someone's yellow balloon floated up in the sky. I floated. Never before. At that moment, Pilgrim and its moonshining violence and fear of change evaporated like a summer's snowflake. I was glued to the window, on top of happy, wanting to fly planes. The noisy engine vibrated my seat. It was my first time sitting on a vibrating seat. Then Uncle Dillard's hand caressed my inner thigh, and he leaned into me. Lust-filled big blue eyes. He'd never done anything like that before. Not knowing what to do, I turned away and talked real loud and edgy, hiding fear. "Look at the church, look, the people—like little ants. That's a fancy rooftop. So steep. Is that the city hall? Uncle Dillard, look at the farm far away. The rows of corn. Yellow. Look. See the creek. Silvery. Look out your window, Uncle Dillard. Look." I moved as far from him as I could, trying to make an inch a mile.

He removed his hand. When we landed, he looked shamefaced and mumbled, "Sorry."

I forgave him but moved out of his house, saying I didn't want to be a burden on them (not wanting to hurt anyone's feelings). Sometime later, Aunt Pleasant said she didn't like traveling on a train with Uncle Dillard, because all the motion and new scenery gets him too romantic. I knew what that meant.

I rented a room—single bed, thin mattress, a dresser, one wobbly chair, three clothes hooks on the wall, each with three coat hangers (more than I needed and worth a chuckle), one loose window, hot in the summer, cold in the winter—real cheap at old Mrs. Felton's in exchange for cleaning her house every Saturday. It was nice having a little wall mirror, where I combed my hair right and proper before heading to work, thirteen blocks away. It wasn't a bad walk on nice days. In six months' time, my words were crisp, and my stomach wasn't so knotted.

IT WAS GOOD being tall until I realized it put off the few boys I liked. They wanted short, ladylike girls. Now I was fair-looking enough (strong cheekbones, eyes okay, just-right lips, a nose not too little and not too big, well-arched eyebrows—my opinion) and was especially frugal with money—my opinion. Any spare change, I'd deposit it in my savings to earn interest. My bankbook lay in my dresser drawer under well-mended hand-me-downs. If there was a penny on the sidewalk, I'd slip it in my pocket. Pennies added up over a year or two could buy a book about flying.

Once I found a dollar on the street—enough for two weeks' worth of bus fare. Then I saw a man wearing a pinstriped suit with his eyes targeting me. He tipped his fedora hat, winked twice, and did some lip movements.

Tipping his hat was okay, but not the other stuff.

"Like them legs, Sugar. You show me more?" He winked again and touched himself.

I dropped the dollar on the ground and walked on with my surest stride.

ONE TIME AT my first job, my boss, who walked slow with a cane and chewed tobacco all day, told me, "Honey, you must live on air and willpower, even when there's a paycheck sitting in your little pocketbook. I've never seen someone never spend money."

"Mr. Semson, there are things I want to do."

"And just what is that?"

"Learn to fly a plane." Just saying those words aloud pleased me.

"A girl fly a plane? That's pure crazy." He laughed, showing no concern for manners. "Honey, you need to get married and have ten children." At least he apologized after realizing he spit black tobacco juice on my white blouse when he laughed all openmouthed. Later that day, he slammed a stack of papers down hard on my desk, startling me. I jumped out of the way, and he laughed.

I sucked it up as a loss when the stain didn't come out. I never told him. And I never told him having ten kids wasn't one of my goals. I hadn't even thought much about marriage, one way or other. But I had dreamed a lot about learning to fly, in spite of Uncle Dillard almost ruining my first plane ride. Flying would take me as far from Pilgrim as I wanted. And if I got a job as a pilot that'd be better than heaven.

I made my pennies go twice as far, and sometimes thrice. Not soon enough, I climbed into the cockpit of a two-seater, one-engine plane and took my first thirty-minute flying lesson with skinny, bald-headed Leon Connell. It was amazing how I was able to ignore all his cursing, but he knew airplanes. He showed me how to line up straight on the obscene-curse-word runway and how to use the curse-word throttle and rudder to control the blasphemous-curse-word plane, how to taxi down the smutty-curse-word runway and, when I got up to speed, how to add up-elevator and how to maintain a simple-curse-word gradual ascent. I knew I'd never forget the feeling of the plane lifting off the ground. It was so good I feared if I got a job as a pilot I'd die of joy. Up in the air, Mr. Connell said I reminded him of his little sister and he was impressed that, in the preflight class, I already knew about the forces in a climb—thrust, drag, lift, and weight, and why a plane can actually fly. I didn't tell him I twice read a book about flying. He said I asked the smartest-curse-word questions and I'd become a curse-word-good pilot. What would my life have been like if I had a father like him?

Philadelphia, Pennsylvania
1941

Jim Lewis

Chapter 2

KEEPING MY EYES fixed on the exit door, I walked out of the induction office, worried everyone was staring at me. With my chin up, shoulders back, nervous hands at my sides, I tried not to clench my teeth and look upset. Would others know I was just rated a reject 4-F due to flat feet, hernia, history of tuberculosis, and was my mother's only support? Problem was, I wasn't missing a leg, wasn't blind or deaf. I looked healthy enough for war. What would I say if people asked? As soon as I stepped outside in the bright sunlight, I paused, took a deep breath, and tried to look calm. After walking a noisy block, I stopped at the street corner and waited for a letup in the traffic. A cold wind blew some trash across the busy street. It was good I had dressed warm.

Two men stood nearby. Their breath condensed in the freezing air. Both were clean-shaven and muscular. Short haircuts. The blond one had a deep voice, broad shoulders, a movie-star face. The taller one wore a heavy jacket; he blew his breath into his big hands, stubby fingers. He asked his buddy, "You ready for war?"

The buddy said, "Ready as ever."

"What about living in foxholes? What if you get trench foot?"

"Not something a soldier thinks about," the buddy said.

"Yeah. Let's drink a beer."

I wanted to join their conversation, but what could a reject say? *Wish you the best? Don't get killed? I'll be thinking of you?* It was troubling how my life had taken another bad turn. I walked down a side street. Coward. Yellowbelly. I could have not said I was my mother's only support and if I was killed she'd have no one. Tuberculosis? I could have lied. It was years ago. I would've served. Coward. It's awful to lose confidence. In some ways, I never had it, except in chemistry classes. Easy straight A's.

I passed by a grade school where kids were enjoying recess. A boy hit another one and kicked him. There was yelling, and a crowd of boys gathered to watch. Even an ignorant girl watched; she probably had ignorant parents.

Their aggression triggered a memory of being beaten by a bully in sixth grade. I had suffered bruises, a cut lip, two black eyes, and a fear for my life. Despite the pain, I had staggered home worrying my mother would chastise me for the blood on my shirt. But she cleaned me up, kissed and bandaged me, and put me to bed.

By the time I got to the end of the street, dread overcame me. My heart beat fast, my sweaty hands trembled. My mouth turned dry as cotton, and my head tightened like it would explode. I wanted to run. From whom? The childhood memory? The schoolboys fighting? The two rugged-looking men heading off to war? The unwanted attraction I felt for the blond man? I was losing control. So I didn't look like a fool, I forced myself to walk at a reasonable pace to the trolley stop. Each step, I counted. Lost count; started over. It took forever.

When the trolley arrived, there was an empty seat by an old man wearing a tweed jacket and a wool scarf. I liked tweed. Why tweed? Why not? Everything seemed like dumb questions with dumber answers. To better share his seat, the polite man moved over; his wrinkled hands shook. Another trembler sitting in the same seat didn't help. My heart was still beating fast. What good was I? Thirty-three years old, looking fit but dying of fright, clenched teeth, armpits sweaty, and smelling of fear. Not wanting the trembler or anyone else to notice, I got off and walked the rest of the way home. Were people looking at me, recognizing my 4-F status? I hated my fear.

If I was like this in Philadelphia how could I ever make it through a war? It was good I wasn't talking to the army now, for they'd reject me just on mental reasons. I ordered myself to calm down, to get some self-respect. The freezing air stung my nose, so I breathed through my mouth. I jammed my cold hands in my pockets and dug my fingernails into my palms. The pain gave me a focus. I made myself notice things—lace curtains in a window; a well-groomed poodle peeing on a tree, the pee condensing in the freezing air; a child crying; an old man bundled up in a thick wool jacket, cap, scarf, and baggy wool pants walking slow; an icy section of sidewalk that made me walk slower than the old man so I didn't slip and fall like a fool; a store owner standing in his doorway, aloof and warm. It all seemed unconnected.

Why was I a jackass? I should have worn earmuffs; my ears were cold. I took a deep breath and cursed my fear. Coward. But I knew I would have served, if they had let me. I would've followed orders, lived in a dirty, smelly foxhole, witnessed death, taken good care of my gun—oiled it daily. Yes, I would've killed the enemy—the bastards, swine, swine offal. Fuck the damn devils. Damn. Calm down, jackass. Damn devils. Thieves. I had no idea how to kill. Or what one does afterward. Do you say a prayer for the soul? Should you pray for an enemy's soul? Do more killing? Can an enemy go to heaven? What if he was heroic? I wasn't breathing. I took a breath.

By the time I got home, my anger had whipped my fear. Seeking solitude, I walked to my room and pulled down the window shade. I changed my smelly shirt. Warming my hands by the radiator helped, but I was exhausted. I looked in the mirror. "You're a handsome young man. All the girls will want you," my father once told me. I had managed a smile because I knew he was complimenting me. I didn't dare say it was boys I helplessly admired. Like Eddie who lived around the corner. It was good he moved away—such a temptation. And young Mr. Atkins, my schoolteacher.

With my elbows on my knees, head in my hands, I sat on my bed, barely noticing the good smells coming from the kitchen. I wanted to lie down and pull the covers up, but that's what a milksop would do. Shameful day. Not something to talk about, but I was good at keeping things to myself. Isn't that something to be proud of? Doing what's needed in life. Functioning. Paying the bills. The two men high on patriotism would soon be on the battlefield, throwing grenades and killing the enemy. May they come home in one piece. Welcome home, soldiers. Heroes. I stood up, and saw my reflection in the mirror. Salute. Coward, relax your hands. Get rid of the strain in your face. My smile looked stupid. Stupid. My hair needed combing. I corrected my shirt that I had misbuttoned.

Mother called, so I walked downstairs into her warm, clean kitchen. I had painted it a pale yellow for her. She was cooking at the stove (a new one thanks to me) and offered me a taste of her meat filling for a pie. It was delicious, giving me fleeting comfort. I shared the news about being classified a 4-F. She, Elizabeth Clarinda Lewis, was a petite woman, with a graceful neck, cornflower blue eyes, and gently arched eyebrows. A very symmetrical roundish face made her look uncommonly attractive. Her red hair hung in a long braid down her back like she usually wore when at home. It was fun to tug on her braid sometimes to show my affection.

"You tried to enlist? When did you do that? You look disappointed." Her voice was soft, as if she couldn't yell if she wanted to. She never did, except when my sister did her terrible thing.

"This morning. Yes, I am disappointed." My agitated voice indicated I was losing control. I turned away, walked over to the steamed-up window and gathered my thoughts. The fear rose again but determination cursed it away. Soldiers. Being a soldier is what normal men do—wear a uniform, follow orders, kill the enemy, shoot their brains out, earn medals. They don't stay home obediently and take care of their mother all their lives. Will I ever have my own life? I had almost gotten married but Mother had insisted I wait until after she died. The girl, Abigail Washington (a beautiful name), was nice looking, graceful, and came from a good family. While she was attractive, I can't say I loved her. What did I know about love for a woman? After two years, I still hadn't married her. My excuses—Mother needs more time to adjust; I need to save more money. Eventually Abigail accused me of play-acting about marriage.

It all seemed like play-acting—trying to tell myself I wasn't attracted to men, that I knew what I wanted. Eventually, Abigail married a lieutenant. Again I felt like a 4-F.

"And how would I take care of everything? What if you were killed, then where would I be? Alone. Did you think of that?"

"Well, they didn't want me." I resisted yelling at her for thinking just of herself.

"And I do. Don't be so gruff." Her calmness made me feel guilty. But she couldn't manage alone. Father had died. Then my sister.

"Supper will be ready shortly." She gave me the evening newspaper.

The front page was all about World War II preparations, boot camp, and the troopships that would soon be leaving all hours of the day. I turned pages, looked at pictures, tried to read, remembered nothing. Would I ever get my own life? Would I ever get married and have children? At supper, I made myself eat so Mother wouldn't ask what was wrong. Afterward, I wrote Cousin Frank—we had grown up together in the same neighborhood, had the same friends—that the army couldn't use me; that I had wanted to serve my country and had hoped we would serve together. I didn't confess I almost died of fright that day. But it wasn't something to dwell on. On with life. Finish the damn letter. I had excellent handwriting. Go to work in the morning. An awful job. Idiot boss. Worst one. Bald. Double chin. Little ears. Big nose. Take a deep breath. Get a hold of yourself. At dinner Mother asked why I was so quiet.

"Headache."

A week later, I got a letter and opened it.

"You look like you're reading bad news," Mother said.

"Frank enlisted. He hopes he'll be sent to Europe." I didn't speak my fear that Frank would get killed. After my sister died, he was like my only sibling, like a brother. We played harmless pranks on each other in high school. Stole liquor one time, got drunk and puked it up. Talked about sex—how it stays hard . . . what you do . . . don't do . . . dirty names for the girl part. Once, I helped Frank cheat on a chemistry test. It was my best subject; I rarely had to study. Frank liked literature and dreamed of owning a bookstore.

"You two are close. I don't know why he had to move up to Brooklyn." She stood there with her mouth half-open. Her hand gripped a can of scrubbing powder. She went back to cleaning.

"All you care about is that I'm not drafted." I was angry with her for not knowing what I was going through and angrier with myself for more than I had the energy to think about. Underneath the anger, my shame troubled me. The combination almost caused a fear but I caught it in time.

She stopped cleaning and faced me but said nothing. Her eyes blinking, looking confused, but trying to be tolerant.

I put the letter back in the envelope, and looked out the window wondering how tolerant she would be if I mentioned my attraction to men. She asked me to take out the garbage. It was too cold to walk, the sky a freezing dusk blue, so I went back in the house. I wished I wasn't over six feet tall and looking as fit as they come. I had broad shoulders. Could I walk with a cane? Limp all day? My ruse would surely be discovered.

NEEDING SELF-RESPECT, I volunteered with the salvage operations and building empty boxes. The empty boxes were depressing, so I spent twice the time helping with salvage efforts. I organized neighborhood kids to collect scrap metals. I put up flyers and set up drop-off places, scheduled pickups. Once monthly, I went to schools and gave short speeches. It gave me pride and a sense of patriotism. The kids liked me. Every so often, I'd treat some to ice cream if I saw them in the corner drugstore. Their chatter was enjoyable—about how pretty their teacher was, how funny looking the principal was, complaints about siblings. I wondered who was the smartest, so I asked questions, but not all at once, not wanting to shame anyone. If they were talking about Philadelphia I asked how it was spelled. If one said he had a quarter I might've asked how many nickels are in a quarter. One boy got most of them right. He must have been the smartest. His father should be proud.

For the first year, Frank sent me a letter every month. He complained about the freezing cold, stinky feet, stinky clothes, stinkier underwear, eating cans of C rations, and D rations. One time he bragged about having a fine meal of Italian farm cat and stolen old wine. There was another about laughing with a skinny soldier who made a joke out of trench foot. Moments after their laughter subsided, Frank heard a blast and turned around. The comedian had been blown apart—his smile scattered. Usually Frank didn't write those kinds of details. I feared the war was getting to him. There were no letters for months until finally one arrived.

> Dear Jim,
>   I'm okay. Got recommended for a dumb medal for a wound that wasn't bad enough to get more than a week of medical leave. Hope everyone's fine. I hate war. It turns good men into brutal barbarians or mute ghosts. Tragic. Not much else to say. I guess I needed war to make me speechless. But then, death is silent. Life's noisy. Give my love to your mother.
>   Frank

The paper it was written on was smudged. I touched the smudge like it was a soldier's spilled blood. Twice I read it, seeking justification for my 4-F status. I poured myself a shot of whiskey, but it didn't satisfy. Neither did the evening newspaper or my mother's gossip about the neighborhood. Claiming a headache, I went to bed early and lay awake, couldn't sleep, hoped Frank didn't get killed. How many soldiers have been killed? Would we be invaded? What would I do? Germans bombing Philadelphia? Shooting up my street? Defeating us. I made a fist, as if that would do something. Me—winning a fistfight? I almost laughed and then felt depressed. Should I have insisted I was fit to serve? Earlier that afternoon, a scrawny brash kid I never saw before called me yellowbellied. He was pale like he never saw the sun. His pimples said he was pubescent and not nine years as I first thought. He deserved a slap across his face but I walked on, cursing him under my breath.

I worked as a laboratory technician running tests and collecting data. It was monotonous, but I was helping with the war effort. I didn't grumble about rationing. I bought war bonds and continued to volunteer with the salvage operations. As often as possible, I sent the best cigarettes, chewing gum, and chocolates to Frank. I wanted to write, *Here's some noisy chocolates and gum*, but didn't know if it was sarcasm or humor, so I didn't. Once in a while I sent a salami. The years filled with guilt, boredom, and fear. The fear was the worst— fear of being conquered, fear of myself, of my sexual yearnings. It was tiresome; I took care that I didn't drink too much.

When it seemed like the war would never end, it was announced on the radio that Germany signed an unconditional surrender in Reims, France, on May 7, 1945 and Hitler was most likely dead. Frank telegrammed he was in Paris celebrating victory and hoped to be coming home soon. I walked to the neighborhood bar in search of my own celebrations. I ordered the most expensive gin and listened to four old men talk dirty—the swear words, sex words, whore jokes. One spilled his drink on the floor, and someone's pretty dog lapped it up. Bets were made as to how much the dog could drink before it couldn't stand up. It was given another drink but it wobbled and collapsed to the floor, not even halfway through it. The whole smelly, smoked-filled bar laughed. I laughed to not draw attention to myself, but I hoped I'd never become a pathetic old man. Then one of the men started crying about World War I. That was too much; I walked out.

Three months later, the newspaper reported on August 6, 1945, and three days later on August 9th, two bombs, named *Little Boy* and *Fat Man*, each flattened a city in Japan. Two-thirds of Hiroshima was destroyed. Nagasaki suffered more damage. I read it twice.

But it wasn't over. How much longer? I read about the new atomic bomb, equal to 20,000 tons of TNT. It gave me chills. A city and its entire people blown to smithereens with one solitary weapon. Then on August 14th, my bald idiot boss, Mr. Murray, ran into the lab, yelling, "It's over. Just heard the news. Japan's goddamn emperor declared surrender. World War II is over. We won. The boys are coming home."

Everyone erupted in applause. Some hugged. I sighed with relief, hoping life would return to normal. I had enough of scrap-metal collecting. Murray was so happy he let everyone off early. No one left. We all crowded into his small office to listen to the details on the radio, with the volume turned up. Barely a word was said until another worker popped in and said he heard that celebrations had started downtown. I left and took a crowded trolley—women holding children, people laughing, old men smoking pungent cigars. A blond woman with banana-curled bangs sat next to me. She wore five rings and was drenched in perfume. When I got off at my stop, I still smelled her. Her perfume had seeped into my jacket. It didn't matter. On this day, nothing bothered me.

The streets were soon packed with people, joyous about sons, husbands, or brothers coming home. There was a woman with two children in tow—holding hands—taking it all in. The little boy had on a blue suit, a white shirt, and red tennis shoes. The girl wore white, and the woman wore red and white. I wanted to ask if they had dressed patriotic just for today. But I walked on because I didn't want her to think I was flirting, especially in front of her children.

"Goddamn Krauts. Hope they burn in hell," a voice grumbled. "They killed my brother."

I turned around to see who the curser was and ended up stepping on his foot. He was thick-necked, had big ears, hairy nostrils, and a scar above his lip. He wore brown pants, a gray-green work shirt with a button missing, and a frayed newsboy cap.

"Beg your pardon. Didn't mean to."

"Yeah?" The man looked cross.

"I'm sorry about your brother. I lost my sister years ago. She was only sixteen. It was awful. I know what you feel. Can I buy you a drink?" I rarely talked about Elizabeth's death and when I did I excluded the awful details. Under the circumstances it seemed to calm the man. Plus it was good to say a word about her after so many years, especially since I probably wouldn't see him again and be asked prying questions. I hated prying questions. But I was getting better at dealing with them. Just take a few words from the person's question and redirect them.

"I'd like that," the man said. "I know a great bar."

It was a short walk. All the man did was to complain about his boss, his neighbors, the war taking so long. A malcontent. Not worthy of my time. The place was dark, crowded, with a Wurlitzer jukebox lit up and blaring. We downed a shot of the smoothest bourbon. "Aged twenty-three years in white oak. Best I have," the bartender said through the haze of tobacco smoke.

After the second shot, I found an excuse to leave, and strolled through the streets. People were shoulder to shoulder, arm in arm, lips on cheeks, lips on lips. I wove a path through the moving crowd. The air was buzzing that America had won. Laughter and waves of chitchat mingled like music. Jimmy Dorsey couldn't compete. The warm arms of history swept me away. Never before had I experienced a crowd of people suddenly all in love with each other. Unforgettable.

A young woman stood close enough to touch. She wore a full-skirted white dress with black polka-dots. She smiled right at me. I smiled. She smiled more and stepped toward me and tilted her head like she was asking for a kiss. Impulsively—not my habit, maybe it was the bourbon—I slipped my hand around her waist and pressed my mouth on her moist red lips. Her slender body offered no resistance. She was so little I could have picked her up and carried her home. She smelled good—a hint of perfume, her wavy hair smelling like she had just shampooed it. Unsteady in her shoes, she walked away, singing, "It's Been a Long, Long Time." She had to be singing about her soldier overseas. As she walked away, swaying her hips, my loins stirred. It's what I hoped for—to be attracted to women. Should I have asked her for a date? She disappeared into the crowd. I could count on one hand the times a woman aroused me. Abigail Washington did a few times. I should have married her. Another was a woman who had boarded a trolley on a summer's day. She wore pink high heels, a pink spaghetti-strap dress with a full skirt. The hem of her lacy slip was just visible. She sat in front of me. I wanted to introduce myself but was too shy. There may have been one other.

Down the sidewalk a man in uniform walked toward me. He looked familiar. Where had I seen him before? Was he the rugged blond man with the movie-star face standing near the induction office the day I was rejected by the army? The one who excited me? There was another man in uniform strolling with his wife, his hand around her waist. She was holding their child's hand. The soldier called his wife "sweetheart" and his child "baby." I wanted my own family. My youth was gone. I was thirty-six.

For weeks afterward, after dinner, I sat on the back porch and sipped iced tea. Under the black, starlit night, flirtatious laughter spilled out of a neighbor's open window. I was humming with need—a pretty wife who knew how to cook, four children, three bedrooms, a big yard, an apple tree, a shade tree, some rose bushes. The hum settled down but it was still there.

Chapter 3

TRYING TO LOOK relaxed and in charge of my life, I put my hands in my pockets, rested my weight on one leg. A good stance. I shifted weight. Frank had insisted I come with him to the party. He had driven down from Brooklyn. A publisher he did business with was celebrating his fiftieth birthday. I had nothing else to do and did like spending time with Frank, but at the moment he was off talking to others. Feeling nervous, thinking of leaving, then staying, I looked around the room. A tall woman opened the door and walked in. She was attractive, not beautiful. Nice lips. Good eyes. She wore a dark blue dress with long sleeves, tight at the waist, and a full skirt. About twenty-five. Was she by herself? Our eyes connected. I thought she would turn away. I returned her smile.

Usually, I was timid with women but there were exceptions, like the day the war ended. The memory kindled some courage to walk toward her. A tall man with a foreign accent got to her first. I stood nearby, listening, trying to figure out if they were a couple. Her blue eyes, light brown hair with a few strands of blond, ruby lips broadening into a melodic laugh caught my admiration. I wanted to meet her, but flirting was not my strength.

The foreigner said it was nice seeing her again and left, leaving an empty space around her. Wondering what I would say and how it would come across, I walked over and asked if I could get her some punch. It surprised me how easily I spoke.

She didn't step back or frown, but accepted my offer. I got her some while thinking her voice had a softness like she enjoyed decent conversation. It wasn't squeaky and high-pitched like some women. I handed her the cup of punch and said, "I'm guessing you can't be Northern, maybe Midwestern. May I ask where you're from?"

"Pilgrim, a little town in Tennessee." She took a sip. "Very good. Who first made punch?"

"Must have been a pretty woman from Pilgrim." I hoped that wasn't corny but I was trying my best. Trying to look upstanding, worth talking to. Just a normal gentleman. I nodded my head ever so slightly because that was what she was doing. Would she think I was mimicking her? I stopped nodding.

"What brings you here?"

"My cousin Frank—the man over there. The shorter one wearing the gray jacket. He said I'd enjoy myself."

"Interesting. I met him at work. He said the same to me. He was discussing atom bombs with one of my coworkers. He called them Pandora's box and they should've never been invented."

"That doesn't surprise me. He forgets the war ended because of them." I was trying to sound patriotic.

"That's true. It's been said President Truman shared atomic secrets with Britain and Canada. It's nice to share."

"Ah, a dry sense of humor you have."

"I've been told that." She took a step toward me. I responded in kind but didn't realize it until after I had done it. My body must have had a quicker will than my brain. Her puffy full skirt was up against me. I took a small step sideways and the skirt made rustling noises—like taffeta talking, like I was touching her body, making sophisticated romance. The slight stirring had to mean something. We smiled in sync—inviting me to forget my shyness. I leaned toward her blue eyes. Not too small, not too large. Good cheekbones. A plump mouth. Straight teeth. She didn't pull back. I was making progress with the chitchat.

We exchanged names. Hers was Iola Boggs. Boggs was strange, like bogland or swamp, but that was okay. Maybe her ancestors lived near marshes. Maybe fishermen. I was never a fan of eating fish, except for cod—the way Mother made it. And Iola? I never heard of it before. It was mostly vowels. Almost odd, but definitely different. Soon we were talking about favorite foods, favorite things to do.

"I was born in Philadelphia. The streets are full of history," I said.

She just moved here, and she liked the city. "It's Northern . . . but not too far from home."

"You don't have a Southern accent."

"I've traveled. You travel much?"

"Boston, Concord, Mount Vernon, Gettysburg, Plymouth Rock."

"I'd guess you like American history."

An astute woman. Hopefully we would talk awhile. Then an overly endowed fiftyish woman in a tight black dress and little white apron, holding a plate of hors d'oeuvres, ambled by and offered freshly made clam fritters, piroshki, and fried cheese balls. We each took one.

"A cute couple like you deserves more. Take more," the matron said. I stuck one in my mouth and swallowed it in two gulps. I popped another one in. To avoid coming across like a lowlife, I said, "Famished. I haven't eaten much all day."

Iola stuck one in her mouth, quicker than I.

It was fun seeing her gobble food, so I gobbled another and I could tell she knew I was enjoying myself. That gave me the courage to ask, "Can we meet again?"

I expected her to politely say no, that it was nice talking to me but she couldn't fit me into her busy schedule. To my surprise, she said, "Love to, Jim." I liked her saying my name in the same sentence with *love*. What did I know about love? Love of parents—yes. Love of sister—absolutely, even after her death.

We decided we'd meet the following week. When she left for a minute to use the ladies' room, I admired the sway of her skirt. It suddenly occurred to me I had forgotten all about Frank. I looked around the room and saw him engaged in a discussion with two people, and decided he was doing fine.

Iola returned, smiling. Had a friendship begun? Then Frank came by with the two people and introduced them to Iola and me. Tony was a city councilman. Fred was the owner of a bookstore in Chicago, who quickly focused on Iola. "You look familiar. I know you. You grew up in Chicago."

My eyes darted over to her. Had she been caught in a lie? Was she a charlatan?

"Not at all. In Tennessee. A small town." Her voice was steady, unwavering. "No crime, but nothing ever changes. It takes them fifty years to accept that inventions like the radio aren't the devil's toys."

"Two questions. What's a devil's toy?" Fred asked. "And I have relatives who grew up in Tennessee. I know how they talk, and you don't sound like them. Just why is that?"

I feared she was a fake. What I most disliked—people pretending to be something they're not. Deep down, I was fake. It was a terrible feeling.

"Two answers for the inquisitive gentleman. First one. Idle hands would be my guess. I'd say it's been that way for ages. Certainly not the radio. Second one—because I traveled a lot—all over the country. Got influenced by how others talk. My family says I talk different now." She smiled with her lips closed, and gave a one-shoulder shrug.

"Yeah, idle hands. An age-old problem, isn't it?" Fred looked at his hands, rubbed them together. "I'd like to idle with you." He winked and mouthed a kiss.

"Looks like it's still a problem." Her voice stiffened.

She took a step back. It was obvious Fred was drunk. I stepped forward, and narrowed my eyes. I decided she wasn't a fake.

Fred laughed so loud, people on the far side of the room looked over. He touched Iola's arm. She took another step back. Frank suggested Fred and the councilman needed to meet someone else. He led them away.

Iola and I agreed we had enough of the party and so we went walking, shared stories. She spoke of growing up in Pilgrim, her first job in Chattanooga. I liked the quick upturn in her voice when she said "Chattanooga," which bordered Alabama, which she also said nicely, and the way she talked about the long, meandering Tennessee River, and the town of Soddy-Daisy. She sounded both quaint and sophisticated. Unusual. She had thirteen siblings—a brother named Friend, another named Buck, one called Sledge. I didn't pay attention to the others. I said I had one sister, but not anymore. Iola opened her ruby-colored lips like she was going to ask a question.

"She passed on." I looked away, and let go of her hand. I ended the silence by asking if she would like a cup of coffee and some dessert. There was a good coffee shop nearby that was open late.

We slowly nibbled our blackberry pie (I never cared for pie but she ordered it, so I did), sipped coffee, got refills, touched hands, and talked until we had the place to ourselves, until the waitress, full of yawns, said they were closing. I liked this intelligent woman with the strange name. I was glad she wasn't beautiful. It would draw attention to me and she'd expect more. We planned the next date.

THE MOVIE WAS Iola's choice. The actors were good, but the theater was crowded and the man sitting next to me was smacking gum. I wanted to ask him to stop but didn't. When the hero's father died unexpectedly in an accident, I recalled the death of my father and sister. I tried thinking of other things. I focused on the gum-smacker. But the memories kept coming back—Father and Elizabeth taking a walk and getting hit by a car skidding out of control. They were critically injured. My sister ended up paralyzed from the waist down. Without a second thought, I had used my savings of eight years, intended for my college education, to pay for the best medical treatment available. I knew the tragedy changed my life. I was twenty-four. A month before, I had been accepted to Princeton University. My plans to earn a college degree in chemistry evaporated. I put the acceptance letter in the safe box along with my parents' marriage certificate, my birth record, my parents' birth records, my sister's, all of the family's important papers. As if by some future miracle, I would need it. A hope. A dream so strong, part of me never let it go.

When the movie ended, I told Iola I had a headache. Talking took concentration and effort, but being irritable was unacceptable. I flagged a taxi for her and we said good night. I walked home. It was late and most of the shops were closed. Few cars were in the streets. A man walked his little dog, which yapped at me as it passed. It seemed safe to not fight my returning sorrow. My headache eased. I half wanted to remember it all. I wished, that by so doing, my father and sister might return. A few days before he died, Father had said, "Promise you'll take good care of your mother and sister. Be sure nothing bad happens to them." My stolid, dependable father, healthy as any until the accident, had worked hard to provide for his family. He bought us good clothes and a small but decent house to live in. It had a little yard in the back where my mother grew vegetables in the summer. We never went hungry. We took summer vacations at the Jersey Shore.

"Oh, Daddy, I love you. Please come back," Elizabeth—she had just turned sixteen—in a wheelchair, had cried at Father's funeral. My tears were embarrassing. Mother said nothing for five days. Elizabeth had turned pale. Her hair went uncombed. She cried at the dinner table with her mouth full of food. In her bedroom, at her piano. Some days, I came home late so I didn't have to see it, depressing as it was. She had been so outgoing and had brought the humor out of me, even got me to dance a few times. Not too long afterward, we heard a gunshot and found her dead in her bedroom. She had taken Papa's gun and shot herself in the chest. Her note said, *I want to be with Papa.*

Mother screamed, then collapsed, and stopped talking for two months. She hardly ate, didn't cook. She smelled and had to be reminded to change her clothes and take a bath. I had to teach myself cooking. I burned food; said I was sorry—almost lost my temper. Somehow, I don't know how, I buried my anger in order to pull my mother out of death. A deep guilt for failing Elizabeth, not keeping her safe, almost overwhelmed me. The day my sister died, Mother had taken the gun out of a locked box. She wanted it taken to a gun shop to sell it that morning, but a plumbing problem demanded my immediate attention. We forgot about the gun and had left it on the table.

I purposely walked out of my way, down a street to the funeral parlor where my father's and sister's services had been held. I wanted to walk in but the front door was closed. It had to be locked. Could they be inside, suddenly come to life, then walking down the steps? For a second, I believed it would happen. That they were embracing me, saying they were happy to be back, asking how I've been. *We missed you. Yes, we're fine. How's Mother? She'll be so pleased to see you. Let's hurry.* I remembered her laugh.

As I walked farther, a girl got out of a car and walked up the stairs to a house with all the lights on. Was a party going on? She looked like she was the same age Elizabeth would've been if she was still alive. Did she like music? Play the piano? What was her name? Did she have an older brother? Would she be my sister? The front door opened and she disappeared inside. I had never been so drawn to fantasy.

I went a few more blocks, more than needed, just to clear my head. At home, my mother was up waiting for me.

"Is there a problem? You seem bothered," she said.

"I have a headache."

"Would you like a cold compress for your head?"

"No."

"Do you want to read the evening newspaper?"

I picked it up and held it as if reading. I wanted to tell her I might have found a girl I'd like to marry. That I wanted to have children, maybe four or five and that nothing bad would ever happen to them because I would protect them. They'd have long lives and be upstanding citizens. Be normal. Especially be normal. And my sons would go to war if needed. That I'd like to bring my girl home to meet her. I'd like my mother to accept Iola. She was tall, smart, trim, not too buxom, looked healthy, pretty enough. Plus if I waited until Mother died, I might be so old no girl would want me.

Mother served tea in a fine-china teapot with two matching cups I had bought for her, for no special occasion except filial devotion, several months after Elizabeth's passing.

After finishing my tea, I laid down the newspaper and said, "I'll be going to bed." I was annoyed but covered it well. I checked that the doors were locked. Mother turned down the heater and we retired for the evening.

Iola

Chapter 4

AUTUMN COOLED THE city of humid summer heat. The sky was an unbounded, unclouded blue. Trees had turned their seasonal yellows, oranges, and reds. Few leaves had fallen. Jim wanted to show me historical Philadelphia. He called me honey and took my hand. First, we walked to the Liberty Bell at Constitution Hall, and he talked about when it was made—1752 and recast in 1753. What it was made of—copper and tin. He looked at it from the right and the left. He gestured with his hand like he was conversing with it. He explained why the bell had cracked.

"It's nice that way." I took a step back. "I'd say it gives it more history. A bigger story. It survived a problem."

"That's right. Of course. It's as if the crack symbolizes the revolution. Breaking away from England. People sacrificed their lives. I never thought of it that way." His eyes brightened.

Arm in arm, we strolled to Christ Church Burial Ground. Jim, the historian, showed me Benjamin Franklin's grave.

"He helped found our country. It pleases me to be here." As he spoke, a demeanor came over him. Not haughty. Almost awe. A love of country. perhaps. Or heritage. Honoring ancestry—not something I was good at doing. As we walked, he pointed out Dr. Benjamin Rush's grave and the graves of three other signers of the Declaration of Independence and those of some Revolutionary War heroes.

When my historian bent over to wipe some leaves off a gravestone, I admired his backside, the fit of his pants, and imagined intimacy. I wanted, needed to get married, to belong to someone, and have a family. I would soon be twenty-eight. It was time to have some security in a man's world that had no more need for female pilots, especially those who wanted to fly as a job, get paid for it, and be proud of her skills. I hadn't yet told Jim I'd been a pilot and wondered if I should. A suitor once dumped me after I told him. And others—I was too tall, too smart, or not ladylike enough. And the good one, Sal Shouse, had died before we had a chance to marry. I held my breath. Had being a pilot inadvertently hurt me? Well, well—what to do now? Why not learn about the graveyard? It was small and wouldn't take all day. I took a deep breath. "Very interesting, Jim. I've never been in an historical graveyard."

"Technically, all graveyards are history." He gave my hand a squeeze.

As we were walking through the cemetery, I turned my ankle on the cobblestones and fell. Instinctively, I put my arms in front of me to brace my fall. I could feel my skirt flying up. I figured he'd like the view but he acted like he saw nothing and immediately went to help me up. He blamed himself. He helped me to the nearest bench while insisting, "A gentleman doesn't let that happen." I protested I should've been more careful. He examined my ankle and then sat beside me and put his arm around my shoulders. We were under a big maple tree. The leaves all red and glorious; no one was around.

Waiting for the pain to settle down, we sat, smiled, held hands, said, "Umm."

"Lovely day," I said.

"Very."

"Which is your favorite gravestone?"

"Iola, you're silly."

"I like the two touching."

"Where?"

"Over there. They're leaning so far they're touching each other. Girlfriend, boyfriend."

"You definitely have a sense of humor." He leaned his shoulder into mine.

"Let's imitate them."

"How do you imitate gravestones?"

"Just touch your shoulder to mine."

"If people knew what we're doing they'd think we're crazy."

"Jim, they just don't know what fun is. It'd be more fun to imitate them a year from now, when they're hugging."

"Like this?"

"Yes, perfect."

Soon we shared a brief kiss on the lips. Then a longer one.

"Umm."

"Umm. How's your ankle?"

"It still hurts a bit, dear."

"I should take you home so you can put your foot up and rest."

When we got back to my apartment, Jim said he'd be right back with something for my ankle. While he was gone, I hobbled about and washed the dishes in the sink, cleaned off the table quickly. A pile of dirty clothes was dumped in a closet. I shut the door to my little bedroom and unmade bed.

He returned with flowers, a cake, and Epsom salts. In my seven-foot kitchen, he brewed some tea, and prepared a pan of hot water and put in the salts.

While my foot soaked, we ate cake, drank tea, and talked of winter, ice, martinis, movies, movie stars, stars, and back to winter, keeping warm, summer. The topics didn't matter. It was fun.

"It's the first time I had a date in a graveyard." I laughed after I realized how comical it sounded.

"It's not any graveyard. It's an American monument."

"That's right. I was just being funny. You know—stupid humor."

"What is stupid humor?"

"Just joking, dear." He seemed to like being called dear.

When I was done soaking my foot, he dried it with a towel. I noticed he caught a peek farther up my skirt. I didn't mind because his eyes didn't catch mine catching his ways. To hide my smile, I looked at the ceiling and put my hand over my mouth. Should I invite him to bed? My bedroom was a mess and the sheets needed changed. It was a narrow bed. My ankle hurt. Plus, I didn't want to give him the wrong impression. I wasn't easy. There were things I wanted. A normal life, a marriage. To be included. Be part of something meaningful and safe that didn't get shut down. Wasn't that reasonable? I was tired of being on my own as a secretary smarter than the boss. I had put up with so much, worked too hard. And what came of it? All the years and money spent on flying lessons, getting my pilot's certification, and then the luck of getting accepted in the Women Airforce Service Pilots. The WASP. Five months I served. It was depressing when it was dissolved and there were no more jobs for female pilots. I couldn't even do it for leisure—not having the money, or the energy to work three jobs to make the money.

I could propose marriage, but Jim could reject me, plus it wasn't something a woman should do. Like marriage was a one-sided decision. What were the things a woman could ask and not be told she didn't know her place? *Shall we eat? Do you like my dress? My hat? My lipstick color? Does my nose need powdering? What would you like for dinner? Any laundry you need done? Ironing? Mopping?* I'd never been satisfied with those types of questions. But it had become lonely living all by my too-tall, too-smart, too-piloty self. One favorite brother dead. The other one living some unknown place, unless he was buried too. I hadn't seen Aunt Pleasant and Uncle Dillard in several years. I was worn out and not even thirty.

A WEEK LATER, after my ankle felt better, we walked along Market Street and then over to Chestnut Street, both of us having long strides. We walked in sync, like the forgotten kid in us had leaked out. It became a game, lasting less than a block. The wind blew my hair into my face, covering my eyes. Through my hair, I saw Jim smiling. He wanted my photograph, so we found an automated photo-booth in a five-and-dime. We sat in it, pulled the curtain closed. I wanted to comb my hair but he liked it tousled. For thirty cents we got six pictures taken. Two looking straight ahead, two with his arm around me, one looking at each other—all smiles except for the one with us kissing on the lips.

"I never had a picture of me kissing before," I said.

"Neither have I."

We kissed again.

"How about six more just kissing?" I tilted my head.

"Just kissing? They'd all be the same."

"Kissing on the lips, kissing hands, fingertips, cheeks. Noses. Foreheads."

When we got the pictures, I whispered, "My mother would say it's pornography. I won't send them to her." I put my hand over my mouth and rolled my eyes.

He looked curious. "Have you ever seen pornography?"

I felt my neck and cheeks getting warm. I was at a loss of words until I blurted out, "Did you ever?" Did he notice I didn't answer?

"Frank and I looked at some when we were boys." He smiled. "Actually, private parts look funny. Kind of ugly. Not something you want to look at every day."

I didn't know what to say; I gave an awkward shrug. I could tell he was trying not to smile.

"That didn't come out the way I meant it," he said.

"How did you mean it, dear?"

He scratched his forehead, looked pensive. Then said, "I'm sorry."

His apology got us back in sync again. That was good. Then he asked if I'd ever been to Washington, DC. He'd be happy to show me. He insisted on paying for the trip. His generosity was a strength.

At home that evening, I was intrigued. My front door was locked. The blinds were pulled down and the curtains were all closed. I went in the bathroom, locked the door, and got a hand mirror. I pulled down my panties, pulled up my skirt, put one foot up on the toilet seat, and looked at my privates. With my fingers, I separated the folds of darker skin, and saw my opening. Growing up rural, I had seen pig and cow vaginas before, but never my own. Interesting. Why did Jim call it ugly? My imagination took hold and I wondered what a woman might do to arouse a man.

AFTER THREE HOURS in the Library of Congress in Washington, DC, we found ourselves in front of a sheet of aging parchment full of words (about thirteen hundred according to my historian) telling King George III we can rule ourselves. Jim talked on and on about the Declaration of Independence. Who all signed it. The disputes and compromises. What got left out and why. He never hesitated and spoke with ardor. I was impressed with how much he knew about American history, but it was boring, so my mind often wandered off. All in all, the day was enjoyable. At dinner, I didn't complain about my chicken and peas being overcooked. "Excellent potatoes, excellent wine." I ran my finger over my lower lip, then touched his hand, and got him to smile. He suggested having a late-night cocktail in a nightclub nearby.

Nat King Cole was singing when we got seated. We ordered some drinks and sat back and listened. Cole sang a number of songs, some of my favorites. "Doesn't he have a lovely voice—smooth and creamy?"

"It's odd. He looks odd. I prefer Frank Sinatra—now there's an excellent singer. And very good looking." He rubbed his chin.

I'd never heard a man compliment another man's looks before, especially never in Pilgrim. But this was a nightclub and Jim was on his third martini and I was on my second. Not a habit for either of us. But it was the end of the evening, and we had become rather jovial.

The next day, we went to Mount Vernon. I wore a wide-brimmed hat. He took hold of it and moved it at an angle on my head. I didn't tell him I had decorated it myself with feathers I found on sale in a secondhand store and a ribbon sticking out of a smelly garbage can. It was on the top and I had washed it well.

We ambled to the ha-haw walls by the Bowling Green entrance, and then inside to the central hall staircase.

"George Washington had walked down these stairs," Jim said. "He might have stood right here."

"He probably did."

"You think so?"

"Of course. Right where you're standing. Maybe talking with his wife."

"Yes, to Martha. What would she have said?"

"'You make me proud, George. First president of the United States. It's good to be first.'"

Jim's eyes brightened. "Maybe this sounds strange, but I feel grounded to this land."

"Let's be George and Martha."

"What do you mean?"

"Just joking, dear." Since this wasn't the time for humor, I said, "It's good to be American. 'God's promised land'—Uncle Dillard liked to say. A preacher I knew claimed heaven has to be someplace overlooking America." I then gave in to my need to say something heartfelt. "I bet this area looks even more beautiful when you're in a plane."

"I've never flown."

"I have."

"Have you traveled a lot?"

"You could say so. It was my job at the time."

"Traveling?"

"Actually—piloting planes."

"A pilot? I thought you're a secretary."

"I am a secretary. Piloting was how I got out of Pilgrim." I hoped telling him wasn't a mistake, but I couldn't help myself. I adjusted my hat.

"You flew a plane out of Pilgrim? You said it lay between two steep hills."

"No. My Uncle Dillard paid for my first plane ride after I moved to Chattanooga. He was friends with the owner of a local airport. A twenty-minute plane ride opened up a new world to me—that life wasn't just backwoods and cooking possum on wood-fire stoves. I decided—this is what I want to do. Fly a plane."

"You ate possum?" His eyes widened and he leaned away from me.

Was he actually reacting more to my possum story than to me being a pilot? "You'd want to fly a plane, too, if you had to eat it. There were a lot of things about Pilgrim I didn't care for. But I liked flying, and Pilgrim had no airplanes. So I decided I was going to learn how to fly."

"Do you still fly?"

"My pilot job ended and there are no more jobs now for a girl pilot."

"I never knew a pilot. I never knew there were girl pilots. What does a girl pilot do?"

"Flies planes and eats possum."

I was glad he smiled. "That flight inspired me. In fact I believed flying would take me as far away from Pilgrim as anything could. I never knew a place more stuck in its ways. *New* was a bad word, unless it was a new crop, new baby, new moon, new moonshine." I looked to see if he showed any sign of disapproval, any frown or narrowed eyes.

"Tradition has its place," he countered.

"I took the best traditions with me."

"But the best are always in the place where you grow up. It's in the monuments, the parks and rivers you visited as a child. The streets you played on. Even the corner drugstores."

"Usually, that's true if the place has good traditions, like Philadelphia. I mean, what kind of good tradition do you think Pilgrim had? Eating possum?"

"Well, when you say it that way."

"A lot depends on perspective. Like probably if I spent my life growing up here, I would've been happy being Mrs. Washington."

My handsome historian gave a look of surprise, surveyed me from head to toe, and nodded. "It wouldn't surprise me if you were a descendant of English royalty."

"My ancestry is Scottish."

"They intermingled."

"Well if that's so, then maybe the king who killed his wives."

"I'm not sure what you mean." He scratched his head.

"Oh, nothing. Just my mind rambling. I'm a bit tired." I had no idea why I said that. Maybe it was some of my cynicism, or him being so thickheaded. To change the topic, to get some optimism, I pointed out a blue jay in a spruce tree nearby. "I like blue jays. But my favorite are whippoorwills. You ever hear one?"

"Not that I remember. What do they sound like?"

"I'll imitate one when we go outside." Outside, I gave a whippoorwill call—the three syllables with the up-accent on the last.

"How do you do that?"

"Grew up around them. They come out in the early morning and at dusk," I said.

"Can you imitate a nightingale?"

"Never heard one."

"Are whippoorwills the best of Pilgrim?

"Very best. Sometimes, I'd wake up hearing them. In fact, if all of Pilgrim was as good as that I might never have left."

"Is that what you took with you?"

"Absolutely." I hoped I hadn't said too much but then he took a hold of my hand. He spoke about how George Washington came to own Mount Vernon. I nodded every so often so he'd think I was listening. To make it look like I was interested, I asked, "How many children did he have?"

His answer took longer than needed. Then he squeezed my hand and changed the topic. "Would you like to meet my mother? We could have lunch with her."

"But of course." Jim apparently had accepted me being a pilot. I could marry this man. We had fun together. He seemed smart. Nice looking. Sometimes boring, but who isn't? Sometimes I've bored myself.

A week later, Jim told me his mother insisted she would cook dinner for us the following Sunday.

"IT'S GOOD TO meet you. Jim told me your name, but I forgot your last name." Mrs. Lewis looked me up and down.

"Iola Boggs."

"What kind of name is that?"

"Scottish."

"You have a calling card?"

"I don't use them. I'm a modern woman."

"Modern?" Mrs. Lewis looked at Jim. "We can all go to the parlor now."

She directed me to sit in chair by a bookcase. Three of the shelves contained American history books. Obviously Jim's. Jim and his mother sat in dark brocade armchairs on the other side of the small room, one on each side of the fireplace, opposite each other. A newspaper lay on a little black table near Jim, probably put there by his mother for him to read at his leisure.

It was an ordered room, with no dust to be seen. The windowpanes, the glass lampshades, the floor, the doorknobs were spotless. There were starched white doilies on every armrest and headrest. The white lace curtains were pressed. Being curious, I asked, "Who plays the piano?"

"My sister did." Jim looked at me sideways and narrowed his eyes and looked away. I opened my mouth but said nothing. I predicted an uncomfortable evening lay ahead.

Finally we sat down for dinner. The embroidered tablecloth and napkins were perfectly ironed. The needlework was excellent, the silverware shiny. Mrs. Lewis served potato leek soup in an antique tureen she said came from England. She said to pass my soup bowl to her. She filled it without asking if I wanted any.

"Where are you from?" Mrs. Lewis asked.

"Pilgrim."

"You're not using the soup spoon. Jim, show Miss Boggs the soup spoon."

"Sorry. Actually, you can call me Iola."

"Yes, of course. Iola."

Mrs. Lewis took tiny bites of food and never used her napkin. She was the neatest eater in the world. My own napkin already had spots on it. When we finished, I offered to help clean up.

"Guests never do that." Mrs. Lewis seemed surprised.

"My guests do if they offer. I guess we have one little difference." I was being diplomatic.

Mrs. Lewis looked as if she'd fallen in a trance for a few seconds. She managed to rouse herself and told me to wait in the parlor while she cleaned up. Jim accompanied her to the kitchen. I went to the parlor, thinking of leaving, knowing I wouldn't. Thinking of taking my fingernail file and making an eensy scratch in the leg of my chair, knowing I wouldn't.

When we finished our visit and left the house, Jim said, "Mother likes you."

"I didn't get that impression." I must've opened my eyes wide in disbelief, the way Jim got defensive and said, "She'll warm up to you. Give her time. She's a bit miffed because this morning I told her I was going to ask you to marry me."

Had I heard him right? Was he asking me now? It was odd, like he didn't know how a man should propose, that it should be romantic. Had he misspoken? When he pulled out a ring with a sweet smile, I managed to say yes. It was peculiar, what with me thinking of leaving him a few minutes earlier.

Chapter 5

MAY 1946. IT was sunny, trees were blooming, a blue sky. Jim was thirty-eight years old and I was nine years younger. His mother, his cousin Frank, and Frank's wife and children attended our wedding in a little Protestant church. My sister, Maude, sent a letter saying she and Lucine didn't have the money to pay for bus fare. Buck said he was coming but called the night before and said his car had broken down outside of Louisville, he got soaked in the rain, and was almost hit by lightning. He was probably lying about the lightning. Aunt Pleasant had to stay home and nurse a sick Uncle Dillard, but they probably wouldn't have made the long trip anyway, as they were both up in years. I had wanted to just invite Papa but he would've refused if Mama wasn't invited. Papa needed to grow some spine. But how do you grow a spine married to someone mean as Mama? I invited them anyway but they didn't come—Mama's feet were too swollen and Papa was sick again, probably drunk.

Jim's mother said just four words to me. "You look nice, dear."

After the ceremony and small reception, the three of us went home in a taxi. When the taxi stopped at our new apartment, Jim said he'd accompany his mother home and I could get out now and he'd be home shortly. Yes, I guess I could. Should I? Wasn't he supposed to open the door for me? Being too surprised to say a word, I obliged.

I stood on the sidewalk in my wedding dress, holding my bouquet, and watched them drive off. A couple walked by and smiled.

"Where's the groom?" the man asked. I said nothing.

As they walked away, the woman said, "Maybe she was stood up at the altar."

With my teeth clenched, and my eyes aimed down at my first pair of white patent-leather high heels, I walked up the two flights of stairs to our apartment, hoping no one else saw me. It took forever. I hadn't noticed before how worn the steps were. At the top floor, a tall man, maybe in his fifties, with a heavy accent and acne scars walked out of an apartment and looked at me.

"You look like you just got married. Where's your groom, honey?"

"He'll be here." I barely looked at him. With a nervous hand, I tried putting my key in the lock but missed the keyhole.

"Your groom isn't here to take you across the threshold. I'll do it for you. Be happy to. You know it's bad luck if a bride walks over the threshold on her wedding day. I like your dress. It's not one of those lacy satin things dragging on the floor. It's simple and elegant. It looks like velvet. Aren't you pretty."

He startled me and so I looked straight at him. He held his arms out, with his palms up, and his face smiley. He gestured with his arms like he was trying to pick me up. It would've been funny if it wasn't so sad. My hand tremored. Holding my right hand with my left hand, I aimed the key to the keyhole and missed.

"You okay. You're not sick, are you? I have a tea that's good for most anything. It smells awful, though," he said. "I'll go get it. Honey, you can have all of what I have. It's my wedding present to you. Name's Spencer Riley."

"I'm fine. Thank you, Mr. Riley." I felt nauseous. If I didn't get the door open soon, I might make a mess in the hallway. I crouched over, and managed to open the door and rushed in. What a humiliating way to meet the neighbor. Within a second of locking my door, I ran to the bathroom but didn't get there in time. My wedding lunch ended up on the shiny floor. I had cleaned the apartment two days before. Windowpanes sparkled. A new dishtowel lay on the spotless kitchen countertop. The blue tablecloth and yellow curtains were washed and ironed. The sink, bathtub, and toilet had been scrubbed. With an old rag, I wiped up the vomit, washed out the rag, reused it, and washed it out again. All evidence gone. There was a knock on the door but I didn't answer it, as it might be Mr. Riley. If it was Jim and he lost his key, he could sit on the floor and wait until I was ready to let him in.

An hour passed and no Jim. I looked out the window and saw Mr. Riley leave the building. I stepped back, afraid he'd look up and see me. Another hour passed. To freshen the air, I opened a window. The neighborhood was busy—a streetcar rattled its bell, a cat in heat seemed oblivious to barking dogs, a mother called her child, someone's phone rang, loud kids playing, car horns, the whistle of a distant train. A woman cursing, "Goddamn prick. Don't come back." I mouthed her words. Usually I enjoyed city sounds, but not this day.

I closed the window and sat down, stared at the ceiling and the tin ceiling-light that somehow reminded me of an old office where I used to work long hours as a secretary for little pay. All my life I had worked hard and respected hard workers. Farmers, physicians, teachers, and shopkeepers who started work at six in the morning and ended at seven at night with tired eyes and sore muscles. I never stole a thing in my life except for vegetables and apples, a ribbon in someone's trash can, and lost change buried in sofas in waiting rooms. I tried not to think of my favorite brother, Zeke. It hurt too much. He didn't deserve to die. He listened to me, didn't care that I was taller than him, told me I was smart, drew my portrait—it looked good. Said he hated Pilgrim. With his eyes intense, he said he was going to move to Chicago and wanted me to come with him. We'd get an apartment and I could have the bedroom and he'd sleep on the couch.

I got up and washed my face. It was refreshing, so I drew a bath. The water running full force out of the faucet whooshed loud. I sat in water as hot as I could stand it. It steamed up the bathroom. The water running full force out of the faucet whooshed loud. The day's humiliation opened up old fears and hostilities, like there were strings in my brain tying them together. One sparked and it got the others sparking. The beatings with a switch by Mama. Seeing Sledge Jr. yelling that he came upon Zeke on the outskirts of another town, doing sex stuff with a strange man. The man, naked from the waist down, ran into the woods, lucky to miss the bullets, Sledge Jr. said. Zeke was all beaten up, moaning in pain. His eyes black and blue. Bloody lips. Then a shot rang out and Zeke went flying backward into Lucine's flower patch. Drunken Uncle Edgar had taken his 12-gauge shotgun and killed him, right beside the house.

I yelled, "You killed my brother."

Mama slapped me hard across my face and squeezed my arm so tight I screamed. "That so you know to keep your stubborn eleven-year-old mouth shut and if you don't, worse'll happen to you. Maybe not tomorrow, maybe not next month, maybe not next year, but there'll be a time, if you say one word, even twenty years down the road. Repeat what I just said."

I was so scared I peed in my panties, but no one noticed as I had a long skirt on and I kept my legs together tight so the pee dribbled quietly down. The ground underneath me got wet, so I stayed still. I wanted to run but I didn't want to get punished for bad behavior. I shut my eyes, and turned mute until Sledge Jr. ordered me to do what Mama said.

I let the water drain out. I was cold sitting in an empty tub, water drops clinging to me. After getting out, I toweled myself, put on my secondhand bathrobe, and walked to the kitchen but had no clue what I wanted. Between the bedroom and kitchen, I shuffled back and forth. It was hard to let go of that kind of past. Another hour passed and still no Jim.

In my bedroom, I opened my dresser drawer and pulled out my bankbook. I read my deposits—$1.22, $3.85, $5.19, and 73 cents. There were pages of them, giving me some comfort. I picked up my wedding veil I had dropped on the floor and started to place it on a table. Suddenly, I ripped it into shreds and the shreds into shreds, opened the window and dropped them, piece by piece. Each one floated down to the narrow alley below. I counted the seconds as the pieces hit the ground. There was powerful lightning out in the distance. Thunder exploded the sky.

I wasn't afraid of thunder. Mama had once locked me outside the house on a hot summer evening all by myself for some misdeed. She thought I was terrified of the dark when there was lightning and thunder. Mama was. I had pretended I was fearful. I pleaded and then I laid my head on the floor and looked underneath the door. I could see Mama's swollen feet walking in the kitchen. Sometimes, Mama made me rub her feet. They were smelly and the skin all dry and cracked.

After the thunder stopped, Mama came out on the porch and said in her slow drawl with melodic upturns on the ends of her sentences, "Here, child, some ayehrr pudding. It won't give you a bellyache." I didn't know what "ayehrr pudding" was but I figured I was getting off easy because whenever Mama was mad, she talked low but a little louder and stronger with no upturns. Mama set the bowl on the cold porch floor. It was empty. It was air pudding. Mama laughed and left me for the night. I noticed a sadness in her laugh and for the first time I got an inkling of superiority. After everyone had gone to bed, I snuck off the porch and over to a neighbor's to steal two apples. I even ate the cores, because I was taking no chance someone might discover my theft. Except most of the seeds I spit in the creek like I was spitting it on the sad-laugher. It taught me to keep my mouth shut. It taught me to read sad-laugher's face, her eyebrows, her mouth, the way she chewed and how long she did, her silence— mean, or tired, or don't-bother-me.

Within ten minutes, a pain pounded my head. I closed the curtains in my bedroom, and put a cold cloth over my forehead. After a while, I fell asleep clothed in my bathrobe on top of my clean white bedspread.

JIM WOKE ME. "Dear, we need to get going to the Jersey Shore."

I squinted, and moved my head back. "Do you know what you did?"

"What did I do?"

I rubbed my teeth over my bottom lip several times. "Well . . . I'll tell you. You left me, your bride, on the sidewalk on our wedding day, standing there feeling stupid, and went off with your mother. Never in my life did I even hear of someone doing that, let alone knowing someone."

"I didn't leave you there. I'm here. It was a beautiful ceremony."

I looked at the clock and saw that he'd been gone for four hours. I looked at the ceiling to every corner, took a long breath, and rubbed my lips. When I was done with the purposeful silence, and with my blood steaming, I said, "You didn't see how upset I was?"

"You were upset?"

"How could you not know?"

"But you looked like you understood. It's what I like about you—your composure. I needed some time with my mother to help her adjust. I told you. It will pay off in the long run. She has no choice but to accept you." He put his hand out to touch me but I pulled away.

"You never told me. And don't touch me."

"I did tell you. Why are you raising your voice?"

"You never said that." I put my mind to lowering my voice but my hand shook. I got up from the bed, and stepped away from Jim.

When we left the apartment for our honeymoon, there was a little brown bag tied with brown twine sitting on the floor by our door. Jim picked it up. *Congratulations* was written on the bag. Jim looked confused.

"Must be the neighbor. He saw me coming in and said I looked ill. He offered to give me some tea that's good for most things. It's mine." I grabbed it out of Jim's hand. In the car on the drive to the shore, I didn't say a word and paid little attention to what Jim said. By the time we arrived in Atlantic City, the sun was setting. The sky was flung with red oranges, red purples, golden yellows, barely yellows, ribbons of red, ribbons of magenta, specks and splashes of shimmering white, all across a blue sky with wispy pink clouds far away.

"Beautiful sunset, best I've ever seen," he said.

"Maybe it's a sign things will improve," this fool said.

"Improve? What's wrong?"

"Nothing. Nothing at all. A perfect day." He might've caught my sarcasm.

After we checked into our hotel room, he suggested a walk along the beach. I had nothing else to do. Not a thing in the world. We removed our shoes and dipped our toes in the sea. He put his arm around me and said I looked lovely. At dinner, he said to the waiter, "My beautiful bride would like the beef Stroganoff." I decided to forget the earlier problem. Did I have a choice? He left a big tip. My historian was a generous man. It's good to know people's strengths. Back at our hotel room, he took hold of my hand and kissed me. As we readied for bed, he seemed surprised I took all my clothes off right in front of him.

His eyes opened wide. "You're not wearing a negligee."

"I don't have one."

"Do you have a nightgown?"

"I have pajamas. You want me in pajamas on our wedding night?"

"Well. Maybe top half."

It was strange, but I had enough of a difficult day, so I went to my luggage, pulled out my pajama top, and put it on, figuring he preferred buttocks over breasts.

Somehow we made it to the bed. He was clumsy. Was he a virgin? I didn't want to know. Did he wonder if I was experienced? I played ignorant. He kissed me but my nose started itching. I scratched my nose. We weren't fitting together well. I needed to move my leg. My arm hurt. He moved, moaned, and soon it was over. He got up and went to the bathroom, closed the door, soon came back to bed. His back faced me.

Isn't there supposed to be love talk on a honeymoon? Not being sure what kind of love talk to say, I said, "That sunset was beautiful."

"Yes, it was nice," he said. When he fell asleep real quick, I stared up at the ceiling. Had there been clues he was peculiar? Sometimes he'd been so much fun. Had I been too desperate to notice any strange habits? I wanted to get up and leave but no relative of mine ever got divorced. I didn't know anyone divorced. I had no energy for it, but wondered if this marriage would last.

It was a very tiresome and messy day, but I had once noticed distress fades by the morning. Something happens in sleep. Let muddy water settle was what some said. Out of sheer desperation or foolishness or something, I would let this very dirty water settle. What's to lose? Good things can start off very bad. Heroes know that. At the end of their long struggle, they feel a pride, and have a good story to tell. Uncle Dillard had told me I planned too much. Always trying to figure everything out. Making order out of every minute. Working too hard. Making others look lazy. I had argued my plans for leaving Pilgrim had worked very well. Maybe it was simply beginner's luck, the enthusiasm of youth, was argued back.

In the dark, this sad fool found it hard to ignore my troubles. It took me two hours to fall asleep.

The next morning my stomach was still gnawed up, but less so. The worry returned. But Jim had kept dating me after I had told him I was a pilot. He had the same regular job for the last six years. Aunt Pleasant had said she and Uncle Dillard didn't love each other when they first got married. She barely liked him. Maybe love wasn't needed. Jim was good looking, wavy dark-hair. Smart. Taller than me. Polite. Clean. Patriotic. My own historian, the walking library. Had a decent job. Knowledgeable about chemistry. He knew the periodic chart by heart. Well read. A good citizen. Always voted. Served on a jury. Never got in trouble with the law. Not a drunk. Not violent. Didn't own a gun. Never killed anyone. Always opened the door for me. Generous. Left good tips. I wanted to swear. "Fuck," I mouthed.

Chapter 6

MRS. LEWIS CLOSED her front door as I was about to follow Jim into her home for our first Sunday visit. With my shoulders back, and head high, I turned away, wondering what to do. I heard the door reopen and her raspy voice. "Aren't you coming in? It's good to see you."

I turned around and walked into the house, giving her a nod. Jim didn't seem to be aware of what had happened.

"You look wonderful," Mrs. Lewis said to Jim. "I have something for you." She left the room and came back with a new suit. She whispered something. Historian kissed Mother of Historian on her pale old cheek, then left the room, holding the suit. Mother of Historian turned and opened the drapes a few inches more.

"Nice drapes you have," I said. She straightened a doily on a chair after barely looking at me. Historian returned wearing the perfectly fitting suit, except the pants needed hemming. She said she missed him.

"You always give me perfect presents," he reciprocated. He left again to change back to his other clothes. Uncomfortable silence. Upon his return, Mother of Historian said Frank dropped by when we were on vacation.

"We weren't on vacation. We were on our honeymoon." My voice was intentionally matter-of-fact—just providing information.

Jim clasped his hands on his lap. The two of them talked about Frank and what he was up to in Brooklyn.

I crossed my legs, shook my foot, stuck my hand under my thigh. I think President Theodore Roosevelt had once said, "Do what you can, with what you have, where you are." That was good advice, so I gave it a try.

Jim and his mother talked about the forecast of rain.

"The weather was perfect at the Jersey Shore." They didn't seem to hear my amiable voice. Maybe they did but tuned me out. *President Roosevelt is shit.* Just to see if I could get some response, I said, "I'd like to live in Manhattan." Nothing. *I once wanted to fuck President Franklin Roosevelt. In the White House.* It wasn't true. I wondered if Roosevelt was a good F-U-C-K-E-R.

Out the window, two birds were leap-frogging through the sky, diving and ascending, taking me back to Pilgrim and the red-winged blackbirds, crows, gnatcatchers, towhees, throaty whippoorwills at early dawn and late evening, and mockingbirds all day. I knew their songs. Males puffed up, showing off for love. Females signaling to the biggest, loudest male—Take me. Rear ends raised. I doubted Jim's mother ever observed that world. Porcelain figurines lined up in order were her preference. Perfect folds. Clean shiny surfaces. Starched clothes. Ironed sheets. Doilies. Calling cards. No dust. Thank-you notes. Excellent handwriting. Evening in Paris perfume.

I sat poised. Who would've known my brain was lit up like primary colors in big stripes and loud zigzags, and wishing Pilgrim's woods and meadows into the room? That all of a sudden, a floodgate of animals would run amuck through Mrs. Lewis's world. As if I brought groundhogs, possums, and raccoons into the parlor and set them loose on her chairs, on the settee, the rug. I would've have laughed my head off as the animals did all their smelly stuff, oblivious of anything else when mating was the driving force. It was cuckoo thinking. My mama said cuckoo thinking was the devil talking. I pressed my tongue against the roof of my mouth.

Jim and his mother sat in matching chairs on opposite sides of the fireplace on the other side of the room. A porcelain tea service sat on the little black table. I never owned a tea service. Mine was a cast-iron kettle and secondhand unmatched cups. I coughed but they just gossiped about someone. I twice clicked my purse open and closed. Diddly-squat. I dropped my purse on the floor. More diddly. More squat. Fuck.

I excused myself to use the bathroom. I didn't have to use the toilet but I pulled down my panties and sat on it anyway. I picked my nose and flicked the snot on the spotless floor. Spotless floors weren't something I needed. I thought about what I've done in my life. I've flown airplanes, and that's not pretend and I knew the difference. How many planes are on the earth? Must be thousands. I'd like to own one—a single-engine, two-seater, any color. I piloted planes to Texas—too hot. I didn't care. North Carolina—too humid. Didn't care. California—beautiful ocean and mountains. Arizona—too dry. I didn't care for cactus. Oklahoma—too flat but good for airports.

Me, Iola Boggs, with no middle name (Mama said she didn't have the time to think of one for me), born poor, who by single-minded determination pushed my boundaries past my limits. Leon Connell, owner of Leander Airport, taught me to fly. I got references. In my interview, I answered questions with a yes and a no and why it was so, at the right times. Hands on my lap, feet together. Got accepted into the Women Airforce Service Pilots. Congratulations. The WASP—helping with the war effort. I caught on quick in training in Sweetwater, Texas, and followed orders. Lots of "Yes, sirs." Although, I did have unexpressed opinions about the arrogance of my superiors. Over twenty thousand applied. Just a little over a thousand girls were accepted. The WASP. Smart. Intelligent. Dedicated. Stupid damn fools. Got no thanks. Had to pay our own way home when it was disbanded because the war was winding down and we were no longer needed. Bye-bye. Have a nice life. Get married. Have children. Cook. Clean. La-de-da.

I got off the toilet, quietly opened the medicine cabinet, and opened little bottles and sniffed smelly ointments. I took a small hairpin and dropped it in the trash. I opened the linen closet and stuck my hand in the clean towels.

Was this what it had all come to? Looking into a hateful old woman's elixirs and pills. Jim and his mother could be heard walking into the kitchen. I looked at my watch—still not time to leave. I flushed the toilet, washed my hands, folded the towel neater than I found it. I spit on the towel. Then regretted it. I rubbed the spot, powdered my face, combed my hair, walked out of the bathroom and into the kitchen. They didn't notice me. I might as well have been dried flea poop. On a shelf there was a tin of Bliss Coffee. Bliss? Mrs. Lewis needed to drink it.

I went back to the parlor and sat in my assigned very comfortable chair, but I refused its comfort. I randomly pulled a book out of the bookcase. The title was *Points of Etiquette*. The first page was missing. The second page said, *"Points Of Etiquette." Designed as a Text Book for the Young.* It was printed in 1881. Inside was written, *To my dearest daughter Elizabeth, on her tenth birthday, from your loving mother.* I thumbed through it. It was dog-eared and well worn. At the back of it were pages of test questions. Hundreds of them. I read a few. What is to be observed in entering particular rooms? When should the young lend trivial services? What is always ill-bred? How should ladies walk in the streets when unattended? How should soup be taken? How is fish to be eaten? How should peas and asparagus be eaten? What caution should be observed with regard to the knife, fork, and spoon? When does dress become a serious evil? What neglect is inexcusable and why? What do careless habits about stamps cause?

I understood his mother better. Almost pitied her. What was preferable— growing up in Pilgrim or having to follow a book that was a prison? I put it back, got up and walked to the window. Outside, two boys played kickball. A tree stood tall and straight. A bird flew perfect. The sun had a good place in the sky. I had an unexpected longing for eensy Pilgrim. I wanted to be by my favorite pawpaw trees, or standing in a creek hunting crayfish with Buck. I smiled, remembering how I'd talked to the pawpaws to practice crisp talk. Only Pilgrim would've inspired that. It wouldn't have inspired the etiquette book. Jim and his mother could be heard walking back to the parlor. I sat down in my chair, crossed my legs, uncrossed them, and clasped my hands on my blue-rayon-dressed lap.

Mrs. Lewis held a tray with tea. "Cream or sugar?"

"What?" Hadn't meant to sound irritated.

"Do you want cream or sugar with your tea?"

"I'd prefer cup of Bliss. Bliss coffee." Oh, did I say that?

Mrs. Lewis frowned. I hid my smile inside my face.

"Of course, tea is fine. With lots of cream," I added. "Sugar too. Lots." It wasn't what I meant to say. I should have just said tea is fine—politely—thank you. To make matters worse I then spilled my tea on the rug. It was obvious I would've failed the etiquette test.

I sat back in my chair, trying to look charmed. Soon ignored. Not thinking, I stuck my hand behind the seat cushion, looking for change—a habit learned long ago. I found a nickel and put it in my pocket. My watch said an hour had passed.

DRIVING HOME, JIM said, "Mother asked if grandchildren are on the way."

"When did she ask that?"

"In the kitchen. Why are you sitting so far away?" He tugged on my arm. I moved nearer, but not so close to touch. My eyes focused straight ahead.

"That was a nice visit."

"If you like being shunned."

"Who shunned you?"

"Your mother. She ignored everything I said. So did you."

"She talked to you. It takes time for her to feel comfortable with new people. She'll warm up. You seem annoyed."

"Oh, not me. No, not me." I picked up my secondhand purse, set it on my lap, and wrapped my hands around it. "I got a letter from my mother two days ago."

"And how is she?"

"Fine. She'll give you the shirt off her back if you need it. She worked hard and raised ten children to adults." I pressed my tongue against my teeth. I was raised not to speak ill of my family and punished if I did. But Mama just won and made me lie, and turned me stupid. I remembered Aunt Pleasant calling Mama mean. Aunt Pleasant called me Sweet Potato.

Dear Sweet Potato,

Been meaning to write. How you doing in Sweetwater Texas? Your Papa said you almost done with pilot training. Doesn't surprise me. You always had a mind of your own. Once made up, no one could change it. You was a bit ornery sometimes. Sometimes awfully quiet. I thought you was sad a lot. You certainly loved the radio when you came for a visit. You liked to say—There's a magic to radios. Voices coming out of the air. All us is doing fine. Write and let us know what you up to and keep yourself safe. Buck came visiting and wondered how you doing. Your Mama wrote and said she sent you some dollars.

Love,

Aunt Pleasant

Dear Aunt Pleasant,

It's not easy but I'm managing. Yesterday, Major Croft read my log notes of a flight. He couldn't identify the signature and asked, "Which pilot wrote these notes?" Imagine! I said real pleased, "Why, I did." He said, "Boggs, what do you mean you did? You're just a trainee and a woman." He thought I was lying but I said, "Sir, that was the way I was trained." He said nothing. You know, I think I turned his accusation around to my favor. I don't like him. He's always rude. Most all the male pilots are. I should be graduating shortly. I have to go. I'll write again. I'm thrilled to heaven being in the WASP. Say hi to Buck when you see him again.

Love,

Iola

Jim parked the car in front of a tailor's shop—the family's tailor—to get his pants hemmed that his mother had given him. He said he wouldn't be long.

"I was thinking about my brother, Buck."

"How's he doing?"

"Last I heard—fine and dandy."

"I'll be right back. Did I tell you—you look nice?"

"I do? You like my blue dress and blue shoes?"

"I do. Are they new?"

"I wore them on our honeymoon. One time I wore them in the bathtub. They look sexy when they're all wet and dripping water."

Jim cocked his head like he wasn't sure he heard me right.

"Just kidding." I half-smiled because that's all it was worth. "I'm going in too." I got out of the car. I quarter-smiled to his admonition. "You should let me open your door."

Mr. Yalonsky, the tailor, was a tall man, taller than Jim, on the slim side, not skinny, with attractive dark eyes and a good head of brown hair, well-groomed eyebrows, thin lips, and small chin. A frayed yellow tape measure was draped around his neck. He welcomed Jim and asked who was the lovely woman with him. He sounded Polish, or German, maybe Russian, not French. I wasn't good at identifying accents.

"My bride, Iola. Had to wait until the right one came along."

Why couldn't Jim have said something like that to his mother?

Mr. Yalonsky and Jim got to business. When Jim went to the dressing room to change his pants, Mr. Yalonsky saw me looking at a photo of a tall man and a short woman. He said it was he and his wife, taken after they had recently come to America from a village near Riga on the Baltic Sea with a few dollars, and one set of clothes each. She was seventeen; he was nineteen. He worked as a street sweeper during the day and as a dishwasher in the evenings. His wife cleaned houses and did ironing so they could save money to open a tailor's shop. He asked me if I had ever worked outside the home.

"I once flew planes."

"Real planes?" He stepped closer. His eyes widened.

"I used to."

"Interesting. It had to be a lot of work to learn to fly." He smelled of mint and cigar smoke. I probably smelled of Ivory soap. Not a bad combination.

"I worked as a secretary for five years to pay for flying lessons and then had to get the hours in to be licensed." I didn't mention the lecherous bosses. "I also cleaned houses on Monday and Thursday nights for Mrs. Marley and Wednesday night and Saturday morning for Mrs. Atwater." I didn't say Atwater gave me old dresses with rips, and seams coming apart, and leftovers to eat—like it was a tip for doing a real good job for little pay. I didn't say there were days I could feel myself on a precipice, not knowing if I was going to cry or laugh, one mood creeping into the other. Sometimes my dreams about flying were all that mattered because that would mean I freed myself of Pilgrim. If unsuccessful, I might've fallen in the abyss and been committed to the crazy house, diagnosed with Too Much Ambition.

When Jim stepped out of the dressing room, I stepped away from Mr. Yalonsky. As he measured and pinned Jim's pants, I noticed his shoes were old and worn but his soles looked brand new. The man was a survivor. Persistent. He finished measuring and Jim returned to the dressing room. Mr. Yalonsky wasted no time saying he had wanted to be a tailor since he was a boy, but his father, who worked for a tailor, died when he was only twelve. His death plunged the family farther into poverty.

He took a step closer. "Were you thrilled when you first flew a plane?" His nose had large pores. His white shirt was well pressed but the collar tips were well worn. Very frugal.

"Was small change compared to getting accepted in the WASP."

He cocked his head. His curiosity was easy to recognize.

"The Women Airforce Service Pilots." I didn't say that after I opened the acceptance letter, I waltzed across my tiny apartment, opened my window, and saluted the neighbor's windows ten feet away. It made no sense but I wanted to hoot and yell but couldn't for fear the landlady would complain. She insisted on quiet. It was hard to dampen the joy of becoming part of something important. My plan was to stand in front of a military plane and get my picture taken. Two were later taken. One I sent to Buck but he lost it. He deserved a smack on the mouth.

Mr. Yalonsky took a step closer, tilted his head, and slowly moved his hand in a circular motion, like he wanted us to touch. "What did you do in the WASP?"

I sighed and leaned an inch closer to him. "I flew planes with targets towed behind them for trainee gunners to learn how to shoot down enemy planes."

"They shot at you?" His mouth opened, eyes amazed.

"At the target trailing behind the plane. I tested new planes, delivered training planes."

Out of the corner of my eye, I noticed Jim had returned. He coughed and said, "We have to go."

"Shortly." I didn't look at Jim.

"You risked your life?" Mr. Yalonsky didn't look at Jim.

"I guess I did. We were meant to free up male pilots for combat missions. I was in for only five months when the government eliminated the corps. The war was coming to a close and there were enough male pilots for both combat and noncombat missions. So we were no longer needed." I looked out the window and rubbed my neck. Mr. Yalonsky was very likable.

"You must've been greatly disappointed."

"I was." I didn't say it felt like years of work for nothing, as if we hadn't ever existed. It was depressing.

"You work as a pilot now?"

"No jobs now for female pilots." His large eyes were dark brown, the whites very white, and his eyelashes were long. Probably what his wife first admired in him. Mr. Yalonsky said he was pleased to meet me.

When we left the shop, I didn't wait for Jim to open the car door for me. Halfway home, I said, "Mr. Yalonsky is awfully smart."

"What was that all about? You certainly talked with him a long time."

"Are you complaining?"

"You never told me you liked flying so much."

"I don't know."

"You don't know if you liked flying?"

"I mean I don't know why I never told you. Did you ever ask?"

"I'm asking you now. Don't be complicated."

"Loved it. Flew over the Rocky Mountains, Smoky Mountains, Great Lakes, Grand Canyon, New York City, all over the country. It was impressive. Is that being complicated, dear? I don't want to be complicated. I'm the picture of simplicity."

He said nothing. At a stoplight, he seemed lost in his thoughts. I had to tell him the light had turned green. "Green's an uncomplicated color."

"What do you mean?"

"Dear, I'm pulling your leg because I don't know what else to say."

Would I see Mr. Yalonsky again? A tall man who enjoyed hearing a woman talk about flying planes. His store was near another store where Jim sometimes shopped. I could find something on sale that Jim might like, walk over to Mr. Yalonsky's, and ask if I could use his phone to call and ask Jim if he wanted it. Then I'd have another pleasant conversation. I clicked my tongue.

Brooklyn, New York
1946

Jim

Chapter 7

IOLA'S TALK ABOUT flying inspired my ounce of wanderlust. When Frank invited us to a party following his third child's baptism, I told Iola we would be taking a four-day vacation in Brooklyn.

Thursday morning, she and I boarded a train to Manhattan. I wore a gray suit, white shirt, and a striped tie. In my breast pocket, I put a well-folded pocket square. She wore a print dress, a black hat with wide brim, a fancy hatpin, and patent-leather heels. It was amazing how good she looked in secondhand clothes. The stirring in my loins pleased me. The few times it happened was when she was dressed her best and out in public.

The car we boarded was half-full. We found a seat away from everyone and sat down, close together. When an old man sat across from us, I moved a few inches away from her and began to read my newspaper. Every so often, I'd look up and Iola was gazing out the window at passing towns, old farmhouses, big barns, a crop being harvested, and grazing cows. She was smiling, like a farm girl might. I had never expected I would marry a farm girl, especially one who ate possum. She looked happy. Was I happy? I wouldn't be happy if I had to eat possum. But then what is happiness? Is anyone happy? Enough questions. At the next stop, more people got on. The old man got off and a skinny man took his seat. He wore gray work clothes and a brown cap, which he tipped to Iola, to reveal dull brown hair parted down the middle. He had a scar on his forehead. Probably a street fighter. I didn't like him.

Once the train got moving and the conductor collected tickets, the skinny man said, "Name's Ray Harris. Would you like to play poker?"

I looked up from my newspaper. "No thank you."

"I'll play Spit in the Ocean poker," Iola said.

"Where you learn to play?"

"When I was a pilot."

"A pilot. Damn. I never met a girl pilot before. Goddamn." Ray grinned.

"I'd appreciate if you not swear in front of my wife." I kept my tone of voice polite-sounding.

"Sir. I'll watch my language." Ray tipped his cap.

After she started playing, I poked her ribs but she kept playing. The stirring I had, ended. I was glad I had a newspaper to read. Every so often I would look at them.

When we disembarked at Grand Central Station, I said, "Don't you know it's illegal to be gambling on a train. And it's beyond me why you'd play with someone like that."

"He looked like Buck, if that's okay. And they don't mind you gambling if you keep it quiet."

"Another passenger could have turned you in. You know that."

"No one did." She smiled smugly. "I won four dollars."

The subway we boarded quickly got crowded—some people smelling of perfume, one of body odor. They wore fancy clothes, or ordinary clothes, work clothes. Someone talked nonstop. A baby cried. It was hard to ignore the man who sat across from us, and coughed, noisily turned every page of his magazine, and blew his nose. He looked like he never was in the sun. His skin was very pale. Maybe he lived underground. A woman wore too much makeup. The subway screeched most of the way to our stop. I hated subways.

Obviously it had rained the night before, cooling Brooklyn of August heat. It smelled like wet stone. Puddles of water remained on the tops of dented garbage-can lids, in the worn parts of old stone steps, in indentations on sidewalks. A ragged-looking pigeon washed itself in a puddle, its wings fluttering. It was missing a foot. Some people eat pigeon; I wouldn't.

We walked past women prettier than Iola, adolescent boys seeking excitement, some poor soul with a pushcart selling cheap trinkets. If he gets to heaven, he'd be happy with a little corner. There were little old ladies hanging on to little old men walking slow, a beggar who wasn't bad looking. Iola gave him some money.

"You shouldn't do that. Did you see his dirty nails?"

"Why not? He looked like he's starving."

"Maybe he's an artist. They like to starve. It gives them inspiration."

"That's ridiculous. You ever go hungry? You ever look at others eating and want to snatch their food? Have just dried herbs seeped in hot water for a whole day?" Hunger's not a sharp pain, like a toothache, but it's consuming." Iola shrugged and looked straight ahead.

"How much did you give him?"

"Enough for a meal."

"I said . . . how much?"

"Four dollars."

"That's enough for four meals."

"Didn't cost us anything. I won it in the card game. See, I had to play poker to win some money to help out a starving artist. Because of me, he might paint a masterpiece. Twenty years from now, we might see his masterpiece in a museum. You like helping people, don't you? You're helpful. Didn't Jesus say feed the hungry?"

What could I say? Nothing. She couldn't have planned it—win a card game so she could give a handout to a dirty beggar . . . like she's some fortune-teller. Forget it—just walk. Walk and forget it. It was only one more block. Too many noisy car horns. Hundreds of people. Some yelling. A high-pitched voice. Someone blew a whistle. It was cacophony.

Upon arriving at Frank's house, I knocked once and the door opened. Frank was saying goodbye to two people, who came out of his house before Iola and I could walk in. Introductions were made. A blond-haired man—Erskine (a strange name; needed a haircut)—was a psychiatrist (they're crazy themselves), and an elderly, white-haired woman—Josephina—wrote poems (I never liked poetry) and walked half a mile a day.

As Erskine and Josephina walked down the steps and went on their way, a man across the street yelled over and asked Frank how he was doing. The two of them talked about baseball, weather. Another man joined in and suggested they play bocce ball next weekend.

"Yes."

"Good idea."

"I'll win."

"No you won't."

"Bet you fifty cents."

"Does everyone know you here?" Iola asked. Frank smiled, shrugged, nodded.

Sarah came to the door and asked why we hadn't come in. She had a nice nose, shapely lips, dark brown eyes, and prominent cheekbones, long wavy black hair. She wore no makeup except red lipstick. She was striking in a different way. I could see why Frank married her. They looked married.

Inside the house were two more people, not striking at all, but attractive enough to not be homely.

"What is this? The party before the party?" Iola asked.

"That sounds like fun—have a party-before-a-party." Sarah elbowed Frank. "I can call up lots of people who'll come. Want to have a preparty now?"

"No."

"Okay. You're right. We don't have the time anyway."

The two strangers were Jill and Mike Something-or-other who both taught at the college where Sarah taught. They were customers at the bookstore Frank had bought after the war ended. The woman mentioned F. Scott Fitzgerald and another author I didn't recognize. The talk turned to Paris, wine, and some French-sounding names. Like the house was full of foreigners. There was laughter at a joke I didn't catch. This was not the Frank I knew as a kid. I relaxed my shoulders when Jill and Mike left.

I walked down the long hallway. The tall bookcases got my attention. Four all crammed full, and more books stacked on the tops. I recognized none of the authors—Albert Camus, Martin Heidegger, Pascal, Kafka, lots of foreign-sounding names, until I noticed Mark Twain and Nathaniel Hawthorne, a few others. Frank had definitely changed. Maybe the war did it. On one wall in the dining room was a collection of baseball paraphernalia, and on another wall were photographs of no one I recognized. Sarah noticed me looking at the photographs and said they were current and past residents of Brooklyn. Some looked like laborers; some looked well-to-do. In one, a man was standing by a street-sweeping machine, along with Frank. There was a crazy painting on the wall. Just splotches of bright color and amorphous shapes. I never knew anyone before who owned a real painting, especially one of those nonsense abstracts. I was tense again. This was supposed to be a vacation. On another wall was a black-and-white photograph of a man standing, looking straight ahead, and holding a cigar.

Frank and Iola came in the room.

Iola commented on the picture—how the man looked quite intelligent.

Frank said it was an original photograph of Sigmund Freud, and it was given to him by his friend, the psychiatrist, after Frank did him a big favor. "Ever hear of Freud?"

"Of course," Iola said.

I once heard Freud was a heathen. He didn't look like a heathen—wild and barbaric. Kids' coloring books, puzzles, toys were strewn over the dining table. My mother would never allow clutter like that but I figured Iola would, because after we got married, she left dirty clothes in a pile in the corner, even after I asked her not to. I always hung my clothes up neat in the closet or put them in the laundry.

The next morning, Iola and I were sitting at the breakfast table. Frank came in, brushing his teeth. He spit in the sink. His legs were skinny; his chest was hairy. He was wearing only boxer shorts.

"Frank, get the hell out of here without your clothes on. We have guests," Sarah said. "And don't spit in my sink."

"Sweets, it's your fault. The aromas made me walk in here almost naked. If you were a lousy cook I'd behave."

"You go to hell," Sarah said.

Frank sat down and took a sip of coffee. "Excellent coffee. Makes me want to take all my clothes off."

"You can go naked to hell," Sarah said.

"No one's naked in hell. You're naked in heaven. All you have is gigantic white cherubic wings. Light as a feather. If you don't want to be naked you have to flap one wing to the front and one in back to cover yourself." Frank put one arm in front and the other behind his back.

"What if you're flying?" Iola asked. "Doesn't one fly in heaven?"

"You're stark naked when you fly. Heaven is a nudie camp. In hell you wear heavy black wool clothes. Very hot. Wool hats, coats, socks, itchy underwear, everything is wool, even black wool sheets."

"So you sleep in hell?" Iola had the barest smile.

"If you can fall asleep on rough wool sheets." Frank sipped his coffee. "Where do you want to go, Sarah—nudie-camp heaven or hot woolen hell?"

"Heaven, but I'd keep my big wings wrapped around me and tiptoe everywhere." Sarah demonstrated.

They all erupted in laughter.

"Jim, where do you want to go—nudie-camp heaven or woolen hell?"

"You're blasphemous," I said.

"Cousin, you're endearing. When you get so serious your forehead winkles. Dear favorite cousin. Dear cousin."

"Just drink your coffee, Frank." I was annoyed.

"It's good to be blasphemous. God likes it because God's funny. God's everything. Nudie God's laughing right now. A very divine ha-ha-ha-luyah."

I didn't know what to say.

Sarah set a plate of pastries on the table and pointed to two. "These are nun's puffs."

"They're served in heaven's Catholic neighborhood," Frank said.

"Frank, shush. This one is a Paris-Brest. It's filled with praline-flavored cream. If you like frangipane try these *Jésuites*. They're named after hats Jesuits wear. The éclairs are filled with *chiboust* cream. This *chouquette* is filled with mousse. And last but not least are the *vol-au-vents*. I made them. The others I bought. We don't usually eat so opulent."

I was taken aback by the abundance and the way Sarah said all the foreign-sounding words with a French accent. I had always thought my mother was the best cook but the only deserts she ever made were fruit pies, banbury cake, or bakewell pudding. Sometimes, she made sad cake but I never liked it for the name, especially after my sister's death. It sounded like a poor man's dessert.

Sarah put more food on the table. "These are both quiche. Jim, it's an egg pie."

"I never had a pie of egg."

"One is filled with ham and cheese, and this one with spinach and cheese."

The baby started crying in her bassinet, so Sarah picked her up, sat down across from me at the kitchen table, opened her blouse, and her big braless breast spilled out for the baby. Then the two older kids, Steven and Louise, sat down.

The nursing display embarrassed me, but I don't think I blushed. Then Steven asked for the *chouquette*, and Louise wanted a nun's puff. They both said it all Frenchy too. Being polite, I said the egg pie was good. Louise said something like "marecee" and Steven said, "Marecee bokoo," and Frank said, "Wee wee." Sarah said, "Wee wee." I knew they were talking French. Sarah was the cause. Her grandfather was French.

"Jim, you want more pie of egg? And a Catholic pastry?" Frank asked.

I took more pie but no pastry.

"It's good. You won't turn French. You've got too much English blood in you to ever turn French. Your blood is superior. When you cut yourself you don't bleed. It's that English control." Iola gave me a slim smile.

"I do too."

"Iola's right, Jim. Remember, one time we had a sword fight as kids, and I cut off your head and you didn't bleed. I stuck your head back on and you punched me."

"You're full of shit."

"Just for you, favorite cousin. I love my handsome cousin." Frank took my hand and kissed it.

I pushed him away.

"Jim, you know what I liked about you when we first met—you pronounce all your syllables. Every single one, crisp and clear. Crisp talk," Iola said.

"It's called the king's English."

"That's right, Jim, you talk like the royals. You'll never turn French." Iola patted my kissed hand.

Sarah said, "Be nice, Frank," but I could see all of them were doing poorly holding back their amusement. Over what? It didn't seem funny. To change the topic, I suggested to Frank that we play a game of bocce ball after breakfast.

"Iola, would you like to join us?" Frank asked.

"I never played it but I once won a tennis contest."

"You competitive?" Frank asked.

"I had to be to get in the WASP."

Frank nodded. "That's right, you were a pilot. That's pretty independent. And smart. I think you'd say that women are equal to men. You like Susan B. Anthony?"

"Where I grew up, people said she did the work of the devil."

"Your family never voted?"

"Never. Not a religious thing to do." Iola shrugged.

"I like Susan B. Anthony," Sarah said. "She got women the vote. And Frank, don't talk with good French food in your big English mouth."

Frank swallowed his egg stuff. "You like the vote?" He looked at Iola.

"I'd say so. I vote."

"You know, I have a writer friend who would love to interview you—write your story. You miss being a pilot?" Frank asked.

"I do, but Jim won't like hearing me say that."

I said nothing but I noticed her suppressing her smile.

Sarah said she was short of good tablecloths and she would be forever pleased if someone would go buy some for her.

Iola immediately offered to go into Manhattan to pick up some damask tablecloths because she could get it for half of what Sarah wanted to pay. She knew of a neighborhood where she could find some because she had visited the city several times in the past. I pulled a ten-dollar bill out of my wallet and gave it to Iola. "If you do that—here, buy something for yourself. Anything you want." She looked surprised.

As she was going out the door, I went over, out of earshot of everyone, and asked her to buy a present for my mother's sixtieth birthday, one week away. I handed her twenty-five dollars. I did it with no smile. My mouth open, eyes relaxed like a baby. I kept my composure even when she narrowed her eyes at me. She deserved it for making fun of me in front of Frank. After she left, I regretted what I did. It wasn't something my father would have done. He was good to me, and my mother, and my sister. I loved him.

Chapter 8

FOLLOWING THE BAPTISM of the new baby, Frank and Sarah's house filled with happy, laughing, noisy kids, and talkative adults who found humor in anything. In the parlor, the hallway, dining room, even sitting on the stairs, adults were kissing, drinking, hugging, saying how much they missed each other, and taking turns holding baby Jeannette. Wanting less hoopla, I walked into the kitchen and sat down by Frank. Soon the talk turned to General Eisenhower and World War II and how he had led the Normandy invasion.

The old poet, Josephina, from two days before, was also sitting at the table. She had several strands of purple beads around her wrinkled neck. She was probably good-looking when young. Her voice was a bit deep, somewhat creaky and she spoke with an accent.

"Wars aren't justified," Sarah said while wiping up something she had spilled on the floor.

"Maybe a few are, but no victory in any war, even a just one, should be celebrated. Innocent people always die. I heard over thirty million total in World War II. Thirty million." Josephine looked at everyone.

"That's right. I never put any credence in war medals," Frank said.

"Is that why you threw away your purple heart?" I asked. "God knows you shouldn't have done that. You fought for our freedom. America is a free country. The first free country."

"Actually the first written accounts of freedom were in Urukagina's reign in ancient Sumeria. They would've said the same thing. And as far as I'm concerned, all soldiers are brave. They should all get one," Frank said.

"That would diminish the medal." I leaned back in my chair.

"I think we're all brave to live in this world." Josephina touched her purple beads. Her English was perfect. That had to mean she was smart. I liked smart people, but I thought her comment was stupid.

Using my calmest voice, I asked, "What was so good about this Uru man?"

"For one thing, Uru man got rid of a tax for burying your dead. So if you didn't pay the tax, I'd conjecture you'd have to leave the swollen body rotting someplace, smelling up everything until the buzzards got to it."

"How does a buzzard eat putrid, smelly rotting flesh?" Josephina asked.

"Maybe they have no sense of smell." Sarah shrugged.

"Catholics have fought lots of wars. They started wars," Iola said. I hadn't realized she had come into the kitchen and was standing by the door. Why did she say that? She looked pretty in her blue dress and blue heels.

"I don't catch what you mean." Josephina stroked her chin. Iola sat down.

"Well, you're complaining about war, yet you're Catholic," Iola said.

"Why do you think that?" Josephina rested her head in her hands.

"Well, you're at a party for a Catholic christening." Iola gestured to all the people in the house.

"I'm not a Catholic." Josephina laughed. "Half of the people here aren't. If they are—not very serious."

"I'm not much of one, but my mother and sister still are," Sarah said.

Iola looked at Josephina and asked, "What are you, then?"

"I'm nothing. I don't think we live after we die. To me baptism is anthropology, a cultural ritual. Plus I love Sarah's parties." She ran her hand through her thin white hair. "Are you Catholic?"

"No." Iola looked puzzled.

"You're here."

Iola sat down by Josephina, touched her arm, and said, "It's interesting. One can draw a conclusion about people and be all wrong. I grew up in a place like that—most everyone made too many conclusions about people they didn't know."

"So you don't believe in God?" I asked.

"I didn't say that," Josephina said. "How would I know if God exists? But it does kind of seem like believing in Santa Claus. Fine for a kid. Most kids are disappointed when they find out Santa Claus doesn't exist. But you know . . . if someone wants to get to heaven, I wish them the best of luck getting there."

"So you wouldn't want to go to heaven?" I asked.

"I just don't see that we live after death."

I'd be damned if I sat in the same room with a heathen, so I got up. As I was walking out of the kitchen, I turned around and saw Iola smiling at Josephina. It gave me angst—the interest she had in someone like that. I blamed it on her yearning to still be a pilot. I knew—the way she'd read every article in the newspaper about planes, pilots, Charles Lindberg. The way she looked out windows when she heard planes flying overhead. I regretted the visit—all the Frenchy stuff, the heathens, the foreign books. I was ready to go home.

Willowsburg, Pennsylvania
1947

Jim

Chapter 9

MY MOTHER DIDN'T answer her doorbell. It was our Sunday visit. I used my key to get in. The house was warm and very quiet. No pleasant aromas came from the kitchen. I called her name but she didn't answer. This was unusual.

We found her lying in bed under her covers. Her slippers were by her bed. Draped over a chair lay her neatly folded white robe. I called to wake her up but there was no response. I went over to her. Something looked different. Her skin had no color and she was perfectly still. I touched her, snatched my hand away, and spun around. My fist, held tight against my mouth, kept me from crying, from fearing what life was going to be like without her.

Iola walked over and touched her. "She probably died in her sleep." She said something about calling someone.

What do I do? Pull the covers over her head, touch her, say goodbye? Can you kiss the dead? I didn't know, but did it anyway. I walked to the window to hold back tears, opened and closed the curtains, and walked back to her bed. My hands tremored. I wished Iola would leave the room so I could be alone. Somehow she must have known, because she left.

An emptiness loomed ahead—no mother, no father, no sister. I was glad I had Iola.

Iola returned with a cup. "It's coffee. Bliss Coffee."

"Bliss? Yes, bliss, she'll be in heaven. She was a good person."

"My mama liked to say you don't have to be a good person to get to heaven—just have to accept Jesus into your heart. She accepted Jesus, didn't she?"

"Are you saying she wasn't a good person?"

"I didn't mean that. Meant as long as she accepted Jesus she'll be in heaven. That's it. Jesus gets you in."

I moved a chair over to the bed and sat down. She looked asleep, as if death had only brushed by and went on its way. Her hand felt cold but maybe deep in her veins she still had the warmth of life. Maybe her soul hadn't left. It would be nice to be holding her hand when her soul departed. How long does it take for a soul to leave a body? Does it leave all at once or cell by cell? Maybe it first leaves the toes, the feet, and up the body. Maybe the soul never inhabits the feet or the legs. It seemed like the right place to leave a body is up through the top of the head. Her head was cold. Her white hair smelled good. Her room always did. Was her soul still in the room?

I looked for signs—a speck of light on the ceiling, the four walls, over the bed, by the floorboards. I thought I saw a flicker of light. Maybe it's a sound. A whisper. Maybe it leaves a sweet odor. I didn't smell or hear anything unusual. I should pray. What do I say? *Please, God, take her soul.* For myself, I said silently, *I did what I could for her and tried my best.* I felt bad that I felt a release from responsibility. It was odd—feeling both free and sad.

Iola placed the coffee on the bedside table for me. I slumped down into my chair and I cried like a child in broad daylight, in front of Iola. Men shouldn't cry.

"I'm sorry, dear." Iola stood awhile. I didn't touch the coffee. I sunk into grief and confusion.

AT THE FUNERAL, before anyone arrived, Iola said, "Except for one of the WASP girls, I've never seen fancy funerals. Those in Pilgrim were always held in the funeral room of my oldest uncle's house."

"And what is a funeral room?" Was this going to be another strange Pilgrim story?

"Custom was the oldest brother would set aside one room in his house just for funerals. The men made the casket. Just a plain wooden box. Over time, everything rotted in the ground. Something planted there—it would grow well. There was the preacher. Prayers, talk, maybe flowers, unless it was winter. Tears, if the death was unexpected, and then enough food for days spread out on the kitchen table. In the summer, flies were a problem."

"Are you saying I should not have bought an expensive casket?"

"No. Just meant things were different where I grew up. You look irritated."

"I was just asking a question. You're here in Philadelphia now."

"Isn't that true. I wouldn't want to be in Pilgrim."

I was glad Iola was with me. Enough people paid their respects to assure me my mother was well liked.

A week later, after I got home from work, I hung a picture of my mother right by our wedding picture on the wall. I wasn't quite sure why I did it, but it was like I still had a family. It had never occurred to me I'd be the last Lewis to survive. I was glad I was married. I couldn't imagine being alone. I wanted to share my feelings with Iola but didn't.

At dinner it surprised me that Iola had used my mother's recipe for a pork roast. "You did a good job. It's better than my mother's."

"Thank you. I'll have to use it again," she said. "Nice picture of her. I don't think I ever told you."

"You like it?"

"Yes, very nice. She was attractive, stunning blue eyes, an excellent cook, knew how to manage a two-story house. Kept it shiny and free of dust, and well stocked. Embroidered sheets, mended clothes, perfect at starching, ironing, mending. She had a list for every day of the week—mornings, afternoons, evenings. Her days were busy."

"She did?"

"You didn't know that? It's amazing how she got it all done. Set a wonderful table. Never cursed that I ever heard. I doubt she cursed even in her thoughts. I curse in my thoughts."

"You do?"

"Yes, dear."

"What do you say?"

"Damn it. Sometimes worse."

"Worse what?"

"Oh fuck. It's important to know people's strengths. Weaknesses are easy to recognize."

"You're saying she had weaknesses?"

"Don't you think? Seems everyone does. I think she may have been someone who would get even for insults in little symbolic ways. Maybe the offender wouldn't even know what she did. Just a gesture to make her feel better. Help her feel she's not a fool, didn't make the worst decision on earth. Help her get through the day, get her chores done. She ever do that?"

"I don't think she ever felt like a fool. Are you saying she was a fool?" It wasn't the first time Iola was hard to fathom.

"Just meant she was probably subtle if she ever tried to get a bit of revenge."

"That sounds like a strength."

"You're right again."

"Now it's just me and you, Iola."

"We'll get by, dear."

I liked being called dear. After dinner, I went through a box of letters my mother had kept in her closet. One was from my uncle written to my father years ago. Two lines got my attention—*Regarding your worry that Jim acts too girlish, I say don't worry, as he's only eleven. Boys can outgrow that.*

I stuck the letter in my pocket, put on a hat and coat, and went for a walk, even though it was drizzling. At the park, I tore the letter up into pieces, and threw bits of it in four different trash cans as I walked around the park. On the way home, I stopped in a bar and had a drink. It didn't lessen the angst.

IN AUGUST 1947, our first baby was on the way. Soon, I'd be a father, and a father needs a house to raise a family. My hope—four smart, good-looking children. Is that too much to ask for?

I finally sold my mother's house for less than expected due to newly discovered problems with termites, and a plumbing disaster. We looked at an old stone farmhouse on the edge of the respectable town of Willowsburg near Philadelphia. It sat at the end of a quiet street. A big maple shaded the wide front porch. I looked up through the maple, to the blue sky, white clouds. The green leaves fluttering, shadows aquiver, the browns and grays of branches, the seedpods looked beautiful and peaceful.

It needed repairs. The wooden kitchen countertop was rotted in places. Most windows wouldn't stay open unless propped up. The roof would need replacing in several years. There was some dry rot on the front porch, and the back door needed to be replaced, but the foundation was strong, and no termites. There was a large basement and two staircases going upstairs. A regular one with fancy banisters, near the front entry, and a steep, narrow, winding one off the kitchen. It had three large bedrooms. One of the bedrooms had a repairable hole in the wall. Probably someone's angry foot went through it.

A small room off the kitchen might have been servants' quarters, since it had a sink and a closet. What would it be like to have a servant? I'd be a decent boss and give a Christmas bonus. I'd never curse a servant or raise a hand. There was a small toilet room by the kitchen, and a bathroom upstairs with a long claw-foot tub. I never lived in a house with one and a half bathrooms. The front door had beveled glass, and a carved design in the oak wood. At the end of the street, a dirt road led onto the farmer's field that bordered the property. Looking at the farmer's field out back, I imagined what life might be like in the prairies. The large backyard had a cherry tree, a peach, and a lilac. I wanted to grow old here. We bought it—328 Oak Tree Road.

All the furniture we needed was in my mother's house. We had a month to pack. Iola held her own, carrying heavy boxes, rarely out of breath. My farm girl, strong as an ox. Ox girl. Ox wife. Horse wife. Buffalo wife (I almost chuckled) was ready to pick up one end of the buffet to move it out the door.

"You shouldn't do that. You're pregnant." Was she ever. Huge breasts and belly like a fertility goddess.

"Women did it all the time in Pilgrim and rarely had a miscarriage."

"Still."

"Anyone else going to help you?"

I FOUND A neighbor to lend a hand. After we had moved in, Iola bumped into the dining table while holding a fork and gauged a scratch in it. I accused her of being careless.

"You act like it's the Last Supper table," she said.

"If that's what it takes for you to take care of it, then that's what it is and God doesn't want you to wreck it. Say some prayers."

"Dear God, is this the Last Supper table? Thank you, God. He laughed and said, 'No. It's too short.'"

"Ah the comedian. You would have done better telling jokes than becoming a pilot."

She stepped back, souring her face. "Don't you say that."

"Well, think about it. Did you get much pay as a pilot? You came out as poor as you went in. You had to pay for your own food, lodging, and uniforms. What good did it do you? End of conversation." My mood changed somehow. I don't know why I got so bothered. Needing time alone, I said I was going to meet some of my friends and told her to save me some dinner. I walked out of the house, got in my car, and drove into downtown Philadelphia. Why? I didn't know. There were two men walking across an intersection on Chestnut Street. Nice-looking. Were they together? I drove past Washington Square, down to Pine Street and Lombard, just watching. There was a tall man, well-dressed, broad shoulders, real healthy-looking. I parked my car away from streetlights and neons, sat and watched various men passing by, and let my mind wander.

So I didn't look suspicious, I drove to South Street, parked, and watched more men. One I couldn't help myself. He was handsome, young, dark hair, and had a quick stride. I wanted to see him naked. It was just thoughts. Can't go to prison for thoughts. I briefly touched myself, but then out of nowhere, a man came up and knocked on my window, scaring me. It was a beggar asking for a dime. Maybe it was my own form of penance but I got out of my car and walked with him to a White Castle and bought him a meal. He smelled awful. His shirt was filthy. It occurred to me that if he was what all men looked like, I might fall in love with Iola.

ON MAY 2, 1948, Iola gave birth to Charles, named after my father. I had never held a newborn before. He hardly weighed anything. His eyes were closed. I touched his lips. He sucked my finger. He smelled of new flesh, maybe lilac, the woods after a rain. Spontaneously I made a vow to be a good and steadfast father. Was this holiness I felt? Pray. Did I do it right? Pray again. Please bless me, God, and make me a good father. Again. I kissed him.

A milestone of this magnitude deserved a picture, so I bought a Brownie camera. I asked Iola to put lipstick on, to powder her face, and comb her tumbleweed hair and put on a decent dress. "One with a full skirt. Look pretty. You're a pretty wife." She sat in a chair, holding Charles with the morning sun shining through the lace curtains. There were lacy shadows on my boy's face, arms and hands, and his white blanket. There were on Iola's arms, hands, and white dress. Her buttons caught the light. The dappled shadows made it hard to tell where Charles ended and Iola started. Beautiful. It might be a perfect picture, but what is perfect? I had her sit by the window, facing forward, sideways, standing, holding the baby in different ways, and used up a whole roll of film. I had her sit out on the front porch and finished another roll.

Later in the day, I watched Iola with Charles. She called him Baby, and vegetables like Pumpkin and Sweet Potato, and desserts like Pudding and Cupcake. He was Little Man to me. When she was changing his diaper, he peed. It shot right up in the air like a fountain. Her bumpy laugh made me laugh. I called him Fountain and felt poetic. I almost laughed—me, poetic? Is a good father poetic? I wished I had a photograph of it. She cleaned the fountain off him. The poem evaporated. She seemed to be a good mother. My ox wife, mother of Fountain. I shouldn't think of her that way. I wished I had a stirring whenever I saw her bent over pulling up her underpants. Once when she bent over, I caught a glimpse of her vagina. And putting on her bra. Her breasts swollen with milk. It was a chore to pretend, but pretending protected me. Men have gone to prison for the wrong kind of passion. It gave me fear, so I refused to think any more about it.

"Honey, you look pretty holding the baby." Ox mother. Please turn into a man just for a night. It'll be our secret.

THE FIRST YEAR on Oak Tree Road was good. I did some repairs, planted two apple trees. One died but that was okay. I'd plant another. I walked down our tree-lined street and met some of the neighbors. Al Peterson worked in a factory in Philadelphia, and his wife, Jill—they lived two doors down. Lester Causley, a large man, owned the bordering farm. George and Edna Miller with the Virgin Mary statue in their front yard—must be Catholics—nice enough. The Mackeys with the Buick Roadmaster and six children. I bragged about my firstborn and showed them pictures. In town, I met the owner of three hardware stores, Mr. Delanet, nice, rich, but plain-looking. The grocery store owner, Luke Something-or-other, and a schoolteacher, Miss Helen Alton, never married, slender, very polite. We discussed American history for an hour. I was pleased to be living in Willowsburg. It was an honest town with clean sidewalks, a town square with a fountain in the middle, and no crime to speak of, and a decent commute to work—to the lab with test tubes and petri dishes, the centrifuge, the IR spectrometer, and guinea pigs. That I was merely a lab technician vexed me, whenever I allowed myself to think about it. I, who had almost gone to Princeton University for a degree in chemistry.

ON MAY 30, 1949, Starla was born, named after Iola's favorite little sister, who drowned at age ten.

"This is a good family—just two children," Iola said after dinner one night.

"We need another," I said.

It surprised me when she said she didn't want a third. Didn't all women want lots of children? For fulfillment? Then she blamed me—that I wasn't making much money as a lab technician. And I had recently talked about possible layoffs at work. "Three kids would put us in the poorhouse, even without you getting laid off. You're crazy." She shook her head.

"I love my kids and a third one is needed. It's enough that I don't insist on five. And I'm in charge and you need to mind me."

"I love my kids, too, and I'm in charge of myself, I'll have you know. And just why is it that you were much nicer to me before we got married? We actually had fun together."

"Well, the courtship is over, so lower your voice, and I'm going for a ride. I'll be back when I'm back." Irked about the poorhouse and crazy accusations, I walked out, got in the car, and drove into Philadelphia.

Chapter 10

I GOT HOME at two in the morning, and so I woke up late. Walking downstairs, I heard the sound of a dove. How could a dove get trapped in the house? I followed the sound toward the kitchen, walking quietly to not scare the bird. At the far end of the kitchen and standing with her back to me, Iola cooed to Charles. Charles made *mmm, mmm* sounds. She reciprocated. Back and forth they went. She said, "Mmm, mmm, mama." He said the same and then giggled like it was the funniest thing he ever heard.

Like an unwitting intruder not wanting to be discovered, I quietly backed out of the doorway and walked out to the front porch. For the first time, I realized why a child's first word is usually *Mama*. It's the easiest two syllables to say. I liked my son speaking. He will have an excellent vocabulary.

It was nice being unnoticed. Maybe I would be more attracted to Iola if I spied on her, like a Peeping Tom. That's perverse. I hated perverse. That's what I am but couldn't admit it to anyone. If I was Catholic I could go to confession and talk with a priest in a dark confessional and he wouldn't know who I was. *Bless me, Father, I have sinned. Isn't that what you say, Father? (Yes, son. Now tell me your sins.) I am perverse. (Why, son?) Father, I imagine having sex with men. Sometimes, it's hard to control. (You must try). I do, all the time, but sometimes . . . Will God forgive me? (Say forty Hail Marys.) Yes, Father. I just want to be normal.*

When Iola took a bath later that day, I picked Charles up and held him, eyes to eyes. I shaped my lips the right way, snapped my lips open, while exhaling, making *pa, pa* sounds. Charles didn't quite catch it, but his wide-open eyes looked intrigued, so I did it again close to Charles's hand so he'd feel my breath. I then put my hand near Charles's mouth. Charles understood and made *pa* sounds. Simultaneously we did it. I said, "Pa, pa" real snappy slow and pointed to myself.

Charles said, "Pa, pa." He giggled like he knew what he'd done and it was even funnier than before. I shaped my lips just right.

I exaggerated the movement right in front of him and said, "Baay beee," and pointed to him.

Charles said, "Bah ba."

I was never into dancing but this was a dance—pointing to myself and saying, "Pa, pa," pointing to Charles and saying, "Baay beee." Charles learned the steps, back and forth in unison, as if we were dancing. He laughed hysterically like it was the funniest thing ever, like we were saints doing comedy.

Charles's three-word vocabulary had transported me to someplace unknown. Getting a Ph.D. in chemistry couldn't have done it better. The elation was almost too good to be believed. I wasn't sure if I'd know how to describe what happened. It wasn't just a lesson in language acquisition. I'd likely get all tongue-tied and Iola would look at me strange. No one had ever done that to me before. I took Charles into the front room where Starla was in her playpen. I set Charles down on the settee, put my arm around him, and watched Starla. I wanted to share the experience with Iola but didn't. I didn't know why. It was pure mystery.

IT WAS NOVEMBER 20, 1951, in the living room, and the lights out. My first home movie began with a close-up of Elizabeth—beautiful baby Lizzy's first birthday—with her eyes and mouth opened wide, taking the world in. Charles stood straight and saluted some imaginary hero. Starla put her arm around her baby sister and then she clapped. Birthday cake was served. As Iola bent over to wipe Lizzy's cake-smeared mouth, her neckline dropped letting her cleavage catch the camera's eye. End of movie.

"You like taking pictures of cleavage?" Iola asked.

"With cleavage like that you could be a movie star."

"Is that why you married me? For my cleavage?" She uncrossed and crossed her long legs.

"It was actually your childbearing hips that caught my attention. You looked like a farm girl capable of any chore. Certainly not you being a pilot. By the way, you look much better with children than in that picture of you standing by an airplane."

"So do stray dogs."

"What do stray dogs have to do with anything?"

"They look good with their pups." She shrugged one shoulder.

"Anyone ever tell you, you don't take compliments well?"

"Not used to getting them. And I know what I'm talking about. I once watched a scraggly stray suddenly look good as she offered herself to her pups. Tails wagged. Bellies filled. She licked them. They loved her licks. Very sweet."

"My parents wanted six children. Did you know my mother had two miscarriages and a stillbirth? I almost had four siblings."

"Never knew that. I know three equals fertile-plus-smart. As a kid, I knew spewing out fifteen kids wasn't for me. Seeds popping out of seed pods to grow more seed pods."

"You sound like one of those Darwin people. They make no sense—saying people evolved from apes."

"You're making no sense. I'm talking about too many kids—not where we came from. I would've done fine with four siblings, five at the most. Thirteen—no way. You want a Boggs history? A brief Boggs history of why three's enough? I'll give you one. Sledge Jr. joined the military and got to sergeant. Thought he was general at home. Ethyl Lou. She's still in Pilgrim trying to bend everyone to her will. Henry—he almost killed Lucine when he hit her hard, and then he was killed in a hunting accident. Zeke disappeared one day. Never came back. Friend became a preacher. I heard he and his wife say grace before having sex."

"I never heard of that—saying grace before sex."

"Suited them, I guess. Maybe it was a fertility prayer. They have ten kids."

"What did they say?"

"How would I know? I wasn't there listening, being some pervert."

"You're talking awfully fast. Do you have to get someplace?"

"Yeah, I'd like to finish my family history. The quicker the better if you don't mind." Iola talked even faster. "Edgar died at age three, Buck my second favorite brother, me, Nelda—too pretty for Pilgrim, Lucine talked too much, my sister Starla drowned in the river swollen by two days of downpour despite Zeke's effort to save her, Cecil—don't know what to say about him other than he mixed up most of his pronouns, Verna died at five days, and Maude—Papa's favorite. Lucine found her out in the shed about to be raped by Friend . . ."

"You mean perversely assaulted. Be careful what you say around the children."

"I mean raped, the kids aren't listening, only thing Papa did was tell Friend not to do it again or he'd beat the living daylights out of him, Lucine got no thanks, just a 'Shut up and don't say a word about it,' plus I had to sleep in a bed with two sisters sometimes three." She exhaled and inhaled two long breaths. "That's my reason. Is that enough?"

"You should be an auctioneer. You could auction off airplanes."

"Go ahead, chuckle. And I'd make more money than you. You can chuckle at that."

I didn't take kindly to her smart retort. After the popcorn was eaten, I set up my tripod and camera to take some photographs of my good-looking children. "Your grandmother would have been so proud. I would give anything for her to be here," I said. I moved furniture about and adjusted my camera. I placed the baby in a chair, next to a small table, where the light from a stained-glass lamp gave a glow. Charles and Starla stood beside little Lizzy. On the table sat a picture of their grandparents—for family lineage. I snapped away.

Iola came over and stood beside the children.

"Iola, not in this picture, please."

She stayed and finger-combed her hair.

When the photos were developed, and she took a look at them, her head was cut off in the picture she was in. "Why did you do that?" she asked.

"Not every photo comes out perfect. Professional photographers will tell you that." I scissored off the part of the picture where she was standing. "See now— no one with a head cut off. It's perfect."

She got an expression of being offended—I've seen it before. I regretted my actions. My father would apologize if he had done something wrong. I loved him. *Sorry*, I thought and walked away.

Iola

Chapter 11

IT WAS UNUSUAL to hear several knocks on my back door. Had someone come out of the woods and crossed the field behind the house? They'd be up to no good. I was alone with my kids. I picked up a butcher knife, held it real tight, and peeked out the window through the curtains. It was Norma Wendall. Six months ago she and her husband, Ron Wendall, had moved into the small clapboard house next door. We usually talked at the property line about nothing in particular—rain coming, making pickles, kids, Willowsburg, stain removal. One time she talked about husband problems. She said she was joking, but I wondered.

I yanked the door open. It hit the wall, making a racket. I hadn't meant to. The door was peeling paint. It had a dilapidated screen with holes big enough for horseflies to crawl through. One time, I had put scotch tape over the holes, but it all fell off.

She looked surprised and took a step back. She had sky-blue eyes, smooth cream-colored Nordic skin, not one freckle, scar, or mole, and high cheekbones, a round face. Her belly was plump, her hips wide. I guessed—mid twenties.

She asked if I'd like some tomatoes. With hands of a laborer—all dry and rough—she handed me a bag, saying, "Beautiful. Aren't they?"

I pulled out an unblemished, ripe red, round one. She said she grew everything from seed, and had seed pots all over her house last winter. Her animated voice reminded me of my little sister, Starla, who got real excited over growing tomatoes until Mama said excitement for physical things is sinning, and she got a little slap.

It was ordinary talk—not about planes or World War II—but it brightened my monotonous morning. I asked her in, if she didn't mind the odor of diapers waiting to be washed. As soon as Norma walked in the kitchen, the dishes soaking in my sink inspired an apology. Then Lizzy cried her hunger cry. Should I tell Norma to leave so I could open my blouse and nurse? I liked having an adult to talk to. Norma must have picked up on my awkwardness because she said, "Feel free in front of me. I don't mind. Ron never liked it when I nursed in front of others. I'm talking about in front of a girlfriend. He was stupid."

"Isn't that true?" I picked up Lizzy and unbuttoned my blouse. Needing to explain my lack of a bra, I said, "I only have two nursing bras and they're both in the laundry."

"I don't mind. Where I was raised, my mother wore an undershirt, sometimes nothing underneath. All of us—my sisters, aunts, cousins. I was sixteen when I first wore a bra—at my wedding." Norma glanced twice around the whole kitchen. Then she quickly pulled up her blouse for a second or two, exposing her bare breasts. "See. Still don't sometimes."

"I've never complimented a woman on her chest before but yours looks pretty good."

"Yours look pretty good too." We had a fit of laughter.

"Ron says nudity is sinful. But he talks one thing, does another. My sister once saw him going in a strip club. Strippers dance until their clothes are almost off. Now I like to dance but not like that. Ron won't dance, so I do the two-step with my broom." She noticed my broom, danced over to it, and danced with it. Her red hair, tied in a ponytail with a green ribbon, swung right and left. Again, she reminded me of my sister, Starla. One time, Starla had danced with a broom. She was so funny I asked her to do it again. A week later she drowned and I cried for days until told to shut up. She and Norma would've liked each other. I hoped Norma wasn't going to drown.

"Where you grow up?"

"Pilgrim. Nearest big city was Chattanooga."

Norma stopped dancing and set my broom down. "I know Chattanooga. I grew up in a little town about fifty miles outside of Chattanooga."

We discovered we both had relatives in Chattanooga, in the same part of town, and once in a while got to visit them in the summer as kids. She sat down at the table. We talked about Jackson Creek with a swimming hole, and the magnolia trees with big white blossoms. I asked if she had ever climbed any of the magnolia trees. She asked if I had ever played belle with the flowers. It became a game.

"Did you go to Harner's corner drugstore and buy root beer floats?" I asked.

"If I had ten cents."

"What about matinees at the Capital Theatre?"

"If I had the nickel."

"Did you ever sneak in?"

"Yes." She smiled wide.

"You ever get caught?"

"No."

"Did you ever shop at Placker's Five-and-Dime?"

"Yes."

We became best friends when she told me she loved listening to the radio when she was a girl. She asked if I ever ate pawpaws. Five minutes we must've talked about them—finding pawpaw patches, their twelve-inch leaves, and pretty maroon flowers. Her favorite was pawpaw custard—once she had it with whipped cream on top—but pawpaw pie would do. Mine was just eating them raw. I didn't ask if her mama ever made baby food by chewing food up and feeding it to her babies. My mama did.

When she asked if I ever ate possum, she was like my sister. We preferred squirrel to possum. Then she said what she really liked in Chattanooga was once hearing her cousin, Cora, sing at the Capital Theatre, and the audience loved her and gave her a standing ovation. "For the first time I felt I was part of something big." Norma sighed.

I held my breath, my mouth open, my excitement spilling out. "I had a relative named Cora. We were second or third cousins, by marriage. She sang, too, like perfection and was the nicest person ever. Her last name was Bevil and she grew up in Chattanooga. I heard she moved to Chicago. She was skinny as a rail and had thick brown hair."

"Good God, that makes us cousins."

Simultaneously, we stood up and hugged each other, for we were family. "Where is she now?"

"Last I heard, she and a colored girl sang together and they moved to France because there were problems—a white and colored girl singing together, even in Chicago. Cora got her life threatened and the colored girl was beaten until she was bloody." Norma almost whispered the last sentence, like it was hard to talk about it.

I wanted to talk about Zeke and how he was beaten until bloody and killed for being homosexual. He was smart and loved me like the best brother ever. I wanted to know more about Cora. I wanted to hear she was okay. I wanted to brag about her—how wonderful she was. But I stood there waiting for Norma to say something.

Abruptly, Norma's mood changed—maybe puzzled, pensive, or reticent about talking. She rubbed her hands together, and finally said, "One time, Ron beat my oldest with his belt real hard, drawing blood." She looked around the kitchen. "Don't tell anyone—but I said, 'If you do that again, I'll kill you when you're asleep.' And I would. He hasn't done it since. Would you kill Jim if he beat one of your kids that bad?"

"Wouldn't hesitate, though I've never seen him raise his hand." I said no more about Cora. I wanted to.

"Sometimes I wondered if Cora and the colored girl were female homosexuals. Now I like women better than men but not . . . you know like . . . sexual." Norma got bright red in the face.

She looked funny but I held my smile. The topic intrigued me because it was taboo, not that I was sexually interested in women, either. I heard one of the WASP girls was that way, but I only talked with her a few times and just in passing. Rumor was she was an excellent pilot. Norma got a faraway look, almost sad. I got sad, and the sadness made me feel more connected to Norma. She sighed and put her elbows on the table and rested her chin in her hands. I did the same. She had almond-shaped eyes, long tawny lashes. Tawny eyebrows too. And those blue eyes. The silence said something—I wasn't sure what. Thoughts about Cora faded.

Out of nowhere, she said, "There's a baby contest in Philadelphia coming up. You should enter Lizzy. She's a beautiful baby. Ron's cousin, Edna—married a lawyer—she plans to enter her baby. I think Edna's a well-wrapped Christmas package with nothing inside. I did that one time when I was seventeen. I wrapped up empty boxes in brown paper tied with twine. Nothing inside, but it made me feel good. We were poor. One time, I was in the checkout line at the A&P and who walks up but Edna packaged in a mink coat. All she did was brag. I wonder what it's like to wear a fur."

"I have one." Her eyes widened and she wobbled her head. It was obvious she wanted to try it on. I didn't hesitate to get the coat. Norma put it on and suddenly she laughed, and said she'd love having one. She turned in circles, like my sister Starla did in church when others were holy rolling. Starla had made herself dizzy. So did Norma. My past had come alive, having someone to share it with. Having a relative actually living next door. It didn't matter she was a cousin by marriage.

"Oh dear me, it must have cost you five hundred dollars and here I'm acting like it's a rag." Norma steadied herself.

"It's dried out. I never put it in cold storage in the summer, as I didn't have the money to take proper care of it. Would you like to wear it for a week? Wear it for two." We went back and forth saying, "Please do," and "I couldn't," until Norma acquiesced.

"What do you think it feels like to be rich? I can't imagine." Norma got pensive again. "Were you rich one time? Now why did I ask you that? Must be the fur."

"Never was. But I was on the other side."

"Yeah." Norma didn't ask me how I could afford a fur and I didn't tell her about the cheap price I paid. She left soon after.

I watched her walk home in the fur, baggy blue pants, and red tennis shoes, slightly limping, her ponytail bobbing. She bent over to tighten her shoelaces. I was happy to have the bag of tomatoes and the baby compliment. I sat down at the kitchen table, sliced a perfect tomato into eight imperfect pieces, and took my time eating, wondering where she would wear my old fur. Would she wear it braless? Once, I wore it in my apartment with nothing on underneath. It felt soft and warm.

I had bought it after the government had eliminated the WASP, throwing me into a depression. Buck saw me dejected and convinced me to go to the horse races with him. I bet a few dollars and won nice money. To celebrate we went to a restaurant and drank whiskey, ate steaks and apple pie. On the way home, we passed a fur store going out of business, and he dragged me into the store. I was drunk, so he easily convinced me to buy a cheap used one. Someone had put it in the store for summer storage; it was left unclaimed. The problem was—where to wear it. Sunday came, and the first place I wore it was to a cathedral in Covington, Kentucky, but I still was downcast, full of grief for the WASP. I sat in the last pew in the back, ignoring the preacher. Just about everything I wore was secondhand, except for my well-mended drawers. Never liked them secondhand, but homemade was okay.

After I finished my tomato slices, I stood up, put the radio on to a music station. The music got me to shimmy my shoulders and sway my hips. Like I was sending a telepathic thank-you to Norma. Norma's good. Honest, no pretense, fun. Then I wanted to cry for no reason, but I was good at holding back tears. Lizzy was gurgling in her playpen. Starla ran in the kitchen and danced like joy. I wasn't joyous but recognizing it in her, helped me feel a bit of it.

THE WORKDAY AT 328 Oak Tree Road was behind schedule. I stood by the sink with my weight on one foot, looking out the kitchen window that had a crack in it. I put tape on the crack—to keep out the wind. To keep it from breaking further. To prepare myself if Jim got laid off at work. That made no sense but so what. Life often didn't. A ladybug landed on the windowsill and spread its black-dotted red wings. Was it saying things would get better? Aunt Pleasant claimed ladybugs were good omens. Aunt Pleasant was good to me.

I looked at the hundred-year-old kitchen sink. Jim had promised he'd replace the wooden countertop that was rotted in places. All he did was lay a dull brown-and-yellow linoleum remnant on top of it. Wasn't Norma nice to not comment on it? It was neighborly of me to loan her my fur. The faucet needed a new gasket or it would keep leaking.

Done.

What I next needed to do was to boil some eggs, marinate meat, wash, bake, mend clothes, iron, hug, scold, caress, tie shoelaces. Think positive, Iola. I had an indoor porcelain flush toilet and food on the table. I had a table and chairs. An electric refrigerator that worked and made twelve ice cubes. A party-line telephone, a gas stove. An electric toaster. A comfortable bed to sleep in. My children had books and warm beds. I'd known worse. I didn't drown as a kid. Didn't crash as a pilot. Wasn't deaf or blind, had all my limbs. It was nice of Norma to not say my hair looked a mess.

The day turned cloudy and gray. I did two loads of laundry in my wringer washer. The motor sounded rough. If it broke I knew how to use a washboard. Lizzy needed nursing again. She sucked her fill, then spit up on me. I pinned a basket of diapers on the line to dry and sang a song. My singing floated up into the treetops. The orioles didn't mind my mediocre voice. The yard turned into an outdoor singalong. A crow squawked like he knew what he wanted. I liked crows—how black they are, their attitude. My flesh was sticky. That was my exciting day. I sang a nursery rhyme for Lizzy. She clapped as best she could; her laughter was sweet. I can be a good mother.

I mopped the kitchen floor. It never would shine. I'd take a needed bath before going to bed unless the hot-water heater broke. If it did I'd heat water on the stove and take a sponge bath. Buck called them whore baths. Had he ever used whores?

Norma and I being cousins, I wanted the relationship not to fizzle. I could bring a decorated cake over to her house and we could sit and talk. Norma could make coffee. After the visit, I'd wait until Norma reciprocated, not wanting to set myself up for being called a nuisance. Would giving away a worn-out fur coat be a nuisance? Maybe Norma would wonder if I had ulterior motives. Now was a good time; she already had it. Despite my doubts, I walked over two days later and knocked. When the door opened, Norma's perfect face was gone. She had a black eye, a bruised cheek, and a cut swollen lip.

"I fell yesterday." Her distressed expression told me she hadn't. She barely looked at me.

I stared and then caught myself. Silence amplified the embarrassment until Norma said she'd get the fur and be right back. Should I leave? Concern for her kept me there. Ron couldn't be home because his car wasn't in the driveway. Norma returned with the coat, saying she had accidently put a tear in it and had no idea how to mend fur. "I'm so sorry. I don't have the money to pay for it. It's a small tear."

I explained again how fur has to be kept in cold storage in the summer and that it tore because it wasn't cared for properly. I said, "You can have it. I never wear it. You like it. Please take it."

"But it cost five hundred dollars."

"No, it didn't. I got it on sale, real cheap. It was secondhand."

Norma put her head down, slowly looked up, making brief eye contact. She said, "Okay." She ran her bruised hand over the coat and said, "Thank you. I have housework to do and I'll wear it while I dust." She smiled like she was trying to be funny, or maybe to keep from crying.

Why I chuckled, I don't know—a tense moment. "I got to go but just wanted to say—anytime you can visit."

Neither of us said a word about the bruises, much less who caused them.

As I left, I turned back and said, "You take care of yourself." There was a muffled thank-you as the door closed.

I was glad to be rid of the fur. I had kept it only because of my practice of rarely throwing anything away. I should have offered more sympathy. It was obvious Ron had beaten her. Last evening he walked in his house with a bouquet of flowers in his hand. To make up for beating her? Why would he beat her? She loved housework and cooking. She didn't want a career. Ron once shot a longhaired stray dog with a BB gun. It yelped and ran away. I now had two good reasons to detest the bastard. Bastard. Fuck him.

Seeking a distraction, I turned the radio on to a music station. I didn't want to be depressed. Lizzy, in her playpen, was babbling, happy as could be, moving her lips and tongue, discovering her sounds.

> Hey diddle diddle, the cat and the fiddle,
> The cow jumped over the moon,
> The little dog laughed to see such fun,
> And the dish ran away with happy Lizzy.

"Do cows jump over moons? Of course they can. Will they do it for you?" I touched Lizzy's head. "They'll jump over the stars for you." I wobbled like I was beginning a dance movement. It started in my neck, then a wobble undulating to my shoulders, spreading out into my hips and then my feet for a step or two. I didn't really feel like dancing.

> Humpty Dumpty sat on a wall,
> Humpty Dumpty had a great fall,
> All the king's horses and all the king's men
> Couldn't put Humpty Dumpty together again.

Who can put Humpty Dumpty together again?
My pretty baby will.
My husband won't.
The wall will fall on Ron and crush him to death.

Lizzy giggled. Later when I hung my laundry on the line, Norma was in her garden. Her red hair looked good among the cornrows. Norma was quiet. Everything was. The corn, the trees, the birds. The day had turned humid. Norma disappeared and then popped back up with weeds in her hands.

Next day, I phoned Norma and said we should visit more often.

Norma cried and then apologized for crying.

I asked her over for coffee. Norma said she couldn't because she had too much housework to do and needed to bake a pie. I had been taught to not give in to tears. It served me well when I was in WASP training. I wanted to cry with Norma but didn't. "I bet you make great pies."

Norma said she'd like to come over another day. "I'll bring a pie."

"That'd be nice. I'll make coffee. We'll talk about pawpaws and Mr. Placker's five-and-dime. Anything we want."

The rest of the day, every so often, I wondered what Norma was doing. Next day too. And some of the next. I wondered if she had it in her to kill Ron if he beat one of their kids. My hunch: she did.

Chapter 12

NEXT MORNING, I retrieved the newspaper from the porch. The paperboy had an excellent throw. The first page had an article about President Truman talking about the Korean War and the People's Republic of China coming to the aid of North Korea. All I read was the first paragraph. I didn't care about Korea unless I could fly a plane there and then I might get involved. Finding nothing of interest, I put the paper down. I made my usual to-do list. At the bottom of the list I wrote—*Tell Ron to pick on someone his own size. Tell the jerk to try beating Floyd Patterson but he won't because Patterson would beat him until his head was bloody pulp and I'd cheer Patterson.* I scratched out the two sentences.

I did a load of laundry but ran out of soap and couldn't do a second load. I sat down to slow my worries but then, out of the corner of my eye, I saw Starla hit Lizzy. I set her straight and called her Bad Girl. Starla cried as she was made to sit in the corner, facing the wall. When I turned around, she had scribbled a stick figure with no hands, tears falling off the face, no ground. After doing some backtalk, she was made to sit a minute longer. She cried and gasped and hiccupped. Then she was made to clean the red crayon off the wall. Between the hiccups, she said she was going to run away.

"And just where will you run away to?"

"Phildelphee. And won't come home."

"I'll miss you."

"Won't miss you."

"Okay. But first you get all that crayon off."

She cried, hiccupped, and sulked, but soon she settled down. I kissed the top of her head. I found some more soap and then the wringer washer wouldn't start. A stain wouldn't come out of a dress that had good memories, bought on sale fifteen years ago. I had always taken care of it but Charles accidentally poured ink on it. I showed the dress to Charles so he would learn from what he had done. His eyes widened.

"What are you going to do now?" I spoke calmly.

He turned mute.

"You're going to sit in a corner if you can't figure out what to do."

He looked at his feet, toes turned in. "I . . . I'm sorry."

"That's so you'll turn out decent and have respect for what belongs to others." Knowing when to give up on persistent stains, I tore the dress up for a rag. I tore up one of Jim's shirts that had a stain on it but I hadn't tried to get it out because I was tired of stain removal.

It started raining hard. There was a load of laundry drying outside. My feet flew to get the white sheets, white pillowcases hanging on the line, blowing like sails in the wind. I got wet. Everything did. My house slippers got muddy. I kicked them off before entering the house. I hung the laundry in the basement. It smelled bad down there like maybe a mouse had died.

Lizzy wanted to be held.

"No, no, no."

She cried.

"No, no, no. Didn't you hear me?" I clicked my tongue.

> Rain, rain go away, come back when I've gone astray.
> Little Bo Peep lost her sheep when a flood swept them away.
> Help me.

Jim came home at the end of the day. It was Friday and I was making beef stew for dinner.

"What's wrong?" he asked. "You look upset."

"Oh, nothing. I'm fine. My day was good."

"Nice."

"I bet your day was fine and dandy." All my words were crisp and distinct, to be sarcastic. But all he did was sit at the table and read the newspaper.

Soon he said, "Did you know that China is coming to the aid of North Korea? China is evil."

"Ron's evil."

"Ron who?"

"Next door. Who else? Do you know he beats Norma? Someone needs to come to her aid. Two days ago, she had a black eye and a swollen lip. It was awful. Poor thing. She didn't say a thing about it, but I knew what happened."

"Now don't go interfering in someone else's marriage." He thumbed through the newspaper.

"He shouldn't hit her. She said he drinks a lot."

"A lot of people do."

"Not like that. I can tell what kind of drunk he is. Someday, he'll kill her. Someday, he'll have a bad day, get angry, get drunk and kill her if she doesn't have dinner on the table as soon as walks in the door. Drunks will do that."

"He's not going to do that."

"How do you know? You ever seen crazy mean drunks? I have. I've seen him coming home. Once, he couldn't park his car straight in their driveway. He parked half in the bushes and crawled out through his window, cursing. When he went in the house, there was yelling and the sound of something breaking. He has a gun. I once saw him shoot a stray dog. How would you feel if Norma got murdered?"

"You worry way more than you need." He finally put down the newspaper.

"He scares me. You don't see that? I'd feel awful if she got killed. Can't you say something to him? I don't think you care. Or maybe you're afraid he'd beat you?" I noticed a change take a hold of Jim's eyes, a stiffened face. "You're afraid of that? Yeah, that's it. You look like you want to hit me. Go ahead. And I might hit you back. And we'll just hate each other. What else has there been anyway? We stay together because I want the kids and you want them too. Kid cement holds us together."

He got up and walked away.

"That's easy. Just leave. Like always. On our wedding day, you left me for four hours. You spent four hours with your mother instead of your bride. Why didn't you bring her on our honeymoon? It still bothers me when I think about it. Things can simmer in me real low, the heat barely on, for a long while. We have one simple unpleasant life."

He turned around and looked at me, like he was looking past me, through me. He said nothing.

"So you fiddle with your test tubes and microscope in your lab, and I fiddle with my soap and scrub brushes and brooms and iron your shirts, hankies, and undershirts. Norma is simple but she's good and doesn't deserve that. She likes me and we have a good time. By the way, I had to throw away one of your shirts. I couldn't get the simple ugly stain out with my simple ugly effort."

He walked out the back door. When he came back in, I, with my head cocked and eyes narrowed, said, "You know if I had to choose between being a pilot or having children and married to you, I'd choose being a pilot."

"Now don't go and kill my kids and run off in an airplane to help the Koreans fight the Communists."

Underneath his stoic face and calm voice, it was obvious he was trying to irk me. I glared. "How could you even say that? Kill my kids. Kill anyone." Although, I kept it to myself that the Communists weren't my worry. I actually had a secret soft spot for them. During World War II, the Soviets had female fighter pilots. They dropped bombs on the Germans. The Germans called them

Night Witches. They belonged to the Soviet Air Force. They flew at night, sometimes turning off their engines and gliding quietly over their targets. Some were as young as seventeen. The Communists weren't totally bad.

"Maybe you have Roman ancestry," Jim said. "Did you know that the ancient Romans could kill their kids or sell them if they wanted? They were considered property. I read that in a history of the Roman Empire."

"You're talking sick."

"Come to think of it, I'd wager Roman women would have become pilots if they had the opportunity."

After giving me a smirk, he went back into the living room, like my temper tantrum had no effect on him. Through the doorway, I saw him sit down at the dining room table with a book to read. Starla ran over and climbed up on him. She wanted to play horseback ride. He got down on the floor and crawled on his hands and knees with her sitting on his back saying, "Giddyup," and kicking him with her little bare feet to make him go faster. He went as fast as she wanted, like he was showing me how much better he was with children. I couldn't remember ever doing that. He snorted like a horse. Or ever doing that. Starla kicked. He snorted. She snorted. Her snorts weren't half as good as his and they seemed to both know because it made them laugh.

I was jealous, then angry that I was jealous, and soon tired of it all.

Dinner was served. I kept quiet because I never liked angry dinners—people yelling at each other. It was hard to keep my indignation quiet. Food was passed around. Little was said except Starla humming a little girl song and Charles telling her he didn't like it.

Halfway through dinner, Jim said, "A young chemist at work had a problem today. He talked to the wall real fast about one subject, and then something else totally unrelated, then something else. He made no sense. I heard he was summa cum laude in his class. The secretary got scared of him. Since he needed to be taken to the hospital, I volunteered. The doctor asked me about him. I said he had gotten his Ph.D. in chemistry and had been acting a little strange for the last week. I think he was psychotic."

"You mean crazy?"

"Well, if your preference is to call the illness crazy. It's called schizophrenia. He had promise. Nice looking—like Errol Flynn. We often had lunch together. We had to work late sometimes on projects. I liked working with him. It was sad."

"One time when I was studying, Papa said too much thinking and book studying makes a person crazy. He said it made his uncle crazy. He was planning to be a doctor, but then news came that he got committed to a crazy hospital for hard study. Papa said his father once took him to visit his uncle and he met patients with all sorts of problems: lost love, church revival excitement, bad son-in-law, sight of blood, loss of leg, wife problems, bad neighbor, ego, kicked by horse. He never said anyone had schiz-o-phrenia. Papa said it could happen to anyone studying too hard. Might be a good thing you didn't go to Princeton. You might've gotten too wrapped up in books. Maybe if you went to Princeton I'd have a crazy husband, or if your preference is to call it schiz-o-phrenia." I never believed Papa on this one, but it was a way to get back at Jim for making me feel jealous and angry.

"The doctor said it's caused by a schizophrenogenic mother putting the child into too many double binds."

"Talk normal, if you know how."

"In some circles, normal is considered abnormal. It can affect people from any walk of life, like King George III."

"King George?" I figured he was trying to irk me in spite of his calm voice.

"The king of England during the American Revolution. Now that I think of it, Nero went insane. He was one of the Roman emperors. I believe he lived in the first century AD. Some historians speculate that President Lincoln had problems. Did you know we had a mentally ill president?"

"You know too many dates."

"If you know history you're less likely to repeat it."

"Dates are only the bones of history. A stupid person knows that." Had I outsmarted him?

"One can make a lot of astute inferences from dry bones." Jim maintained his calm.

No more words were said except for the kids' banter. Starla only wanted to eat the carrots. Charles wanted more fried chicken and no carrots. Lizzy shoved the peas off her plate onto the floor. One pea was left. She threw it. It went right toward Jim. He opened his mouth in time to catch it. Charles, Starla, and Jim giggled like the funniest thing in Willowsburg just happened. Charles threw a pea at his father and he caught it in his mouth. Life had turned hilarious for everyone except me. The laughter went way longer than needed.

"Cut it out," I ordered, as unruffled as I could, which took huge effort.

When I went upstairs, it was eleven p.m., quiet except for Jim snoring and the sound of me peeing in the toilet. I was glad the boring, hard, stupid day was done. I entered my bedroom and unpinned my hair. It didn't feel like my bedroom but my things were there; my side of the boring bed, my five pairs of resoled shoes, my wedding dress in my cedar chest, along with the clothes I wore in the WASP. I undressed and then, quiet as I could, I opened my cedar chest, took out my WASP clothes, and slid them on. I went downstairs and imagined I was sitting in the cockpit of a plane. Not being one to dwell long in fantasy, I went upstairs, changed into my nightgown, and lay in bed under sheets that should be washed the next day.

But I needed memories. I had landed a B-25 plane at the army air base in Salinas, California. It was a cute town. An officer gave me a martini. I drank half of it and got woozy. There was sunny Santa Monica, California, and the A-24 I flew. Good flight. Seeing the Pacific Ocean for the first time. My three hardest landings. The easy ones. The flight that almost killed me. The colonel at Walker Army Airfield in Victoria, Kansas, who grabbed my breast before I boarded a B-17. I removed his hand and said stoically, "It's called a breast. They're common. Babies suck them." What else could I have said? *Asshole?* What could I have done? Kicked him in the balls? No. I had a plane to fly.

Jim was snoring, sprawled over the middle of the bed, taking more than his share. I soon fell asleep.

At two in the morning, I woke up to the sound of a car. It stopped, a door opened, and then I recognized Ron cursing and a door slammed shut. Was he going to beat up Norma, who was probably in a sound sleep? My crazy great uncle never did that, not that I heard. Jim never did. My life wasn't that bad in spite of persistent stains, peas getting thrown, the asshole colonel, the broken washing machine, laundry needing ironing, losing my temper. It's stupid to lose your temper. It can mess up your day. A full moon was sharing its light with my dark boring bedroom. The picture on the wall was barely visible. The darkness was good for listening. I wanted to hear spring peepers and not the neighbor's yappy dog scaring away raccoons. Jim had stopped snoring. There was no sound of his breathing. I touched his body to be sure it was warm. Being a widow was not in my plans. Far away, some animal howled on and on, making me feel sadder.

Chapter 13

LATE RISING WASN'T my habit. I pulled off my nightgown, grabbed the nearest housedress out of my closet, and threw it on. Downstairs, it was obvious from the empty cereal bowls and juice glasses on the kitchen table that Jim had made Saturday breakfast. I took the dirty dishes to the sink and wiped up the puddle of milk on the floor.

The radio was playing static. I tuned in a station. A commercial announced that Reverend Billy Graham was coming to Philadelphia to preach God's word, and then some singer sang a few lines of "Just as I Am." It had no rhythm, no sway, no clapping in the background. I never liked that kind of music.

I walked to the front room and pulled the curtains back. Out the window, Lester Causley in his old black pickup truck with a load of hay drove down the street. Bits of hay flew into the sky, onto the street. I knew different types— alfalfa, timothy, oat, clover. I liked the smell of hay, mountain peaks, and the top floor of skyscrapers.

The wind was in the trees, the birds in the wind, birds acting like the wind, like they owned the wind. A large tree branch had fallen in a neighbor's yard across the street, two houses down. Good thing no one was under it or they'd be dead and not be able to sit out on their front porch drinking beer at noon, like they liked doing. It was sunny in between the clouds.

Charles, Starla, and Lizzy were in the front yard. They looked like puppies chasing each other—exchanging gargled growls and higher-pitched yaps. Two-legged puppies in clothes, horseplaying, jumping up, challenging gravity. It was like unadulterated life risen from nothing, doing nothing but fun, on top of nothing but dirt. Since childhood, I enjoyed life moving.

At six, I had admired water skeeters stepping across summer water.

At ten, I envied an owl owning the night sky.

At twelve, I noticed gnats chumming around under a tree. Hundreds. I wondered if they were figuring out what to do. Smelling the air? Where's the food? I walked into them but they made way for me. I passed by, and turned around. They were back at it like they hardly noticed me. A day later, they were in the same place like it was their home. I was drawn toward them; they moved a speck away. I got rude and walked into their party. They acquiesced, having better things to do than squabble with a pig-tailed girl.

At fifteen I watched metallic-colored dragonflies having sex in the sky. I wondered about their male and female parts. I decided dragonflies brought good luck, but Mama said it was heathen thinking.

I opened the window and had the urge to yell out my love to my children. I closed the window but hadn't meant to slam it. By the way of thoughts, I sent them my love. Was I a good mother?

Back in the kitchen, the radio program was about senate hearings held the day before by Senator Joseph McCarthy and his committee whose aim was to rid the country of Communists. There was mention of a man who had been subpoenaed. He was ordered to state his name and where he worked. I sat down and listened to the interrogation.

Suspect Man said his constitutional rights were being violated. "The First Amendment states that Congress shall make no law respecting an establishment of religion or prohibiting the free exercise thereof or abridging the freedom of speech, or of the press or the right of the people peaceably to assemble and to petition the government for a redress of grievances. Would you like me to state for you the other amendments to the Constitution or would you even recognize them?"

Never before had I heard a person repeat a whole constitutional amendment by heart. If my memory was correct, there are twenty-two, maybe twenty-three amendments and the first twelve are called the Bill of Rights and the fifth one has to do with protection against self-incrimination and the nineteenth gave women the vote. I had learned that in my civics class in tenth grade that I got an A in with little study.

Senator McCarthy said he didn't like the man's attitude and ordered him to just answer the questions. "Did you ever attend a Communist Party meeting?"

"I exercise my constitutional rights."

"Did you attend a Communist Party meeting?"

"I have peaceably assembled at lots of meetings—the PTA, the ACLU, the Elks, VFW . . . and I was wounded in World War II. Were you wounded in World War II? Did you even fight in the war?"

I turned off the radio to lower my stomach tension. I had no idea why it started—McCarthy interrogating the man, the truck with the load of hay, the fallen tree branch. How could McCarthy have such an effect on me? How could the man he was interrogating pique my interest, make me miss flying planes, capture half of my admiration, scare the piss out of me? Zeke getting killed had terrified the piss out of me.

He was so sure of himself under pressure. I hadn't caught his name. What might he look like—handsome, ugly, old, young, pockmarked, bulging veins in his forehead, long nose, short neck? He sounded like he was in his fifties. Would a confident voice belong to a good-looking face? Was he clean-shaven with deep-set eyes, who had affectionate conversations with his wife, listened, did good sex, and had a good job? I poured some cream in a cup and then poured in hot coffee so the cream would mix by itself. A custom I learned years ago when I only had one spoon; that way I wouldn't waste time washing the spoon. If I met McCarthy's victim—Mr. Subversive, Stand-up-for-your-rights man, To-hell-with-McCarthy man, I'd shake his hand and say, *Pleased to meet you.*

Jim walked in the house. "I see you didn't kill the kids last night."

"I see no one killed you last night."

"Good thing we're not living in Pilgrim. I'd be dead and buried and no one would say a word." He laughed. Ha-ha-ha.

I moved slightly; barely opened my mouth. Did Jim know? Had I talked in my sleep about Uncle Edgar killing Zeke with a shotgun, his red blood splattering everywhere? Some of his flesh landed on my arm. I covered it with my hand like I was protecting his life, like I could put Zeke back together. Not much was left of his face. A chicken got splattered with his blood. My family figured it was evidence, so they killed it and plucked its feathers. My uncles and the older boys buried the body and the chicken feathers in the bottom of Uncle Edgar's new cesspool he had just dug, and poured lime on top. Chicken was served for dinner that night. I had a hard time eating it but the rule was clean your plate. I ate as if I was in a space no one knew I'd fallen in.

No one ever said a word about it, except Uncle Edgar, when he was drunk, would sometimes whistle around the crime scene. I was ordered, "Keep your mouth shut—forever. Repeat it." . . . "Again." I couldn't say it was one of the main reasons I had left Pilgrim. I haven't been back in years.

The memories aggravated my gnawed-up spot. Grocery shopping was an escape, so I listed several items we needed. Jim didn't seem to care. He was more interested in making funny faces with the kids. I got in the car and drove into town and out of town. Zeke was good to me. To get rid of the images, I put on the radio and hummed. I counted. One, two, three, four, five.

I found myself driving east. All lights at the intersections were green. I saw a store advertising a sale. I parked my car. The salesclerk found what I wanted right away—a pair of navy blue slacks that fit perfect except they needed someone like Mr. Yalonsky to hem them.

In Philadelphia, tall Mr. Yalonsky, with the wide smile, remembered me, and insisted I was good luck, and he had two excellent weeks after meeting me. He was happy to hem my pants. We talked about our children. I remembered the names of his. He praised my good memory, my smile, my choice of pants.

After I put on the pants so he could measure the hem, he said they looked like uniform pants. "Didn't you say you were in the service? It had an unusual name."

"The Women Airforce Service Pilots. The WASP."

"Yes, yes, that's wonderful. The Women Airforce Service Pilots." He spoke slowly as if the name itself deserved respect. He asked what kind of uniform I had worn. I told him about my dress uniform, but I didn't wear it when flying. He was all wide smiles and asked if I still had it.

"It's packed away."

"I'd love to see you in it." He was obviously flirting. "Can I see you in it?"

"We'll see." I went into the dressing room, changed, looked at myself in the mirror, and came back. Before he stooped down to pin the hem of my pants, he touched my arm with the tip of his finger.

As he did his work, I noticed how small his tidy shop was. A narrow staircase led up to his living quarters. Someone was singing in a foreign language upstairs. His wife, most likely. Was she pretty? Homely? Dumb? I could feel his good-looking hand on my long leg. I never had a man hem my pants before. His young-looking hair was thick and dark brown, giving me the urge to run my hands through it. I rubbed my fingertips together. His shop had a pleasant smell.

If he came on to me, I'd tell him I was married and had children, but in a way not to hurt his feelings because he respected me and listened to what I had to say. Buck had taught me how to find crayfish in the creeks and where the wild pawpaws were. He taught me how to shoot squirrels, make a fire, and cook them in the deep woods. I wondered what I might learn from Mr. Yalonsky.

On the way home, I stopped at the grocery store, and reviewed a mental list I had learned long ago so I didn't waste paper and pencil. Beans, bread, butter, carrots, celery, coffee, meat, milk, oatmeal, oil, onions, potatoes, peas, salt, soap, sugar, sundries, vinegar. I bought needed items as fast as possible. When I got home, I kissed Jim to allay any concerns he might be harboring. I planned to see Yalonsky again. It was hard to bury excitement.

Jim didn't seem to care I was gone for hours. He seemed to like the kiss and put his arm around my waist.

The phone rang.

I didn't let on that I liked the interruption. It was a wrong number.

Starla, Lizzy, and Charles burst open the door. Starla slammed it against the wall. A porcelain figurine, my wedding present from Aunt Pleasant and Uncle

Dillard, fell off a nearby table and shattered. Starla and Charles stopped in their tracks, almost tripping over each other.

Jim picked up the broken pieces and laid them on the table.

"What's that going to do? Is it going to mend itself? That's Limoges porcelain—our best wedding present. Is there anything nice I have that doesn't get taken from me?" I asked the last question twice.

Jim told them to go to their rooms. He nudged them in the direction of the stairs.

"You pray and ask God's forgiveness. You stay upstairs till dinner," I yelled, but managed not to go over the edge.

Jim said he needed to take the garbage out.

When he came back in, he sat down at the table. "I'm getting laid off in three weeks."

I dropped what I was doing and spun around, folded my arms, took a step back, and leaned against the sink. "What did you say?"

"I said I'm getting laid off in three weeks."

"When did you hear that?" I clenched my teeth.

"Beginning of the week. I've been looking in the want ads for a job. I'll get one."

"And what will happen if you don't?"

"You worry too much." He picked up the newspaper that was lying on the table.

"I suppose you think I'll take in ironing and do house cleaning. And then I'll come home and cook your meals. Is that what you think?"

"Never thought that. Calm yourself down."

"You put the damn paper down."

"Lower your voice and stop your cursing. I'll get a job. I have an interview next Friday. It'll pay more. No doubt I'll get it."

"Pretty sure, huh? What dream are you basing that on?"

"My boss told me about it yesterday. He said he'd give me his best recommendation."

"Why didn't you tell me that first?"

"I said lower your voice."

"You didn't answer my question." I heard a noise by the kitchen door. The kids were all standing there, staring.

"I told you to go to your rooms. Get up there now."

They disappeared.

At the dinner table, I served half portions.

"What's all this about?" Jim asked.

"If you're going to be out of a job I figure we're going to have to tighten our belts. It's starting now. When you get a job, we'll get regular portions."

"Are you going to lose your job?" Charles asked.

"Is Daddy gonna lose his job?" Starla asked. "Are we not going to get anything to eat?"

Lizzy started crying.

"See all the trouble you caused." Jim looked at the kids. "My job is just fine. I'll be getting a better one. Don't you worry." He divided his dinner into three portions and gave one to each of the kids. Then he got up and walked out of the house.

"Daddy, don't leave," Lizzy said.

"I'll be back."

When Jim came home, the kids were in bed. I was sipping a cup of tea. The first thing Jim said was, "Frank and Sarah and their kids are coming in three weeks."

"Since when?" I asked.

"Since they planned it."

"Don't play your games. When did you know?"

"I told you a week ago."

"You never did. How long are they staying?"

"Overnight."

"And you think we have enough room?"

"Of course. Frank and Sarah can sleep in the girls' room and all the kids can sleep on the floor."

"Why are they coming here?"

"They're my only family. At least they're visiting. Your family ever visit you?"

I ignored the troublesome question. "And why are they coming?"

"They're on their way to North Carolina . . . Morehead City. Vacation time."

"Be nice to take a vacation."

Jim

Chapter 14

THE DAY WAS warm, with a breeze, billowing clouds heading east. Clouds do a lot—bring rain, cool things down in the summer, warm things up in the winter, look nice. Some say they have silver linings. Don't be stupid. Iola and Norma sat on the porch swing, talking.

The porch was good for surveying Oak Tree Road—the Buick Roadmaster in the Mackey driveway, the best car in the neighborhood. The Wendalls' old Plymouth, the newly painted Peterson house. They hired someone to do it—a pale yellow. Girls playing hopscotch, lawns being mowed, the shade trees. A neighbor will talk to you when you're on your porch. They'll wave and ask about your day from across the street.

I went back to reading my book on the American Revolution. Hearing the sound of a plane in the distance, I knew Iola was looking at it. She always does. There was no need to confirm my hypothesis. I liked the word *hypothesis*. I kept reading.

Every so often I listened to Iola and Norma saying how to make the best potato salad, or how they both liked this or that when growing up. Iola had a nice voice—a little deep, with a slight Southern accent. She had served iced tea, with a lemon slice, and the right amount of sugar. Then a light green Pontiac with shiny chrome and big round headlights pulled up our gravel driveway. It was the best-looking car I ever saw—the color, the chrome, and the shape. Better than the Mackeys' Buick Roadmaster.

The car stopped and three kids piled out. Frank and Sarah ambled out. Sarah wore a white sleeveless blouse with red polka dots, white capri pants, red leather belt, and white sandals. Her black hair almost reached her waist. I was impressed. Iola used to look that stylish, before we got married. Frank's hair was uncombed and his shirt was hanging out. That was often how he looked when we were kids. It occurred to me how much I had missed Frank.

I had recently painted the porch floor—Charles, my boy, my firstborn had helped me and did a good job. It was long overdue but what with company coming, I had taken my time and used a fine-bristle brush and expensive gunmetal gray paint that was on sale. I had replaced the wooden kitchen countertop that was rotted in places, that Iola kept pestering me to fix.

After all the kids went off to play, more tea was served. The talk turned to the beautiful weather saying summer is here and the fruits forming on the trees saying we should get buckets of cherries and peaches. Then it turned to cherry jam, peach pie, hot dogs, the Poconos—I liked the Pocono talk because my family took vacations there when I was growing up. Then it was swimming, swimsuits, beauty pageants. I never watched a beauty pageant.

There was a pause in the conversation until Norma asked, "Now, what actually makes something beautiful?"

"What do you mean? It's a strange question," I said.

"I never thought to ask it," Iola countered.

"I think it's a good question." Frank rubbed his nose.

"One of my students asked that question." Sarah leaned back in her chair, looking thoughtful. "We were having a discussion about physical beauty. One student said something about social beauty. That got us talking about social beauty."

"What do you teach?" Norma asked.

"Twentieth-century literature. Sometimes French literature."

"My favorite book was *Alice in Wonderland*," Norma said.

"I never heard that—social beauty." Iola looked curious.

"She made it up."

"You can't make things up. Not like that. How can you say that, Sarah?"

"Sure you can, Jim. That's how culture changes." Frank sounded real sure of himself.

"Good culture doesn't change." It surprised me, what I was hearing.

"Of course it does. It's all relative." Frank nodded.

"Eleanor Roosevelt wasn't good looking, but look at all the good she did," Iola said.

"Don't remember what she did, except being first lady." Norma ran her hand down her ponytail. She did that a lot.

It occurred to me Norma was very pretty with the bluest eyes, and light reddish-brown eyebrows that were perfectly arched, and not too thin but not bushy. She had the smooth complexion of a child. And I never saw a nicer looking mouth and nose. I could take her picture. But she needed something other than the muumuus she wore. She reminded me of an oil painting I once saw, of a bosomy naked woman, by one of those Frenchy artists. I imagined Norma naked and me taking her picture. I wouldn't have wanted to do anything else with her. I didn't know what I would even do with the photograph. Give it to Ron? I almost smiled, thinking these things right in front of everyone.

"She pushed for the government to form the WASP." Iola looked at Norma.

"Who?" Norma asked.

"Eleanor Roosevelt. I'd say she was smarter than Franklin. Everyone knows he was born into wealth. She was too." Iola took a sip of tea and spilled some on her white blouse. She often spilled stuff.

"You know she was orphaned when she was a child." Sarah had a mild Brooklyn accent.

"Never knew that. Knew they were cousins. Knew she wasn't a good-looker." Norma jiggled her head.

"You like good looks?" Frank asked.

"Don't everybody?" Norma shrugged. "I was a good-looker in high school. People said I looked like Louise Brooks, so I got a bobbed haircut like hers. My mother said I looked cute. Then got married, had a kid, moved up North, and had two more. Look at me now. I put on weight looking at food." Norma looked down at her torso and said, "Speaking of the ugly well-to-do, the rich Delanet kids aren't beautiful. I've seen them. I'd say the oldest is downright homely. I hear he's so smart he'll go to Harvard. Smart and ugly. I don't mean to be mean but he ain't here to hear me."

I knew the boy—polite, smart, hardworking—and I didn't like Norma putting him down.

"You had a senator named Delanet, didn't you?" Frank stroked his chin.

"That's right—the grandfather. His son owns several hardware stores," Norma said. "Big shots. Only live about four miles away in a fancy house."

"I know what makes the boy plain. He's got thin lips and small eyes," Iola said.

"That's right." Norma kept nodding like she was extra agreeable or maybe couldn't sit still. She didn't seem like the nervous type.

"Come to think of it—the boy's father. He has thin lips, flat cheekbones, and a long, skinny nose. From the side it looks like a beak. Now I don't mean to be cruel, either, but as Norma says, he ain't here." Iola looked at Norma.

"I just realized that boy is the reverse of the colored with the big noses and huge lips. They got too much face but the Delanet boy has too little," Norma said.

"Now think about what you're saying." Frank did another chin stroke.

"I am thinking."

"Good." Frank swatted a mosquito that landed on his arm.

"My mama used to say that even the colored are cute when they're little." Norma leaned back into her chair and clasped her hands behind her head. She crossed her feet and wiggled them. "Now the Negroes, they all look alike."

"Negroes don't all look alike. You haven't looked." Sarah barely smirked.

"I haven't looked? What does that mean?" Norma sat up.

Sarah picked up the newspaper lying on one of the porch chairs. She flipped through it and then held up the front page of one of the sections. "See this picture here of Negroes playing jazz. These two with very dark skin. This one with a round face, and this one long. You see? This one has lips of ample size but not big. The end of his nose is delicately formed. The other one's actually thin and chiseled-like. His face is long; lips thin but not too thin. Nice. Large eyes. Right here. I think they're quite good looking. Yes. This other one does look like your Negro stereotype—big lips, wide nose."

"They must have white blood in them," I said. Sarah's comment didn't surprise me. She always was a bit odd. Iola was odd sometimes. Did I attract oddity?

"Doubt it. They have very dark skin." Sarah barely smirked again.

"Well . . . I don't know why the paper has to write about them. Jazz is Communist music." I preferred talking about Communists than thinking I attracted oddities.

"Oh come on," Frank chortled. "Jazz is American. You sound like Senator McCarthy."

"What's wrong with him?" I fidgeted with the coins in my pocket. I noticed some derision in Frank's voice, which he had no right to do, being he was at my house. My perfect day was disappearing. And who was directing this conversation? It became a free-for-all. Should I not be directing it?

"He's insane." Frank chuckled.

"That's awful. He's a patriot." I stopped coin-fidgeting when I remembered reading that money carries germs. But people that wash their money—that's going too far. Iola wouldn't care about germs.

"What point are you making?" Norma asked.

"You mean about McCarthy?" Frank looked at her.

"I don't care about McCarthy. About the Negroes." Norma wrinkled her forehead.

"You should care about McCarthy." I threw her a look.

"You know, a colored soldier told me that white people all look alike," Frank said. "At the end of the war—we were in Paris talking about war and drinking the best Bordeaux wine, the best champagne."

"We do not," I said.

"We do?" Norma looked surprised. "I mean . . . ?"

My eyes darted from Norma to Sarah.

"I'll show you." Sarah picked up the newspaper again, thumbed through it, and held it up. "See these pictures of white people. Lips are very thin, like a fine line. Almost not there. Cheekbones flat. Beak noses. Bridge of the nose is almost squared off—sharp, angular, plain-looking—if you recognize the white stereotype." She turned the page. "This white boy right here—lips are thin. Too thin. See. See here. And his small eyes are set too far apart. Same for this girl. Sliver lips." She turned another page. "This man has sliver lips, too, and flat cheekbones, small eyes. More white stereotypes."

"You saying white folks have their own way of being ugly?" Norma looked confused.

"I don't think you should say that—call white people ugly. Plain, if you must." I crossed my arms, uncrossed them. I think I scowled.

"I'm sorry," Norma said.

"You're saying white people are never ugly?" Frank asked.

"I didn't say that." There was agitation in my voice. I was losing control. Control was important in life, especially of temptations that could cause me to do something regretful.

"Well then, what did you say?" Frank opened his eyes and mouth wide, like he was curious.

"I mean don't compare white people to the colored." It was hard to talk calm while agitated.

"You're missing the point. Lots of white folks have flat cheekbones and not enough lip. Top lip is barely there, like chicken lips. And long, pointy noses, like a hawk beak." Frank looked square at me—full-on eye contact with a slight smile.

"Chickens don't have lips," Norma said. "What are you talking about?"

"Exactly—chicken lips." Sarah rubbed her finger across her lips.

I stared at Frank.

Sarah turned another page. "This white girl is quite pretty but she has full lips and not much of a bridge to her nose. See her high cheekbones. Color her black, frizz her hair, and you'd say she was a Negro and all of a sudden call her ugly because you can't see what's in front of you. Beauty's beauty. If you have too little it won't work. If you have too much, won't work. Probably if you have too little here and too much there, that might look odd. Just have to look at what's there."

"I never heard any Negroes say we all look alike," Norma said.

"You ever ask them?" Frank raised his eyebrows. Smiled. Tilted his head side to side, like he was poking fun, poking a finger. I knew his ways. I wanted to sock him.

Norma's mouth dropped open, and then she said, "No, I never did."

"You two sound like you're defending the colored. Like you're one of them," I said. I noticed something going on between Sarah and Frank—the way they looked at each other—little secret signs, both rubbing their chins, tilting their heads, communicating something. I rubbed my bottom lip against my teeth.

"Oh," Norma said.

"Yes. Oh. Lots of good ohs," Sarah replied.

"What does that mean?" I asked.

"What?" Sarah rubbed her hands together, like she had something up her sleeve.

"The ohs."

"I have no problem with the ohs. Do you?" Sarah asked.

"No oh-problem here," Frank said.

"Frank, you sound like a Communist. I wouldn't be surprised if you grieved Stalin's death back in March." I furrowed my forehead but Frank just smiled. I was not a violent man, but I wanted to get up, walk over, and sock him in the mouth. It would be the second time. We once had a fight as kids. But then Charles came up on the porch and sat right beside me. I secured my hands in my pockets.

"Stalin . . . a despicable tyrant. Glad he's dead. But did you know that white Communists all look alike?" Frank looked at his coffee cup and asked for a refill.

It was funny but I refused to laugh. "You're going too far. You're making a mockery of what I say."

"But it's fine mockery. Come on, Jim." He laughed.

Sarah smiled and squeezed Frank's arm. She leaned toward him but looked straight at me. "Let's talk about North Carolina. It's a beautiful state. Isn't that what started all this?" She commented on Morehead City and how this was the second time they were going down South. "Would you like to come with us on our next trip? Think about it. Long beaches and big beach umbrellas, blue skies. Doing nothing but lying about and eating fish caught an hour ago. We always have a wonderful time. We eat crabs and shrimp and flounder and take long walks at sunset."

Well, well. Wasn't it nice of her to shift into pleasant. I was wary of Sarah.

"Do you ever eat whale?" Charles asked.

"I never ate one. That would be a huge dinner. You like whales?" Sarah asked.

"I like Jonah and the whale," Charles said.

"You know that story?" I loved my beautiful boy.

Charles looked up to the sky like God was listening. "Jonah didn't want to go to Nineveh. So God told the whale to swallow him and take him there. God can talk with whales. It was Jonah's job to save Nineveh but he didn't want to. When he was inside the whale's belly, he prayed."

"Oh, you're a smart young man," Norma said.

"What kind of whale was it?" Charles asked.

"We don't have that information, dear." Iola smiled sweetly.

Steven, who was Frank's oldest and had followed Charles up on the porch, asked, "Where did you learn that?"

"I learned it in Sunday school." Charles looked pleased with himself. "What did you learn in Sunday school?"

"We don't go to Sunday school." Steven shrugged.

"Do you go to church?" Norma asked.

"Not much."

"Oh, dear, oh dear." Norma leaned back in her chair.

It bothered me that simple talk about summer and beauty pageants had turned so damn haywire. And in my house. And on a day that was supposed to be good.

"That was a wonderful story, Charles. I liked it when I was a child. Sounded magical," Sarah said.

"There's no magic in the Bible. Only miracles," Norma said like she was an authority.

"That's right. No magic." It was peculiar—me defending Norma.

"From a child's viewpoint—that's what I meant—how a child sees the world." Sarah leaned back, and rubbed her hands together.

Norma left soon after, looking confused. Things quieted down and we mostly just talked about food and weather.

Later when Sarah and Iola were making dinner, I picked up the newspaper to have another look at the jazz musicians. Was Sarah right? I had to admit Negroes didn't all look alike. Part of me was amazed at how something can be right in front of you and you don't recognize it. Part of me didn't want to think about it. Part of me did. The curious part that I was wrong. I nervously scanned the page and noticed down in the corner a small article on some organization called the Mattachine Society, founded by a man named Harry Hay. It said Hay was a Communist, organizing meetings, seeking rights for the homosexual. I focused on the last five words. They have rights? Have meetings out in the open? In public? Have a mission and purpose statement? I discretely read the article twice to be sure I read it right. I had to read it again.

Before retiring to bed that evening, Iola showed me a photograph and said, "Look here. I have high cheekbones, plump lips. You know I have relatives on my mother's side that go back to South Carolina pre-Civil War. I just might have a great great-great grandfather who owned a slave. What might he have done to her? You know what I'm saying. I might have a great-great grandmother who was his slave, and had his child. Looks to me like I could pass for a Negro if my skin was dark and my hair was black and frizzy. Someone once told me I look like a white Billie Holiday." She hung the photo back on the wall and smiled.

I didn't know what to say because I was tired, had no interest in an argument, what with my confusion, and my curiosity about the Mattachines. I felt ignorant.

Next morning, after breakfast I said, "It's time for the kids to get together so I can take their picture." I gathered them and took several pictures. All of them together, then just the girls, next just the boys, just my kids, just Frank's three standing in front of his beautiful mint green Pontiac. I wished I owned one. I'd drive it only on weekends.

They left for North Carolina. "Goodbye. Wonderful visit."

"Yes, it was."

"You need to come with us next year."

"We will."

The kids waved goodbye.

Iola waved goodbye. "Please come again."

It made me recall the times my family went to the Jersey Shore for vacation. They were some of my best childhood memories. My father brought home crabs for dinner. We had often stayed up late, laughing and playing games.

Sarah yelled out a thank-you as they headed out. Kisses were blown. When they disappeared down the street, I said, "I heard Sarah has relatives in France. You know the French like the colored." I looked off down the road. "I'm disappointed in Frank. Maybe you're right—next time they want to visit, we might be too busy. I think one day both of them are going to get themselves in deep trouble. You have to look ahead and know how to stay safe."

"I like Sarah and Frank—"

"Did you hear what I said?"

"I did. What are you—predictor of the future?"

"I guarantee they'll get in trouble."

"No, they won't. Come to think of it—Sarah reminds me of when I was a kid. I'd visit cousins, the Bevils, who had a radio. My mother heard a rumor Alma Bevil had a second cousin, maybe third cousin, Cora, who sang on stage with a colored girl in Chicago. I didn't care; Cora was wonderful. I met her only a few times, but to me, she could do no wrong. Then Mama wouldn't let me visit them anymore. I liked listening to their radio and hearing Amelia Earhart talk about flying. I finagled a job doing ironing for Alma. I told Mama I'd give her all the nickels I made. She gave in, and I got to listen to the radio again. She didn't know my other reason. I liked Alma. She was real nice. She changed my life. I like today."

"What does that mean—you like today?"

"It means—it's a good day. And I like the way Sarah was dressed and I'm going to buy me some white capri pants and a white blouse with red polka-dots."

"Why do you need a new outfit?"

"I don't but the last time I splurged was years ago."

"We can't afford splurges."

"Did you know that Amelia Earhart was a social worker before she became a pilot?"

"What does that have to do with anything we're talking about?"

"Nothing. Absolutely nothing. It has to do with what I want to talk about. It means she was likely nice and not like most of the male pilots I knew when I was in the WASP."

"And she got herself killed all by her nice self. I call that stupid."

She stiffened and said, "You don't know that. She may be alive someplace, hoping to be rescued. She'd be patient."

I almost chuckled. Iola got up and walked in the house.

I sat in the rocking chair, wanting a Pontiac, like Frank's. All the things said, the day almost turning bad. I seemed to have no control over my thoughts. Harry Hay and the Mattachines popped up. Then homosexual rights. Communists. Chicken lips. Whites all looking alike. My father had chicken lips. Feeling stupid. My wife possibly being the descendant of a slave. I hated feeling stupid. I didn't know what to make of it all. I folded my arms across my chest. A headache came on, and then a fear. The grass needed mowed. The car needed an oil change. The fear worsened. I stuck my stupid, nervous hands in my pockets. I had a boss one time tell me I had nice-looking hands—good for holding things—and then he licked his lips. I liked him, but I quit the job to avoid unlawful relationships. Fear is awful, so I just sat there and ordered myself to calm down. I ordered myself to do it for my kids. Be a man. A good father. To myself, I kept repeating the names of my three children. In a minute or two, the fear subsided.

Iola

Chapter 15

I WALKED TO the back fence to pick some flowers for the dining room table. Clouds dappled the sky. A fox raced across the field. A train whistled in the distance. While I was stooped over picking flowers, I heard the sound of a tractor. When I looked up, burly Lester Causley was riding his green tractor down his field on the other side of the fence. He was predictable every season— plow, plant, weed, harvest, turn under. He kept riding over to me. He never did that before. He tipped his straw hat. When he got to the fence, he came to a stop and smiled. "Nice day, isn't it? I think they'd call it balmy. And the birds singing."

"Why yes it is." I kept picking flowers.

"You look nice with flowers in your hands."

"Thank you."

"What kind are they?"

"Daisies, zinnias."

"Aren't they pretty? I just wanted to tell you anytime you'd like to come for a visit you'd be welcome."

I was at a loss for words but managed to give a nod.

"The wife's not home this week. She and the kids are visiting family in Ohio. You could come visit and have some coffee and cake, if you like, and we can get to know each other. You could tell me about you being a pilot. I'd guess female pilots enjoy excitement." He winked and looked me over, head to toe.

I dropped the flowers and bent over to pick them up.

"You look nice bent over."

Feeling thankful the fence was between us, I took a step backward and almost curled my lip. Despite my discomfort, I managed to say, "Well, I don't have the time but thank you." Then I walked with my shoulders back, my head up, toward the house, and a firm grip on the flowers. In the kitchen, I looked out the window and Causley was headed on. How did he know I was a pilot? Who told him? Norma? Jim? It alarmed me. I sat awhile. Had he ruined my pride of being a pilot? I thought of lots of curse words. "Asshole."

Not liking bad feelings, I baked a cake, taking extra time, trying to slip into a good mood. It had four layers and two fillings—strawberry preserves mixed with cream cheese, and the other was chocolate custard. It had whipped cream icing, shaved chocolate, and silver sprinkles. It was the best-looking cake I ever made. On a whim, I walked to my bedroom, pulled the door shut. I pulled my torn window shade down slowly so it wouldn't tear anymore. A dead fly lay on the windowsill. Had it starved to death or died of old age? Probably starved and shriveled to death. I'd starve before ever visiting Causley. I pulled my WASP clothes out of the cedar chest, took my housedress off, put on my WASP pants, shirt, and leather jacket, and lay down on the bed for a while, doing nothing but daydreaming.

I undressed again, took a bath, gave myself a manicure, and painted my toenails red. Never in his life would Causley see my toenails. Starla and Lizzy yelled at each other, but they were easy to ignore, and they soon quieted down. "Asshole." I styled my hair, ironed my prettiest dress. That got me to put the flowers in the bedroom. It helped get rid of the bad feeling. I put on some shiny earrings, then cooked a roast for dinner. It turned out succulent. Everyone liked it. The children couldn't wait to eat the cake. Jim had a big slice and got icing on his lips.

"Jim, did you ever tell anyone I was a pilot?"

"No. Why?"

"Just a thought."

"What made you think that?"

"I don't know. You know how thoughts can be."

That night we shared a conjugal bed. Jim pressed down on me, making my knee hurt, making my nose itch when he kissed me, making me have to pull away and scratch, like we weren't made for each other. Soon he was finished, said good night, and turned over. It was quiet, except for an owl outside. I said, "Jim," as if that would give me some satisfaction but he had fallen asleep. What if the owl was now soaring through the sky? What if it turned into a plane? And I was at the controls flying to California?

Divorce? I'd lose my children. It'd be another failure. No longer a pilot. No longer a wife and my children gone. Jim did pay the bills and made sure the car was always working. He mowed the grass, pruned the trees, put up the back fence I was glad I had. He took two full weekends, getting sweaty, and he didn't even go have his usual Saturday breakfast with his buddies in Willowsburg.

I got up and tiptoed downstairs to the front room. I should've been sleeping instead of having needs and reminiscences. Salathiel Shouse. A strange name, a fine man, large brown eyes. I was fine with strange. He liked being called Sal.

Chattanooga in August. "I need to be with you, dear," Sal had pleaded. And so we went riding, all the car windows rolled down to get some breeze against the heat. He knew of a swimming hole off a backcountry road. Did I dig my toes into the cool bottom as he wrapped his arms around me? The sky was bleached white by a blazing sun. There were cypress trees dipping their roots in the green pond. Pollen wafted through the air with no place to get to and plenty of time to do it, but that might've been another day. We went back there three times, maybe two. He sounded like a boy in love. Then sweet nothing itself slipped and slid like sweet voodoo. He stuck the tips of his fingers under my swimsuit.

"Marry me," he said.

"I will, but I want two months to plan it."

His body, dripping water, pressed against me. "Love you."

"I know you do."

"Kiss me again"

Again?"

I made sure the shades were pulled down, the curtains closed. I turned out the light, and listened for anyone stirring upstairs. The hooting owl outside was easy to ignore. Then my hands played with myself under my nightgown. I inhaled and exhaled. Soon I smoothed my nightgown over my long, hot legs. Like someone lost in deep space, I sat in the dark doing nothing but thinking of the cool green pond. Not a sound but the clock ticking. Had it been five ticks, or twenty, or one hundred? Knowing Jim was upstairs carried me back to Oak Tree Road. A little light from the moon was all.

I turned the lamp on and looked at my wedding picture on the wall. Jim's lips were on the slim side. He had well-shaped, adequate-sized eyes and finely chiseled features. He looked white as could be.

"Chicken Lips," I whispered. He didn't know about Sal, other than I had dated an engineer for a year and then he died when a steam pipe exploded. Third-degree burns. Jim never asked further questions.

I tiptoed into the kitchen, got a bottle of whiskey Jim kept on a top shelf, and poured a shot. It was smooth all the way down. Jim liked buying the best for himself, unlike the moonshine Buck made. I was not much of a drinker. To cover my breath, I drank milk. I went to bed and lay there. Some would call me a pervert. When I was in the WASP, I knew a pervert.

"Miss Boggs, what do you think about having sex with a friend of mine and I watch?"

"I can't do that, Major Croft."

"If you don't I could get you court martialed."

"You can't do that because I'm not officially in the military. I'm in the WASP. And if you could, well then . . . you court martial me."

After two hours of thoughts, broodings, worries, I fell asleep.

In the morning, Jim noticed the flowers. He stood there, fiddling with them, and said, "Mother used to make sure there were always cut flowers in the house in the spring and summer. She'd put a vase in the parlor and the entry but not in the bedrooms."

As I walked right out the bedroom, the cold floor creaked. Outside a window, two sparrows were fucking like experts on the windowsill. Nothing made sense. I didn't mean to slam the door hard.

"Why did you do that?" he yelled. "Sometimes, I just don't understand you."

A DAY LATER, Norma told me God is white and bright as light. Since humans were created in the image of God, she figured every human, if they weren't already, will turn white and beautiful as soon as they enter heaven. She said the good-looking Negroes are just one step closer to becoming white and that's 'cause they were good people and minded their manners and she will love them in their new white skin in heaven but right now they're making up for sins. She told me people's eyes will turn blue and hair turn blond in heaven if they weren't already. She won't have red hair but she might miss it a little—if missing things is allowed in heaven. She hoped she could keep her ponytail. Norma went on how the only colors in heaven will be sky blue, golden-yellows, mint greens and God's light shining bright. Maybe a few pastels under your feet. Not a red, black, or orange to be seen because they're the devil's colors. That's why the red-light districts use red lights. All heavenly bodies will be covered with robes spun from light, the soft leaves of the manna bush, and God's pure love.

"Now how do you know that?" I narrowed my eyes.

"A preacher once told me. Guess what else he said. Sex is the work of the devil and there's none of it in heaven. Adultery, murder, promiscuity and . . ." Norma paused and then whispered, "Masturbation. It makes men lose their minds. It'll send a lot of men to hell. Pain and torture fill the halls of hell. A shame. Boys need to be taught . . . to save their souls."

"Norma, I'm real busy. I have no time for this crazy nonsense."

"You don't have to be so nasty about it." Norma walked back to her house, grumbling loud enough to be heard.

I watched her go home and slam her door shut. I wanted to yell, *There's no skin in heaven, you stupid idiot.* I turned away and sat at the kitchen table. An iridescent black fly caught my attention. It took jerky steps, fluttered its translucent wings, stopped, took more jerky steps, and stopped at a crumb to nibble. I slammed my hand on it. It gave me some comfort that my aim was good, but its blood and oozy guts were on the table. I cleaned the table, washed my hands, and worried I'd been too rude. Norma was, after all, my distant cousin by marriage, my friend. Was I not good at keeping family or friends? I had tried and written letters to stay in contact with WASP girls but got no answers. Once I was told I worked two times too hard and made others look lazy. What is this life? Awful questions. I promised myself I'd be real nice to Norma next time we talked. I could look after her kids awhile so she could go shopping by herself without them begging for candy.

Pilgrim, Tennessee
1952

Chapter 16

THE MORNING MAIL contained a letter from Ethyl Lou. I dropped it on the kitchen table. The trash can was two steps away. I walked out to the front porch and sat in the rocking chair. I rubbed the back of my neck, not that it was sore. Usually I opened all my mail. Ethyl Lou would've accused me of lolling about. In Pilgrim, lolling about was a means of resistance. Folks might agree to do something, but never follow through.

I finger-combed my hair while rocking in the forest green rocking chair. I liked green forests. Toward the end of the street, a dirt road went off into Lester Causley's field. Last spring a fox had chased a rabbit across the field and killed it. The tree in the yard was bright with autumn leaves—its leaves scattered over the yard and into the street. The air smelled like cut grass before a storm. I heard the sound of Causley's tractor, a dog barking, a train's whistle, crows squawking—the land's music, Buck often said. In the Mackeys' driveway, their Buick Roadmaster was parked. Jim said they never graduated from high school. In one of the neighbor houses across the street, the shades were always pulled down—to hide something, maybe. Maybe not. Don't be paranoid. How did Causley know I was in the WASP?

Alone on my porch, alone on an empty street except for two little girls two houses down playing hopscotch. There were dark clouds on the horizon that could become a storm. Where might the storm hit first? On the faraway hill lit up with a sunray? Pass me by? Hit my house with a lightning strike? Strike Lester Causley riding his tractor and kill him? He'd deserve it. Dribble into nothing? My stomach tightened.

My face not powdered.

No lipstick.

Pale gray housedress on.

Dark gray sweater on.

Same color as the clouds coming my way.

Hole in my sweater.

I felt gray like I could blend in and not come back, being swallowed by gray. It was cuckoo thinking, like I was some crazy patient diagnosed with too much marriage. Sometimes cuckoo thinking was relaxing, like daydreaming.

I got up and upturned the overturned tricycle lying on the porch. It needed a new pedal. Jim hadn't fixed it. A neighbor's black dog chased a black cat up a tree with yellow leaves. It wouldn't stop barking. Soon a door opened and the neighbor woman ordered the dog into the house. A storm-smelling wind came up and lightning struck off in the distance. It was jagged, beautiful, dangerous. Was it a sign the letter was bad news? Maybe someone died. Maybe someone lost a leg? Lost money and needed some? Making guesses feeds curiosity. I went back in, picked up the envelope, and forced my long fingers to rip it open. I tapped my fingers on the table and read the letter.

In handwriting with every letter written as it should be—curved, straight, dotted, crossed, slanted, or circular, all legible—a talented hand. Ethyl Lou's *L*'s were large and well looped. Her *R*'s and *A*'s had a creative swirl at the bottom. She wrote in pencil with lots of misspelling. The irony of perfect yet incorrect. She never admitted when she was wrong, except to Jesus, which sometimes brought tears to her eyes.

Ethyl Lou wrote that Mama was badly sick and I should come home to see her before she passed on to her eternal home in heaven.

I phoned Ethyl Lou's neighbor, Swannie, and asked if she would get my sister who, of her own choosing, didn't have a telephone. Swannie said she'd recently got one; she politely gave me the number and said not to bother her again. I called and got the operator, and the operator had to connect us. Ethyl Lou said Mama caught pneumonia and didn't look like she's going to live. "Figured you might want to come home and say goodbye. Everyone here except for Buck, you, and Maude."

"When did it happen?"

"Three weeks ago."

"And you just wrote me."

"Well . . . she was doing better and then got worse. Sledge agreed he'd call you."

"He's never good for his word. You're always complaining about that. Why didn't you call me? You have a phone now."

"Long distance costs too much. Now it be nice if you want to hear what we doing for her. Changing her sheets every five days . . . like she always like."

"She never did that. Sometimes she didn't change her sheets for weeks. You're the one changing your sheets every five days."

"And I'm the one a making sure her room smell clean. The one braiding her hair every day. Would you like to know how nice she look with her hair braided?" She said the last three words loud.

"Old, I suppose," I said, louder.

"That all you can say? Now if you come down, you could braid her hair too." Ethyl Lou talked louder.

"You don't want me there."

"Stop telling me what I want." Ethyl Lou got even louder.

"You don't want me there," I said softer, knowing she'd go over the edge of superiority if we got in a shouting match. Plus, it wasn't worth the effort to expend the energy.

"You can't say that. I want the whole family here."

In my own laid-back superiority way, I said, "I say what needs to be said. But whatever. I'd come down but we don't have the money. You win. How's Papa?"

"Fine and I'm not winning."

I smiled because I knew I had gotten under her skin. I was glad she was on the other end of the telephone because my smile would've been a provocation. "Fine. You're losing. How's Sledge doing? I heard he got real sick."

"Who told you?"

"Buck."

"You two talking? I heard him and you had a falling-out."

"You believe what you hear, do you? Tell Mama I love her. She was the best mother a person could have."

"Didn't think you knew that. Haven't heard from you in a long time."

"Ethyl Lou, I said . . . you give her my love. You got a problem with that?"

"She don't hear no more."

"Dying people can hear. They just don't have energy to respond. It's all they can do to breathe in and out. You hear from Maude?"

"She out in Hollywood losing her soul."

"She'll find it," I shot back and then wondered why I defended the pretty ingrate. "How your children doing?"

"Fine."

"Charles had the measles awhile back. You think they'll come up with a measles vaccine? They're working on one for polio."

"That's interfering with God's plan."

"Nothing in the Bible one way or other about vaccines."

We talked some about the wonders of telephones. Ethyl Lou agreed they were convenient and she could get used to it. We said a few more words, a somewhat cordial goodbye, which was significantly better than past conversations. It seemed like a mend might be on the way. But a mend would never be complete unless she took back what she said the day after Zeke was murdered—that he was now screaming in hell.

Then the storm let loose with sheets of rain, pounding the windows and front porch. Lightning lit the sky. Thunder boomed. And again. It sounded closer. Soon the electricity went out and it looked like dusk. I stood there, staring at the black phone and the wall cubicle where it sat. I wanted the phone to ring again, like it possessed a magnetism and would connect me to what I needed. It occurred to me I might be more connected to the world by my phone than by my neighbors or Willowsburg. It made me feel lonely. Thunder boomed again, almost scaring me.

I went in the kitchen, sat down at the table, picked up Ethyl Lou's letter, and put it back in the envelope.

Pretty Lizzy came in and lay on the floor and rolled over a few times, reminding me of holy rolling. As a child, I liked holy rolling. I lay down on the cool floor. Lizzy rolled toward me and I rolled toward her. She giggled. It'd been a long time since I giggled. There were several wads of gum on the underside of the table. A neighbor kid most likely. Or messy Starla with a mind of her own. Takes after me. The legs were scuffed. If I were lying underneath an airplane, I would never stick gum on its belly. I'd clean and polish it. Underneaths have their own use—holder of secrets, holder of pent-up feelings. Jim would think I was crazy if he came home and found me on the floor.

Down the hallway was the front door. It had nine panes of beveled glass, a brass doorknob, oak wood with a little bit of swirly carving. The door lied. It said this was a house with beautiful things. The sofa with a tear in the upholstery, the ugly kitchen linoleum, the wooden floor in the parlor full of scuffs and a big black ink stain, and two adults with little in common—they all said you're a damn fool to come in. I never liked liars, but it was a lovely door. I might open it and walk away, but then something didn't feel right like a feeling had slithered into the house and passed through me like I wasn't home. Then the feeling got stronger and I realized if I opened my beautiful door I wouldn't have known where to go. It seemed some feelings are best ignored.

Lizzy squeezed my flesh, trying to get herself in a position to nurse. She had a hurtful grip for a child old enough to no longer need breastfeeding. She'd cry if she didn't get it. I got up, sat in a chair, and pulled Lizzy to my lap. As soon as I unbuttoned the front of my dress, Lizzy's little mouth opened. My nipple went in.

Humpty Dumpty sat on a wall,
Humpty Dumpty had a stupid fall,
All the king's horses and all the king's men
Couldn't put Humpty Dumpty together again.
Is my baby going to learn how to put Humpty Dumpty together again?
No. You'll do best to marry a rich man.

Two contented eyes stared at my mouth, then up to my eyes. Her perfect mouth pumped. Very pretty Lizzy, with the flower-petal skin, rosy cheeks and lips, soon had her fill. I was tired of nursing.

It wasn't my best day for love but I said I loved her. I whispered, "You're going to win Miss America and I'll be the first to clap." When Lizzy fell asleep, I whispered, "I never got what I needed from my Mama . . . (Why?) . . . Don't know, Baby. Nelda got what she needed. Ethyl Lou did. So did Friend and Sledge . . . (She not love you?) . . . Never said she did. (Awful thing to do.) . . . Wasn't it? She said you don't have to be a good person to get to heaven. You just have to accept Jesus into your heart as your personal lord and savior . . . (How can mean people get to heaven?) . . . Doesn't make sense does it? Do you know your father applied for a promotion? . . . (Did he get it?) . . . No. Didn't bother him. He just went and lay on the sofa. Then he bought a TV your brother and sister begged for. Now the four of you sit watching some show every night while I clean up. Who do your love more, me or your father? . . . (You) . . . Love you too."

I looked around to be sure no one heard my cuckoo one-person conversation. Being so tired, I was ready to fall asleep. Jim had snored and snorted last night, keeping me up.

It didn't feel good anymore saying, *Go to hell, Mama.* I couldn't cry. Mama never cried, never said she was sorry—except to Jesus. Mama should've said she was sorry. I wanted her to say she loved her hard-working daughter who had the courage to go out in the world, like an explorer might. I felt like cursing. Uncle Dillard once said cursing's not a sin if it's only your thoughts because God allows for a little upset. Well then, Goddamn it twice.

After my upset, I laid sleeping Lizzy to bed. I made brownies for Charles—his favorite. I made macaroni and cheese for Starla—her favorite; made stew for dinner—Jim's favorite sometimes. I marinated the meat in red wine, garlic, onions, and hot peppers. I got inspired and added raisins. Another inspiration suggested finely chopped carrots and celery. It smelled succulent. A bit later, I found a fly floating on its back in the marinade. It wiggled its feet up in the air, trying to escape, fighting for its brief life. I placed a piece of paper at its feet. It grabbed on; its wings were soggy. I dropped it on the floor and stomped on it. It was a good thing I found it before Jim did. He'd refuse to eat the whole stew. I added more wine to kill the germs. I noticed two of my fingernails were dirty. Jim would refuse to eat if he knew I had cooked with dirty nails. I stuck my fingertips in the stew and then cleaned up.

Jim came home after working all day. Dinnertime was pleasant. He said the stew was very good and took two servings. "I'll have to make it again, dear." Without the fly in the marinade and the dirty fingernails. I smiled about my little mean joke.

The next evening, Ethyl Lou called and said Mama died on the same bed she was born. With the same pillow, exactly how she would've liked it, spending her whole life in Pilgrim, like it was attached by an umbilical cord to heaven. Ethyl Lou had a poetic way of talking sometimes. Sometimes I had a poetic way of feeling, but rarely let on.

My muscle tension and clenched jaw were like red stop signs that keep the best neighborhood streets free of chaos. One after the other, down the whole stretch of road. Every fifty feet, muscle and sinewy signs were giving me signals, but I seemed to keep on going as if my aches and pains were misinformation that must be ignored in order to pay attention to family responsibilities.

I called my brother, Friend, and asked him to buy me flowers for the funeral. He required my double promise that I'd send the money by the next day. Friend did most of the talking. His voice was husky. It was the best I could do—not being there for the passing on. I had only seen one person actually die—Zeke murdered by Uncle Edgar. I wasn't there for my grandma's dying—being sick in bed myself, too many miles away in a little room I rented in Mrs. Felton's house. Plus, I'd been saving all my money for flying lessons.

"Sweethearts, I love you. Don't you look beautiful," I said to Charles, Starla, and Lizzy when I put them to bed that night. I kissed them, prayed they'd wake up in the morning, and I'd bake them a beautiful cake.

In the middle of the night, my muscles got flaccid and I fell out of a plane and my smelly-footed mother was flying a transport plane to Korea where she was going to drop three atomic bombs on the Communists. There was a silvery crescent moon. A billion stars lit up— the Milky Way stretched across the sky. My mother was a hero; the whole United States of America loved her, and President Truman gave her a gold medal, bright as the sun. People stood up and clapped. My mother laughed at me. The laughs kept getting louder. I woke up in a sweat. An hour later I was still awake.

WAS IT MORNING? Light in the window, a dog barking. I opened, and then closed my eyes. I couldn't remember much that happened the day before except for Mama dying and I needed to send money to Friend. When I had told Jim, he had said he was sorry and asked how much the flowers would cost. I closed my eyes to the intrusive sun but the insides of my eyelids glowed reddish. In that sliver of one-dimensional space between sleep and wake, I got up and closed the drapes.

I crawled back into bed, not quite ignoring the sound of a chair being pushed across the floor downstairs, some voices, a door being opened. A little world intruding—Mama dying, the fly in the marinate. The one-dimensional sleep-wake space ended.

The milk truck rattled noisily as it stopped in front of the house. Forest Huling made his usual sounds as he left three bottles of milk in a wooden box on the side of the house. The children loved opening the box. They wanted the cream scooped off the top of the milk and put it on their cereal. Forest had a good name for a man. He was polite, skinny, strong, had a crooked nose, small eyes, weathered skin, beautiful blond wavy hair that his wife must like running her hands through. I had noticed lots of his good details. He worked a dairy farm when he wasn't delivering milk. He had one wife, four daughters, no sons, and thirty cows. Guess he preferred the female world. I laughed aloud. Should I be a comedienne? Ha-ha.

One spring, when the cherry tree was blooming, I had tried to mess up his schedule for the rest of his route because I'd been annoyed all morning. I had talked about gossip that might interest him—things about Lester Causley. Three times, Huling said, "Got to go." Then he turned around, got in his truck, and drove off. I regretted doing it.

A glass of milk would be nice. The phone rang. I jumped out of bed and ran downstairs. It was Ethyl Lou. I should've known and not answered. I was ready to chew her out for calling so early in the morning but Ethyl Lou said she was sorry for what she said two days before. We had a few nice words and then hung up. Mama dying certainly changed things. I put flower money in an envelope to send to Friend. Mama was dead.

The phone rang again a few hours later. Was it Ethyl Lou? Was she going to take back her apology? It was Mr. Yalonsky saying he was giving me a free account because he had two excellent weeks after he hemmed my pants. He was sure it was due to me because when I had first come to his shop with Jim, he also had two excellent weeks afterward. He called me good luck. He said he could tell just by looking at me, and my lovely voice.

That was so good of him to call. It was like he was a friend. I said I'd bring all of my alterations to him. No one had ever told me I was good luck, like I was better than the Irish Sweepstakes. I might have to go buy something that needed alterations just to help him with good luck—just to see it happen, just to be his friend.

I believed it was Mama talking to me through Mr. Yalonsky because she was too stubborn to give me a complement, and people in the afterlife are free to do lots of things live people have a hard time doing. I didn't know Mr. Yalonsky's first name. That was okay. I made a draft of a plan—to buy something needing an alteration to have a reason to go see him again. It was something new—having my own tailor. The smell of good luck was sifting through the air.

Willowsburg, Pennsylvania
1952

Iola

Chapter 17

I WAS THINKING it would be good to see Buck or Maude. Aunt Pleasant said if you want something, wish with all your heart and be humble. But Papa was humble and he had trouble most of his life. I decided to give it a try and imagined myself as ordinary, average, run-of-the-mill. Then I humbly, like a beggar, wished Buck would knock on my front door. Several hours later, the phone rang. I got excited but prepared myself for a wrong number. It was Buck. Oh my. Aunt Pleasant!

We talked about missing each other, my children, Mama's death. We wished we could have gone to the funeral, but we both knew we were lying by a drawn-out inflection on one word—*wished*. Each doing it. His voice, coming through a telephone wire strung across states, hadn't changed. We had a history of knowing what the other was thinking by slow inflections. It was the first time we talked on the phone, so we talked about phones. Better than letters . . . Modern . . . Hearing your real voice back and forth . . . Magical . . . Like being together . . . Where've you been? . . . Mississippi . . . You like Mississippi? . . . No, too hot, too humid, and too many bugs.

"Where are you now?" I asked. "Been wanting to talk to you. So glad you called."

"Richmond, Virginia. What you been up to besides married and three kids?"

"Isn't that enough?"

"Enough for me. Maude came to visit me here in Richmond."

"When was that?"

"When? Umm. Month ago. She took me out to White Castle."

"That didn't cost her much."

"I like cheap."

"She didn't come visit me. Richmond isn't that far from Philadelphia. I've been there."

"When was you here?"

"When I was in the WASP."

"That so? She said say hello if I talk with you. Said she tried to call you couple of times."

"That's all? Nothing else?"

"Nothing."

"Did you tell her to visit me?"

"She don't like being told to do things."

"She don't like paying her debts. She still owes me fifty dollars. She go to Mama's funeral?"

"Said she was."

"I heard otherwise."

"Iola, why you ask me if you knew?"

"I thought maybe you knew for sure."

"She got a small part in a movie."

"Doing what?"

"Being a maid."

"Poor thing. Doesn't she want to be a star?"

"Cinderella was a maid and Disney made her a star."

"I don't think she wants to be a cartoon."

We talked some about making ends meet, the weather, his travels. He said he had turned his life around, was behaving himself, and he'd like to visit if he could.

"Please do, brother. You still playing guitar?"

"Still am."

"You working?"

"I've gotten some good carpentry jobs."

We did more catching up on this and that. Then Buck said the phone bill was going to be too high if we kept talking like he was rich. He gave me a number where he could be reached so we could keep in touch. He missed me. I said the same.

"Love you."

"Love you. Bye."

"Bye."

I hoped Buck would follow through on visiting. I was so pleased he called. Was it just coincidence that Buck called and it had nothing to do with wishing and being humble? Frank would say it was coincidence. I liked Frank. There were times I wished for something with all my heart, and it never came through. Mama liked to say everything in the universe happens for a reason. It's one big plan by God and he even has a reason why you have the number of hairs on your head. That sounded dumb to me—all that useless planning.

When putting dirty clothes in the hamper, I found twelve dollars in one of Jim's pockets. I hadn't wished for that. Without a doubt, I was going to use it to buy white capri pants and a white blouse with red polka-dots I had promised myself after Frank and Sarah visited. Was I stealing Jim's money? Didn't I deserve a few dollars for all my hard work? If it needed alterations I'd take it to nice Mr. Yalonsky who had promised me free alterations. I hadn't wished for that. Deep down, I knew I'd go out of my way to buy something needing alterations.

The day turning out good meant coincidence might be leaning my way. I cleaned my kitchen and opened wide the windows. The wind chime jingled its same-changing repertoire as the breeze wafted through and disappeared. The pink and yellow tea roses sent out aromas. The children were playing outside. Their laughter merged with a crow calling, a cricket singing, red robins joining the cricket, the neighbor's brown dog howling to the wail of a siren, another one howling, the radio playing a song. Lovely cacophony. It'd be a perfect day if a whippoorwill sang, for I hadn't heard one in years. I got inspiration and baked a cake with chocolate icing, cream cheese filling, and blackberries on top.

It looked like a party cake, so I made party hats out of newspaper—five simple folds. I tied balloons to chairs and set Kool-Aid on the table. Since the table needed flowers, I set down my African violet—a present from Norma after I gave her the fur coat. I picked some geraniums and white roses and set them on the table. Upstairs, I put on my pink dress and pink high heels.

I called my kids in and Norma's three—Ronnie, Jimmie, and Irene. I invited Bruce Ott, whose family had recently moved to the neighborhood. He wore cute red tennis shoes. Little Nina, with a yellow bow in her blond wavy hair, and skinny Earl in navy blue shorts, from down the street came in. I set the cake, lit with candles, on the table and suddenly there were nine ohhs in unison.

I sang, "Happy birthday to you." To who? Not the right song. Okay. Happy Birthday to everyone. Everyone sang, "Happy birthday everyone." The children blew out the pink, blue, and yellow candles.

"Do it again," Nina said.

"Again, you want?" I lit them again. Everyone sang again. We blew them all out.

"Do it again."

"Again? We're crazy." We did it again, all giggles. Everyone got a slice of cake. A red balloon popped. Nina squealed. Boys laughed.

I entertained, "Little Bo Peep lost one of her sheep.

"She found it hiding inside everyone's birthday cake."

Using their fingers or forks, Nine Kool-Aid kids searched for the sheep hiding in cake. A yellow balloon popped. More boy-laughs at the girl-squeals. A Mad Hatter party had risen at 328 Oak Tree Road.

Nina's cake slice fell on the floor. Red-tennis-shoe Bruce offered to share his. I offered mine. I hadn't touched it.

Kool-Aid spilled on the table.

"Messy mess," Irene said

"Yucky yuck," Lizzy said.

"Messy mess, yucky yuck," Starla said. She made a yucky yuck face. Everyone did, even me. I wiped it up with an old rag.

"Old Mother Hubbard lived in a shoe.

"She cleaned her shoe with an old rag too."

All of us were drunk on fun. A celebration of Kool-Aid puddle and little-kid noise, cake, cakey fingers, singing, and yucky-yucks. Earl gobbled cake down. Nina preferred tiny bites. The yellow curtains blowing in the cool breeze, the air, a dog barking, sunlight turning the kitchen bright, the African violets, sweet-smelling roses, earthy-smelling geraniums. I could see that Charles, Starla, and Lizzy loved their mother having a fine day. I sat down. I, who had escaped Pilgrim, was deeply happy. Did others know this joy, yucky-yuck joy? How many on Oak Tree Road? In Willowsburg? Pennsylvania? On the planet?

The phone rang. It was Norma asking for her kids to come home because they needed to bathe and get cleaned up. She bragged, in her girlish voice, about Ron getting a promotion to shop manager. "He's only worked there two years. He just found out. They said in another two years he could get promoted to supervisor. We're going to spend a couple of days at the shore to celebrate. We're leaving as soon as Ron gets home. Thanks for the party."

Hiding my feelings, I congratulated her. My gnawed-up spot that had disappeared now messed me up. Jim never got promoted. He got laid off. And contrary to what he promised, his new job paid less than his last one. Envy stole my happiness. I was angry with Norma—getting all excited about Ron, like his beating her never happened. The woman was a damn idiot.

I announced the Wendall kids were wanted home and the party was over. Everyone had to go. I was angry with myself for being jealous, but that didn't diminish the jealousy.

Starla looked surprised. Lizzy finished her cake, wiped the icing off her plate, and licked her fingers. Charles watched all the neighbor kids walking out the door. "Why's it over?" he asked. Five minutes before, the house was full of singing. Now, it was only he and his sisters. He got no answer. He asked again.

I turned and walked away. Before I went into the front room, I looked back at his bewildered face.

What had happened? How did my miracle feeling fade so quickly? Was it real? I had felt graced with goodness. Was it just my imagination? Charles and Starla walked outside.

I walked to the window, looking at nothing, lost in thought. I always had to work more than anyone else to get what I needed. Jim was late for dinner three times last week. Was he going to leave me? Quiet types do that. Just walk out and never come back. I hoped Ron would beat up Norma again—just one black eye and bruises but no broken bones or cut lip. I felt guilty.

Lizzy ran over to me, whining that she wanted more cake. I wanted to swat her; had the awful thought to kick her. Despite my pink leather shoes with petite bows, I still had size ten feet that could deliver a strong kick.

Lizzy grabbed on to my pink dress, soiling it with her fingers smeared with cake. "Mommy, pick me up."

"No, you pick me up. How about that, damn it." I was close to yelling.

Lizzy grabbed on harder and smeared more icing on my dress.

I pushed her shoulder. She lost her balance and fell to the floor. Her eyes closed, her forehead tightened and her mouth popped open to a high-pitched wail like her world had fallen apart. Was I on the verge of falling apart? Alarmed, tired. I walked to the bathroom and sat on the toilet, got up, and sat down. I got up, locked the door, and sat down again. The cool seat soothed my bottom. I tried to pee but nothing was there. I wanted to cry but had no tears. I flushed the toilet and let it fill up only to flush it again, for the sound of water. I ran the water in the sink like it was a baptism. Flushing away my sins, but that was wasting water, which was money down the drain. What about the miracle feeling? Real? Crazy?

After a short time in the bathroom, I finally peed; I walked out and told Lizzy, "I love you. You know that. I'm sorry. You stop crying. You hear me. I love you. I told you I'm sorry. If you stop crying we'll go shopping this weekend and I'll buy everyone something." I picked her up and the crying stopped.

We went to Montgomery Ward and I bought white pants and a white blouse with red polka-dots and something for each of the kids. Being a dollar short to buy the blouse, I purposely dropped it on the floor. As I was picking it up, I wiped it against the bottom of my shoe to smudge it, to bargain for a cheaper price. A trick I'd learned from Buck. Not something I'd admit to. A bit fearful of getting caught. Glad I rarely did it. It made up for having my happiness fall off a cliff and I was good about taking out spots. The pants needed to be turned into capri pants. I'd take them to Mr. Yalonsky, who had a big smile. Then I pulled out two dollars I had buried in my pocketbook for an emergency and we all went to White Castle for burgers, fries, and milkshakes.

That evening I needed to talk to Buck. I called the phone number he'd given me. "Hello, sir, may I speak to Buck? . . . You say he's not there? When will he be home? . . . Oh, he doesn't live there anymore . . . Do you have a forwarding address? . . . Well, thank you anyway. Goodbye." It unnerved me because the man said he had no idea where he was and Buck owed him money.

Philadelphia, Pennsylvania
1952

Iola

Chapter 18

LOOKING IN HIS shop window, I could see Mr. Yalonsky bent over working. As soon as I opened the door, he dropped what he was doing, came to the door, and opened it wider. He brushed off a chair for me, said he hoped I would sit and stay awhile. How was I, how were my children, and how was Jim? he asked.

"We're all fine."

Yes, of course—a very lovely family, he said. Would I like some tea; he had just put water on to boil.

"Yes, tea would be nice."

He went into his back room and returned with a porcelain teapot and two cups on a tray. "It's not the best. I'm sorry. There's sugar and lemon here or, if you prefer, fresh cream. If you would like a tea biscuit have as many as you want."

I took a sweet biscuit. He had a bowl of sugar cubes. I put in one; he smiled. I put in another; he smiled more. I put in two more; he smiled and we both laughed. "A lovely spoon," I said as I stirred my very sweet tea.

"It's silver. My wife stole it twenty years ago. It had fallen in the kitchen trash in a rich man's house." Yalonsky had a very expressive face.

"A bit of stolen property makes the day more intriguing."

"And what intriguing thing have you stolen?"

"I could steal your spoon."

"I'd be pleased to give it to you. You look wonderful when you smile."

I ran my hand through my hair. "Your wife would miss it."

"She would."

"We don't want her missing things."

"No. No. But I wouldn't tell if it turned up missing. If she asked I'd say, maybe it got thrown in the trash." He raised his flirting eyebrows, cocked his head, and leaned toward me. "And what brings you here today?"

"Can you turn these pants into capri pants?"

He took them, held them up, fingered the fabric, and laid them down. He pulled over a chair, sat down, and complemented my taste in clothes. Had I been born in a stylish city? Had I studied fashion? he asked. His brown eyes opened wide. Suddenly, he threw a hand up in the air and said, "Ahh." His head wobbled. "Ahh, I now remember, you said you once lived in Chattanooga. If my memory is correct, Chattanooga is in Tennessee? I've always liked geography."

"That's right. But I grew up in a very small town."

"I should've known. There are women who come from very rural backgrounds who are born with style."

I wondered if he was making this up, but his enthusiasm was an invitation to describe Pilgrim.

"Interesting name."

"But very small. Two-hundred-thirty people give or take the yearly deaths and births."

"There are no secrets in small towns."

"I learned to keep quiet."

"Quiet is smart."

"Very smart."

"Very smart is excellent."

"I left after high school to get a job. If I hadn't gotten a ride into Chattanooga with my brother Buck, I would've walked even if it had taken me a month."

"Smart plus determination is unbeatable. One needs both in life to get anywhere."

"Isn't that true. It was hard but I knew what I wanted. Nothing could've gotten in my way. My Papa said I'd be homesick. I doubted it. I was right."

When Mr. Yalonsky's face turned serious, I feared I said too much. Then he smiled. "I know . . . I know what you mean. It was an excellent decision." He moved his chair a few inches closer to me. He looked charmed, captivated, and more attractive. "I, too, grew up in a very small village, a half village. A hamlet . . . barely there. We were poor. Our whole village was. The animals were. The ground was. Sometimes, it seemed our village was the path to death."

"Yes, when we first met, you said it was near Riga near the Baltic Sea."

"Ah, Mrs. Lewis, you have an excellent memory. Yes, yes. We had a one-room house with no indoor plumbing. And freezing winters." He pretended to shiver. "They could kill you. Three of my siblings died. We had to be careful."

"We had two wood-burning stoves and lots of wood, so our house was warm, and we had a hand pump in the kitchen for water. But the water sometimes froze before it got to the house. And an outhouse that was very cold in the winter."

"It's like we came from the same cloth."

"One that can be rewoven." I laughed.

"Rewoven. I like that. And you have a lovely laugh."

"And you have lovely tea."

"I think we're having a lovely time."

He talked about Latvian *buberts* and sorrel soup. I talked about vinegar pie and honeysuckle jelly. Then it was Philadelphia and leaving home. We agreed on much and sidestepped our differences.

Finally, he remembered what brought me to his store. We took care of business. When he bent over to pick up his tape measure that he dropped on the floor, I noticed the seat of his baggy pants was worn to a thin shine. Not a man who spent money on himself.

Just before I left, Mr. Yalonsky said, his voice just above a whisper, "May I ask you something? Please forgive me . . . if I shouldn't ask this, but can I meet you someplace else whenever you bring me alterations? I'm not flirting. I love my wife, but she's jealous of you."

"But she's never seen me."

"I talked about you. I know you're good luck. My shop always does excellent after you come here. Plus, my wife wants me to charge you. If I did that I know it would ruin my good luck." He looked up at the ceiling. "She means well. I don't say anything to her because she has poor health and stresses easily."

"Yes. I understand. It's important to take care of good luck. Treat it right and it'll stay longer." I found myself thinking of Mr. Yalonsky as a widower, as a husband, my husband. I had never planned to think these things or much less to enjoy the thoughts.

"Wonderful. You understand. I could take your future alterations and do them without you coming here. I can take your measurements now . . . the ones I don't have. Like inseam, chest, waist, hips, arm length, a few others. For future alterations. I have them for all of my customers." He pulled out from his desk a notebook of names and measurements; he had superb, legible handwriting. "You'll be bringing me more work? Yes?"

"Of course."

"Wonderful. If we meet at . . . like a park. A store. Wherever you like, it might be awkward to take your measurements . . . you know, in public. But you could give me the item needing alterations."

"How could I refuse? You're so kind and don't charge me, especially now . . . money has become tight. Jim didn't get a promotion he hoped for and we have more expenses with three growing children. I don't know how we're going to make ends meet."

"Do you ever consider getting a job? A woman like you could get one easily."

I nodded and then rubbed my ear.

Mr. Yalonsky nodded. He took my measurements and barely touched my body.

"It's almost like we're family, aren't we?"

"Yes, you could say that. And I've known you not as long as I've known Jim." With a trace of a flirtatious smile, he put a closed hand under his chin. "This is very interesting. I was just asking myself . . . who do I feel more connected to—you or Jim? I think you and I are from the same cloth. Jim is so lucky to have you." Before I left, we decided on a Woolworth store where we could meet. I didn't mind his flirtations. There was excitement to it.

Willowsburg, Pennsylvania
1953

Iola

Chapter 19

I JUMPED OUT of the bathtub, wrapped myself in a threadbare towel with ragged edges, and ran downstairs to answer the phone, dripping wet, thinking of Yalonsky, stubbed my toe, cursed out loud.

After the usual greeting, Frank said, "We're moving to France." He gave a stiff laugh.

"You're joking?" It was more of a statement than a question. With my free hand, I tried drying myself but the towel dropped and I was naked in view of the front door. This was the first time I was naked outside my bedroom or bathroom. May no one come knocking.

"I wish." He sounded tired.

I covered myself again, and held the towel tight to my body. "But you love Brooklyn. Your bookstore's there. Why?" Would I regret my question?

"Senator McCarthy." He paused. "You know him."

"This isn't sounding good." I leaned against the wall, preparing for the worst. It was a difficult conversation to have while almost naked.

"He's targeted Sarah."

I almost dropped the towel again. "What is she accused of?" Unpleasant silence. I leaned hard against the wall and pressed the phone to my ear. It was good the kids were upstairs. I wanted to sit, but there were no chairs within reach. I slowly slid down the wall until I was sitting on the hardwood floor with a big ink stain on it that I disliked but didn't mind it now. My bare bottom was on the floor, but not a time to think of sanitation. While trying to stand up, my bottom got exposed. I must've looked ridiculous.

"It's nice you call it an accusation. But she actually attended two Communist meetings several months before McCarthy began his witch hunt. She was curious to see what it was about. Two months ago, a colleague of hers reported that she'd heard Sarah talking about having gone to two meetings."

"Was it on the radio? Her being targeted?"

"Just mention of it. She's not a huge prize."

"I once heard McCarthy interrogate a man. The man stood up for himself. Asserted his rights to free speech and peaceful assembly."

"If McCarthy's not downright paranoid he's willfully ignorant."

"He sounded hateful."

"*Nefarious* is a better word. I could go on. Sarah will be losing her job at the end of the term . . ."

I didn't hear what next he said because I was cold and concerned someone would come to the door. "But why France?"

"A relative of hers lives in France and connected her to a job in Paris."

"Jim will say you're un-American." Frank took a very audible breath.

"Yes, my very conservative cousin." He filled me in on the details of Sarah's new teaching job, starting in the fall. With a somber voice, he said, "There's so much to do. That's why we waited telling you. And actually . . . I wasn't sure how to tell Jim. I kind of put it off."

I was envious of Sarah finding work so easy. My high school teacher had recommended I become a teacher, but Pilgrim had them but no pilots. Being a pilot meant I was completely free of Pilgrim. I didn't want to be envious of Sarah. I wanted to be supportive. I wanted Frank to think when he hung up the phone—how nice it was to talk to me. "I'd like having a job."

"I might be able to get you one in France."

"Well thanks but . . . how are you going to adjust to . . . a foreign country?" I bit my lip, thinking my question insensitive.

"After the war ended in Europe, I managed to stay in Paris for a month. I liked France. I'm going to try to open a bookstore for both French and English speakers. Maybe . . . maybe just English. I know some French but I'm not close to being fluent. It'll be hard selling my bookstore. I'll miss it." His voice trailed off.

I broke Frank's atypical silence. "It's a lot. I mean . . . this is a huge change."

"Very big. We're trying to do what's needed. Interesting that Sarah and I were actually planning on taking a trip to France in a year or two." His voice picked up.

I noticed cobwebs on the ceiling. Later, I would get on a chair and remove them. Or maybe not. I was cold and jiggled myself to warm up.

"Would you and Jim want to buy my bookstore? I'll sell it with a small down payment. I meant to tell Jim first. I guess I just needed to talk. You know me. I like talking. And . . . well, it was easier telling you than Jim. Can you have him call me when he gets in?"

"Of course."

"And about getting a job—you'll find one, easily."

It seemed like a good time to ask a question I'd wanted to ask for a long time. "Did you suggest I come to that party years ago so I'd meet Jim?"

"Absolutely. I thought you'd be good for him. He was still grieving for his sister and father. They died so unexpectedly. Her suicide really traumatized him. He blamed himself. I feared he might die from guilt. Watching it was painful. Afterward, it seemed like Jim and his mother retied the umbilical cord. Whenever I visited, they seemed to talk without words. They drank tea at the same time, ate little, ate at the same pace. If they talked it was to ask a question that could be answered with a yes or no. I think it made them feel very close—accepting each other's silence. He felt totally obligated to do what she wanted."

"I didn't know. He almost never talks about their deaths."

"There was some improvement after he met you."

"Really?"

"Yes. One time when you two were dating, he asked my opinion about you having been a pilot, like it wasn't a good thing."

"What did you say?"

"Something like—sounds good to me. Probably means she's smart. It's good to have a smart wife."

We talked some about his time in Paris. It was the warmest conversation I'd had with Frank. I was pleased he was family. Afterward, as I walked upstairs and dressed, I let myself realize it was kind of fun being naked near the front door, except for feeling cold. But I'd never do it again.

WHEN I SERVED dinner to the children, I set some aside for Jim. Lizzy only wanted to eat carrots and meatloaf. Starla called her dopey. Lizzy screamed. Both made their ugliest, angriest faces. When told to behave, they didn't. I ignored them. Let them figure it out for themselves. Charles yelled at them and raised his hand. They quieted. I didn't reprimand Charles for threatening.

Jim came home late, looking tired. He threw his hat on a chair—not his custom.

I wasn't sure how to approach him with the news and all he wanted to do was talk about setbacks at work on a lab test for the drug they were developing. If it was successful, there probably won't be any layoffs. If not, well . . .

I interrupted him and talked about Frank. He floundered. All drug discussion stopped. "Is this one of your silly jokes?" He loosened his necktie.

"Call it what you want. My suggestion to you—call Frank."

He stood there silent, looking right at me as I shrugged with the palms of my hands held up implying, *Believe what you want. I don't care. I really don't care.* He looked around the room, as if searching for something.

"Call him. He's your only real family other than us."

"I told you they were going to get themselves in trouble. I warned you. If I call him we'll be targeted."

"No, we won't. By the way, Frank asked if we would like to buy his bookstore. It makes more money than you do. I'd move to Brooklyn. You love books . . . it's meant for you. I'll help run the store." I intentionally spoke with a wifely voice. "When I learn the business, I can run it entirely, and if you want to work for a chemical company, there's got to be some in New York."

"I am not leaving the Philadelphia area. I grew up here."

"And I suppose you'll die here?"

"As a matter of fact, I will. You know the kind of problems you would have in Brooklyn? Do you ever want to settle down? Know your neighbors? I've never known anyone who's lived in so many places as you. Norma is the only neighbor you talk to. I don't understand what you see in her."

Jim's comments made me bristle, but holding steady was my strength. "It's an opportunity."

"The bookstore?"

"What else are we talking about?"

"It's not for me." Jim sat down and removed his necktie, took off his father's gold watch, and laid it on the armrest. He leaned his head back on the chair.

"Tomorrow morning you'll forget you left your watch there and spend a half hour looking for it."

"You'll remember. You remember everything."

"No, I don't."

He picked it up and put it in his pocket.

"What about the bookstore? You love books," I said.

"Reading them. Not selling them. I'm no salesman. I should have been a chemist."

"Well then, we're staying here in wonderful happy Willowsburg and I'm going to be looking for a job. It'll be good we have two incomes. You never know. Never know. You might be targeted and get fired, get laid off, get sick . . . die. You could die. I could. Remember when we met. Neither of us expected we'd be getting married." I used the cheeriest of tones when I said the last four words.

"What does that mean?" he asked.

"It means you never know what will happen—good or bad. Better to be prepared."

"No wife of mine works."

"I've worked since I was a child. I was working when I met you. Life is work." I wiped my forehead, then ran my thumb over my lips. "And I don't get paid for my work here. And if you have a problem with me working, then I'll somehow buy Frank's bookstore. I'll move to Brooklyn and you'll have to visit me and the kids up there. On the weekends. 'Hello, dear. Did you have a good drive? I sold four hundred books. Yippee.'"

No response. Jim just sat with his head back and his mouth agape, his eyes closed. His dark brown hair was still thick and wavy and as good-looking as it was when we first met. But this day, he was unattractive. I had a physical need to be away from him.

JIM CALLED FRANK the next evening and got the details. When he was ready to hang up the phone, he looked morose, maybe angry. Top lip curled.

I asked if I could speak with Sarah and we talked, mainly about the children but some about seeing new places, especially Paris. How to say hello in French. Bonjour. How to say it with a French accent by directing some of the sound toward the back of my mouth or maybe up toward my nose.

BY THE TIME Frank and Sarah obtained all the documents they needed, it was early June. They next had to travel to Paris to find a house and a place for a bookstore. I suggested I could help them by coming to Brooklyn to babysit their three kids while they were gone, if my three could come with me. Several weeks, maybe a month, was doable, without Jim feeling excessively abandoned. It took some effort to not sound excited.

Jim objected and said nothing at dinner.

It was easy to oblige the silence because I disliked argumentative meals. When dinner was done, I brought it up again.

He refused to drive me to Brooklyn because I'd be putting us in danger of being targeted by McCarthy. Frank's house might be under surveillance and they'd see me coming and going and I'd be targeted and then we would all be targeted here in Willowsburg. "You want to wreck our lives?" He threw his hands up and scowled.

"Why would he target me? You say he's a patriot. Why would a patriot target me? I'm married to a patriot. We live in Patriotville. We go to patriot church, shop at patriot stores, and wear patriot clothes. I served in World War II." I noticed Jim had the start of a smile but he suppressed it.

"He would target you for visiting Frank."

"I won't be visiting Frank. I'd be helping him leave the country. Isn't that what McCarthy wants—ridding the country of Communist sympathizers?"

"I will. Not. Drive you."

"Yes. You. Will."

He walked out to the front porch.

I followed him. For a while it was quiet except for the birds nesting for the night. When a neighbor's dog barked, I said, "Goddamn it. Frank's your cousin." We exchanged scowls. Our little war. He looked like an angry granite statue, until he blinked.

"So be it. If you don't drive us, we'll. Take. The train. If you don't drive us to the train station, we'll. Take. A taxi . . . When. You're. Working. Simple. Thank you."

He didn't say another word. When he stood up to go inside, I said, "Good night, dear." I knew he acquiesced. But within an hour he'd likely be planning some retribution.

Brooklyn, New York
1953

Chapter 20

FRANK AND SARAH'S three-story brownstone house, second from the corner, number 506, had impressive nine marble steps up to the leaded-glass oak front door. The wrought-iron railings were ornate. I had grown up in a row house with not an inch of front yard and only two concrete steps up to the door.

I stared at it.

"What are you waiting for?" Iola asked.

I walked up the stairs. I assumed, when the click of her high heels stopped, she and the kids were standing behind me. I knocked and soon Frank opened the door, and welcomed us. He took our bags and asked how the trip was. Iola said something, but I didn't pay attention to a word.

Sarah showed up with more greetings. The affection was unnecessary. Steven, Louise, and Jeannette came running. Charles and Lizzy hid behind me but Starla was ready to play.

Their home was different than I remembered. In the front parlor, lace curtains covered the tall leaded-glass windows. My mother loved lace. Some toys lay on the floor. Sarah was as messy as Iola. The sofa and two plush armchairs were yellow. Yellow was my least favorite color. An oriental rug lay on the floor. Not American made. I'd forgotten that the walls were made of hardwood paneling. The house had long rooms, tall ceilings, and parquet floors. They had bought it after Frank sold a handwritten note signed by Abraham Lincoln, which was tucked inside an old book he bought. Why couldn't I find books like that? My life was bad luck. They'll miss this house. Sarah caused all of this, going to Communist meetings. Damn woman.

I don't remember much of what I said at lunch other than thanking Sarah for the hamburger, and I'd be leaving soon, as it was a long drive. I didn't say I was glad she hadn't served Frenchy food or that I couldn't wait to go home. As I was about to walk out the door, Lizzy ran to me and cried, "Don't leave, Daddy." She stopped crying when I picked her up. A lovely child.

Sarah said if I stayed overnight Lizzy might adjust better to her new surroundings and feel more comfortable. Iola nodded. Lizzy wrapped her arms around me tight as she could, trying to keep me from leaving. I gave in; plus I had a headache, and was tired.

Sarah offered us the guest bedroom on the second floor. It had a four-post bed and its own bathroom. It's uncomfortable feeling jealous. Iola said something about wanting to take all six children sightseeing. They said other things that I paid no attention to.

When Frank and Sarah were going over a list with Iola in the kitchen about what needed what, and who needed what, I walked down the long hallway lined with four bookcases. I ran my hand along some of the books, perusing titles. There were lots of authors I didn't know—Camus, Heidegger, and Kafka. Then *Das Kapital* by Karl Marx. I looked twice to be sure my eyes weren't fooling me. My God. Were they Communists? Finally I saw Herman Melville, Jack London, Stephen Crane, Mark Twain, Nathaniel Hawthorne, and *The Federalist* by Hamilton, Jay, and Madison. I took out *The Federalist* (I had always wanted to read the letters they wrote to the people of New York) and read the first page of the first letter written by Hamilton, on October 27, 1787. I stopped when I got to: "Happy will it be if our choice should be decided by a judicious estimate of our true interests, uninfluenced and unbiased by considerations foreign to the public good." The public good? It sounded like Marx. Could Hamilton have liked Marx? I put it back. I might've frowned. *The City and the Pillar* by Gore Vidal caught my attention. I'd heard of Vidal. Unusual name. Didn't he write about American history? What could be bad about it?

I sat in the parlor and opened the book to a random page—just to get a feel for the writing. I expected history but I got a young man named Jim who seemed to be falling in love with a man named Bob. I closed it. I looked up, making sure no one was in the room. I opened it and fingered the page. I started at the beginning, read to the friendly naked wrestling, then returned it to the bookshelf, noting that it was on the third shelf, near the left end. In the evening, after dinner, and after everyone went to bed, I read a few more chapters. Chapters about men who loved men. The queer bars. They called it natural and had no shame. Natural? No shame? I went to bed, laden with curiosity. It was hard to fall asleep, even harder after waking up after having a male-love dream. What a name—Gore Vidal. I took a deep breath as quiet as possible. Holy shit.

On the following morning, Frank opened and closed his suitcase three times, checking that he had everything. Sarah, in a blue suit and white shirt, said she was glad to be leaving the United States of America. Sad-looking Frank said they were determined to make a go of it.

Iola told Sarah she would miss them. They hugged tight, rocked back and forth a few times. When they stopped, Sarah had teary eyes. Frank clenched his jaw; their children cried again. Frank got all Frenchy and said ,"Oh revwar." It was hard to watch, so I loaded their suitcases in a taxi that was waiting to take them to the airport. What could I say? Nothing, if I was polite. *You'll regret this*, if I was honest. *Damn it. It's all Sarah's fault*, if I was rude.

"Bon voyage," Iola said. "It's going to go well for you."

When downcast Frank looked out the taxi window as they drove off, emptiness welled up in me. Frank and Sarah's children cried. Iola assured them their parents would be back to get them. She said she'd bake a cake and they would have an oh revwar party. She said, "Everyone must have fun so loved ones who have left on a trip stay safe. We do it for them." Why had she suddenly got so much imagination? She got all six to promise. When she was preparing for the party, I found a book by Freud and switched its cover with the Gore Vidal book. While the party was going on, I read more of *The City and the Pillar*. I wanted to finish reading it, but I had to leave soon to go back to Willowsburg. When switching back the book covers, *Das Kapital* caught my attention again. I took it and stuck it in my bag. When the party was done, I drove home. When I was in New Jersey, I threw *Das Kapital* in a trash can at a gas station.

IT WAS WEDNESDAY, so I called like I promised. I needed a reason to go back on the weekend and finish reading *The City and the Pillar*. I asked about Lizzy, and if she had adjusted or was she still crying?

"No, she's fine. We did some sightseeing," Iola said.

"Edna Miller down the street just died of cancer. The one, five houses down, with the Virgin Mary statue in the front yard." I never cared much for Edna, but she was a good way to keep the conversation going.

"The Virgin Mary . . . Mother of God, they say. How does God have a mother?"

"It makes sense to them. Well, you have to believe something in this world."

"True, whatever makes sense to you. That can change, though."

"Sometimes it does. I heard she refused pain medications because she wanted to suffer to honor Jesus, who died for the sins of mankind. That's going too far. There's nothing wrong with pain medication. I'd take it."

"I would too."

"In the end she said Jesus was at the supermarket and he liked Cheerios. She asked to have a box of Cheerios by her bed. I almost laughed. Jesus and Cheerios."

"I think he'd prefer Wheaties."

"Why that?"

"I was just being silly, dear. Where'd you hear all this?"

"From Norma. She was at the store. She looked like she lost some weight. She heard Edna was all swollen up and the tumors were everywhere. She died at home. She asked about you."

"Edna?"

"No, Norma."

"I knew of someone who all of a sudden felt pain and dizziness and then spoke gibberish."

"They say pain confuses the mind."

"Are you going to the funeral?"

"I don't think so." I missed Iola but was uncomfortable saying so. It's not like I loved her. But she had my respect. I'd miss her if she died. How would I take care of everything? How many things would I have to do? "Maybe I should come up this weekend to help with all six kids. Are you being targeted by anyone?" I was glad I got that said.

"No one. Why would anyone target me?"

I almost said, *Why do I bother talking to you?* but I wanted to be polite. "I just wanted to be sure you're okay." The image of me in the house all day washing, ironing, sweeping, hanging clothes on the line, cooking, making beds seemed ludicrous, unsuitable. I never did any of it before except cooking and not very well, when my sister died and my mother fell apart. Women like all that stuff.

"No problems and not to worry."

"I might come up this weekend."

IT WAS AN exhausting drive to Brooklyn after work on Friday. The weather had turned stormy. Roads were flooded causing detours. I feared I might have to stay overnight in a motel but I made it. After four days of rain, Brooklyn was soaked. Yellow daffodils growing in the planter box on the front windowsill had acquiesced and were face down in soil that was getting diluted in a water puddle. Iola saved some dinner for me. I ate and went right to bed.

In the morning, Iola was dressed nice, but her hair needed combed. Doesn't she ever look in a mirror? The children whined and argued.

"What's going on with them?" I asked.

"Well, they've been stuck indoors for days." She shrugged.

Steven asked why they had to move to France.

Charles said they were Communists and Communists can't live in America. Defending her brother, Jeannette hit Charles. Charles smacked Jeannette in the face. Iola was livid with Charles. Starla called Charles ugly. Iola told her not to do that.

"Why?"

"What comes around goes around."

"What does that mean—comes around goes around?" Starla asked.

"Means merry-go-round."

"Shut up, Lizzy."

"You be quiet," Iola corrected Charles.

She handled the kids well but I didn't tell her that. I wanted to. But that seemed to be my history—not following my urges, not expressing feelings. It was safer that way. There was a knock on the front door. I quickly walked down the hall and opened the door. Julie, a neighbor from several houses down, was standing under a red umbrella. She wore a yellow raincoat, black galoshes, an orange cap.

Was she trying to make a fashion statement? Before Sarah and Frank left for France, Sarah had introduced her as very helpful, if needed. Julie invited all six kids to a rain party.

"A rain party?" I asked. "I never heard of that."

Julie had a lovely oblong face, dangly blue earrings, and an expression that went along with her comical outfit. "I made it up to trick them," she said. "It's funny how they're easily fooled by a different name. One word changes everything. It'll only be my two, yours, and Sarah's. Send them down in thirty minutes."

Without the kids in the house, I could read more of *The City and the Pillar*. I helped Iola get all six ready and waiting at the door. Charles, Starla, and Lizzy had to share umbrellas. Iola and I stood at the front door and watched them run to Julie's. After they disappeared into her house, I noticed a man wearing a black jacket and a white shirt sitting in a black car across the street. He looked at Iola and me, and then took off his glasses and put them back on.

Were we being watched? Were we now under surveillance? The man looked like FBI. I knew it was a mistake coming to Brooklyn. Was McCarthy going to destroy us next? This could change my whole life. Would we also have to move to France? Leave my home? There was really nothing I could do because I couldn't take all the children back to Willowsburg. It was hard not to panic.

"That man over there is watching us. He's FBI." I squeezed Iola's elbow. "I knew this would be a mistake. Damn it. Why don't you ever listen to me?" My heart beat fast. It rained harder. My mouth got dry.

Iola's eyes widened as she looked at the man. Quietly, she followed me back in the house.

We peeked out the window, behind lace curtains. An old woman in a raincoat and rain hat—head hung down, shoulders stooped—came walking down the sidewalk. When she got to the black car, she saw the man. Her mouth dropped open and she waved her hands in the air. He jumped out of the car. She hugged him profusely and kissed him several times on each cheek. They got all wet. He wore bright green pants. Where does a man buy green pants? He got a suitcase out of the trunk, and he followed her inside her house.

"So much for surveillance and the need to keep a low profile." Iola chuckled. Probably just to irk me, she opened the curtains wide and stood there looking at the drenched neighborhood. I didn't care. It was a complete relief, not having the FBI to deal with. I sat in the parlor thinking I worry too much. Then Iola went to the basement to do laundry. Her footsteps were audible as she descended the stairs. They would be audible when she came back up.

It was an opportunity to read *The City and the Pillar*, as Iola would start on dinner after she finished the laundry. I read a few chapters—just wonderful. Gore Vidal wasn't a pornographer; he was a respected writer, but still I would never tell anyone.

When the kids came home, all happy with a box of cookies, Iola phoned Julie and thanked her. I had put away my Vidal book. I said to Iola, "I have to admit, you were right about helping out Frank and Sarah. It was a good thing to do. Maybe we'll all go out for breakfast tomorrow morning. Would you like that?" It was making up for reading Vidal, for feeling aroused, for wanting male love. For wondering how many men like myself I might find in Brooklyn. In Philadelphia. Willowsburg. On Oak Tree Road. Oak Tree Road would surprise me. The man in the green pants wouldn't surprise me. I wondered if he was like me.

Iola was peeling potatoes at the kitchen table. I went over and kissed the top of her head. Her hair smelled good. She let all the peels fall on the table. It was messy but Vidal's Jim character wouldn't have cared. He probably wouldn't have noticed. When she was done, I picked up the peels and put them in the trash.

I didn't read in the evening as the kids were running all over the house and wanted my attention. It's good not to push one's luck.

Sunday breakfast was perfect, especially with six kids. Imagine if they were all mine. Iola looked nice in her blue shirtwaist dress, tight at the waist. She had done her hair special. Her ruby lipstick. Her shiny yellow earrings. Very colorful and pretty. The kids told me the rules of a rain party—you have say something about rain. Real or pretend, but has to be happy. "You get to wear a yellow coat."

"Everyone can shower outside at the same time."

"You can play in puddles."

"You can get a pet whenever it rains cats and dogs."

"Sugar cane likes rain."

"Take a train in rain and you won't have pain."

It didn't matter what they said. It pleased me to hear kid-talk.

When I drove back to Willowsburg after lunch, Vidal might as well have been in the car with me, reading his book out loud. It was all I was thinking about. All the stuff I read, particularly about some men having families and children, and straying just once in a while. What was wrong with that? I planned to finish reading it on my next trip. Sometimes on a straight road and no other cars around, I closed my eyes for a second and tried to imagine a sex scene. That night when I was in bed alone, alone with Vidal, I envisioned all sorts of sexual contact and the queer bars, the freedom, talking loose. Then I played with myself, like my bedroom was the back room of a queer bar. And having a partner. Then another. No modesty. Nothing held back. But only in my thoughts. Good God, I loved it. I never thought to call myself queer.

THE NEXT WEEKEND, a trip to Brooklyn was out of the question, as I was needed on Saturday at the lab to help correct a problem my stupid boss caused. Owning a copy of Vidal's book could be hard evidence. And the library didn't have it; at least it wasn't there in the card catalog. I didn't ask the librarian, who might ask questions. It was a boring week. I returned to Brooklyn the following weekend when Frank and Sarah were scheduled to come home. They were tired but encouraged. They had decided on renting a place in Paris, since they had not yet sold their house. They said some other stuff but I paid no attention until Frank said, "I think it was meant to be—that we move to Paris. Now it's—pack, sell our house and bookstore, and move out of the United States of America." He snidely elongated the syllables in *America*.

"If you say so. I hope it works out for you. I guess it's the best move." It was sad—them leaving.

"Well, I'm blacklisted and won't be able to get a job here," Sarah said.

"And Frank might see an FBI agent checking out the bookstore every so often." Iola looked enigmatic—not sad, or sarcastic, or happy. She could be that way—just ball herself up, all secret-like. Funny how we were alike in some ways.

Frank laughed, and then Sarah did. I didn't quite catch the humor but I laughed so I wouldn't stand out. Was Iola making fun of me? Had she talked about my fears of the FBI watching me? Knowing her, she'd do that. We left the next morning because Jeannette got ill, and Iola didn't want her infecting our kids. Would I ever finish reading *The City and the Pillar*?

Chapter 21

A SECOND TRIP to Brooklyn was needed, as Frank and Sarah hadn't yet sold their house or bookstore. A promising offer had fallen through and then their realtor died. Charles might miss a week or two of first grade but he was already reading at second-grade level. Jim drove us up, and said he would stay at least overnight, maybe two nights. We would go see a Broadway show.

It was good weather; Starla sang, Lizzy waved to passing cars, then all five of us counted red cars. Jim said if we counted twenty, everyone gets ice cream. Twenty-five were counted. Even with our ice-cream stop, we made good time. Upon arrival, Frank was packing a box of books. There were stacks of boxes already sealed; the bookshelves were almost empty. After Jim brought in the luggage, he said he had changed his mind and he would leave shortly.

"You're not staying overnight?" I asked. It seemed strange that he changed his mind so quick. He looked like his happy mood had collapsed.

"I just realized there might be a problem with some data at work. I should go in tomorrow and check, before our Monday meeting." He soon drove home.

IT WAS THE end of July and the humidity and ninety degree temperatures turned the city sluggish. Sarah had already left because she had to start her job in Paris a month before the school year began.

After two days in Brooklyn, Charles said he didn't want to miss any school and didn't like the noisy car horns. He especially disliked sirens, and he wanted to sleep in his room with his own things, without Steven bothering him. He read most of the time, insisted on going to church on Sunday, and, on his own, gave a nickel to the collection basket. He said, "God told me to."

"When did God say that?" I asked.

"Last night when I said my prayers."

He surprised me, and not knowing what to say, I said, "You're a good boy."

Three-year-old Lizzy was fine if she got held enough. She sat by me, played by me, talked to herself, talked to me, was more talkative than usual. She had a better vocabulary than I would've imagined, as she was generally very shy and quiet. Each day she asked, "Is Daddy coming this weekend?"

Starla spent time in Jeannette's room with the door closed and came out in costumes, in masks, with dolls. She came out with her arm around Jeannette. Dancing. Marching. Laughing. In and out like it was an ever-changing stage show. Hunger and sleep were the only things that slowed them down. That and an extra harsh word or two if they got too rambunctious. Starla said she liked eating at Cousin Frank's because everyone talks at dinner and laughs and tells knock-knock jokes. She had learned ten and made up some of her own.

Three siblings raised together but so different. It was enough to make me think—kids must raise themselves in some ways.

Early September, Frank sold his bookstore. The house had not yet sold, but that wouldn't prevent them from moving. A lot of their things were already packed in boxes. He bowed to me, thanking me profusely. I bowed. He did it again. I did. A warm hug. If it was a flirtation I enjoyed it. He took us all out to eat at a French restaurant. It was the best restaurant I'd ever been in. Soft-spoken smiling waiters in short white jackets and black pants. A four-page menu in French. A page of just wines. A page of desserts. Very expensive but Frank didn't seem to care. Different silverware for every course. Two crystal wineglasses. A lit candle. A tiny bowl with salt at each setting. Royal.

"What is *fromage de tête*?" I asked. What is this, and this? How is this pronounced? The food with strange-sounding names was wonderful and so were my three glasses of wine.

Lizzy asked, "Mommy, do you like Frank better than Daddy?"

"No. I love your Daddy." Honesty was unacceptable. I wanted to go to France.

THE LAST WEEKEND, Jim drove up to Brooklyn. Sarah returned before they would all take a plane to Paris, after the movers came. Jim didn't talk much. Finally, he said, "I don't like this living in France. Soon you'll be speaking French all the time."

"I'm sure they'll write to us in English," I said.

Jim looked confused. He pulled a photo out of an envelope and gave it to Frank. He had taken it when they had visited us in Willowsburg. It was of Frank's children and ours.

"It's a wonderful photo. I didn't know you had such talent. The lighting, the way the kids are standing, their happy expressions."

"You think so?"

"I don't know how someone, who can be so void of feelings at times, can take such a lovely photograph," Frank said.

"That's a backhanded compliment." Jim stepped back and rubbed his hand against his chin. "I love my children. I'd do anything for them. It was the reason I got married. I wanted to have five kids, but Iola probably did some of her tricks to keep that from happening. It wouldn't surprise me if she had an abortion and didn't tell me."

"What's an abortion?" Starla asked.

My jaw dropped. My head bent forward, looking at everyone's feet. Jim was wearing his best shoes. Frank wore old loafers. Mine needed polishing. How to respond? I noticed a string lying on the floor, and picked it up.

Sarah quickly said, "I agree. It's a beautiful picture. You have a talent." She touched Jim's arm.

"I don't want to go home. I want to stay here." Starla ran into the kitchen. I followed Starla and tried comforting her. Jeannette asked if Starla could come to Paris with them. Lizzy and Charles wanted to go home. It was a difficult thirty minutes. Jim said we needed to get going; it was a long drive and he had to work on Monday. I wondered if I'd ever see them again.

"I don't want you to go."

"We have to. We have no choice," Frank said sadly. He walked us to the front door.

"We always have a choice," Jim said. He picked up our luggage.

"Not always," I said. Jim muttered something, opened the door, and walked down the steps to the car. Charles followed.

I kissed Frank, Sarah, and their kids, turned and walked to the car with Lizzy and Starla.

ON THE WAY home, Starla said she was going to move to Paris when she grew up and she would see Jeannette there.

"They're Communists," Charles said.

"You behave."

Jim smiled. "Maybe he knows something." When we got to Camden, Jim said his only other words the whole trip—"We need gas."

Willowsburg, Pennsylvania
1954

Iola

Chapter 22

WHEN AN OLD Rambler came up the driveway, I knew it was Buck. Very typical—showing up unannounced. All excited, I ran downstairs and outside, saying, "Buck. Buck. Buck Boggs. You know how long it's been?"

"Thought I never find you."

"And what brings you?" We hugged when he got out of his car.

"After talking to you on the phone, I realized I had a need to see my sissy dear."

I gave him a sideways look. "Couldn't be too big a need—we talked months ago. You always had two reasons when you had a need." He looked skinnier than usual.

"Might be true. Might be smart thing to do."

I called my children, who were playing with Norma's kids, to come on over. The kids met their uncle, and Buck shook Charles's hand. Starla put her hand forward.

"Little girls don't shake men's hands," Buck said.

"Starla's a modern girl."

"Being you're her mama, I guess there's nothing else she could be."

"Now your Uncle Buck has old ways, but he taught me to stand up for myself when I was growing up." I didn't say he had taught me to steal the neighbor's apples, how to fish for crayfish and roast them over a fire in the woods if I'd been served only bread and water for breakfast for some misdeed.

The kids went off to play and Buck followed me into the kitchen, which had a sink full of dirty dishes. "Nice kitchen. Warm for the spirit." His voice sounded like Pilgrim talk. He pulled a cup from the sink and washed it. "I'll have some coffee if you would. After you finish what you was doing would be fine. I'm known as patient."

"You're known as lazy by those who know you. And you look rawboned."

"You known as too smart for your pretty britches by those who know you." He sat down. "You still good looking, Iola." He stretched his legs out. His pants had a hole in one knee, and the hems were ragged.

I made a new pot of coffee and served him some cookies, of which Buck had four. "Have more. I made them for you."

"Knew I was coming?"

"When I woke up this morning."

He laughed. "And the husband? He around?"

"He'll be home at five-forty."

"Looking forward to it." He lit up a cigarette. "You smoke?"

"I gave it up after hearing it might cause cancer."

"Not worried about cancer. When your times comes, it comes."

"You'll die of cancer."

"Said when your time comes, it comes." His fingernails were yellow with tobacco stains.

"It's painful, they say."

"So's life." He exhaled smoke.

"Better than death." After we had enough of cancer talk, we talked about shoofly pie and eating possum, and squirrel. We agreed squirrel tasted best. We talked about the creeks in Pilgrim, the times they flooded, and the rats coming out of their holes, and the family that died in a fire. Two kids drowning. One dying from scarlet fever. Then June bugs, long black snakes slinking past outhouses. We talked about wood-burning cookstoves with music fruit cooking in a pot. He said *ain't*. I said *isn't*. He said I talked different, like I wasn't even from Pilgrim.

"That's fine with me."

"Sounds like you don't appreciate Pilgrim talk. Once I listened to Pa talking on the porch in the quiet moonlight. Just the sounds. The up and down and slow and fast. It sounded like a melody. I liked Pa. Too bad he was sick so much."

"You think Mama made him sick?"

"She made him something."

Buck had helped me get through childhood. I relaxed my sore shoulders.

He said he liked my stone house with the two floors and my downright modern Formica table. The kitchen had turned hazy with cigarette smoke.

"Pilgrim was barely a town."

"Bigger than some, Iola. It had a church, feed store, general store, a meetinghouse, the post office. A school. The schoolteacher's house. Up her road a ways was where we got the wood for Friend's barn. The old one that half burned down, we dismantled. I lost my good hat there. It fell in the creek and was swept away."

"I remember that. I remember when Mr. Clamon gave me a newspaper with an article about Amelia Earhart. Mama threw it in the trash pile, in the rain and claimed she hadn't meant to. She did."

"Did not."

"You weren't there. Mama never did like me."

"And she ain't cotton to no one, but I did hear her say nice things about you, and you was her favorite."

"Favorite to whip."

"You was always mouthing off."

We said nothing for a short bit, to quiet down the quibble. I let it go because I did love seeing Buck. I touched his hand. "Cockeyed fool. Good to see you. I missed you."

"Yeah. We's close."

"True."

"I feel like a misfit."

"Wait. I'm telling you I missed you, and you're saying you feel like a misfit. Where'd that come from?"

"So you can't talk about different things? You can't be one-track in a ten-track world. Not much happens on a one-track. You need lots of tracks for something to happen. So I was saying I felt like a misfit growing up. Misfits do things we shouldn't—just to keep our heads above water. Then people slam doors in our face. Whack."

"Never heard you being called a misfit but one time Mama said you weren't allowed on the Most Respectable Street Corner, where there was no drinking and carrying on—you often being drunk."

"Forgot about that. Amazing what one forgets and what one don't. Pilgrim had its ways. Had a street sign for it. It only had one intersection. Didn't like that corner anyway."

"So are you still drinking?"

"You still flying?" With his hands, he mimicked flying and then crashing. He laughed. "Glad you never crashed. I can honestly tell you, honest as ever, I've given up bug juice and bird-dogging cheap girls."

"So you drink good stuff now and don't use whores?"

"Drink nothing and have me a good girlfriend. I said I turned my life around."

"And why?" I was doubtful but wished I wasn't. Buck and I had some good times. After Uncle Dillard took me on my first plane ride, only Buck wanted to hear about it. When I had told him I was going to fly planes, he had said, "Girl, who wouldn't want to fly?"

"A reason? Is that what you want?"

"I think I look like I'm listening."

"That you do. I don't got to, but I'll give my Iola what she wants." He lit up another cigarette and took several long drags. He leaned back in his chair and aimed his little brown eyes at me. "You know what a landlord is?"

"Is this going to take forever? I don't have all day, and don't blow smoke in my face."

"Every once in a while, everyone needs an all-day day. Being this ain't your all-day day, I'll give you my short, with no smoke in your face, since you don't like no smoky face. You look pretty with a smoky face."

"Don't get sidetracked."

"Yes, ma'am. I was on the third track. You want me back on the first track?"

"Tell your story."

"Ma'am—the first track for my Iola O."

I had always liked his nickname for me.

"The uppity landlord evicted my body out of my one-room cold apartment filled with empty liquor bottles. Had no job, no money, no girl, no nothing. Hit rocky bottom but slid sideways 'cause I had a knack. Sold my carpentry tools for beer, my guitar for whiskey, shoplifted. Spent a month in jail. Maybe two. At least I got three hots, if you could call them that. Got out, got homeless. Sang for pennies and nickels. Sweated hard for whiskey, stole a guitar, sold the guitar, sold my car, stole a car, wrecked it, walked away from the wreck. Call me lucky . . . I should write a song." He got up and went outside to get his guitar out of his car.

His walking out the door reminded me that the last time I had a family visit was in Memphis before I was accepted into the WASP in 1944. Afterward, none of my family seemed to have much time for me except Buck and Maude. Then Maude drove with a boyfriend across the country to Hollywood to be a movie star. Mama refused to read any of Maude's letters and called her bad names but no four-letter words, since she didn't use cheap language.

When Buck came back in and sat down, I pushed aside the unpleasant memories. He sang a few lines, then gave up, saying the words were good but the melody needed work.

I saw a hint of a grin.

"I turned my life around."

"If that's so, you tell me, brother."

"I will. Just for Iola O, I will." He laid his guitar down, leaned back in his chair, looked up at the ceiling, then me, and nodded like he was falling off to sleep.

I knew his habits. It was like he was inviting the words to come out on their own free will.

"One day" (he repeated, prayer-like, almost singing), "I was passed out with a whiskey bottle in my hand by the front gate of some big fancy school in Greenville, South Carolina. I don't know how or when or what got me there, but I woke up, my mind undone. Out in the grass I was. Like a tired animal." He closed his eyes. "Could've been eaten up by wild bears. Could've been facing the everlasting knock." He opened his eyes. "Someone from the school passed by, I held out my hand, he threw me a blessing and two bits and I said, 'Thank you,' and he said, 'Don't spend it on liquor,' and I said, 'I won't and thank you again,' and I asked God to bless him for his kindness and he said, 'Thank you.' I said, 'You're welcome. God bless you again and again,' and he said, 'You need help. I'll help you. Get in my car. First brush yourself off.'

"Just like that I went from lying on the cold ground to riding in a warm Cadillac—I think it was. He drove me to an AA meeting. You know the AA?"

I nodded.

He nodded. "First time I rode in a Cadillac. Luxury seats. Nice. Plush. It smelled rich. Like good pipe tobacco. The man opened the windows with a push-a-button, probably to get rid of my smell. It had a pullout cigarette ashtray. Oh my. Tinted glass. That's what did it. The smell of luxury saved my soul. I promised I'd pay luxury back. It was like the sweetest woman I ever met, so I washed my body, my raggedy clothes, and got a haircut. Went to lots of AA meetings and said, 'My name is Buck Boggs and I'm an alcoholic. This is my story.' I should write a song. And I got rid of my lice. How's that, Iola? You ever have lice?" The whole story he said slow and preacher-like sometimes, fast and zippy other times.

"Never," I lied, smiled, laughed. "Yes."

"It's like old times. Want to go squirrel hunting?"

"No."

"Want to eat ramps?"

"No."

"Pick pawpaws?"

"None around here."

"No pawpaws? Oh well, we got rid of our lice and I got rid of my vice and when I get back to Richmond I got me a preaching job on skid row. I'm a good preacher for skid row. Know it all—drowning in booze, living on the streets, and finding salvation. Been a hard life." He stretched his arms over his head. Then he lit up another cigarette.

"You got a job?"

"That's right. Got one a waiting."

"Why'd you come for a visit?"

"You tired of me already?" His voice turned raspy until he coughed. "You want me to up and go? You afraid I'm a Communist?"

"You like the Communists?"

"Don't care one way or other. They don't bother or help me."

I noticed my gnawed-up spot was rising up again. "Sometimes you didn't follow through with promises."

"I never promised you anything. What I promise you? I promised you something?"

"Where do I start?" I had the urge to break a forced promise. I wanted to talk about Zeke getting killed. I wanted to ask Buck what he knew. If he ever had nightmares. Did he ever hear what town Zeke was in when Uncle Edgar discovered him doing sex with a man? I wanted to tell Buck that sometimes I had walked to the cesspool where Zeke's body was dumped and said a prayer for him. I missed him. But I kept my oath of silence my mother forced me to take, and left me with a fear I was an accomplice to murder. Plus it hurt too much to think about it.

"You promised you'd do something with your life," I said. "I wish you would. You're the best guitar player I know. And a good carpenter. You made a cedar chest one time that was the prettiest piece of furniture I ever saw. Wish I had it." I didn't ask if he was just another Pilgrim boy afraid of success.

"Pretty sister, I'd give it to you if I had it."

We talked some more and then he helped me clean up the kitchen. In the evening, when Jim came home, they sat down to talk. After a short while, Jim said he wanted to read the evening newspaper. The headline was about Senator McCarthy. Jim looked over at Buck, sitting quietly, and asked, "What do you think of McCarthy? I say he's a patriot, keeping the government free of Communists."

"That's true. Yeah. The Communists is doing the devil's work. Should all be sent to prison for life."

It pleased me that Buck knew what Jim needed to hear. I wanted him to stay for a while.

In the morning at breakfast, Buck said, "The Communists are trying to take over the world and if they succeed, the second coming of Jesus will happen."

Jim looked up from his fried eggs. "I don't know about the second coming but we'd lose our freedom."

"That be true, but it also be the second coming."

"Well it's obvious you care about this country. I like that." And then Jim soon left for work.

On the weekend, Buck helped Jim clean up the yard and mend a fence, which Jim said he did very well and did most of the work. Three weeks went by and he was still staying with us, smoking his cigarettes, helping out with chores, playing guitar. At dinner, Jim told him he had to live in the garage because there was no room in the house for him, and the sofa wasn't a bed.

It was no problem for Buck. He liked the garage. "It's half-indoors and half-outside—close to God. I hear heaven's like that. Inside-heaven is a big golden tabernacle, and outside-heaven is the stars in the sky." A week later, he asked if he could turn the storeroom, which was off the side of the garage, into a small place for himself. He'd build shelves in the garage for things that were in the storeroom.

Jim said that was fine but he wasn't going to pay for materials. Buck put in a window and a wooden floor from stuff he found at the county dump. He nailed up fancy solid wood paneling on two of the walls. The other walls he covered in cheap stuff but he painted it nice. He went into town and came back with a secondhand bed, and a table with two legs missing. I asked what he was going to do with a two-legged table.

"Chisel two legs from a scrap two-by-four."

Buck put up a raggedy sheet for curtains and a threadbare rug on the floor. He ran a water line over and put in a sink he found in someone's trash. The last chore was to put up a chimney pipe and a little wood-burning stove that he found at the dump. Then he got a part-time job at the dump. Two months later he added a small extension for a shower and a toilet.

I ASKED BUCK to babysit the children so I could get some grocery shopping done without them begging for candy. When I came home, they all said they loved Uncle Buck.

Next Saturday Jim asked Buck if he would paint the garage.

He took his time, sang, made no mess, did a good job, and cleaned his brush.

I asked him if he would take the clothes off the clothesline because it had started to rain and I had a sick child crying.

When he came back in with a basket of laundry, he was singing about taking sheets and undies off the line. It had clicks and hoots, with rhymes and unexpected twists and turns of notes, high sliding to low, low careening back to high, a yeah, yeah, yeah, the sheets are clean and fine, undies aren't mine, and a high-note squeal ending real soft. A beautiful tenor voice.

"How do you do that?"

"Just comes to me." He shrugged.

"So songwriter—when will you start your preaching job?"

"I said it's waiting for when songwriter's ready. Preaching . . . it's something you can only do when you ready. Every evening late I quiet myself, and listen, and one day I'll hear the spirit. The words will flow. I'll have the grace. They told me take my time, and the preacher they got will retire when I get there. Why you asking?"

"Just curious. Don't be so pinched." Would Frank and Sarah like Buck? If Buck met them and he gave them a hard time, I'd tell Buck to shut up. If he got nasty I'd tell him to leave.

Jim

Chapter 23

AFTER SEVERAL MONTHS, a letter arrived from Frank. Was he now a French citizen? Wearing a Frenchy beret? I opened all the other mail, but not his. It lay on the kitchen table. My curiosity about what he had to say was not as strong as my fear that we'd be targeted for getting letters from a Communist. I wanted to make the best decision, so I let it sit awhile thinking—benefits versus risks. Benefit—family news, maybe good news. Risks—losing my job, being blacklisted, having to leave the country. It was difficult to write *Return to sender* and drop it back in the mailbox. Perhaps paranoid? That wasn't a word I'd willingly use to describe myself. Was Frank right? I thought of myself as not taking risks. Protective. Cautious. Prudent. Getting by in life, but it's tiresome living in a prison.

When Iola came home from shopping, she walked into the house, shaking her head, with the letter in her hand. "What's this all about?"

She scoffed at my explanation. "That's foolish. It's crazy."

"McCarthy could destroy us."

She tore it open and read the letter aloud.

I knew she was going to do that. I knew. Sometimes I knew her so well. I listened intently.

Dear Jim and Iola,

 We are settled somewhat in Paris. It hasn't been too hard for Sarah to adjust as she speaks fluent French. Me—I'm trying to learn ten new words a day. We have mini conversations—half-English, half-French. *Je vais for une promenade. Est-ce-que tu* want me *acheter* something? You get the idea. The kids are learning easier than I, but I'm motivated.

 Yes, obviously we miss Brooklyn and our friends and especially you, dear cousins. Words fail to say how much we appreciate the help you gave us. And Iola, thank you again for your help. You made the move easier. It was a stressful time. Having you both come to Brooklyn, staying in our house meant a lot to us in another way. We had several friends who wanted no part of us. They feared if they even talked to us they'd be targeted. One very good friend, who was always on our side, and had lunch with us several times, has told us he was never targeted. Fear is strange, isn't it? Contagious too. *Destructive* might be a better word. But courage inspires. Thank you both for your courage.

I didn't realize how hard it is to immigrate, even with Sarah speaking fluent French and having a job and relatives here. And even with me having been in France during the war. I can't imagine how much more difficult otherwise. I'm struck by how much of culture is made up. It's like fiction agreed upon by many. Things we took for granted. So many differences in the details. It's another language, different greetings, different gestures, different preferences, if you know what I mean.

We're looking for a house to buy now that our house in Brooklyn has sold. We're taking our time. We'd love to have you come for a visit after we get a little more settled. Give our love to the kids.

Love,
Frank and Sarah

I had self-doubt, but then, when didn't I? Frank called me courageous. Was I? I missed him. I found *The City and the Pillar* in his house.

"That was a nice letter." Iola put it back in the envelope real careful, like it was a letter from the president.

"I don't know about them living in France, and we're not going there."

"Well what else could they do?" Iola put the letter in a drawer, in the back under a stack of papers as if hiding it.

Later that evening when she was putting the kids to bed, I got the letter and put it in the trash. It was a precaution to protect my children. I'd do anything for them. Give my life to protect them. The sight of the letter lying in the trash confused me, so I took it out and put it back where Iola had left it.

A FEW WEEKS later, Iola said that she had read in the morning newspaper that the Senate passed a resolution condemning Senator McCarthy for abusing his power.

"I was right. I said they never needed to move. It was Sarah. She was the one who wanted to move to France."

"You never said that."

"You don't ever listen to much I say. You just do what you want to do."

A strange look came over her face. "I guess I didn't mean to accuse you. I don't know." I rubbed my hands together. "Why don't you write them back? You're better at writing letters."

Later that day, she asked me if I wanted to sign my name to the letter. "Yeah, why not."

Soon enough, a letter arrived from Paris.

Dear Jim and Iola,

Thank you so much for your last letter. We appreciate the news about McCarthy. We've told our new friends about him. They, in turn, told us about their work in the resistance and living in the hills hiding from the Vichy militias during WW II, and dealing with cold and hunger. And who to trust? Who wasn't a Nazi collaborator? Sarah wouldn't have been able to teach. Women were considered useful only as mothers. Democracy didn't exist. News was very much controlled. Jews were rounded up and sent to their deaths in gas chambers. Without a doubt it could've been worse. Of course, believing that things will improve certainly helps. And that belief makes one more receptive to new possibilities.

Well, you're probably wondering if we regret the move. Yes and no. It was hectic, worrisome, and nerve-racking, trying to get everything done. Some things we still miss—my bookstore, Brooklyn, our friends. And of course—we miss you.

And next—our progress. We've made new friends. My new bookstore is up and running. Sort of. It brings in a little money and pays its rent. Sarah loves her job. She says she would've had a hard time working around her former colleagues (one was a very close friend—we thought) who tried to destroy her. We both like France. There is so much to do. We plan to take a trip to England. My maternal grandfather was born and raised there.

All our love,
Frank and Sarah and the children

I left the letter on the table for Iola.

Chapter 24

A FEW WEEKS later, Buck and the kids were sitting on the front porch. Iola had gone shopping with Norma.

As soon as I stepped on the porch, Charles said, "Uncle Buck said in the Bible there were first-class wives and second-class wives and Mama's a first-class wife."

"And why did he say that?" I asked.

"Because she's not a concubine."

"What did he say a concubine was?"

"A second-class wife. They're like live-in maids and they always have to do what you tell them. They have to clean your room and wash your clothes."

"And who cleans your room and washes your—"

"Was just doing a little preaching. Just to get in practice. I told them about Ishmael and Isaac. How Isaac's mother stole the birthright from Ishmael, but Ishmael's mother was a concubine. You don't know the story?" Buck put his hands behind his head and leaned back in his chair.

"Go on."

"Good thing I'm here—to teach some Bible. Your son—he asks good questions. Like he's thinking about things. One thing followed another. I was just Bible talking."

"Well, watch what you talk about."

"I love Uncle Buck," Charles said.

"You do, do you?"

Buck asked if they wanted another story. In unison, the kids said yes.

"Well, I'll tell you about the miracle of the loaves and fishes. Now a miracle is a work of God, an extraordinary event. Something humans can't make happen. Now Jesus took five loaves of bread and two tasty fish and he multiplied them right in front of a thousand hungry men's big wide eyes plus all the lovely women and children until everyone was stuffed to the gills. Now gills are the way a fish breathes but it's just an analogy, and an analogy is making a connection between two things that don't seem connected. The first big picnic it was, and more food than needed and only thing missing was music but they didn't need no music. It was the best fish and bread ever served on the face of the earth. The bread tasted fresh out of the oven even though there was no oven and the fish tasted just caught and cooked perfect even though there were no cookstoves around. The fish were about a foot long, the flesh was sweet, and needed no seasoning. It was a pleasant place—green and grassy, sunny, and the weather was warm and it was a wonderful place for Jesus to do miracles. And Jesus had the most heavenly voice—like fine music on a balmy day."

I had to admit Buck was a good storyteller, almost like Frank but with Jesus talk.

Buck looked up to the heavens, closed his eyes and inhaled deep. He opened his eyes and looked at the kids and said they all needed to stay focused on heavenly goals.

He said to Lizzy, who had her feet up on her chair, "I can see all the way up to your underpants. Your Mama has told you better. A girl keeps her legs together, even if you got a pair of long-legged pants on 'cause it's a temptation to the boys. You gotta be aware of your body. You gotta help the boys be aware the body leads us all to hell. Mark my word. Every day you watch your body. Hell's an awful place to be. Hotter than scalding. Forever. My Lord." Then he talked about Moses on the mountain and the Ten Commandments.

Charles said he knew them but he could only repeat four.

"Smart boy, I'm amazed you knew four. Enough. I've preached enough."

I never heard Buck talk with a cadence like he was a quarter of the way to singing. I figured he might make an excellent preacher. The kind that gets the congregation feeling like they've been transported to the gates of heaven with a peek inside. I wondered if that's what is meant when they say the preacher is only the vehicle. Not that I was ever enamored of preachers.

After we all had lunch, Buck said he wanted to treat everyone to dessert, if I would be so kind and drive us all to a drive-in.

Buck ordered twenty-cent milkshakes. He called the kids the Neapolitans because Charles liked vanilla, Starla liked chocolate, and Lizzy only ever liked strawberry.

Buck told Lizzy, "You don't slurp. It ain't polite. How many times your decent loving mother—my decent loving sister, your father's decent loving wife, decent as decent can be—told you—don't do that."

She stopped slurping. Buck smiled and then started up again. "Most people go to regular church. Today, we had church on the porch. There's porch churches and living room ones and outside ones. I'm good at knowing where outside churches are. All across the country. In Pennsylvania, I found one right by Lake Erie and could feel it in the air. In Ohio one was edging the Ohio River, and in Kansas by some fields with the tallest, prettiest, tastiest corn ever. And even in California. I know of one by the blue Pacific Ocean with the waves lapping at the white sandy shore—where the sunsets are the best I ever seen. It was holy. No plagues, no leprosy, nothing but pureness and tiny miracles, like the mosquitoes not bothering you and no flies around."

He lit up a cigarette and said he never smokes when he's preaching or if he's in a regular church. He let Charles put an unlit cigarette in his mouth. "Girls should never smoke and shouldn't even have cigarettes in their purse, even if it's to give to the boyfriend if he got a need."

Driving home, when I waited for the light to turn green, Starla threw her empty milkshake cup into the open window of a parked car. Charles snitched. I told her not to do it. Buck laughed, "That's just a little funning. Don't mean nothing. God's okay with harmless funning."

I shook my head but said nothing. Buck was Iola's family. And Frank was gone. Buck seemed to like me. It was like I had a brother in an odd way. He was folksy, energetic, and liked the kids. Like a Pecos Pete, or a Paul Bunyan. I could write a story about him, a child's story. It could be an American fable.

When we got home, Buck said to me, "You got a preacher there. Your son will be a preacher."

"He'll be a chemist." It was the most emphatic thing I said all day.

WHEN IOLA CAME home, Charles said, "Uncle Buck said I'm going to be a preacher."

"No, you're not. You're going to be a pilot. And you're going to fly around the world."

"And he'll preach wherever he lands. Be a missionary pilot. They're the best." Buck sounded real sure of himself.

It occurred to me I could make Buck a religious Pecos Pete character riding a tornado while he preached the Bible and loved America. A child's story. I could title it *The Tornado Preacher*, maybe taking place during the American Revolution. If I got it written Frank might recommend a publisher. I went to my desk and made a few notes of things Buck had said. He would never know I was plagiarizing him.

Chapter 25

IT ALL REMINDED me of a picture my mother had of a family together—a child playing on the floor by the door. The parents at the table, with the other children. There was my Starla, the tomboy. If she were outside she'd be playing in the dirt. Charles, the neat one, was across the table reading a book well above his grade level. I loved having a smart boy. A pretty girl sitting next to her mother—Lizzy quiet and watching Iola prepare dinner. Iola was making cabbage rolls. It was nice how she laid out the pale green cabbage leaves, added her stuffing, and rolled them up. Cabbage rolls weren't my favorite, but Iola's were tasty. She carefully lined them up in a pan. With the light overhead, the shadows, Charles's fine features in profile, Starla's red dress with blue buttons, Lizzy's yellow dress, the light on Iola's face, her deep-set blue eyes, a nice-looking family all together—I wanted to take a photograph but didn't.

Iola had an attractive face, worked hard every day, and never got sick, made beautiful cakes. A good wife. Suddenly, I fantasized that she wasn't a woman but a man, and that we slept in the same bed and talked about the kids while holding hands. And . . . I'd likely love her if so. Him? Yes, love him. Her name—his name—Isaac, Ivan, Irvin? Io is one of Jupiter's moons. I wouldn't care. Any name would do. Sam, Jack. One thing I had never liked about *The City and the Pillar* was the main character having sex with strangers. Lots of stranger sex with hardly a word said. No. I wanted a family and someone to love and talk to. I wanted to come home and sit on the porch, having intelligent conversations about raising the children, American history, even chemistry. What if he was a chemist? But I was confused—two men. Who would be the mother? Who would cook and clean? It wasn't nice—thinking this in front of Iola. What if I started calling her Io? Would she know what I was thinking?

Having all three kids around me reminded me why I worked at a job that was beneath my intelligence. They gave me a degree of normalcy.

Buck walked in, pulled up a chair, lit up a cigarette, and held it near his mouth. In his plaid shirt, and sitting by the light, suddenly it was obvious he was nice looking—good cheekbones, a nose like a museum statue, his brown eyes just right, good eyebrows. He had put on some weight. He looked a bit like Errol Flynn.

"Why do people wear clothes?" Starla asked.

How does she come up with those odd questions? Takes after her mother. Out of nowhere, I thought of Buck removing his shirt and being naked, then having sex with him. Wouldn't that be incestuous? Adulterous? Shameful, thinking that in the kitchen, in front of my kids.

"Because it's sinful not to," Charles said. "Don't you know—Eve ate the apple in the Garden of Eden and gave it to Adam. They had to start wearing clothes. We have to die because of Eve. We have to die because of girls."

"Tell you, he be a preacher." Buck exhaled smoke rings. Lizzy watched them disappear.

"No, he's going to be a chemist." I willfully got rid of the shameful thoughts.

"Boy talks like a preacher."

"He asks questions like a chemist—what is the air made of?"

"Oxygen." Buck shrugged.

"In part. Also nitrogen, carbon dioxide. That's ninety-nine percent of it. There's other things in air. Yesterday, he asked me, 'What makes fire?'"

"Devil in hell." Buck laughed. He stretched out his legs, and Iola almost tripped over them on her way to the sink.

"Damn you," she said. I liked it when she cursed. It made her seem more like a man.

Buck was now getting on my nerves but his preacher talk made me think again of my story—Tornado Preacher. A child's story should be fanciful. So Tornado Preacher could be someone who hops on beneficent tornadoes. The tornado could be a disguised spirit. One time, the tornado could make a swath through a meadow and tear out all the big rocks and set them down as a rock wall for a young man who needed a field cleared for farming. The tornado would change into a preacher who would say to the man, "You're going to end up leading this land into an independent country." The man's name would be George Washington. Another time, the tornado would just touch the soil and till it for a young farmer, and the spirit tornado would turn again into a preacher, and say to the farmer, "You're going to end up becoming president and you'll keep the country from falling apart." The man's name would be Abraham Lincoln. That would be the gist.

I was amazed I could come up with such ideas. It had to be a combination of my love for my children, my interest in American history, and the influence of odd Buck, and my odd pilot wife.

Everyone turned their heads to a loud knock. Charles answered the door and in walked Norma wearing a blue muumuu, and sunglasses with rhinestones on the edges. The sunglasses looked silly and the muumuu just made her look fatter. What would I think of her if she was a fat man? Could I love a fat man? What if he was a chemist? A genius? A fat genius chemist who loved American history? What if he was a colored man? A fat, colored, genius chemist who loved me? A good-looking one? And won the Nobel prize? I'd be in love. Why am I intrigued? And aroused? As she walked in, she stepped over Starla, still on the floor. She dropped off a letter the postman had wrongly delivered to her house.

Norma was limping and said she had sprained her ankle. She saw Buck sitting at the table. "I knew when I first saw you, you were Iola's brother. I knew you weren't Jim's."

"How you know? No one ever thinks we are. You a fortune-teller?" Buck took a drag on another cigarette. The kitchen was hazy with smoke.

"It's not that you look alike but it's like you got the same kindred spirit. Some say I have an extra sense. I got to go. Have a pie baking." Norma stepped over Starla again as she walked to the door and left.

"There was something wrong with Mrs. Norma," Starla said.

"There certainly is, plus she figured you're Iola's brother because you have a Southern accent." I chuckled. "Anyone could figure that out."

"No, a fortune-teller she is," Buck said. "Plain as day. Plainer as night."

"She had a big dark bruise on her legs, by her underpants," Starla said.

"That's shameful looking up a woman's skirt. If I catch you doing that again, I'll swat your fanny and you'll have a big bruise. You hear me? Get off the floor." Iola gestured with her hand.

"But she walked over me."

"You should've closed your eyes." Iola frowned.

"It wasn't her fault," I said. "Norma should have known better."

"Girls are stupid," Charles snickered, making a snorty sound, then he laughed.

"Enough of you two."

Starla headed for the door and went outside. Lizzy followed. Then Charles.

"I think Ron beat up Norma again—and way up on her legs." Iola put her cabbage rolls in the oven to bake. "A bruise up there. You know what that means. Plus she was wearing sunglasses to cover up a black eye. She never wears sunglasses. I wish something bad happens to Ron—beating her."

"Wishing bad on others is a sin," Buck said.

"You keep quiet." Iola turned her back to him.

I wondered if I could include Iola in my tornado story. Maybe the spirit tornado would see a little girl in Pilgrim eating possum and swoop down and take her for a ride and tell her she's going to learn to fly and never have to eat possum again. I thought again of Iola as a man. Io.

Charles suddenly came back in and said, "Starla's playing with worms. She's digging them out of the ground, giving them names. Lizzy said they have a mother and father and brothers and sisters. Starla said the mother and father had gone to heaven but the brothers and sisters are alive. Are there worms in heaven?"

"Not a one. They got no soul. Only people got souls," Buck said

"Why?"

"Way God made us. And who would want to share heaven with the worms?"

"I've read that in India, they believe all life forms have souls," I said in a matter-of-fact tone, like it was a reasonable comment.

"India is full of heathens. You didn't know that?" Buck crossed his arms, looking straight at me, like he was perplexed, like I had spoken heresy.

Iola opened the door and ordered the girls inside to wash up for dinner. During dinner, Starla hit Charles and so she got no dessert. She was sent to her room after she did her chore and wiped the table clean. Poor thing cried herself to sleep.

The next morning, Starla said, "I heard music before I fell asleep last night and I saw myself on my bed. I floated out the window, and over the maple tree, and the big trees down the street and down to Willowsburg. Over the water fountain in the middle of town. I floated in the sky with two white birds flying beside me. Near the five-and-dime store, people were talking."

"Don't be silly. You just had a dream," Iola said.

Starla looked at her feet.

"Stupid had a stupid dream," Charles said.

"Stupid Number Two needs to keep his mouth shut and know his place." Iola was stern.

I put my arm around Starla, who seemed like she was about to cry.

"Don't feel bad," Buck said. "I have stupid dreams too, flying around kingdom come. Getting chased from cloud to cloud by giant buzzards. I had a dream one time—I was sitting on the wing of an airplane and had to fly that way from California to New York City. Was frozen stiff. Famished when I got there; all day I ate lettuce and peas 'cause that was all there was. Lettuce and peas. I was glad I woke up. But I tell you . . . people that have flying dreams like yours—it means they'll get good fortune."

"You don't know what you're talking about."

"Now, Jim, you don't have to know a lot of stuff. You just have to have faith and feel the Lord as your personal Savior." Buck put his hand over his heart.

"Stop your preaching." Iola wrinkled her forehead.

"You don't like preaching?"

"Not in my house, not all the time. You're obsessed."

"And I'll be obsessed as I enter heaven. Then I'll sit back and relax and enjoy the fruits of my labor. Yes, ma'am. Obsessed on earth. Free in heaven to the end of time. After time ends, eternity begins."

"Eternity has no beginning or ending. It's timeless but time can exist within it, like a second within a century. But that's not an adequate analogy. It's more like a second within a trillion centuries and that's not even adequate. How about a millionth of a second within a trillion centuries," I said, using the most unassuming voice I could muster.

"You're talking about infinity." Buck frowned.

"No, infinity means unending distance. Nothing stops it," I said.

"You missed my point."

Actually, I had intentionally avoided his point. I was ridiculing. Buck deserved it. He was just plain odd. But then, I married odd. A pilot. What normal man marries a female pilot? I wanted normal. My children weren't odd. They were good. And they'd be normal adults and get married to someone they loved. I went to my desk and wrote some notes for my spirit tornado fable. Like the color of the tornado, what people would say about it, any other historical figures involved, the towns involved. If I would include Iola some way. If I ever got it written.

Iola

Chapter 26

IT TOOK ME a second to recognize Mr. Yalonsky's voice. He asked how Jim and the children and I were doing, how things were in Willowsburg. "Philadelphia is sunny."

Did he call to talk about the weather? Was he bored? I was. Was he going to ask me out on a date? I wanted him to, just to know that someone found me attractive. I'd tell him no but in a way to not hurt his feelings.

"Mrs. Lewis, I have a question for you?" He coughed nervously. "I bought a dry cleaner's in Willowsburg. It was a good deal and I'll need someone to take care of the shop on Fridays and Saturdays. Well. So I thought of you, since you and Jim live there. Would you work for me? I'd be pleased."

He talked fast like he feared I'd say no before he could finish saying what he wanted, so I tried to sound interested. He went on about how I had once mentioned having money problems. He'd need me ten hours Saturday and Sunday. He described the job duties, then exhaled loud, and said, "You can have a week to think about it."

I wanted to say yes right then. I wanted to say I felt like hugging him but that might give him the wrong idea. I said I was interested but I should talk to Jim and would call him back within a couple of days. It was obvious he wanted to talk more because he suggested I take my time, then he asked about my kids again. When I asked about his wife, he said she liked Willowsburg and then he said Willowsburg was a wonderful town and he mentioned the town square with the fountain and the pretty elm trees. He was very cheery. He didn't say another word about his wife. "And why don't you call me Wilhelm? Will is fine. You'll make me feel like family."

"I can do that. You call me Iola." I knew he was flirting. I did a little bit, by a sweeter voice, and a little hip wiggle, but he didn't see that. After we said goodbye, I decided good luck was floating my way.

NEXT DAY, I was pinning laundry on the clothesline. Norma was in her garden, and when she saw me, she yelled, "Something must've changed because you're smiling again. I bet you got a job."

"You think so?" I walked toward her.

"Just figured. You seemed nervous after you said Jim might get laid off again and then . . . well with you talking, you know, about getting work. Well, did you? I predicted you would." She clasped her hands when I gave her the news. "People tell me I have a sixth sense. Sometimes, I think I'd like a job other than cooking, cleaning, and talking to my kids. And Ron doesn't ever listen to what I say. Be nice to be a fortune-teller. Two times, I used a Ouija Board and was good. You give people news of the future and how their lives will turn out fine and they pay you. Easy as pie."

"The offer came out of the blue."

"You know what that means?" She walked over to me. "Out of the blue means it was meant to be and you have to take the job so good things will happen. Jim okay about you working?"

"I didn't tell him yet."

"Oh. He doesn't have a bad temper, does he? He ever hit you? If not, you take the job. If he objects, worst he'll do is yell."

I said real quiet, "I never told you, but I worry someday Ron's going to hurt you bad. I wish you had someone who appreciated you."

Norma looked away, fiddled with her hands, stuck them in the pockets of her red-and-yellow muumuu. She finally said, "So do I, but you know—I don't. I have three kids and nowhere to go." Neither of us said a word.

Norma looked uncomfortable, almost tearful, and said, "I never told you but Ron saved me. You can't tell anyone but his father raped me. I was sixteen and feared he got me pregnant. Ron's mother was a witch and she would've called me a slut and killed me if she found out. So I had sex with Ron because we were friends. I figured it'd look better claiming Ron got me pregnant. I hoped he'd marry me. He was nice then. We eloped. Then he changed. If he hadn't married me, though . . . well I try not to think about it." She looked at my house, her garden, her shoes, the blue sky, everything but me. "Day's nice, isn't it?" She finally looked at me. "You know what my prediction is—someday, I'll be a paid fortune-teller and one day you'll fly again and you'll give me a ride. At sunset. I don't know why but I'd like it at sunset." She gave a stiff smile.

I had crossed a line. Not knowing what else to do, I said, "If I fly again, I'll give you two rides." Then I invited her over for coffee, but she had too much to do. I know I had embarrassed her and hoped I hadn't damaged our relationship.

After I hung all my laundry, I called Mr. Yalonsky and told him I'd work for him, starting Saturday. He was all excited.

I got the whiskey bottle Jim kept on the top shelf in the kitchen and poured a shot to celebrate. I sipped it slow, and made a plan as how to tell Jim in the morning.

Jim

Chapter 27

THREE RED LUNCH pails were lined up on the uncluttered kitchen countertop. I would have liked having a red lunch pail as a boy. Then there was Iola in a blue full-skirted dress, and her white apron with the ruffle at the bottom. Cinching her waist was a pink belt. I liked her wide waist. Men have wide waists. She was wearing a bra. Why didn't she some days? Likely her upbringing. Maybe when I'm old I'll love her. She wore pink high heels, not her gray house slippers with a hole in the toe. Her dangly pink earrings were sweet. Should I jiggle them? She might not like it. Maybe kiss her? I couldn't remember the last time. At the kitchen table sat Charles, Starla, and pretty Lizzy, all eating cereal for breakfast in white bowls my grandmother gave to my mother. This was the way things should be. I sat down.

Iola, smiling, served me fresh-squeezed orange juice, fried eggs sunny-side over, crisp bacon, toast, butter. A jar of raspberry jam. Had she made it? Ironed napkins. The morning newspaper lay by my coffee. I should appreciate her more.

I asked Charles questions like my father asked me. "Did you complete your homework for today? I have big plans for you—to become a chemist." I wanted him to be prepared for life—to learn how to do well. I wiped a spot of breakfast off Lizzy's chin.

"What are your plans for me?" Starla asked.

"You would do well to marry a chemist."

Lizzy looked just like my sister did when she was her age. I wished I had six children sitting around me. I wished I loved Iola. She wasn't evil. She gave me three good kids. She was right that four would have been too many, but I didn't admit that to her.

Mornings such as this would definitely help me deal with stress and headaches at work, my stupid boss yelling like a lunatic, like I was his slave—do this right now. There have been days I wanted to quit. Just walk out, telling him—go to hell; do it yourself. Asshole. Fuck yourself. And worse names.

I finished eating, kissed Iola on the cheek, and the kids on their heads, said goodbye and headed to the front door. While putting on my fedora hat and coat

I heard Iola coming up behind me. As I put my hand on the doorknob, Iola put her hand on mine and blocked my way.

"I need to talk." She smiled.

Insisting I'd be late to work, I pulled the door open, nudging her aside. Why did she pick the strangest times to flirt? I hoped she wasn't going to want to have sex later that night.

She yielded and stepped back. "I know you like being punctual. I could call you at lunch and we could talk about my new job. I'm starting Saturday."

"What do you mean?" I closed the door.

"Working for a paycheck."

"Don't be facetious." I kept my hand on the doorknob. "Where did you get this idea?"

"I told you the day Frank said McCarthy was targeting Sarah and they were moving to France. You had no problem with it then."

"You're making that up."

"No. You had come home late from work. Remember? You complained about setbacks on a project being developed. If it wasn't successful, you said there might be layoffs. I said it'd be good if I got a job."

"Doing what?"

"Working for Mr. Yalonsky."

"Yalonsky? In Philadelphia? And when did you ask him for a job?"

"He asked me."

"He asked you for a job?"

"No. He asked me if I would like a job."

"He came here and asked you? When?" I stepped away from the door. Before she answered, I asked, "And how are you going to get to work?"

"Buck said he could drive me, and if he can't, I can walk Fridays. It's only a couple of miles. I've walked longer. Saturday I'll use our car unless Buck can drive me. And if I have to—I'll walk again. I have to be there by eight thirty."

"So Buck already knows."

"It's only Fridays and Saturdays—eight thirty to six thirty. Yalonsky bought a dry cleaners in town. I'll be getting twenty hours of work in two days. He was very accommodating. He was thinking of us with money being tight."

"How does he know that?"

"I told him when he hemmed my pants."

"You're paying him to hem your pants?"

"He does it for free because I bring him good luck when I come to his store. I told you."

I opened the door and walked out.

"You have anything you need hemmed?" she yelled as I was getting in the car.

I ignored her. Bitch. I would never call her that. It was the way I was brought up. On the way to work I said it again—aloud. It didn't help, though.

At five p.m., I called home and said I had to work late. I went to a restaurant and ordered dinner. "You like working?" I asked the slender, curly-haired waitress.

"Helps pay the bills. My husband and I can save enough money to buy a new car. You do what has to be done. It's okay. Can't complain. Yeah, a spanking brand-new one." She smiled.

I went to a movie. Had I been too hard on Iola? What if I could afford a spanking new car? I've read that some people like being spanked. I imagined being spanked. Am I getting perverse? Spanking? It's not for me. I sat through the whole boring cowboy movie. Why would any man want to be called boy? Hey, boy, take care of the cows.

When I showed up at ten p.m., Iola said she would heat up my dinner.

"I got a quick bite at White Castle."

"I'll be using the car tomorrow. Anything you want me to pick up from the store?"

"No, nothing." I yawned. Feeling tired helped me control my anger. My anger made no sense.

SATURDAY I GOT up at six a.m., washed, shaved, dressed, put my wallet and a hanky in my pocket, got in the car, and drove into town. Iola would be concerned that I left with the car, for Buck had left the evening before for a few days, so she couldn't use his car. I knew Norma and Ron were gone for the weekend and so Iola couldn't leave the kids with Norma. Would she get into a frenzy, fearing she'd get fired if she didn't show up for work? If she tried to take the kids with her she'd have to rush to get them dressed, comb three heads of hair and her own, and make four lunches and whatever else she has to do. It would take them at least an hour to walk to town. The children had never walked for an hour. She'd have to hold Lizzy most of the time. Was I being mean? Shouldn't be that way. She deserved it—always making me feel inadequate. But I often feel inadequate. Don't think that. Well, she's smart enough to call Yalonsky and say she'd be late.

I went to Boyd's Coffee Shop and had breakfast with Bobby and George. Then rich Hugh Delanet, who I heard just bought his fifth hardware store, joined us. George said he heard a rumor the mayor was cheating on his wife. Bobby said his cousin cheats on his wife, and his father probably cheated on his mother. Delanet said the French are always having extramarital affairs. Even the women, was what his father told him. He grinned. The talk made me feel uncomfortable—men having sex with lots of women. I didn't even want to have sex with Iola. I looked at my watch, excused myself, and left.

As I drove down Oak Tree Road, there was my family walking down the front path to the sidewalk. I pulled into the driveway and rolled down my window. "Where are you going with the kids? You weren't walking to work, were you?"

Iola looked dumbfounded, and then locked her eyes with mine. "Where were you?"

"I met Bobby and George at Boyd's Coffee Shop. We met earlier to accommodate you. I told you that."

"You never told me."

I parked and got out of the car. "Thanks for making their lunches," I said real polite. As she drove off, I told the kids to wave goodbye. I was mad, in control, calm. Men are supposed to be in control. I've never felt in control.

She drove off and we went in the house. I was mean to Iola but I didn't want guilt to ruin my day, so I pushed the thought aside. Lizzy wanted to play giddyup. Starla wanted to play Simon Says, and Charles wanted to walk in the woods. So I said, "Simon says we should all take a walk in the woods and I will tell a giddyup story." I amazed myself. We took a walk across Lester Causley's fields out back and into the woods and I started my story.

"Paul Revere was riding a borrowed sleek black horse on a frightful rainy night, no moon out, dark as could be, on April 18, 1775, to warn the colonists in Medford, Lexington, and Concord that the tyrannical British in their bright fancy redcoats were coming to take away their liberty and kill them. He rode at lightning speed, saying giddyup to his horse, and even the smart horse knew it was a matter of liberty. At one turn, trees had fallen down and were blocking Paul Revere's path. But a tornado appeared. The tornado was a spirit and it cleared the path. Then the spirit turned into a man who jumped out of the sky, and he was the Tornado Preacher who told Paul Revere, 'Your name will never be forgotten and you will always be a hero.'"

"Always?" Lizzy asked.

"Always."

"What's a hero?" Lizzy looked like a captivated audience.

"Daddy's a hero." It pleased me to hear Charles say that.

When we got back at the house, Buck had come home earlier than expected from his trip. Buck suggested I have some time to myself and he'd take Charles, Starla, and Lizzy for a ride.

I said, "Why don't we all go for a ride." Everyone agreed.

While driving past a church where a bride and groom were having their picture taken with lots of people, Buck said they all looked happy and one time, Jesus turned water into the best wine at the Marriage at Cana. He then asked if anyone could name any other of God's miracles.

"The loaves and the fishes," said Charles. "Jesus fed everyone. And Jonah and the whale."

"Any others?" Buck paused. "Okay. Here's one. Out on a lake in a storm, Jesus walked on water. The waves were high but he stepped from wave to wave, and his royal white robe never got wet. This story is making me thirsty, so how about I treat everyone to milkshakes." The back seat erupted with yells. We went to a drugstore and Buck told the pretty soda jerk that he had the Neapolitan kids with him, so what kind of milkshakes did they want.

She said, "The boy likes vanilla, and the older girl likes chocolate, and the little one likes strawberry."

"Good Lord, with brains like yours, you should go to Harvard." Buck tilted his head and flirted some but she didn't flirt back.

Needing to show off, I said to the girl, "I heard you make the best milkshakes ever. Real creamy and sweet."

She smiled real big, and then lowered her eyes.

I liked it when girls did that bashful stuff, keeping some distance.

When we were all done, and back home, Buck said he had to do something in Philadelphia and would get back late.

For dinner, I warmed up what Iola had made. It was good; nothing was left on their plates. I said they would each get fifty cents if they all helped clean up. In thirty minutes, the kitchen was spotless. By six o'clock, they were all tired out.

When Iola came home at seven, the kids were sleeping and I was reading.

"How was your day?" she asked.

"Fine."

"And the kids?"

"Fine." It was obvious—she wanted to talk.

"Any problems?"

"The day was uneventful. They were good."

"Don't you want to know how my day was?"

"I suppose it was fine. You'd tell me if it wasn't." I was angry with her for making me feel inadequate, but knowing I had been mean. Why was I mean? She wasn't a bad wife. Who else could I have married? A man? What a preposterous thought. It was funny, though. I mean would I be the wife or the husband? I pressed my hand against my mouth to suppress a laugh.

Iola

Chapter 28

LIZZY SKIPPED INTO the kitchen, and said, "There's swingy music coming from Uncle Buck's place. I peeked in the garage. Then his door open, and a woman came out, wearing a black dress and red shoes. She look for something. Then Uncle Buck came out, and grabbed something on the shelf. They went back in and then the door shut."

She couldn't have been making it up because she'd always been a guileless child. After ordering her to stay put, I walked out of the house, closing the back door quietly. When I got closer to the garage, I walked real slow and tiptoed to his door. If I knocked, that would give the woman a chance to hide, and then what could I say when Buck opened the door, *You're playing music too loud?*

I hesitated. Just to cover myself, in case Lizzy made it up, I knocked and then opened the door and saw naked Buck and a naked woman doing stuff I never knew people did to each other—heads in each other's crotches. They looked startled and embarrassed. I was more embarrassed. What I tried to say came out stuttered. I had never before come across two people doing sex stuff, so I stood transfixed. My mouth agape.

The woman pulled the sheet over her. Buck pulled back on the sheet to cover himself. Buck and the woman kept pulling opposite ways. Buck didn't say a thing and then he blurted out that she was his girl—they were getting married soon and shut the goddamn door.

Having guilty doubts, I looked off to the side of the bed, and eyed an open bottle of whiskey sitting on a table. My indignation welled up. I walked over to the table, grabbed the bottle, and emptied it on their bed. Buck and the woman tried to get out of the way but they weren't quick enough. Then I saw an empty bottle on the floor by his bed. I snatched it up and saw another empty one barely under the bed. I hurled both of them on the floor. They weren't the only things that shattered. Buck deserved a hard smack across his face—lying to me, claiming he was done drinking.

"Sis, what's wrong with you?" Buck said loud and looking like he wanted to pop me hard. He wrinkled his sweaty forehead and squinted his bloodshot, hateful eyes.

"Liar," I said. "You have one day to move on. I knew you didn't change." Aggrieved, I looked at the naked woman and pointed my finger within inches of her eyeballs. "You—you put on your sleazy slut clothes and get out today or I'll have you arrested for obscene behavior in front of a child."

As I stepped toward the door, Buck jumped out of bed, holding the sheet in front of him, and yelled, "Don't you call her a slut." He threw a punch at my shoulder.

After I caught my balance, I did nothing but glare. In a low, slow voice, I said, "You have twenty minutes to move on." Barely holding myself together, I stomped back to the house and took a hold of Lizzy. "Don't tell your father. He'll be upset." I squeezed her shoulder just hard enough to make a point. "You hear me? Don't you tell anyone."

Lizzy let out a little cry.

"Shhh. Be quiet or you'll get bread and water for dinner." I wanted to curse Buck but Lizzy would hear. It shocked me that I had threatened bread and water.

In the kitchen, I sliced a piece of cake and poured myself the last cup of the morning coffee, put in more sugar and cream than usual. I sat in the living room, in the overstuffed armchair with a big stain on it, and put the radio on. Roy Acuff sang about lost love. I was angry, agitated that I had to see two people—my brother—drinking and having sex in the light of day. But it was the booze that most upset me, even more than the punch in the shoulder. It was his pattern—get sober for months and then go drinking for a year, go broke, and lose everything. I'd been lied to and made a fool. I whispered, "Fuck you, Buck." My eyes teared. The image of my naked brother having crazy sex with a real pretty, naked girl on top of the bed covers wouldn't go away. Jim would never do that with me—all naked, everything hanging out, groaning in pleasure.

Lizzy came into the room.

"Go away. Leave. Me. Alone."

Lizzy went and sat on the bottom step of the staircase. "I bad?"

"No. You're good. Go. Away." My monotone voice was an attempt to calm down. I sat back in the chair with my legs stretched out and my hands rubbing the fabric of my seersucker dress that had a little hole under my arm. I stuck a finger in the hole and made it larger. That was stupid. I hated mending. I gazed off through the curtains and out the window to the billowing clouds racing across the blue sky. Pumpkin, our new orange cat, jumped on my lap. He had a broken leg when Jim had found him in Philadelphia and took him to a vet.

"The kids will like him," he had insisted. I rubbed my hands over his fur. My mean mother had hated cats.

His purring reminded me of the sound of a one-engine plane off in the distance. If I was flying a plane I'd forget about Buck. I petted the cat to keep the sound effects going. My hand slid down the length of his back, then to the tip of his tail, and again. He purred, like a duo, Roy Acuff and Pumpkin. It would be nice to listen to Acuff in a plane. I heard Lizzy walk several steps up the staircase.

I finished my cake and coffee and walked up the steps right past Lizzy to my bedroom. Just before shutting the door, I heard Lizzy say, "Mama, am I bad?"

Soon I looked out my window and saw Lizzy in the yard, dragging a doll. Buck and the woman were getting in his car. It started but then stalled. Buck got out, slammed his door shut. "Fuck it." He opened the hood, cursed again— so loud the neighbors probably heard. He fiddled with the engine, slammed the hood back down. Lizzy waved to Buck but he ignored her. He got back in his car, which started up. The woman scowled. I watched them drive off as a million miles separated Buck and me. All that sibling love for naught. Had I overreacted? Buck was a grown man, getting some sex. It was the liquor, the lies, the lies to himself. I was a trusting fool.

Lizzy pulled the head off her doll and threw it down. Guilt made me turn away from the window. I wished Lizzy never told me about Buck and the woman. I'd hold Lizzy after dinner and maybe sing to her. Say I was sorry.

BEFORE DINNER, I told Jim, "Buck left. He found a job in Richmond."

"Why did he leave so suddenly?"

"I don't know. Job required it." I once heard that the best way to lie is to use the fewest words. They're easier to remember.

"Actually, I'm glad he left. You started sounding like him. Same drawl. Plus he bored me."

"Then why'd you let him stay?"

"He was your brother. I thought maybe I'd learn something about you. If he's typical for your family I'm amazed you're as smart as you are."

My mouth dropped open. Silence. Then I blurted, "Buck worked hard to get by in life . . . He was a good carpenter. He built someone a house and didn't get paid. Got ripped off by city folk. He fixed broken-down cars. He respected his family. Drove me to Chattanooga."

"And I suppose Pilgrim was a decent place to raise a family."

"Damn right. My mama worked hard to raise ten children to adults. She cooked three meals a day even if it was only potatoes and ramps."

"And possum?"

"That's right and don't you forget it. My mama took us to church every Sunday." It was awful—me defending Buck and Mama. Like I lost control and my swollen-footed mother had won and made me lie, made me act like a fool. And Buck's lies—it was too much. A headache soon came on.

After dinner, Jim played with the kids—giddyup, Simon Says. I cleaned up the kitchen for hours.

At eleven at night, Jim yelled down to me, "When are you coming to bed?"

"When I want," I yelled back. Just to be stubborn I sat in the front room and drank tea. I fell asleep in my chair and woke up at one in the morning. When I went to bed, Jim woke up and said, "You need to act normal and come to bed no later than ten."

I was too tired to say anything. But a knife came to my hand and the knife went through Jim. It was an awful thought to have in bed. But a stranger was in bed with me. Who would believe he was a stranger? I couldn't get rid of the criminal thought. Real quiet, I got up, so as not to wake up Jim, who had fallen back to sleep. I walked down to the kitchen, but there was nothing to do. I came back upstairs and woke up Lizzy, who was snoring loud for a pretty little girl and said, "I'm sorry. You did nothing wrong. You forgive me?" Feeling her smooth warm skin helped. If she had a bigger bed I would've crawled in with her.

Chapter 29

I HAD TO walk to work on Friday since Buck was now gone to whereabouts unknown and I no longer had a car to borrow. I walked so fast my stomach cramped. To catch my breath, I slowed down. Forty minutes and I'd be there. It was raining hard and the wind upturned my umbrella, making it almost useless. Sometimes, it was necessary to walk out in the street to avoid puddles. They were splattered with rain, which made concentric circles—lovely, if I wasn't cold and wet. A car pulled up slow beside me. Ron, Norma's husband, with a cigarette hanging out of his mouth, said, "Give you a ride. Where you going?" He winked. "You look nice, even with your dress all wet and clinging to your pretty, long legs. I like long, wet legs." Several times, he tapped his tongue to his top lip.

I was speechless but wanted to say I hoped Floyd Patterson would beat him like he beats Norma, and turn him into mincemeat. But that would just get Norma another beating. I needed to respond; otherwise, I'd come across weak. So I looked straight at his eyes and said, "Your wife is the nicest person. I'm happy to know her. I know she loves you. You must be a happy man. About your offer—I need some exercise, so thank you but I'm going to walk. Thank you much," I said calm and unflustered.

His thin-lipped mouth dropped open. His crew-cut hair emphasized his odd-shaped head.

I walked on, not waiting for his response. Out of the corner of my eye, I saw the car driving on. I imagined him getting in an accident with a cement truck with a full load. Wet cement covering him as he clawed for air, terrified his life was ending. Was it even safe for my kids to be in his house? What else could I do? Norma didn't charge much, and Ron was mostly at work when my kids were over there. Then I remembered one time Norma said that he hasn't hit any of his kids after she threatened to kill him if he ever hit his kids hard again. Did he learn his lesson? I was thankful Norma had agreed to babysit my youngest, still not in school, and the other two when they got home. No one else was available. My kids would certainly tell me if something bad happened. I'd ask them.

I looked straight ahead, with my chin up, feet hitting the ground, telling myself the day was going to turn out good. I had a job, three good children, a roof over my head, and hadn't gone hungry in years. Goddamn Ron. I put one foot in front of the other, with my shoulders back. There were some sidewalks where tree roots buckled up and I had to be careful not to trip and fall and make a fool of myself. Goddamn Ron. By the time I got to the cleaner's, I was exhausted, cold, and had soaked shoes. My stomach was knotted.

By eleven, there hadn't been one customer. By noon, I feared my bringing Mr. Yalonsky good luck might be ending. I did what I could to earn my salary. While standing on a chair, I dusted the top of the light fixture. It was coated with dust. During a letup in the rain, I threw out the trash and washed the insides of the smelly garbage pail. I checked for any clothing that hadn't been picked up for over three months and set them aside. I cleaned counters and drawers and did my best because excellence might bring back the good luck I brought to Yalonsky. I pulled out all the drawers to sweep underneath with a whisk broom. One of the bottom drawers had a yellowed envelope taped to the back of it. The tape was so old the envelope came off easy. It was dated 11/20/1950 (same as Lizzy's birthdate), which was without a doubt a good omen and most definitely meant it should be opened. It might as well have had Lizzy's name on it.

I rubbed my hand across my stomach, took a deep breath, and walked to the back of the store. I pulled down the shade, and then sat awhile thinking about the envelope, then Buck, then Aunt Pleasant until it was time to pry into Yalonsky's business. Another minute passed. I counted to ten. Inside the envelope was a second envelope with two hundred and forty dollars in twenty-dollar bills wrapped inside a carbon copy of a bill marked *paid* and signed by the previous owner's wife. I counted it thrice to be accurate. Again for the pleasure. Then just to feel joy. Oh my, sweet goddamn. Sweetest goddamn. I sat for a few minutes doing nothing but feeling the money in my hands. I stuck the money in the bottom of my purse.

Remembering a purse-snatcher had been in the news, I took the money out of the envelope and stuffed it in my bra. I tore the envelope into pieces and flushed the pieces down the toilet. Twice, I flushed. Then it was clean the toilet. After wiping the drawer clean so there was no evidence an envelope had been taped there, I put it back. Worrying that someone might come around one day looking for the envelope, I cleaned every drawer, trying to make them look all the same—if that made any sense. Then it was mop the floor in between waiting on two customers who finally came in. Soon it got busy.

A good omen meant things couldn't go wrong. It meant the money didn't have to be given back because I needed to put a down payment on a car now that Buck was gone and I had brought lots of good luck to Yalonsky. The money had to have belonged to the previous owner and was most likely never included in his sales contract. It made sense. And if it didn't I'd make it up to Yalonsky in the future. I tried to relax.

At the end of the day, to alleviate some guilt, I bought a new mop and a top-of-the-line broom for the shop. I bought a glass jar and filled it up with hard candies of different flavors for customers because fancy stores did that, and because Yalonsky deserved respect. He had been very kind to me. Even his flirtations weren't over the line. He never touched my backside or anything else off-limits.

When I walked home exhausted, worrying I might see Ron, it had stopped raining, though there were still lots of puddles and when the wind blew, drops of water fell from trees on my head when I walked under them, but I didn't care. I didn't care that my shoes got wet again. I hid the money in the bottom of the broom closet, until I figured out a story to tell Jim.

ON SUNDAY, JIM drove into Willowsburg to buy some part to repair the lawn mower. I walked into Buck's place for a couple of minutes, like I was doing something there. When Jim returned, I said, with the money in my hand, "Look what I found under Buck's mattress. He must've forgotten it. And we don't have to return it because we fed him for months, he paid no rent, only did a few chores, and I need a car." I almost said he'd gone off the wagon and violated every sense of decency, but didn't because that would've required explaining.

To my surprise, Jim said he'd help find a good used car. He said if one is patient and looks around, one could get a good deal. He offered to drop me off at work next Saturday and then shop around, even if it took him all day.

"Who will watch the kids?"

"I'll bring them with me."

"All day? They'll be bored and grouchy."

"I'll deal with it."

"You like buying a second car, don't you?"

"It doesn't mean much to me, one way or other."

I didn't say any more except to be agreeable. But I wondered if he actually wanted to help me out or if it had more to do with status of a second car.

ON SATURDAY, HE dropped me off at work. At the end of the day, he had found a shiny 1948 black Kaiser in good shape, had low mileage, a nice radio, a defroster, a heater, and white sidewall tires. It had just been brought in a few hours before Jim saw it. Jim insisted on driving it home in case there might be a problem with it. The kids wanted to go home with him. He told them to go home with their good mother. What a nice compliment. He had a sweet smile. I gave him a hug.

As I drove our old car home, I sang all the way. My singing got the kids singing, like a party was happening. I was so pleased I cooked steak and potatoes au gratin for dinner. We were intimate that night after the kids were asleep. Like always, he was done in no time and I asked if sometimes he could take his time so I could—"Well, you know, enjoy it more."

He seemed surprised and said, "Women don't have sexual desire."

"What makes you think that?"

"Well . . . you're made different. I mean women don't . . . you know . . . ejaculate."

"I do too."

"You ejaculate? No, you don't."

"I mean enjoy. I have sexual feelings."

"Women don't get sexual feelings. You get emotional feelings."

"No, physical too. Like the opposite of pain. Like the pleasure of eating cherry pie a la mode. You know—yummy. Physical."

"Since when?

"Every so often."

"Where do you feel it?"

"Where? You want to know where. Gee. Sometimes my nose, or my feet, my elbows. Once my fingernails and when I filed them—Oh my, did that feel good." I ran my fingernails across my arm, closed my eyes, and took a long, slow breath. I didn't smile or laugh or let on that it was the funniest thing, most ridiculous, cuckooest thing I ever said.

"What?" He had a look on his face that was as strange as ever.

"If you're wondering if I'm being snide, then think why you're asking me where I feel it. Where do you think?" I wanted to say I had had orgasms. But then he'd ask when and where and I'd have to say with Sal Shouse, a long time ago. Or myself one time . . . maybe a few.

"With you nothing is simple." He turned over and went to sleep.

I turned the opposite way. Obviously, my sarcasm had no effect other than to make him think I was nuts. But I was pleased with the car, which was far more important. I predicted he'd want to drive the new car to work and leave me with the old one. No problem.

But next morning he said, "You drive the Kaiser because the kids are with you more often than me and it's a safer car. I wouldn't want the kids to get hurt."

Chapter 30

WHILE I WASHED the front window of the cleaners, a man came into my view. As he came toward me, he smiled and walked into the store. I picked up my wash bucket and squeegee and followed him in. He was tall, lanky, and his hair was a bit on the long side. His leather jacket, khaki pants, and black leather boots got my attention.

"What can I do for you?" I asked, real curious.

"You work here? I'm sorry. I thought you were the window washer."

"That's right. Plus janitor, clerk, cashier, wait on customers, and, oh . . . open up the shop, close it, Friday and Saturdays only. Ten hours a day. Can I help you?"

He looked embarrassed—a bit of silence, mouth dropped open. He apologized, then handed me a navy blue suit, and said he hadn't worn it in years; his secretary died. "I need something for the funeral. Think this will clean up?"

I took the suit and said it looked mostly like years of closet dust. "I'm sorry to hear about your secretary dying." As I talked, I rubbed my fingers on his suit. "I would guess you work outdoors—being that you don't wear suits often and you have a bomber jacket on." I stopped my finger-rubbing.

"Smart observation. Although I could say I'm indoors when I fly planes."

"Flying planes . . . I own a jacket like yours. Haven't worn it in years."

He said he was in a hurry—late for an important appointment—and would be back on Monday afternoon to pick up the suit. He left.

I watched him walk out the door and disappear down the street. I hoped he'd be wearing his bomber jacket when he came to pick up his cleaning. But he said he'd be back on Monday when I wouldn't be working. It would be nice to see him again.

Ten minutes later, he returned for he had forgotten to take the ticket for his suit. We started talking and he asked why I had a bomber jacket, as he never knew a woman who wore one.

"I was a WASP." Would he know what that was?

"I know about the WASP, but not a lot. What did you do?"

I sighed and looked straight into his brown, not quite small eyes, and thick eyebrows. I always liked thick eyebrows on a man. They just did something to me. I might've done a faraway look. I couldn't look at his eyes and his eyebrows and jacket for long, for surely I'd give away my curiosity. I clasped my hands to steady myself. "Where do I start? I brought a plane in when it lost three engines. I flew in icy conditions, storms, lightning. I chauffeured a pompous general across the country at night. There was one nice-looking colonel I avoided if I could—his bad breath. It smelled like old garbage."

"Good looks are worth nothing if someone has bad breath. Now if God had one fault and it was bad breath, no one would want to go to heaven."

"That'd be a problem."

"It would for many." He had an infectious smile.

We exchanged names. His was Harry Olson. He owned a small private airport and flying school.

We talked about preferred types of planes. In five minutes, this man turned my past alive. Then he turned my present inside out with "Would you like a job as a secretary at my airport, assuming you can type?"

"Type?" I paused and wondered if I heard him correctly. Of course I had. "I've done that. Ninety-five words per minute . . . about that."

"You have the job. You want it?"

"Do I want it?" I took a deep breath. "I already have a job and my boss has been good to me."

"What if I paid you more?"

"He'd probably offer me a raise just to keep me."

"He must like you. Another reason I'd like to hire you."

We looked at each other. I went back to finger-rubbing his suit. He rubbed his lower lip, and tilted his chin up, a pleading look in his eyes. "Every so often, I'll take you up in a plane. Can you work full time?" He opened his eyes wide, raised his eyebrows and nodded his head as if he was imploring me to say yes. He offered a decent salary.

I turned away, looked out the window, turned back, looked at him still nodding his head. I looked at the counter, my hands, his well-shaped hands, his jacket, his collar, his eyes looking at me. "That definitely changes everything. I'd have to say . . . yes. Are you kidding?"

"Nope. If you want to come by the airport I'll introduce you as the new secretary. Now I'm real late for my appointment."

"Sorry." I looked downwards like I was sorry, except my smile said otherwise.

"By the way—when can you start?"

"Start? I have to give my boss notice. At least two weeks. He'll need time to hire someone else. He's been so nice."

"That's a while." He wrinkled his forehead and grimaced, then smiled. "I'll be patient. Here's my business card, and if you lose it, I'm in the phone book—Olson Airport, three miles outside of Willowsburg, on the west side."

"I've seen it."

"You should have dropped in."

"You're right."

When he left, I had to sit down to rest my excitement. It was the easiest job interview I ever had. The job would bring me close to planes, maybe to actually flying. "Oh my God. Norma's right?" I whispered. I remembered Norma once said if a job comes to you it was meant to be and you have to take the job so good things will happen. "It was meant to be. Meant to be," I said aloud, and clasped my hands and took a deep breath.

I figured my good luck was moving like a spirit from Mr. Yalonsky to Mr. Olson. Aunt Pleasant told me that good luck does that sometimes—goes from one person to another. To hold on to my good luck, I tried not to even think about flying, which was hard to do. I got up and walked to the back room, sat down, and held his suit, hoping no customers came in for a while.

I looked at the dustpan, the broom, my tennis shoes, my socks that have holes in the heel and needed darning, the window I didn't finish washing. The sun was shining through the window, but the sunlight made me think of flying, so I looked at the basement door. That made me think of turnips in root cellars. Turnips were my least favorite vegetable but I ate them, especially if I had a day's hunger. What didn't I like about turnips? Bitterness? Yes. Wild ramps were good but your breath smelled awful after eating them. There was a candy wrapper lying on the floor. Who brought it in? Did the wind when the door opened? I let it lie there. This man had disrupted my hard-work morning. I didn't finish washing the window. It was clean enough for the day. A customer came in and I treated the irritable, bleach-blond snooty woman like royalty.

AFTER DINNER, I said I got an offer to work almost full time as a secretary. Jim objected but I assured him I'd still take care of all my household duties. Very neatly, I had written down my increased salary. "Within six months there'll be money for a new roof and a new lawn mower. We can save some money. And can afford taking our cars to a mechanic when needed. You dislike doing car repair, don't you?"

Jim leaned toward me looking pensive. His head nodding ever so slightly, a little grimace—I knew he was going to say, "I hate fixing cars."

"I know you do. I understand. Yes . . . think about it." I showed him the numbers I'd written down, real neat. He checked them. I knew he would.

Sensing some resistance, I said it must be awful having all that pressure of making enough money to pay so many bills. I complimented him on the good job he'd done so far but sometimes, he seemed so tired and needed a vacation.

He agreed and suggested we could go to the Smithsonian in Washington, DC for four days.

"That's a wonderful idea." It didn't matter where we went because my new job would be a vacation.

MR. YALONSKY LOOKED excited to see me on Monday, my day off, until I spoke about resigning my job. I couldn't remember the last time I saw someone change his face so quick from debonair to shock to anger.

"This is a joke?" he asked. When he understood I was serious, he said I was abandoning him. Those were his words—*abandoning me*. Not *quitting*, not *leaving*, but *abandoning me*. "You're like family. I bought this business so you'd have a job. To help you and Jim."

"I didn't know that."

"You know now. Are you staying? Answer me." He took a hold of my wrist.

"I thought you'd understand. It's at an airport. I'll have a chance to take a plane flight a few times." I stared at my wrist, like I was politely asking him to let it go.

"That means nothing."

"I'm sorry. I must. It's twice the hours."

"More hours you want? You can have full time if you like." He took a step closer.

"I won't quit until you find someone to replace me." I stepped back and tried to pull my hand free.

He responded with silence and a hurtful grip.

"I'm sorry. To be able to go up in a plane again, even a few times . . . it means the world to me. I'm quitting. Can you let go of my wrist?" It took effort to keep my voice calm. "Please, no violence."

He stared like an old used bullet—hard, cold, misshapen. His nostrils flared. His body puffed up, lowered voice, narrowed steely eyes. He let go of my wrist, and pointed his finger within an inch of me. "You no longer have a free account. Nothing. You get nothing. As of now, you're no longer working for me." He demanded his keys back and he paid me what was due me up to the minute. He gave me back the new broom and mop I bought and the candy in the jar. He threw five cents in the bucket in case any customers had eaten a candy.

I was right about my good luck leaving Yalonsky. He was crazy, acting like I belonged to him. When I got to my car, I threw his pennies on the ground.

I WORKED ALMOST full time at the airport—seven thirty to two thirty, off on Sunday and Monday, with a working lunch so I could pick up my two oldest when they were done with school and Lizzy who was babysat by Norma.

After the first week, I walked into a warehouse with Mr. Olson. It was noisy with hammers clanging, things popping and banging, but then everything got quiet except for a faint murmuring sound. The warehouse opened up into a garden with the tallest trees I ever saw. Olson, in his bomber jacket, said he wanted to fly me to New England. He pointed to snow-capped mountains under a blue sky. We packed a lunch; he touched my arm. We flew over the mountains and landed by a calm blue lake. The snow-capped mountains disappeared. The lake spread out in ribbons over the land. I knew I was dreaming. Then I woke up. Jim was snoring and I wondered if he ever dreamt about other women. If he even wanted another woman. Martha Washington or Dolly Madison, maybe. I didn't laugh out loud because I didn't want to awaken him. He never spoke about his dreams but neither did I.

Chapter 31

I REDESIGNED THE filing system, found a cheaper source for some supplies, talked with customers, smiled, greeted, did the usual. I met the mayor of Philadelphia and a state senator on his way to Harrisburg. The governor shook my hand when he came through. A Miss America flew through one time with a three-person entourage.

"Are you the cleaning lady?" she asked me.

"No, but I'll be happy to clean your plane. And if you like, if your pilot didn't do a preflight inspection before your left, I can do that too. I can check that all the instruments read properly. Pleased to meet you."

Olson was off to the side and gave me a knowing, supportive smile.

I spent not one penny of my paycheck on myself. Jim got a new top-of-the-line lawn mower and we almost had enough money saved for a new roof on the house. We hired a mechanic whenever one of our cars needed work.

HARRY AND I were now calling each other by first names, but he had not kept his promise he'd take me for a plane ride. Had he forgotten all about it or had he lied? He didn't seem like a liar. But if he had lied it wouldn't be good to mention it because that would be challenging him. But if he forgot? I wanted it so much but didn't want something bad to come out of asking. After I perfected a plan, the airport got too hectic—a reckless pilot almost crashed his plane on landing. The next day, Harry was out of the office. On the third day when Harry came in, I said, "Be nice to be in a plane again one of these days." Then I looked out the window and watched a plane depart. I sighed. "Beautiful plane. It's nice to fly."

"Well, gee. Why didn't you remind me? I told you I'd take you on a ride if you worked for me. It got suddenly busy after you started, I got distracted and then forgot. I'm sorry."

"You did tell me that, didn't you?"

"Tomorrow okay?"

LATE AFTERNOON, WE climbed into a four-seater plane. As I took my seat, I put my hand on the stick. I tapped my feet to the floor and touched this and that, the same enthusiastic way I did when I took a plane ride as a girl. I looked over at Harry and he was smiling.

"Let's take off," I said. "You don't know how much this means to me. This is a good day."

"Isn't that true." Harry spread his words out slow, like they had connotations. "Doesn't get better."

"Even when you got accepted in the WASP?"

"That was an excellent day but I had no one to share it with. Just me in a small apartment with one window, with a view of a brick wall."

When we reached full ascent, he touched my knee, not my hand or forearm but a part of me he never touched before. I barely moved my knee up into his warm hand.

Harry asked, "Would you like to fly the plane for a bit?"

My mouth moved but no words came out. Finally I said, "Oh my. Oh my. God Almighty. It gets better."

"You want to?"

My eyes closed, I inhaled. My hands aquiver. I exhaled.

"Consider that you're just putting in the hours, and I'm your instructor. You can't say no." He put it on automatic pilot, got up from his seat and motioned to me to take the controls.

"Ohh, ohh." I slid over and took a hold of the stick. I placed my feet near the rudder. For minutes, it was just me and the plane. Planes don't talk, but I heard the engine whir like it was music. Maybe it was just my imagination but my whole body felt it moving through space, its speed, the aerodynamics. In its own way, the plane said everything I wanted to hear. I looked at the dashboard and the VOR, the heading indicator, the DME, the altimeter and the artificial horizon. I made sure I was flying at least a thousand feet above a small town with a town square, a tall white church steeple, and roads leading out in four directions. Over a farmer's field with rows of yellow grain—maybe oats—I dipped down to eight hundred feet, well within the legal limit. There was a farmer riding his tractor down a fallow field.

I glanced at Harry. It was obvious he understood my gratitude. I turned the plane around to head back to the airport. We switched seats again and he landed the plane. Then we just sat and talked about when we first rode in a plane, first time we flew one, favorite planes, places we've gone, places we'd like to go. He touched my hand with the tip of his finger and said, "Unfortunately, we have to get back to work." I let out a sigh.

At the end of the day, I wondered what Jim would say when I told him I'd flown. On the way home I said Harry's name aloud, maybe seven times. I lost count.

STARTING THE SUMMER by flying gave me energy I didn't know I had. I tried my hand at gardening and planted tomatoes, zucchini, and cucumbers. They did okay, but not nearly as well as Norma's, but she never gloated. Though I was tired most evenings, I managed okay and didn't scold Lizzy for smelling like a puppy after not bathing for four days. I made Jim a cherry pie and he licked his fingers. Harry often licked his fingers when he ate lunch. I wanted to make another pie and bring it to work and watch Harry eat. I didn't. I stopped ironing bed linen and Jim's cotton undershirts. He didn't notice. That inspired me to stop ironing his handkerchiefs. He noticed, but I shrugged and said I didn't have the time. Then I handed him my paycheck.

Jim

Chapter 32

OAK TREE ROAD was lined with fine sycamores, stately elms, and poplars. One large oak. A maple shaded our house. Large yards, and wide front porches. Box hedges served as fences. Leaves shimmered in the breeze cooling the hot summer day. Only one yellow dandelion on our lawn. Saturdays I mowed it unless it rained. The Mackeys in their Roadmaster pulled out of their driveway. Probably going shopping. Rumor was Mrs. Mackey was a spendthrift. Iola wasn't. We had a nice savings account. Seven hundred and sixty-eight dollars. Al Peterson, a nice man, had his old bald head under the hood of his Ford. A dog barked. The Miller boys were playing catch. The older one caught the ball every time. Rumor was he had a talent for baseball. One day he might be famous, and I'll say I knew Joey Miller when he was a boy. Oak Tree Road was one of my best decisions. Was I feeling happy? Seemed so. What is happiness? My sister was happy before . . .

Now, I didn't want to think that or I'd get depressed. Stop the thought. How? Just think something else, anything. Jim. J. Think something else. Summer. Balmy. B. Autumn. A. Colorful. C. Harvest time. Marigolds bordered the walkway. Lizzy wore a red dress when she had helped me plant them. Our maple turns bright red in October. Winter will bring white snow concealing everything. A blizzard would be nice. And quiet days, but doesn't sound travel best in the cold? At night with a full moon, ice will glisten in naked trees. Spring is green, and all the flowers. The rose bushes and daisies I recognize, but the others that the neighbors grow? Whatever they are, they are pretty, red, yellow, white, purple. Yes, Oak Tree Road was one of my best decisions. It was good.

I didn't share my thoughts with Iola because she might think they were silly. She looked lovely in the afternoon light. I wanted something to say. "There's only one cloud in the sky." That sounded moronic.

"Interesting. It looks like a figure getting ready to throw something. If you believe clouds are oracles, that might mean something." Iola looked up from her sock-darning.

"Clouds aren't oracles."

"Dear, use your imagination."

Use my imagination? Umm. "I might try taking some photographs this winter."

"You like taking photographs?"

"I don't know why."

"Why do you need to know why?"

"It seems better."

When Iola got up to go make dinner, I realized I liked sitting on the porch with her without much talk. I wouldn't like living alone.

After dinner, we ended up on the porch again and watched the stars unfold in the moonless evening sky. Did she like sitting with me?

"In Pilgrim, the sky was thick with stars," she said.

"Same number is everywhere."

"Twice as many you could see. That was one good thing about Pilgrim. I hope our children have a good life. You know, rich kids can have problems," Iola said.

"That's right. Bad things can happen to them. Remember Charles Lindbergh's baby getting kidnapped and killed?"

"It was barbaric. The man that did it deserved to die. What was his name?"

"Bruno Richard Hauptmann."

"That's right. Bruno Hauptmann."

"You ever meet Lindbergh with all the flying you did?"

"Would've liked to."

"He was heroic. And how do we ensure our children have a good life?"

"Just try our best." Iola shrugged.

"Isn't that what we're doing?"

"I hope so."

"What do you mean—hope so? You're not trying your best?" I narrowed my eyes.

"Sometimes you don't know. You think it's the best, but later, things might turn out so it's not. They can go completely haywire. End up in an unexpected way."

"You think something we're doing could end up hurting them? Nonsense." I got up to go back in the house, remembering the gun that was left out on a table long ago and my sister found it and shot herself. It upset me to think about. Put it out of mind.

"Why do you always have to walk away when you hear something you don't like?"

I turned around, faced her but said nothing. Maybe it was the light through the window on her and her hair pulled back. No makeup. She had a smudge under her nose—like a thin mustache. She was wearing dark pants and a loose gray shirt. Was it my mood? She looked almost mannish. I wanted her to be a man. I had done it before. I had learned how to think of her that way for sexual performance. Generally I could not close my eyes and visualize something simple like a color or the shape of a tree, let alone Iola as a man. Thinking of sexual words helped—*penis, scrotum, testicles, sperm, Adam's apple.* What really helped was dirty words—*arse opener, bum tickler, cream stick, ding dong, nimrod.* And for buttocks—*full moon, ass, parking place.* Often, to myself, I called her Robert or Steven—men I had been attracted to in the past. I could get the glint of a picture.

A few times I got a stirring when looking at her when she was dressed her best, in white high heels, a yellow dress with a full skirt. Her hair done up. Shiny earrings on. Her ruby red lipstick. I liked the color; I liked saying it. Home alone one time, I took her lipstick and put it on. I powdered my nose, put rouge on my cheeks, and clipped on her earrings. It was fun—violating rules—but it was not my history and if Iola walked in on me she would've divorced me. I could've been one of those men sent to prison when their secrets were discovered.

Since it never did any good to dwell on those things, I went in the house and pulled out a book to read. Iola telling me to use my imagination; how do I do that? Closing my eyes, I tried to visualize the shape of a tree. I realized if I took my finger and drew the outline of a tree, with my eyes closed, I could visualize its shape—the tall trunk and the branches spreading out. I did it for a house. And a car. A penis. Goddamn. A nice long penis. I had a better imagination than I had thought.

Iola

Chapter 33

DURING MY WORKING lunch of a baloney sandwich made with bread ends, a bruised apple, and a half pint of milk, Harry walked into my office, carrying his lunchbox, and sat down, looking worried, like there was a problem. He put his hands behind his head and smiled. He was plainly up to something. He said, "I've been meaning to ask. What inspired you to become a pilot?"

I'd never thought about it as inspiration. It had always been a way to escape drunken, violent, crazy, murderous Pilgrim, but that wasn't something to share. My response—"Hearing Amelia Earhart on the neighbor's radio and Uncle Dillard taking me on my first plane ride."

He stroked his chin. "I had an aunt who was like Earhart in some ways—innovative and thought for herself. She had lived in Paris for a couple of years, traveled through Europe until the war started. Then she headed over to Stockholm. My mother said she was a loose woman because she lived with a man."

"A customer this morning said he wanted to fly his plane to New Orleans and listen to jazz."

"You changed the topic. Maybe you prefer not talking about my favorite auntie living with a man in Paris." He tilted his head and smiled.

A bit intrigued, a bit pleased, a bit hesitant, I put my elbows on my cluttered desk, and my chin on my hands.

He moved his chair near me, and laid his right arm on my desk. His hand was a few inches from my elbow. "You know where I like to listen to jazz is in a club with a martini in my hand." He moved his fingers, like he wanted to do something.

"I haven't been to a club in a long time," I said. Harry sitting so close gave me the urge to finger-comb his messy hair. His shirt needed to be tucked into his pants. I had no urge to help with that but had the thought. His brown eyes had several thin green lines.

"I'd love to take you to one."

"You're flirting."

"Can I keep doing it?"

"You drink a lot?" I did a topic change to avoid temptation.

"About twice a week, at the most. You?"

"About once a month before I got married. Not much now. I have a cousin-in-law who likes jazz. His wife is Catholic. I went to the baptism of their youngest child." I did another topic change.

"I went to Catholic school. My sister's a nun." He followed my lead. "We were never close. There're ten years between us."

"Me and my sister, Ethyl Lou, are miles apart. The most she ever traveled was twenty miles from home. Anything farther might as well've been China. She denounced me becoming a pilot. Most of my family did. It was then I knew for sure I didn't fit in." I noticed Harry had barely moved, like he was listening to my every word. Those thin green lines again in his brown eyes, the crow's feet by his eyes, the tiny mole by his eyebrow were hard to ignore.

"You like being different?"

"From Ethyl Lou? Yes. Actually I like the Catholic baptism. Just a sprinkle of water on the baby's head. Most it does is cry." Why—I wasn't sure, but I needed to tell a story I never told anyone before. I leaned back in my chair, looked out the window, like Pilgrim was nearby. I said, "When I was baptized, I got immersed in a creek."

"An immersion baptism. Never knew someone baptized like that."

"It's the way Pilgrim did it. Reverend put his hand on my head, pushed me into the water, and then squeezed my breast. He had his back to the congregation standing on the shore. When he let go, I popped back to the surface and wanted to scream. But I couldn't with most of Pilgrim there supplicating to God. A few were holy rolling." I hoped I wouldn't regret telling the story.

"You tell anyone?" Harry looked sympathetic.

"No one would've believed me. I didn't know if he just did it to me, or every girl he ever baptized. Grabbing my breast for a few seconds. What good did it do him?"

"He got a sensation to masturbate to later in the evening."

I looked out the window again, hoping he'd end the masturbation topic, even though it intrigued me.

"Can I go back to something you just said?"

"Depends."

"About people supplicating. What is that?" Harry rubbed his forefinger on my desk in a circular motion.

The circular motion seemed like the subtlest, most sophisticated, respectful flirtation I'd ever seen, like sign language he knew I'd recognize. I still had my chin in my hands. "It's raising your hands above your head and swaying a little with your head down and your eyes closed or if you prefer looking straight up to heaven, assuming heaven's up."

"You mean like this?" Harry stood up and gave it a try. He exaggerated the supplicating and I laughed.

"Some would say you're irreverent."

"You think I am?"

"Absolutely."

He sat down and, being full of surprises, he pulled two fancy pastries out of his lunch box and put them on my desk. Two had to have meant he planned it. He gave me one of the pastries. He ate his in two bites. I took my time and enjoyed the flakiness, sweetness, the creamy cheese filling, spices, almonds.

"You got powdered sugar on your lips," he said.

I slowly wiped my lips. To keep the flirtation from becoming blatantly palpable, I talked about the first time I flew in a thunderstorm. He talked about his most difficult flight, how scary it was. I talked about fear and courage. Finally, I said I hadn't done any work for a while and needed to earn my pay.

"You're working. You're inspiring me."

Heat rushed into my cheeks. There was a quiet pause letting things settle. I knew he noticed—by the tilt of his head, slight smile, and long breath. No one ever told me before I was inspiring. It made me imagine possibilities. We were alone, close enough to touch. I had tried my best to keep some distance. But there were signs.

He was a tall, lanky male.

He had given me compliments and a fancy pastry.

We both had the same passion for flying.

Both intelligent.

Nice looks—even better when happy.

We both needed something we didn't have.

He said he was curious about something I said earlier. "That some of your church members were holy rolling when you got baptized. Just what is holy rolling?"

"I guess moving about like you're touched by the Holy Spirit."

"Like anything goes? Every dance movement squeezed into one?"

"What do you mean?"

"Like the tango combined with square dancing, thrown into waltzing, jitterbugging, the two-step, twirling, jumping?"

"You could say that."

"Like abandonment to the spirit-rapping abracadabra, dividing infinity by zero and getting anything you want?"

"That's right. The abracadabra. Anything so long as you're moving. We had our own way—jumping, twisting, moving, and, if you like, rolling on the floor. Some churches just did floor rolling. It's letting go . . . I guess. Letting the Spirit in. No one ever asked me before."

"Would you show me how to holy roll?" He leaned toward me, raised his eyebrows, and nodded his head. Then he looked funny, dreamy, had faraway eyes, but they were so close.

"I'd be embarrassed."

"What if I try it and you tell me if I did it right?"

"Sounds good."

Harry got up and did an interpretation all over the office, slow and jerky at first, and then he shimmied his shoulders and jumped and twirled and shimmied his hips. I almost fell out of my chair; the chair tipped but I caught myself. Tears of laughter streamed down my cheeks. Then I got up and shimmied my hips and twirled, and he twirled over to me. He took hold of my hand and led me into a waltz. It was the eye contact that caused a love to slip out of the air, like it had been there all along and could no longer hide itself and slid right through me. It was in the smile of his mouth and in his male arm around my receptive waist. It was all over me. An illicit love was set loose. Not a word was uttered. Not a thought about Jim.

My upbringing and fear that someone might walk in on us changed the topic again. "It's time to get to work." I stepped away.

"Yes. Yes. Great idea." He pulled on his ear like he was massaging it and took a deep breath. "I'm glad you got us back to work. You should be the boss." Then he rubbed the tip of his nose and touched my nose with the tip of his finger, like it was the shortest step away from kissing. "We didn't holy roll on the floor. Maybe next time?"

I raised my eyebrows. "Umm," I said.

"I like the way you say umm. Say it again."

"Umm."

"Again."

"No." I smiled, but just barely.

WHEN I FINISHED my beautiful day, I walked toward my car. I turned around and Harry was watching me through the window. We waved and I walked on to my car. He was probably still watching me—the slight sway of my hips. My plain ordinary navy blue skirt rippling, like a flirt. My long legs. I purposely dropped my keys so I'd have to bend over to pick them up. He'd enjoy that all evening when he was alone thinking of me. And the way I opened the door wide. And the way I sat in the car, leaving one foot hanging out for a bit, while I dug something out of my old plastic purse, just to be in his view longer. I looked over at him. He was still there in the window smiling, watching. We waved again. As I drove away, I wondered if that was the closest I'd ever get to him. I was married and had never seen myself as having an affair. How to ignore the delicious joy, pleasure, a strong physical craving mixed with a calm sadness, some worry, some trepidation? Not easy. Too much to ponder. At least I got to work with Harry five days a week. Sometimes we stood so close we shared scents.

No one ever told me I should be the boss. On the way home, the craving wouldn't let go. My imagination took hold, so I paid little attention to driving. There was the cloudless sky and a flock of blackbirds, the meadow and a flock of blue flowers, the green hills, a flock of trees and a deer by the road. The deer's lovely mate was probably up the hill, eating some acorns while patiently waiting for her. I stopped the car at the top of a hill and watched the sunset. It was the best hilltop in a good world. Unbridled in thought, I hummed and hummed. Further down the road, I drove through a stop sign and almost caused an accident. I swerved and feared my car would tip over. The other driver blasted his car horn at me.

Chapter 34

HOPING HARRY WOULDN'T mind, I took my children to work with me. It was Saturday and Jim had to work at the lab and Norma was sick. In the morning, three customers cancelled their flying lessons because a storm was predicted. It started raining. There was nothing for kids to do. Harry said he'd pay them each a quarter if they dusted his desk and cleaned the bathroom sink.

"I don't want to clean. I want to take a plane ride." Starla swayed her arms over her head.

"We could manage that if the weather clears and you behave yourselves," Harry said and then swayed his arms. Then Lizzy did. Then I did. We did it again and laughed.

Since I craved a plane ride more than Starla, I bribed the kids to behave themselves. Later that day the clouds disappeared off in the distance, and we all went for a thirty-minute plane ride. Starla pressed her face against the window the whole time. She pointed out silvery streams, barns, hill after hill, treetops, patchwork fields, colors, cars, a farmer riding his green tractor, tractor tracks, a road, more roads, a house, anything that caught her eye. "Look at that, look at that," she said. There was one cloud in the sky. She said the cloud was there just for us, so the plane wouldn't be lonely in the big sky. Her excitement reminded me of my own first plane ride.

Lizzy got nauseous and wanted to go home. Charles counted all the churches we flew over. I didn't say a thing, but I kept smiling at Harry. And the smile turned into joy, a wave of calm evenness that spread right through me. It took my breath away and gave it back. It did it again.

"Another great day."

"Better than before?" Harry asked.

"Two great days are three times better than one."

"Would you like to fly the plane again for a little bit?"

"Oh my. You know I would."

He put it on automatic pilot and we switched seats.

I took a hold of the stick and rested my foot gently on the rudder. It was just the plane and me. I hardly heard Harry and the kids talking. After an hour or maybe it was a day or maybe two minutes, I glanced at Harry. My life had changed. Soon we switched seats again and Harry landed the plane. I wondered what Jim would say when I told him I'd flown for the second time. I'd tell him it was only for a few minutes.

Back in the office, Starla told some little-kid jokes. Harry told some. I laughed, infecting everyone. Charles mimicked me. Starla was unable to get off the floor she was laughing so much. Lizzy, no longer nauseous, un-shyed herself and danced. Harry clapped. Charles clapped. Starla jumped up and took center stage. Every part of her danced.

The young know best the pleasure of movement. I understood what deep happiness was. It made me serene. No cake. No candles. No singing. No planning, but a celebration had risen on its own. This man was gentle.

That evening, when I told Jim about my ten minutes flying, he said nothing.

THE FOLLOWING MORNING, when I walked in the office, Harry said, "Good morning, Iola O."

I came to a complete stop, and my mouth dropped open. My eyes widened.

"You don't like me giving you a nickname? Sorry."

"No. No. My brother Zeke came up with that name. I loved it. He disappeared one day and never came home. He and Buck, another brother, were the only ones who ever called me that … just the two of them. And now … and yes, you too. Please do." Other than that, we behaved ourselves all day. But it was very busy, people coming in and out.

IT BEING A school holiday and Norma not at home, I took my kids to work again. Harry wouldn't mind. Charles told Harry what he learned in Sunday school. Miss Beatrice, his teacher, said Jesus rose from the dead and went to heaven and is coming back. He went on with a Miss Beatrice said this and Miss Beatrice said that.

"You like Miss Beatrice?" Harry asked.

"She smells holy."

"Even on hot humid days?"

"Always. Miss Beatrice said she wasn't married and she was waiting for the right one to come along. I think she'll marry a preacher. I'm going to be a preacher when I grow up."

I knew right then that Charles would never become a pilot. I'd be lucky if he became a teacher.

"You'll make a very good preacher," Harry said.

Behind Charles's back, I shook my head, wishing Harry wouldn't give him ideas.

"I don't want to be a preacher," Starla said. "I want to be a singer."

"I'd be the happiest man on earth if you'd sing me a song." Harry laid his hand over his heart.

Starla did a little jig with her head, like songs inside were figuring which one would go first. Then she took her place in front of everyone. Center stage, she looked at her sister, her brother, Harry, and me, and sang "Frère Jacques." She knew all the words and never missed a note. Her performance ended with a bow.

"Excellent," Harry said.

"Excellent," I said.

Like a copycat, Charles said the same. Starla twirled herself in a circle. Lizzy got shy again, but she was happy sitting on Harry's lap, though it became a busy day, so he wasn't around much in the office.

In the afternoon, Harry came back in with an oil stain on his jacket. I said I knew of a cleaners I could take it to.

"Where we met?" Harry jiggled his head.

"Yes. I'll take it there." I mimicked his jiggle. He reciprocated. Simple fun was the purest and didn't cost a penny.

I took it to Yalonsky the next day. Since I no longer had a free account, I expected to pay. He refused to take my business even with my offer to pay twice the price to help mend his hurt feelings. He gave me no eye contact and acted like I wasn't in his shop. Well, well. Just for that—I was glad I'd taken the two hundred and forty dollars I found hidden in his cleaners a while back. I walked out, let the door slam shut, and took the jacket elsewhere.

Jim

Chapter 35

HALF FEARING I was doing something crazy, I drove the car up the driveway. It was Monday, so Iola was home. Peter Blythe was with me. Needless to say, the man was a genius. He was tall, skinny, had brown hair, perfect eyebrows, strong cheekbones, and a cleft in his chin. I liked clefts and smart men. I liked Peter. I said, "Let me do most of the talking." We both got wet in the light rain as we walked into the house. A few dirty dishes sat on the table. A mop was leaning against a wall. I turned the blaring radio off and put the dishes in the sink.

Iola yelled from upstairs, "Why are you home at noon? Have you been laid off again?"

I hoped things didn't become a disaster. It was taking a chance bringing Peter home, but the decent man needed a place to stay, what with him having wife problems.

Iola bolted downstairs and almost tripped when she saw Peter. It was funny but I didn't laugh.

To keep things civil, I introduced Iola as my lovely wife. Peter was just Peter Blythe who I worked with. "Right now he needs a place to stay for a little bit."

"What did you say his name was?" Iola leaned an ear toward me.

"Peter Blythe."

"You need a place, you say. For how long?" Iola scratched her neck.

Her voice was polite, but she had narrowed her eyes. Peter looked at me. "I told Peter he could stay in the little garage apartment that Buck built. It won't be for long."

"Is that so?"

Iola, all worrisome and fretful, but when wasn't she? Maybe she was embarrassed she was wearing a sack of a housedress, no makeup, and her hair uncombed. Her face was drawn with fatigue. Was she showing her age?

"My brother built that apartment for himself."

When Iola picked up a towel that was on the floor, I nudged Peter and he said, "Thank you. I appreciate it. Is he expected back soon?" He stood straight and clasped his hands behind his back.

"I doubt it," Iola said. "His habit is to come in your life for a while and then be gone for longer. But you never know."

The rain suddenly turned into a hard downpour and there was lightning and thunder not far away, so Peter and I sat at the kitchen table until the storm passed. We talked about the latest drugs on the market and how Thorazine was developed in France and it became the first drug for schizophrenia, and about the new drug we were working on. If it passed the final trial it would be on the market maybe in a year, and the insane who didn't get better on Thorazine might do well on our drug. I liked listening to Peter talk about how he thought our drug actually worked on brain chemistry. He used lots of chemistry words that Iola wouldn't recognize.

Iola stayed in the kitchen cleaning up but she said nothing. Every so often I would look over at her. Mostly she seemed focused on cleaning. Sometimes, she'd look at Peter like she was trying to figure him out—maybe how smart he was, or if he was up to no good. She could probably tell he was smart because he answered every question I asked. Peter's answers were brilliant. I loved brilliance. It inspired me. Plus Peter gave me credit when credit was due and once told our boss that I could easily get a Ph.D.

After the downpour subsided, I took Peter out to the apartment so he could get settled in. He was fine with the accommodations. I told him to take his time unpacking his two suitcases, putting away his books and papers, and a bag of groceries because he might be too tired to do it in the evening. I'd be waiting for him in the car. I wanted to put my hand on his shoulder but didn't for fear of it leading to something. Oh, but to share my life with Peter. But where? What city? New York was too busy. Hollywood was too crazy; we might as well live on the moon. And my kids—I'd be lost without them.

When I came back in the kitchen alone, I told Iola, "Peter needs a little time away from his wife and he'll probably be gone in a month or so."

"Is that so? Be nice to have a month or so away from all the family responsibilities," Iola said. "Think you could find me a place to rest? What do you think?"

"When he's gone, you could stay in Buck's apartment."

"Oh . . . is that what I can do?" She spoke slowly like she was being sarcastic.

"If that's what you need."

"So he's a chemist?"

"He has a Ph.D. He's working hard trying to find a solution to a problem we're having at work. Then he started having difficulties with his wife and it was interfering with his work. I just found out he slept in the office all last week.

You know, not all marriages are perfect like ours." She didn't seem to recognize my sarcasm.

"Is he going to get fired and end up living here? How old is he?"

"Late twenties. You worry too much. He has an excellent mind for chemistry. You know, I once had a plan of getting a degree in chemistry."

"Can't he stay in a hotel?"

"He doesn't like them. His father died in a hotel room and wasn't found for two days. Buck's empty apartment is exactly what he needs. We can go to work together, since Peter doesn't have a car as his wife uses it, and she needs most of his salary for a sick child, so he's happy with something cheap."

"Am I expected to cook for him? We don't have money for extra food."

"He offered to pay me for dinner and rent. He said he could do his own breakfast and lunch, being there's a small refrigerator and a hot plate. He said it would be nice if he could borrow a blanket and sheets."

"I guess so." She went upstairs and got some. When she returned she asked, "What wife problems is he having? Doesn't he have any family he can live with?"

"No."

"He has no family?"

"They all live back in North Dakota."

"Was he the one at work you said had schizophrenia a while back, and you had to take him to the hospital?"

"That was someone else."

"What kind of people you work with? He looks crazy to me. What is this? Crazy people working on crazy pills."

"There's nothing crazy about him. He's fine. Just some wife problems. I said he offered to pay me for helping him out. He's very bright."

"Bright doesn't eliminate crazy. How much he paying you?"

"Fifty dollars a month."

"What do you plan to do with it?"

"What?"

"The money. What else are we talking about?"

"Pay for his utilities, food, and wear and tear. And if you like—buy some new clothes for the kids."

The phone rang and I answered it. "Well, well, how are you, Buck? . . . Yeah, we're all fine . . . Is that so? . . . You're out in Arizona? When did you get there? . . . Oh, after you left here . . . You need some money? Is that so? Iola said you got a job in Richmond . . . You didn't . . . That's too bad . . . Maybe Iola can send you something . . . Do you want to talk with her? . . . Yeah, good talking to you too. Here's Iola." I handed the phone over and left to give Peter the sheets and blankets. The rain had stopped.

When I returned, Iola had hung up the phone. "I thought you said Buck got a job in Virginia."

"That's what he told me." Iola rubbed her neck.

"So he lied to you. He seemed like that. A liar. Why did he think you were angry with him?"

"I don't know."

"What did he say to you?"

"Not much. Mostly talked about having car trouble."

"He sounded drunk to me. Didn't he give up drinking?" Iola got a strange look, like maybe she didn't like what I said. Not wanting an argument, I said, "Peter and I will be going back to work now. Don't forget to set an extra plate." I walked outside looking forward to the ride back to work, the forty minutes or so Peter would be in the car. No interruptions. Just the two of us.

Peter was already sitting patiently in the car. He had a hint of a smile. I had a bigger hint. We looked at each other like we were both thinking romance but trying not to be obvious about it. The inches between us were more than scintillating. As soon as I pulled out of the driveway and onto the street, the air could have lit up. First we talked about the latest drugs on the market. It was the opposite of an icebreaker—it was a way to cool down the titillation—the way we talked.

"Drugs can improve your health."

"Everyone likes to be healthy."

"Who doesn't like to feel good?"

Both of us all smiles.

"Everyone needs to feel good but disappointments can get in the way."

Both of us taking a deep breath.

"That's true. Marriage is a disappointment."

"Isn't it."

"Are you happy?"

"Right now? Absolutely. You—now?"

"Absolutely."

"When at home?"

"No."

More simultaneous laughter. A touch on the arm. A touch on the hand.

"Except for the kids."

"Yeah, my oldest loves going to parades. Doesn't Philadelphia have a Mummers Parade or something like that?"

"We do. It's where men dress up as women."

I shared a brief history of the Mummers.

"Did you ever dress in women's clothes? I did once, when my wife was visiting her family in Boston and the kids were with her."

"What did you wear?" My curiosity mushroomed.

"Her panties, her garter belt and nylons. Her bra. I stuffed the cups. One of her dresses. It was like a costume. Getting all dressed up. Becoming something else. All these things women have to wear. They seem to like it."

"That they do."

"And the makeup. Eyelash curlers, hair curlers. Like every day is a crazy party. Once was enough."

"I never wore any of Iola's clothes but I put her makeup on one time. You know—lipstick and stuff. Just to see how it looked." The honesty was pure catharsis.

At Peter's suggestion, we took the long way to work. Back at the lab, we agreed to go for a drink after work and he said something that pleased me to no end. It was so special—something to always keep secret—just between the two of us.

IT WAS EIGHT p.m. when we got home.

"We had to work late. Thanks for saving dinner for us."

"You should have called me." Iola sounded like she was trying to control her annoyance.

"I should of." I kissed her on the cheek. "I'm sorry. We had so much work to do, I forgot."

Peter was even more apologetic, was humbly grateful for dinner, praised her cooking, and cleaned his plate. He retired to his apartment with his briefcase after washing and drying the dishes and wiping clean the kitchen table. I wanted to spend the night with him in a warm bed, the room dark and quiet, just us talking about life. Love.

Chapter 36

PETER MOVING IN, drunken Buck begging for money, me almost getting caught in a lie, and now Harry was three hours late to work, and no message from him. I hoped disaster wasn't looming. When Harry stepped into my office at noon, he had an expression I'd never seen before. He said we needed to talk. I must've had an awful expression as he suggested we both sit down. I noticed his hair was uncombed, and he had on the same khaki shirt he wore the day before. I feared I was about to be laid off work. I folded my arms against my chest to help deal with bad news.

Harry leaned back in his chair and said, "Dan just told me he'll be leaving in six months. I'll need a pilot to replace him. So I was thinking . . . you interested? It'd be the same he works—five to ten hours a week. And doing the usual— transporting cargo, taking people for plane rides. Occasionally flying some rich guy someplace, or ferrying someone's plane to another airport. You'd cut back on your other work, but knowing you, you'd do it anyway."

Did Harry say he needs a new pilot? Did I hear him right? I pressed my tongue against the roof of my mouth. I tried to talk, but my words evaporated.

"You okay?"

I unfolded my arms, and my worry suddenly turned into suspicious excitement. "Yes . . . that's right. I'm fine."

"Glad you're fine but are you interested in the job?"

I ran my hands through my hair. How should I answer a question with an obvious answer? Was he fooling me? Joking?

He looked at me with his eyebrows raised, and his hands upturned.

After restraining my excitement, I said, "Yes . . . You know once you fly it's always in your blood. You serious?"

"Yes."

"Where's Dan going?"

"Colorado."

"I was in Colorado—La Junta Army Air Field." I pressed my hands down my thighs to steady myself. "He's going back . . . in six months you say?"

"Six months. About one hundred eighty-three days. I know you no longer have your pilot's certification. You'll need to put in the hours to get it."

"I don't have the money for lessons."

"I'll give you free lessons, not that you need them. Would that mean yes?"

"You're making this awfully easy."

"Real awfully easy, so you can't say no."

I took a deep breath and said, "I have a neighbor, Norma. Norma predicted I'd get a job flying again. She made me promise . . . she made me prom, promise that if, if I did, I'd give her a plane ride. Would you let me do that? Give her, give her a plane ride?"

He nodded his head; I smiled—not full, still a bit fearful he was toying with me. I made a fist and placed it in my other hand to anchor myself. Then a gloriousness brightened, jumped and sang in a tiny space in my brain that had almost gotten too small for glorious things to jump and sing. The little gloriousness was like a Mexican jumping bean interrupting my speech. "Oh dear. Oh my. Never thought. Never thought it would happen. Geez." I didn't ask him why he was late to work.

Harry sat there smiling, saying, "Gee gee, geez." Then I did. We went back and forth like teenagers making fun of an anxious substitute teacher.

Harry said to be at work an hour earlier on Thursday. He knew I could fly a plane once it's in the air, but he'd never seen me take off or land. No doubt I still had the skills but he needed to be sure before giving me the job.

"Six o'clock? Five? Four?"

"I prefer six thirty. We'll see how you do. You don't have the job yet. But you do make the best secretary I've ever had."

All day I did my job—phone calls, typing, billing, talking to a potential customer about crop dusting, stuffing envelopes, sticking on stamps, ordering parts, throwing out trash, sweeping a clean floor, sweeping a cleaner floor until Harry ordered, "Take a rest. By God, you're driving me crazy." At the end of the day, when I rode home, I sang along with whoever was singing on the radio. I noticed a fence with a line of black crows taking a rest. They all flew off together in the same direction, giving shape to the wind. It was a good omen. Crows are smart. They know what they want.

As I drove, I thought to tell Jim I'd be flying again, but it wasn't set in stone. I'd wait. I'd tell him. Telling him would be the right thing to do. Maybe.

"Will you get a raise? Jim asked as we sat down for dinner.

"Good idea. You're so smart. I'll ask for one. If I get the job we could buy you a new car. Maybe take a vacation to Boston. You like Boston. The Boston harbor. Throwing the tea over. We could throw teabags in the water just for fun.

You know, dear, you look nice smiling. And maybe you could find some antique books up there. You're smiling more."

He said dinner was good. I got the kitchen cleaned; the kids behaved. A nice family evening. I went to bed with the little jumping joy bean still in my heart. It took me two hours to fall asleep.

THURSDAY, I GOT to work one minute early, hoping I didn't look overenthusiastic. Harry and I checked the winds, the dew point, turbulence, and any chance of thunderstorms within the next few hours. Calm and sunny was the forecast. We had a cup of coffee and some pastries. He knew I liked them. I hardly remembered what we talked about, something about local politics, maybe something about the mayor, then I told Harry he had powdered sugar on his lips. He licked his lips. I noticed his pink wet tongue.

He said, "Time for a flight," and so we went outside, and he watched me do a preflight. I started in the cockpit making sure all the paperwork was in order and my instruments read properly. I checked there was sufficient oil and fuel. I made sure there was no smell of fuel, which could indicate a leak. That there was no smell of kerosene. I ran the controls to check they were working properly. Then it was check the seat-rails, the fire extinguisher, and windshield. I got out of the plane and checked the empennage for signs of fuel leakage, working rivets, skin wrinkling, soot or oil, the doors not closing well, antennas missing. With the same level of thoroughness, the wings, the landing gear, the tail assembly, the cowling and nose were all checked.

"You remembered everything a preflight should entail. I'm impressed," Harry said.

I didn't tell him I had reviewed a book and some notes I had saved from when I was in the WASP. We climbed into the cockpit.

Harry smiled and touched my elbow. "We're going to have an excellent day."

"Umm. Have you ever been anxious, hopeful, and happy all to the same degree at the same time?"

"You'll do fine."

I taxied to the runway and up to the hold short line. After making sure no one was coming in any direction, I announced on the radio that we were departing. I pushed forward on the throttle to full speed down the runway, and the plane was airborne. There was just the sound of the plane's engine. The controls looked perfect, the view looked perfect. My hands were in control of the plane. Just the plane and me. While briefly closing my eyes, I took a deep breath. Harry took a deep breath. Maybe it was his eyes, or his lips slightly open, or the silence that was like a striptease artist getting excitement going. "How'd I do?"

"You know you did excellent." Then as he pointed out a few details worth noting about the instrument panel, his hand, in passing, gently rubbed against my arm for longer than needed.

He had nice hands—long fingers like mine. He was a slightly odd-looking man with a tan face, like he spent a lot of his life working outdoors. A pleasant sensation coursed up my abdomen.

We talked about dangerous flying conditions, birds flying into engines and causing accidents, about long flights. I said I'd love to circle the globe, landing only to get refueled and have a little break.

"You're ambitious. I like that. Iola O—another Amelia Earhart. You must've been an excellent pilot when you were in the WASP."

"I like being called Iola O, but not when anyone else is around."

"It's our secret."

"That's right."

"What else can I call you? In secret."

"What do you want to call me?"

"You really want to know?"

"Maybe not." I looked out the window. Would I beg if told I didn't get the job? Begging wasn't my strength. "Thanks for the compliment. I do my best." I checked the controls.

"I have more compliments waiting for you."

I loved his flirtation but didn't say. "I enjoyed working in the WASP. Then the government did away with the program. They said we weren't needed anymore. The war was winding down and there was less need for fighter or bomber pilots. So the excess male pilots took our jobs. I never worked harder in my life. I was so angry when General Arnold deactivated the WASP I could've killed him."

"You actually thought about killing him?"

"For about thirty seconds. Maybe a minute. Maybe two."

He laughed. "Twenty?"

"Two. I thought I'd shoot him with a stolen gun. Whose—I had no idea. At night, a moonless cold night—three in the morning. Then I figured I wouldn't get away with it. Plus it wouldn't have changed anything and where would I be?" I shrugged.

"For real?" Harry almost had an unseemly grin.

"Oh, not really. I'm being dramatic. You know what stopped me. I shouldn't tell you." I tried to read his face for any sign that he might think poorly of me, but he just had those friendly eyes again and his lips slightly open.

"Now that you've intrigued me, you have to tell. But if you don't want to, that's okay." He touched my hand. I kept my hand in his touch. "How many secrets do we have?" he asked.

"They seem to be growing."

"I only know two."

"So, you want to know why I didn't kill Arnold? It was knowing my mother would jam her finger in my face and say, I knew you'd bring us shame."

"Were you least favored?"

I took back my hand.

"My brothers were favored over me for as long as I can remember," Harry said.

"Would've made a bad name for myself. Anyhow, I wouldn't have done it. It was only an angry thought." I feared I'd said too much, but somehow didn't care. Talking was good. "They should've never dissolved us. We did a great job. There were just over a thousand of us. To this day most people don't know we even existed."

"Afterward, did you ever try to get a job as a pilot?"

"No one would hire a woman. A man laughed when I had applied for a pilot's job. It took me several months to get over it. Still bugs me sometimes."

"You loved doing something that few people even knew about. Like being a hero, risking your life and no one knows it."

"There're lots of unrecognized heroes."

"Excuse the question, but what did you do?"

"We transported planes, tested them, towed targets, tracked weather. I mostly transported, and towed targets for gunner trainees to practice shooting at. A novice gunner hit my plane once. I feared he was going to shoot my plane down. It was the best job I ever had. Not that I don't like working for you."

"What about piloting for me?"

"It'd be better than the WASP except the planes would be smaller. But my boss would be . . . nicer."

"Is he? What if he turns mean?"

"He won't." I hadn't meant to whisper. Did he think I was flirting? I looked away, then back at Harry. Just those eyes and a smile. "I really did like helping with the war effort." No more whispering. "Sometimes I wished they would've let me be a bomber pilot. But then maybe I wouldn't have liked it." I laid my head on the seat back. "Did you ever drop bombs?"

"Never."

"Well, I thought I would've if I was ordered. Did you know the Russians had female bomber pilots during the war? They were good. The Germans called them Night Witches."

"I heard about them."

"But then . . . maybe I would've been intimidated. I suppose it's different when you see a bomb exploding in a city and knowing you've just killed hundreds of people. I once thought I would've dropped the atom bomb on Hiroshima, if asked. One bomb and a whole city was gone. Another one and Japan was on its knees." I then recalled Zeke being murdered, and how I had buried my feelings. I looked out the window, as if there was an answer flying alongside the plane, waiting to be called upon. I knew the answer. Too much pain.

"Why were you so driven?"

"Don't know. But it tired me out. At one point, after the WASP were dissolved, I just gave up and decided I should get married."

"I like a woman who admits to feelings of violence. We all have them."

"How many people have you wanted to kill?"

"Thousands." His voice sounded like a jokester's, his eyes looked like a friend's. "How many planes did you fly?"

"Not enough. Anyway, if men can be bomber pilots, why can't a woman? It doesn't take much muscle to pull a lever. But then . . . I'm glad I wasn't. So much killing. I think it would've gotten to me. It got to some soldiers. They came back with blank stares that never stopped. Combat neurosis. War-crazy. Honestly, hearing myself talk . . . I wouldn't have made it as a bomber pilot. It's cuckoo thinking." I felt perplexed, sighed. He sat there quietly like he was waiting for me to continue. "Honestly, I think I became a pilot just to prove I was somebody. I've worked for you for how many months and we're just now talking about all this. Didn't you wonder before about all the things I did when I was in the WASP?"

"Mostly, I was taking your lead. I also needed to protect myself."

"From what?"

"From you. You're married and if I started talking with you about everything you did in the WASP, I'd be dying to take you out on a date."

"How long have you been in this line of work?"

"You changed the topic but change is good. Twenty years, to answer your question. Ten years flying supplies for a company. That's what got me into the business. I'd like to see how you handle some of my other planes. At least one more. We'll go up again in a week. Tomorrow I'll be leaving on a trip for five days. I'd like to teach you the business so when I'm gone, I can depend on you." He leaned toward me.

Being almost speechless, "Thanks" was all I could manage, but I knew what had happened, and what had to happen. There were rules that needed following, and so I set about repressing fantasies, and sensations as I sat in the pilot seat. Several inches of space separated us. He could've touched me, if I asked. Kissed my neck. Smelled my hair. He could've leaned over and so could I. I'd have no resistance if he asked me to his bed and I wouldn't be able to stop something falling into place that I wanted to fall into place.

When I landed the plane, the wheels touched down the same time the stall warning horn sounded.

"You landed the plane perfectly. Impressive."

"More likely it was good luck."

After we got back in the office, nothing happened. I wasn't sure what to do next, still grappling with words like *adultery* and *scandal*. Not wanting to take the first step that had already been taken. Maybe we were savoring the moment where words don't add much. Something we could remember in our bones years from now. *Remember when. Yes, wasn't that so? We were so hesitant.*

He lit up a cigarette and offered me one, even though he knew I'd given up the habit.

"They say it causes cancer."

He put it out and said, "Wouldn't want to get cancer now that good things are coming my way."

I didn't ask him what that might be because I wasn't quite ready and anyway it was obvious. "Tell me something about your childhood."

"Anything?"

"Anything."

"My younger brother divorced his first wife and married an Englishwoman. It was the scandal of the town."

"Doesn't surprise me you chose that topic."

"You don't like it?"

"Are they still married?"

"Still are and still in love. I see them once every five years when I take a trip to England. My brother seems to like it there. The king of England abdicated his throne so he could marry a divorced woman—an American. I forgot her name."

"Simpson—her last name. Quite a scandal. Where did you grow up?"

"Umm, topic change. Nortontown, Pennsylvania. A blue-collar town. They'd help you, even if they never laid eyes on you before. If your car broke down they'd stop to help get you on your way."

"So you had a great childhood?"

"Not bad. First thing that comes to mind. The father of a high school friend of mine beat his wife. My friend finally got tired of seeing his mother beaten and he punched him hard. He wanted to kill him. He hated him. They arrested him for hitting his father. His mother got him out of jail. But after that, his father didn't beat her anymore."

"My neighbor gets beaten by her husband. She wants to be a fortune-teller and she predicted that I'll be flying again."

"That's easy to predict. And your childhood?" Harry asked.

"Poor. We mostly talked about the weather, planting crops, hunting, making pawpaw jam, Jesus, keeping outsiders out, death, food, ways to cook wild meat."

"Who died?"

"A few siblings. A family in a fire. Old people. Newborns." *My brother was murdered but I can't and don't want to talk about that.*

"Any fights?"

"When there was too much moonshine, too much rotgut. Awful stuff." I made a squeamish face.

"You know what I liked about you when I first met you? It didn't seem that life was cut and dried for you. My sisters don't have that. They still live in Nortontown. Happy as married clams, raising baby clams. Except for the one who's a nun. No complaints I've heard."

"Maybe they're too afraid to express them."

"Nope. They like their beliefs. They know what they have to do. It's all laid out. Auntie, who went off to Europe and lived with a man, makes no sense to them, likes she's from another planet."

"Oh, I could tell you stories."

"I'm listening."

"My family would not help you if they never saw you before. They ordered strangers to get out of town. There's a name for it—xenophobia. That was Pilgrim. A sickness. Small-plot farming. A few stores. A church, a school. The county sheriff came by once in a while. Fear of the outside world. It took some time for me to recognize it. I believe . . . it seems that's why my family had little to do with me when I took flying lessons and especially after I became a WASP. What I loved, they hated—that is that their sister, their daughter was in the military. I was grown but not married. I was only in a paramilitary outfit, but paramilitary was military, they insisted. Except my brother Buck and sister Maude—they never cared. She went to Hollywood. I haven't heard from her."

"The others stay?"

"Most of them live in or near Pilgrim, except for a sister who married a doctor and moved to the city. They're okay with that because the doctor bought some land for two of my brothers. I heard they put on a party for him. They roasted deer, cooked their best dishes, and hired a fiddler to entertain."

"What inspired you to leave?"

"A plane ride. I realized there was more to the world."

Harry then looked at his calendar and he scheduled the next flight for me in a week. He said when he got back from his trip he'd start teaching me more of the business.

On my way home, I couldn't help myself. I imagined spending years with Harry. Maybe Buck wanted to spend years with the woman he was having crazy sex with on top of his bed. Maybe the two of them were planning to get married, like he claimed. Maybe I'd been too mean that day. I softened and forgave Buck for falling off the wagon. That was what really had angered me. I forgave the sexy-looking woman. Then a feeling came over me that I didn't know what to do with—that I half enjoyed seeing two naked people having sex. I didn't remember feeling that way at the time.

Chapter 37

I WAS AT the airport one minute early. I crossed and uncrossed my legs, shook my foot and fiddled with my pencils. Harry hadn't arrived. Had he changed his mind? Thirty minutes passed. I didn't mean to slam the file cabinet drawer shut. I sharpened a pencil and then broke the point. And did it again. Fiddled with more stuff. Opened my desk and put things in order. Waited. Waited. Sixty minutes passed. Had he found another person for the job? Tricked me? Was I going to lose again? Loser. Don't think that. Loser. Stop it. I wiped up the coffee I spilled on my desk. Soon, I came down with a headache.

Harry walked into the office three hours late.

Modulating the worry out of my voice, I asked if he might've forgotten what was on the schedule. He asked if I had gotten his message about postponing the second flight. My anxiety worsened, but then he explained his trip had complications. "Tomorrow," he said. "Sorry, but after dealing with hot, humid weather, poor sleep, and food poisoning in Florida, I'm tired and there's other stuff I must do."

I sensed he had no desire to hear any whining, and it was good he was back. I had missed him, but had signed up two new students (one old, one young), scheduled three cargo transports, and arranged for someone to hanger his plane at the airport, and the man said he'd tell his friends about us. I would tell Harry during the next flight.

THE NEXT DAY—it seemed like a week—we (I, in the pilot's seat) were moving down the runway. Then the plane was airborne. At three thousand feet, Harry said, "You've got the job, Iola O, as if you didn't know. You just need to put in the hours to get your certification."

A string of thank-yous followed and the first words of sentences I was too excited to complete. I looked out the window. A creek snaked through fields, and the land lay flawless under the early light. The sky was a rich morning blue. A small hill, illuminated here and there with oblique sunlight, was covered with a blanket of yellow flowers. More hills undulated as if they had been moving like the ocean and then frozen still.

"Do I really have the job?"

"If you keep asking I'll take it away."

"Well then—it's mine. Holy sweet Moses. Norma was right. I owe her two flights. She wants it at sunset. You've flown at sunset?"

"They last longer when you're flying west. I think time slows a bit when you're flying. Isn't that what Einstein said? The faster you go, time slows. Go as fast as the speed of light and you get there before you leave."

"Too fast for me." I touched my chest with the tips of my fingers.

"You like the trip more than getting there?"

"Both do me fine."

"Me too." Harry touched his chest the same way I did, but slower. It was like he was saying he wanted to touch me.

"A plane flight might break up Norma's marriage. Might give her ideas. Dump her husband for beating her. My first plane flight gave me ideas—not to let Pilgrim beat me. People need ideas. One idea can change your whole life."

"You know what impresses me?" He touched his chest again. "You."

"Remember the day we met?"

"Sure do. Your white blouse, what you did with your left hand, and where you were standing, what you said." He leaned over and I knew he was going to kiss me and I'd be entering a whole different world.

"Love you." He sat back in his seat after the kiss.

Just silence.

"When did you first love me?"

"When I graduated from high school."

"You're crazy. You didn't know me then."

"But I knew what I wanted then. My oldest brother was a pilot and one time he met Amelia Earhart. At least he said he did."

"Your brother knew her. What did he say about her?"

"He said Miss Earhart said, 'One day, your younger brother Harry is going to meet Iola O who will be a better pilot than him. She's going to take Harry's breath away and he's going to fall in love with her.'"

"She said that?"

"She did and she said, 'Your younger brother will love Iola O's voice.'"

"And what else, did she say?"

"I know what you're thinking. You want to know if she told him his younger brother was going to share his bed with Iola O."

"Did she?"

He grinned. "Actually, she didn't but I'm wondering if it's going to happen."

"What do you think?"

"I'm hoping. What are you thinking about now?"

"How nice it'd be to have some soup. Norma makes good tomato soup."

"You're not thinking that. But I'm okay with you telling a lie because your smile is telling the truth. Would you bring some of her tomato soup to work tomorrow?"

"I can do that."

"Do you want to eat her soup with just me or with everyone who works here?"

"Just you."

"Can't wait."

WHEN I LANDED the plane, the wheels touched down the same time the stall warning horn sounded.

"God damn. Second time in a row, you landed the plane perfectly. That's not luck. That's knowing what you're doing." Harry's eyes had that sweet look deserving reciprocation.

He had an appointment with a student for flying lessons. I had hoped for a cancelation but the student arrived early and was talkative, excited, and full of praise. I took care of the office while Harry gave the lesson. We waited until the student and the mechanic went home and we walked into his well-dusted office. We had made love months before—in my thoughts.

I closed the curtains and he shut the door. I'd often heard the metallic click before, but now it elicited a kiss and the touch of his hand around my waist. I slipped my wedding band off. He put it on a table. I unbuttoned his wrinkled shirt. He unzipped the back of my plain cotton dress. It fell to the floor. I unzipped his pants. He unfastened my bra and slipped my nylon stockings and panties down to my feet. He touched my toes; he laid my panties and stockings on a chair. When he pulled down the covers on his daybed, a love was laid open. The second Garden of Eden. The sheets had embroidered edges. Pillows were goose down. They felt brand-new. Ten minutes, thirty, was it an hour, or a day? Silence enhanced the talk of touch and those other sounds.

When we were done—happy, carefree, perfect, flawless—he got up and pulled a scarf out of a drawer. He claimed it belonged to Amelia Earhart. She had left it in an office and his brother found it and had meant to return it to her, but then she disappeared over the Pacific two weeks later.

"How did you get it?"

"He didn't want it, so I took it and now I'm giving it to you."

I got up and put it around my neck. It was silky and it draped down the middle of me.

He must've loved the way I looked for he said, "Oh my. A naked woman in love. Oh my."

While getting dressed, we talked about nudity. Martinis and Oreos when sitting back in my office. We ended up talking about airports. Then I told him about all the business I had done the five days he was gone.

"Doesn't surprise me," he said. As we were closing up for the day, he said, "Don't forget to put your wedding band back on before you leave."

Driving home, I hummed the whole way—barely audible sounds vibrating my throat, then long breaths. I liked the stoplights because I could have a little extra time to savor the reverberations.

By the time I walked into my home on Oak Tree Road, I knew I would always dress like a secretary going to the office, always coming and going on schedule seven thirty to two thirty, ho-hum, a doldrum day, glad I'm home. How's everyone? Jim, did you have a good day? Same kind of white cotton underwear, same work dresses, same work shoes, no earrings, and no lipstick and keep the wedding band always on, so I'd never forget it. I planned on some days I would complain to Jim that work was getting monotonous. My few gray hairs would remain gray. Nothing would cause suspicion, especially to those who might notice a brighter smile, a fancier step. Yes, I knew how to keep a secret since I was a girl and saw my uncle murder Zeke. I had learned to act like nothing had ever happened, how to walk across the crime scene and smile against my fears.

But secrets have a heaviness. What if I tired of the constraints and slipped up one day? Left unintended clues? Gave myself away and a scandal tightened around me? Would I welcome the scandal and walk right through it to the other side in spite of the consequences? What if on the other side Harry changed and became someone I didn't recognize? What if he then dumped me and I'd lose everything? I decided to put those questions off for a while. Six months later would be fine to reconsider. For now I would do what was needed to keep love hidden.

HARRY LIKED TEASING me. Sometimes, when a customer turned and faced the opposite direction, Harry touched my butt—one brief pat. Still, it angered me. I threatened to quit. He knew I wouldn't but he acquiesced. One day he gave me a pair of panties. They were pink silk with lots of lace. I'd never owned fancy panties. They were seduction panties, not drawers or underwear. They were meant to heighten love and make me look like a goddess. It was a temptation to slip them on, but I gave them back because I knew the rules of keeping secrets.

"But you can wear them here just for me."

"I said I want no evidence around."

ONE DAY THE mechanic was sick and a student cancelled. We had a whole long hour together. We talked about anything but business. We talked gossip, slang, fun words. The fun words got us to using some dirty words, but they didn't sound dirty to me, not the way Harry said them. The dirty words got us all romantic. We went into his back office, undressed, and laid down on the daybed and joined together.

Afterward, I said, "I wish I knew you way back, before I got married."

"Love is there for those with courage, Iola O. The king of England abdicated his throne for Wallis Simpson. It was a huge scandal in England. And then there was Ingrid Bergman and Roberto Rossellini—what an uproar—both married . . . to other people. My auntie said, 'The world loves a scandal.'"

"Your auntie's probably right. There was a rumor Eisenhower had an affair with his driver. He didn't look the type."

"Poor Mamie. Think she knew?"

"No. Eisenhower would've known how to keep it secret from poor Mamie."

"Charlie Chaplin was divorced three times. The fourth marriage seems to be lasting," Harry said.

"Didn't he marry a young girl?"

"Oona O'Neil. Eighteen years old. Daughter of Eugene O'Neil. Apparently Eugene didn't like him." Suddenly Harry said, "I want to marry you."

"But I'm already married."

"But you're very innovative. Innovative women get divorced."

"I rubbed my hands together, my thoughts and feelings all jumbled. Finally I said, "Give me a year to think about it."

"A year? Such a long time."

"You can do it, dear."

Later, I called home. "Hi, Charles, I love you. Tell your sisters I love them. I'll be home to cook dinner."

"You feel guilty?" Harry asked.

"Somewhat. Maybe. I do."

"We can stop if you want. You'll still have the job."

"I don't want to stop."

"That makes me very happy."

"I'm glad. First time I was very happy was the day I left Pilgrim. It was a risk to leave—being an unmarried girl, but at the time I didn't see it that way."

"You're drawn to risks. Learning to fly. Being in the WASP."

"Not reckless ones."

"Might you be interested in another risk?"

"Depends." I was curious.

"Parachuting?"

"From flying a plane to jumping out of one. You serious? And who does it other than the military?"

"It's become a sport. Think about it awhile. No rush. Let's kiss."

"You're lovely, dear. Kiss me again. You do it so well."

A MONTH LATER, when only Harry and I were in the office, Harry picked up my skirt with his foot, exposing my underpants. "Pretty legs, pretty butt. So sweet."

I spun around, and pointed my finger at him. "Don't ever do that again."

"Sorry . . . but your legs are beautiful. And no one else is here." He looked innocent, but guilty, confused—like a child.

I caught myself before I exploded. I stopped the finger pointing and held back the cursing. "Sorry, I didn't mean to raise my voice. I did, didn't I?"

"You did, but not a big thing. I'm sorry."

He didn't cause my reaction. My mama had. The Pilgrim memories flooded back—I was sixteen. My mama said to a neighbor woman whose mother had just died, "Sorry about your mama. Was a God-fearing woman. If you a giving things away, my Iola need some clothing. She not one to keep stuff in good shape. I'll take the drawers for her. Thank you."

Mama took all of my underwear and burned them. She said to me, "Child, you got way too much pride. Here's a cure. You wear these." And she handed me the dead woman's old yellowed drawers. Next day, Mama lifted up my skirt to check I had them on, right in front of my whole family. Being that time of the month, there was blood on them.

I needed to say something bad about Pilgrim but not the embarrassing underwear story. An emotion welled up. Suddenly I talked about Zeke who Uncle Edgar had killed with a 12-gauge shotgun. He shot him from the side—five feet away. His nose and lips were gone. Part of his jaw was hanging off. Blood was coming out of his ear and his neck. It was everywhere. He moved his hand before he died with eyes open, trying his best to stay alive. Two white chickens got splattered with blood. The men buried the body. No one ever talked about it other than my uncle whistling sometimes when he walked over the ground where Zeke had died. Sundays and Wednesdays, he went to church. He was good at the public confessions especially about being drunk too much, but never about the murder. It was ugly.

I took my time telling the story. Every detail I could remember, I described. Why Zeke was shot. How my mother slapped me hard across my face, squeezed my arm real tight, making me scream, and threatened that something bad would happen to me if I ever told. How she ordered me to repeat her words, but terror turned me mute. How a second terror—Sledge Jr. slapping my face, saying, "You do what Mama said." That gave my voice back but it wasn't my voice. It came from some place afar, like an echo without a source.

I described the weather, the flowers in bloom, the clear blue sky, other people present, me being so scared I peed in my underpants. Ethyl Lou saying Zeke was now burning in hell. His body being dumped in Uncle Edgar's new cesspool that had just been dug. Two bags of lime that were thrown on top of his body. Me doing everything I was ordered to that day. That week. That month. Saying very little except for my yes ma'ams. At the supper table, how I waited silently until some dish was passed down to me. With no appetite, I was the last to clean my plate.

Harry listened to every word, every pause, asked a question here and there.

A weight lifted. Why had it taken me so long? Why? What a waste of worry for so many years. Fatigue overcame me, and I wanted to sleep.

Jim

Chapter 38

SINCE PETER HAD gone for a long walk, I opened the door to his apartment and peaked in. He expected to leave in a month or so, and I could then turn his place into my study. It would be good to have all of my books in one place. What if he didn't leave? What if we told Iola to leave? But where would she go? In ancient Greece, Peter and I could have lived together. But Willowsburg? No, we had to be careful or we'd be arrested. Imprisoned. Beaten in prison. We were always very careful.

Everything was neat and it was definitely large enough for my needs. Several people told me, with my knowledge of history, I should write a book. A desk and reading lamp would be needed. A picture of George Washington to hang above the desk, for inspiration. My typewriter was gathering dust. One whole wall could be turned into a large bookcase. I made a mental list of the materials I would need—plank lumber for the shelves, a file cabinet, notebooks, typewriter ribbons. The usual.

And what topics to write about? I hadn't done much with my Tornado Preacher story for children. Maybe I could compile all the letters I could find that were written by Civil War soldiers. I'd prefer writing about the Revolutionary War. Maybe I could compile examples of all the colonists' complaints against the English that were listed in the Declaration of Independence. A research trip to Boston and Washington, DC, or New York City would be needed. Maybe Peter could get away and meet me there. We could rent a hotel room and share a bed all night.

I closed the door as Lizzy walked into the garage, wanting something to do.

"Would you like to take a trip?" I asked.

"Irene took me on a trip."

"Where did she take you?"

"She took Starla and me down the street, to a footpath. One day we saw Mr. Peter walking. I like him."

"Isn't he nice?"

"When we got to a big tree, we sat down in the dirt by yellow flowers. Irene said, 'Yellow flowers smell like honeybees.' And then we stuck our noses in them. Starla agreed with Irene. I said, 'Pooh.'"

"I'd say pooh too."

"Not pootoo. Pooh."

"I stand corrected."

"I want to take a walk."

"Where to?"

"Down the street. I'll show you where the pooh flowers are."

"Good idea. Let's walk. Mr. Peter is taking a walk. Maybe we'll see him."

"Irene made up a game with rocks she found on the ground." Lizzy took hold of my hand. "They had lines going through them. And then she gave one to Starla, and me. And then Irene said the lines meant there was mystery in the rocks and we had to figure out the mystery. Then she said her rock came from a witch's house."

"Where was the witch's house?"

"Don't know."

"We don't need to know that."

"She said if she follows the lines on her rock with her fingers, it gives her magic powers but only on Monday and it wasn't Monday, so she couldn't show us the magic. And then Starla said her rock was from the moon because it had a round white spot on it, and she'll bring it to Mrs. Norma next door. Mrs. Norma can see the future, and Starla hoped maybe she'd say Mr. Peter will leave. Starla doesn't like him. I do. He let me sit on his lap. He said you can get polio from creek water and you'll live the rest of your life in an iron lung. Mama says he looks crazy."

"He's real smart and a real gentleman."

"Daddy's always right." She skipped ahead and then skipped back, in and out of the sunlight shining through the tree branches overhead. It would have made a lovely photograph. My temptation to skip surprised me, but I only managed two quicker steps. I didn't remember ever skipping as a child. It's probably just something girls do.

"What was your rock's mystery?"

"Don't know. I didn't like that game."

"You don't have to play it."

"Starla found a shiny green beetle. And then Irene put it on her blouse like it was jewelry, but it flew away. Then I found a bright blue flower. Irene said her father buys flowers for her mother after he hits her. And then Starla said little blue flowers can turn into a flying carpet if you say *mumbo jumbo* a hundred times on Monday."

"Did you say mumbo jumbo?"

"It wasn't Monday. Irene said she convinced Joey Miller to eat some leaves so he'd turn into a giant. He fell for it. Then we laughed because he never became a giant."

"That's not nice."

"I'm nice to Daddy. Irene said her teacher is a witch. She knows everything."

"No one knows everything."

"You do. She promised she'll show us how to put lipstick on. And then she said she was going to become a cowboy when she grows up and she'll wear red lipstick. She said she once put a little round ball of snot on her teacher's chair."

"What would you like to do now?" I asked.

"Be with you."

I whistled a tune. My father had whistled.

"I want to learn to whistle."

I tried to teach her. Hers was more of a high-pitched breath blown through a curled tongue, but she was pleased.

"Now don't whistle in front of Mommy, she won't like it. She says whistling's cheap."

"Why?"

"Don't know, honey. But she says it gives her the willies. Are you good at keeping a secret? How about we whistle only when she's not around."

"Mommy said it's good to have secrets."

"She did?"

"Yep."

"Does Mommy have a secret?"

"She don't tell. I ask."

"You ask her again. You tell me."

"Someone calls her every Monday. She don't tell who calls."

"Who do you think it is?"

"Don't know."

"When does she get the call?"

"Around lunchtime."

"Always?"

"Mostly."

"How long does she talk?"

"Long time."

"Does she ever laugh those times?"

"Sometimes she giggles."

I wondered if Iola was cheating on me. Was it Harry? So long as she didn't file for divorce. She was my family, my respectability. I wasn't going to lose my kids, lose Lizzy, my perfect girl. I'd kill Iola before I let that happen. How do you kill? I had never considered murder. What if I got caught? Then what? Awful thoughts. I took a hold of Lizzy's hand.

"I like having a secret with Daddy. One time Charles and I were near the pond and he said he saw someone moving in the trees and it was a murderer trying to catch us. I screamed and ran all the way home. When I got home, I told Mama, 'Murderer trying to catch us. Charles saw him.' 'Where is he?' she asked. Then I said, 'By the pond.' And then Mama picked up a knife and ran to the pond. She came home with Charles. He said it was a deer. Then he said he tried to tell me but I didn't hear him because I was screaming so loud."

"She never told me that."

"Mama likes secrets. She said I can't tell you she told Uncle Buck he had to leave because she found him with a lady in his apartment."

"I'll never let her know you told me." When we got back to the house, I took her picture and said, "Lizzy, honey, the older you get, the more you look like my sister Elizabeth when she was your age." I wanted to believe in reincarnation so I could have my sister back with me. I bent over, kissed her head, and enjoyed her scent. For a moment, she erased my failure to go to college, to fight in the war, to marry someone I loved, to have a job worthy of my intellect, to share more of my life with Peter.

Chapter 39

PETER AND I were alone in the lab except for the secretary out in the front office. Gray-haired Miss Sally—she liked being called that—had worked there for decades. She knew where everything was—under what pile, in what drawer, on what dusty shelf. Nothing seemed to rattle her, even when a previous boss threw papers at her and threatened to fire her. She just picked up the papers, filed them, and went back to typing—so the story goes. It was good she was petite because she had to work in a small space.

She would be leaving early for the day. The thirty minutes she took to finish her phone conversation and clean up her desk seemed to take forever.

Peter was checking the data, making notes about our apparent success of the final trial of the new drug. His back was to me. His white shirt was wrinkled, almost like he had slept in it, his shoes unpolished. Being well groomed was not his strength. He was sitting by the infrared spectrophotometer, near the window in the lab. It was good there was only one small window in the back lab—better privacy in case we could sneak in some intimacy after Miss Sally left. On the desk, Peter had a stack of files on some of the three hundred volunteers for the drug trial. Thirty-four percent had improved with the new drug, with few side effects. Amazingly good results. Peter had questioned if it was too good. That was why he was checking data. He was such a competent researcher. I was proud to work with him, to be a part of the project.

I enjoyed sitting behind him, watching. God he was handsome. How many times had I admired him? His backside, his shoulders, slim hips, long legs, his oval eyes, fingers, ring finger. I should buy him a ring to wear. I'd slip it on his finger. Usually I didn't like a ski-jump nose; I liked his. Can I say love? I was almost beside myself when Miss Sally finally opened the door at two p.m. and said she was leaving for the day. "See you tomorrow."

"Yeah, you have a good evening, Miss Sally."

"Oh, I always do."

"You're a sweetheart."

"Now don't flirt."

"I always like flirting with you, Miss Sally."

She smiled and closed the door.

Was this going to be the sixth time Peter and I had sex? The first time in the hotel, when Peter undressed, he had holes in his socks. I gave him some new ones the next day. Peter made jokes about the socks. "Umm, what do I put in here?" Like it was a penis warmer. "Am I that big?" It was funny the way he had said it. The other times, it was in the lab—late in the evening, in the back corner behind the four file cabinets, and the front door locked. We were careful that no one unexpected came upon us. Pants could be zipped up quick if a noise was heard. We had pulled out two drawers of the file cabinets in case we needed to look like we were both hard at work, looking for a file on something.

Peter stretched his head far to the right, to the left. He pulled his arms back over his head—probably getting rid of muscle tension from working so hard. The dedicated man could work for hours. Suddenly he turned around. Had he known I was admiring every inch of him? He wasn't smiling. In fact, he looked bothered. Was the data wrong? Had he caught an error? I would've hated making a mistake around Peter.

"Is there a problem with the data?" I asked.

"Yes and no. There is a problem . . . but not with the data. I guess."

A problem. There can't be. And what does "I guess" mean?

He took a deep breath. "Jim, I have to tell you something."

I thought—Oh, he's going to do one of his jokes. Maybe a pun. Sometimes he's so corny, maybe because he grew up on a farm.

Peter paused, touched his mouth, then grasped his hands together, folded his shoulders in. "I just got another job offer. It's near my wife's family. I'm sorry. We can still see each other but not as often. It's in Boston."

Boston? I said nothing.

Peter looked up at the ceiling, looked at me, and opened his mouth as if to speak. He ran his hand through his hair. He was young to be going bald—a perfectly round bald spot on the top of his head that I once kissed. Did Einstein ever go bald? Did Antoine Lavoisier? Or Thomas Graham? Or Pierre Curie? Why did baldness matter? Scientists can't go bald? That makes no sense. I was trying to find something to say. Why was I having a hard time talking? I had been hit hard.

"I'm very sorry. It pays more."

"Oh." I closed my eyes. "Yes, I can see you feel bad. I suppose it's time that we separate . . . Things being what they are. You do what you have to do." My voice flattened so much, I noticed. "You know. How else can one live?" My eyes were still closed because I found it easier to talk if I didn't see Peter.

"Maybe we could see each other in New York. Say we're on business."

If Miss Sally came back into the lab, the awful discussion would end but she had gone home early. My eyes were still closed.

Peter kept talking about his new job—being the director of research. It was hard to listen to. Then he said, "I have some good news. I talked to the boss and suggested you take over supervision of the department. But don't tell him I told you. I think he wants it to be his idea. You worked hard on this project."

"His idea?"

"That he's promoting you. He'll tell you."

"That's great. Some good news." I opened my eyes, pressed my closed fist against my mouth, and nodded my head. Good news? I rocked myself like a little child, but it must've looked dumb, so I stopped. "When will you be leaving?"

"Two weeks."

Did he say two weeks? Did he say his wife's family live in Boston? I thought they were having problems. "Well, Peter, what can I say?"

"Yeah, it's a change. I'll miss you."

"Right. Same here." I didn't ask how something so perfect could fall apart so quickly. Only a few months, not even a year.

No sex was had. I said no when he asked. Not even a kiss. He went back to work. I couldn't do a thing I was so nonplussed. I pretended to read. Sometime later, my boss called and asked me to come to his office. He told me he was offering me a promotion. It took effort to show some enthusiasm. I thanked him and shook his hand.

THAT EVENING, I didn't say much at dinner. Peter ate quickly and excused himself, saying he had some things he had to read. He took his dish to the sink, washed it, and left. Just as I pushed my chair back from the table, Lizzy said, "Daddy looks upset."

"Are you upset, Daddy?" Starla asked.

"No, girls. Just tired. Actually I have good news. How about that. Just before I left work, the boss asked me to come to his office."

Iola looked up—her doubtful eyes on me.

"He was pleased with how I helped on the new drug development. He said I helped solve the problem we were having in our research. Seems like we got the results we wanted. So he said he was giving me a promotion when a position comes up soon. It's mine if I want it. See how it worked out. I'm getting a promotion. It worked out. I knew it would." I tried to smile.

"That's great. It worked out." Iola wrinkled her forehead and carried dishes to the sink.

"You don't seem very happy. You're not pleased?"

"I'm happy. I'm just tired."

I went in the front room and sat down with a book but didn't open it. Was Peter reading now? What was he doing? Will he miss me? I was thankful no one discovered the affair. It would've been a scandal. Think of the repercussions—a ruined life. Even going to prison. Homosexuals get raped in prison and the guards sit by and do nothing. Might even watch and laugh. Probably beat them any chance they get. Too horrible to think about. I opened the book and read a sentence but didn't remember a word. A stupid book. I forgot the title. My life was stupid. Peter, I love you. The man didn't deserve me—what with him moving out of my life. Telling me the way he did. At work. In the lab—so impersonal. That's Peter for you.

What's tomorrow going to bring? What will I say to Peter in the morning on the way to work? Talk about data? The age differences of the volunteers? About Boston? Maybe have lunch with Miss Sally by her desk. She's always polite with her creaky old voice. Bet her three grandnieces love her. There's a picture of them on her desk. Act like nothing happened. Just work. What is tomorrow? Thursday. Week is almost over. Glad of that. I read a page of the book. I forgot what I had read and looked at my watch.

In bed, I whispered to Iola, "I love you." I needed to say those words . . . she was my wife. She wasn't, she was. Wasn't my lover. We shared a bed. She said nothing. Had she fallen asleep? It surprised me when she rubbed my hand. Her silence was fine. I wanted Peter.

We said good night. I turned over and watched the shadows of tree leaves on the window shade. It was windy outside, so the shadows moved a lot. In two weeks Peter would be moving to Boston. He'll be directing the whole research program at one of the best pharmaceuticals in the country. If I had gotten my Ph.D. I'd be doing something like that. But my sister and father had to take some stupid walk in the afternoon and get hit by a car. I had to spend all my college savings on their medical care. Then my father died soon after. Then my sister shot herself. Both of them wasted my hard-earned money. All the guilt, anger, angst gave me a headache and churned my stomach. Hope it works out; I love you, Peter. Damn you. Go to hell. And don't come back. I tried to distract myself by listening to the clock ticking in the dark, and the hushed sound of Iola breathing.

The next morning on the way to work, real calm, I told Peter it was time for him to move back in with his wife. Not much else was said.

Iola

Chapter 40

DURING ONE OF our working lunches, Harry again brought up the topic of parachuting. I pushed back from my desk covered with work and looked out the window at one of the planes landing. He must have recognized my reluctance, as he suggested if anything it would be a way to expand the business by offering parachuting lessons and I should know something about it.

"There's nothing like it around here, for miles. And I could give you another raise. Think about it."

The raise caught my attention. Jim and I now had over five hundred dollars in our savings account. We just bought a new refrigerator, and a new couch and armchair—top of the line, so comfortable to sit in, not that I had the time. Jim was much nicer, although recently he seemed downcast. I worried less, even though it was hard working full time. Some days, I was exhausted. If I could just work as a pilot and give up the secretary job, I'd have a whole lot more energy.

We agreed to let the idea settle but at the end of the day I asked Harry, "Why do you think I'd like parachuting?"

"Because you became a pilot, something women don't normally do. You're pioneering."

It was nice being called pioneering, so I thought I might give it a try.

I told Jim after dinner, and he got annoyed for I'd be risking my life jumping out of a plane. "It's irresponsible. Why, you have children to care for. It's a stupid idea."

"I'd get a raise."

"What good will a raise do if you're dead?"

I said nothing but rubbed my eyes to stay awake.

WE FOUND A small airport that taught parachuting. Harry said it was mostly for my benefit. All he needed was a little brush-up having done it before.

First lesson was how to hit the ground. Kurt, our instructor, said, "Let the ball of your feet hit first, then the side of your calf muscles, the outer thigh, the side of your chest with your arms up and wrapped around your head. Then roll your body." Rolling my body took me right back to Pilgrim and holy rolling. I almost wanted to stop because Pilgrim now had a connection to flying. Maybe Harry saw my surprise for he whispered to me, "It's like holy rolling." His goofy smile assuaged my concerns.

Next was getting fitted with helmets to protect our heads when landing, goggles to keep wind, bugs, or dirt out of our eyes during the descent, and gloves so our hands didn't suffer frostbite at high altitudes. It felt good, like being in the WASP again.

I learned about the main parachute and the reserve and if the main doesn't open, how to deploy the reserve. For the first five jumps, there would be a static line—meaning the ripcord of my chute would be attached to the static line, which would be tied to the plane. Seconds after I jumped out, the static line would pull out my ripcord, and the chute would deploy without me doing a thing. While it sounded easy, it was a risk. What if the static line didn't work?

When hearing about the five jumps, I almost laughed because I figured I'd do it maybe twice at most. I should at least know what it involved, but I'd never try to get certified as an instructor. Plus, Jim would quiet down. He still seemed downcast—and complaining of headaches and stomach upset but he refused to see a doctor. It was worrisome. What if he had cancer? Cancer was an awful way to die. I wasn't wishing his death, but Harry had asked me to marry him. A few times, I almost wished.

Next it was learning how to step out of the plane and how to let go.

"It feels like someone slammed on the brakes real hard when the chute opens. If the harness isn't very snug on you, it'll grab you in the crotch and it hurts, but not so much for a woman." Kurt didn't look at me when he talked about crotches. He pulled a little red flag out of his pocket and said, "After the parachute opens, you need to signal to those on the plane with this here flag. It lets them know you could've pulled the ripcord if there wasn't a static line to do it." Kurt was clean-shaven and had smiled when we first met him. Otherwise he was real serious. I had noticed he had a picture of himself and his four kids on his desk, all of them nice-looking like him—all smiling.

Harry didn't feel he needed the static line, since he wasn't a novice. He talked about the times he parachuted in the war. Kurt never interrupted him and waited until Harry was done talking. He then politely said since it had been some time since Harry's last jump, the lessons would end if we both didn't use static lines. I hid my smile.

On the ground, we practiced falling on landing again and again. We put the main parachute on our backs, and the reserve chute was fitted over our abdomens. Kurt checked everything. He was very professional, likeable, and answered all my questions and then asked if I had any others.

Finally, we were ready to go. While over the drop zone, at an altitude of 6,000 feet, Harry jumped. I ignored my heart palpitations and sweaty hands and jumped. After a few seconds of jarring deceleration, it became quiet. I looked up at my open parachute. As instructed, I gave the little-red-flag signal. It didn't feel like falling. This was above birds, trees, and hills in the middle of the sky with no ground to stand on. There was no altimeter, nor artificial horizon, nor VHF, or VOR, or DME. I might get to like it. Harry was several hundred feet away, waving to me. We both landed with no injuries, except for a few bruises.

I told Jim that night. Just as expected, he looked stunned, then he wrinkled his forehead and narrowed his eyes. "You could have been killed. It's reckless. Irresponsible. You need to think of the kids."

"One is more at risk of dying in a car accident than parachuting. And it could potentially bring in more business and I'd get another raise."

He said nothing the rest of the evening, except a few words to the kids. Then he went out to the garage. What was he going to do out there? He didn't seem like himself. I looked out the window and saw the light was on in Buck's old apartment. I had the thought that he was going to move out there. I could get used to that.

HARRY GOT REAL excited when he bought parachutes for our next jump planned for a couple of weeks. With Kurt present, he practiced packing a parachute. He did everything, step by step, and looked like he knew what he was doing. Kurt said he did an excellent job. He added that one should pack a chute only when you can give it your full attention and have no distractions.

I learned how to pull a ripcord, how to deploy the reserve if the main chute didn't open. There were so many things that could go wrong. But Harry had such enthusiasm and he'd done it before.

We did a fourth and fifth one. My heart no longer beat fast and I no longer got sweaty, but my stomach still got tense. I had progressed to using a ripcord. Everything went perfect. Kurt said, "You're both ready to go. Don't need me anymore."

I lied to Jim about what I'd done. Keeping up with the lies could be hard, so I decided I'd stick to flying. And I did have three children to raise. Plus, parachuting four times had given me enough knowledge that I could talk intelligently to customers. I could help expand the business and I'd get a raise and Jim would be satisfied.

SINCE BUSINESS WAS slow, it was a good day to clean up the office. Two of the employees went home early, leaving the whole airport almost to ourselves. Only the mechanic was there but he was out in the hanger working on a job that needed to be finished soon.

While I sat at my desk and put things in order, Harry pulled up a chair and sat down. He was holding a bag. He pulled a tea candle out of the bag, put it in my empty coffee cup, and lit it. "You look lovely in candlelight." It wasn't the first time his flirtation was unexpected.

Playing hard to get, I stood up and opened the curtain, saying, "Maybe the candle would like some sunlight."

"Poor candle doesn't like sunlight."

"It doesn't? It's a nice looking candle." I sat down. "Tell me about poor candle."

"It loves being lit and shining in the dark." Harry sounded serious.

"But is it happy?" I said more serious.

"When it inspires romance. Poor candle needs some happiness."

"How do we make the poor candle happy?"

Harry picked up the candle, took hold of my hand and led me into his office. He set the candle on his desk. We undressed, and lay down on his daybed and joined together. Nothing was said until we were done.

"Is poor candle happy?" I asked.

"Very happy."

All satisfied, he said a dirty word sweet as ever, and I surprised him and said one. He said a dirtier one. I said "front bottom," thinking he didn't know what it meant but he did. I never heard of *meat whistle*. He said he'd love to sleep all night with me.

"The only way that could happen is if we're married."

"Since that won't happen right at this very moment, how about parachuting again?"

I couldn't refuse a naked, smiling Harry a sixth jump. "It'll be the last time. Who's going to fly us up?" I asked.

"I'll call a pilot to come in."

"A waste of money."

"So? We'll each have to drive a car to the drop zone and leave one there for later. We'll drive the second car back here." We got dressed.

He pulled out our parachutes to check them. While he was repacking the chutes just to be sure there were done right, I touched his arm and asked, "What if I get divorced? What would you do then?"

He spun around and took hold of me. "Marry you. Make you my business partner."

"How much would it cost to be a business partner?"

"Nothing. I'll even help pay for your divorce."

"I'd lose my children."

"Why?"

"Adultery."

"Anyone know?"

"No one that I know of."

"Claim he's hit you. Lots of times."

"I can't say that. The kids would know I lied. Jim loves them. And what if he lied?"

"You don't know what you want." Harry turned around to finish repacking the chutes. He stopped, and spun around, cupped my face in his hands and said, "This will work out. Listen—this is what you'll have. A man who loves you, who respects your intelligence. A career you love. You can't fight to keep your children?"

"I don't know if I can do this. It would destroy Jim. I can't do that."

"You brought up the topic." He turned away and finished packing the chutes. Without looking at me, he said, "Make up your mind."

THERE WERE CLOUDS on the horizon but they were moving east. The west was clear, as was the weather forecast for the day.

We put on our chutes and checked that everything was correct. Well out of view of the pilot, I kissed him to make him smile.

We boarded the plane. As the plane climbed into a blue sky, Harry apologized for getting angry earlier. "Forgive me?"

I took a hold of his hand. "Tell me something."

He talked about his time in World War II and being stationed near Oran, Algeria, and then at Youks-les-Bains, and again in Italy where he got shot and had almost gotten captured. "Later I got captured."

"The Italians?"

"You captured me."

I groaned, smiled. "Umm." He gave me a quick intimate pat, making sure the pilot didn't see.

He repeated what I had to do from jump to landing.

"I'm fine to go." I hoped there would be no problem but I worried too much.

Soon the pilot yelled out that we were six thousand feet up and over the drop zone. When the door of the plane was opened, the wind made it almost impossible to hear anything. I could barely hear Harry say, "You ready?" He looked happy.

"Ready as ever," I yelled.

"Wait ten seconds after I jump and then follow." Harry stepped to the open door, and was gone.

I jumped, and after five seconds of free-fall, I pulled my ripcord. I gritted my teeth for a hard opening. My head jerked forward and then backward as the parachute deployed above me. It got very quiet. I fell into a sigh of relief. I looked for Harry whose chute still had not opened. It was supposed to be open by now.

Harry kept falling and falling.

My heart pounded so fast I feared it would give out. Open it, open it, Harry. I watched long second by long second as his body became a little speck and no parachute, not even his reserve chute, ever opened. He hit ground. I closed my eyes. When I opened them, a person was running over to him—he took forever.

I screamed but it got sucked up into my parachute. A terror struck through me. I got sick to my stomach and threw up. Part of it landed on the front of my shirt and the rest floated away. It was uncomfortable seeing my vomit messing up the sky. Did anyone else ever defile the sky? Then I had an overwhelming fear for my own survival, for my children, and for hour-long seconds I went through Harry's directions: Pull your knees together and keep your feet together. Hit the balls of your feet, the meaty part of your body—your side, your calf muscles, your outer thigh, hip, and your arms wrapped around your head. Bend your legs a little, and don't let your joints hit the ground. Then roll. We don't want you to get a broken leg. It happens sometimes. When you hit, it hurts but if you do it right you don't get injured. Don't let your joints hit. Harry had a wonderful voice and a deep laugh. The man was gentle. We don't want you to get a broken leg. It happens sometimes. We don't want you to get a broken leg. A broken leg. It happens. Tell me you're okay. Harry. Please. Harry please get up, get up. I remembered I was supposed to land with my canopy facing into the wind.

I held my breath and hit the ground, landing a distance from where Harry lay. I landed as instructed. The ground was cold. I shivered but managed to get up and unbuckle my parachute harness with trembling hands. My whole body felt chilled. I tried to run over to Harry. My legs were weak. I stopped and couldn't breathe. I had to catch my breath. My stomach cramped. I walked holding my stomach, limping, fearful, panicked, with my hands shaking, my cries stuck in my throat. My heart beat fast and my legs shook. I tripped and fell, got up and cried until I finally got to Harry.

Something wasn't right. One of his legs was so broken that the sole of his foot was facing him. He wasn't moving. Blood was coming out of his nose and mouth. His helmet was cracked and broken. There was a pool of blood on the ground underneath his head.

"He's not dead, is he? Tell me he's not dead," I pleaded with the man who had run to his aid. My lips tremored; my voice cracked.

The man shook his head. As best as he could, he covered the body with his jacket. "I'm sorry. No one survives a fall like that."

"Oh, God. Why didn't his chute open?"

"He got a cigarette roll. Maybe he didn't pack it right. Maybe he misrouted the cable and reserve or maybe it was defective. My hunch—it was defective. A total malfunction. Second time I've seen it happen. I'm sorry. Be thankful yours opened."

I wanted to lie on the ground next to his body and touch him, but that would tell the world we had loved each other. I trembled and cried.

The police came and they took his body away. It left a slight indentation in the earth, still moist from a rain the night before. After the police finished talking to me, I drove Harry's car to the office and watched my hands rummage through Harry's desk to find his brother's phone number. Since he lived in England, I had to figure out how to dial out of the country. Listening to my weak voice sound like someone else's, I told the brother what happened. He cried. I cried, not something I often did. He said he loved Harry. I had to keep my love secret; I said he was a good boss.

I sat huddled and cold, wanting to quit my job, but to whom could I quit? To whom could I leave a letter of resignation? Tim, the mechanic, asked if he could help me. I said nothing and then finally, "No, thank you." I fell into a fog.

"I can't fly today. I'm sorry," I managed to tell a student who arrived several hours after the accident. He had once told me I was an excellent teacher. After hearing what had happened, he asked if he could help me in some way. I stared and turned away. A minute of silence, then he wrote a note—*Please call me if I can help*—and he left. I wanted Harry to walk in and say it was a bad practical joke. He's going to walk in. He'll be wearing his khaki pants. He'll say he loves me. He hands me a fancy pastry. He says Iola O. I want him to. He's dead. I had to hide my tears.

Dusk gave me some direction. I drove toward home, away from home down a road, any road would do. There was no place to go. Somehow I found myself by a field with two black-and-white cows standing still. The setting sun was behind them—oranges, reds, red clouds. Too much color. I wanted grays, shadows, and dullness. I wanted a thick door to shut, to lock myself in.

I drove up Stenton Avenue, to Blue Bell Road, down Route 9, to Walton Road, to Sandy Hill Road, going way out of my way into Nortontown because Harry liked where he grew up, back down into Conshohocken. I found a place to park by the Schuylkill River, dark and swollen with rain from the day before. I would drown quickly if I jumped in, but suspicions would arise—for a boss she killed herself? Something must've been going on. I drove on, into Philadelphia and then Fairmont Park and sat there. Maybe hours. A robber, a murderer could come by and make me the victim of a heinous crime. *I caused Harry's death. I did. I did. Did he know? Was that his last thought?* I left my door unlocked and waited. It was cold. Too cold. A car drove up and parked beside me. I wasn't scared. *Murder me. I won't resist.* But it was only a boy and girl on a date. I have children. One, two, three. They haven't eaten dinner. Lizzy loved being held. I felt old, near death; I drove home and took out some steaks for dinner.

Jim said everyone had already eaten. He asked why I was late.

"Parachuting accident. Harry Olson died. His chute didn't open." I started tenderizing the meat with a wooden tenderizer.

"Were you parachuting too?"

"Yes."

"I said it was dangerous. You risked your life. What's wrong with you?"

"I won't be doing it again."

"We've already eaten."

I pounded and pounded on the steaks until they looked like chopped meat. Half of it went flying. Bits of flesh were splattered on the wall, ceiling, my blouse. Every once in a while I'd say, "He died. It didn't open."

"What are you doing?" Jim looked wide-eyed and fearful; it was too much to absorb, so I turned away.

"Making dinner." Tears wet my face.

"You need to get a hold of yourself. It's not like one of our kids died. He was only your boss. I can understand tears but you're getting crazy. What's wrong with you?" Oppressive silence filled the kitchen. Jim took the children to their rooms.

The meat that stuck to the ceiling stayed there. I cleaned the wall.

Next evening, I made dinner. "Lizzy, help set the dinner table. You're a good girl. You give me no problem."

"Yes, Mommy."

"You're so pretty. I love you, dear. One, two, three, four, five . . . one, two, three, four, five."

"Mommy, why do you count?"

"Because I need to." I sensed concern in her voice.

"Why do you need to?"

"I don't know why, dear. No idea. Don't ask me questions."

At Harry's funeral, all I did was count in my head—one, two, three, four, five . . . one, two, three, four, five.

AT HOME, I never opened the front door unless I first looked outside to see who was or wasn't there. My fear was that the police would come by and arrest me for causing Harry's death. Before the accident, I had told him about the time I had been ordered by my mother to never talk about Zeke's murder or something evil would happen to me, sooner or later. If I had kept my mouth shut Harry would still be alive.

I didn't say much and didn't disagree or agree with anyone. My small talk and all my opinions vanished. I forgot what laughter was. Being responsible, I found a job as a secretary. I spoke, typed, took notes, ordered supplies, mimeographed, greeted. Hello, goodbye. You're welcome. I'll do that right now. Can I help you? My boss might've given me a lewd once-over every day, but I barely noticed. He might've stopped. My smiles were an effort. I ate my lunch at my desk, while ordering supplies or talking to customers. One day, near quitting time, I called home and spoke to Charles. I told him I had to work late. He said, "Okay. I'll tell Daddy." He was a good boy.

"WHY YOU TAKING it so hard?" Jim asked. "It's not like he was family. I've never seen someone grieve so hard for a boss." He looked at me strange like he wanted to ask more questions, like he was suspecting something.

"Am I taking it hard?" I sensed his suspicion. Covering myself, I said, "It was just awful to see. Awful. The way his body looked. Blood coming out of him. And realizing it could've happened to me." It made me nauseous to talk about it, but I didn't want Jim to know and then divorce me and take the children. I'd be left with nothing. All for naught.

Weeks later, I cleaned the meat off the ceiling.

ONE MONDAY, AFTER I got home from work, I noticed a police car driving up my driveway. I got scared but walked to the clothes tree, put on my coat, and opened the door. The policeman looked familiar. He asked me if I knew Buck Boggs.

"He's my brother."

"You're Iola?" He took his cap off.

"Yes." A chill stung me, in spite of my winter coat.

"I'm sorry, ma'am, but he was killed in a car crash in Arizona. Your name and address were in his belongings. In this envelope is some information. It was a one-car accident. His car slammed into a tree. He likely died on impact. It's assumed he was drinking—there was an empty whiskey bottle in his car. Here's a phone number you can call for more information and where his body is. I'm very sorry, ma'am."

"When did it happen?" Wasn't that a reasonable question? It shouldn't arouse suspicion.

"One week ago. If you have any questions later, give me a call at the police station. I'm sorry." He left.

I looked at him getting into his shiny clean police car, and backing out my gravel driveway. I watched until his car disappeared from sight. So Buck died in Arizona. He was the only one in my family who still visited me after I became a WASP. He had congratulated me and told me I was the best. I stood there in the doorway, with my limp hands at my sides. It wasn't right.

When the neighbor across the street pulled into his driveway, I closed my door, stood and looked at the beautiful front door that lied and said this was a beautiful house. But it wasn't a beautiful house. It was ugly.

"I'm packing my bags," I said to my ugly house.

In ten minutes, I packed some essentials, whatever was nearest. I got within a few feet of the beautiful door and stopped. Where to go? Everything looked awful.

"Where are you going? I want to come with you." Lizzy looked concerned, shaking her hands by her sides.

I threw down my bags, and picked them up again. I wanted to leave. I turned around in a circle several times, dropped my bags and then walked into the small room off the kitchen. I latched the door, took off my coat, and lay down on the wooden floor. It was comforting. I got up and lay down again. My head was pressed against the floor.

My view under the door encompassed the kitchen-table legs, the bottom of the cabinets, and the refrigerator. There was crud on the floor. I should've done a better job sweeping. Dinner was cooking in the oven in an old cast-iron pot. It didn't matter. If it burned it wouldn't cause the house to burn down. Maybe smoke up the house and scare Lizzy. I got up, opened the door, and turned off the oven. I returned to the room and latched the door. A potato chip was on the floor.

Jack and Jill fell down the hill and the world tumbled on them.
Jack and Jill died and their home collapsed.

Footsteps. Please, no footsteps. Had Lizzy followed me into the kitchen? I lay down again on the cool floor and looked under the door. Her bare feet were visible. What does she want?

"Mommy, Mommy," Lizzy called.

She tried to open the door. She lay down and our eyes met. I'd never seen her that way.

"Go away." I turned over. My mind wasn't working. Something smelled like cabbage cooking in bleach. Why did I cook cabbage in bleach? I'd never done it before.

Is that someone crying? It's so far away. Who's crying? The question sputtered. A word or two dangled out of my mouth trying to find a simple sentence. I fell in on myself to a dark space. My heart pumped out a haze of confusion to every ugly vein in my ugly body. I was bugged out, sinking into the clutches of evil and the arms of grief.

There was a noise happening off in a distance. Something not important; it could be ignored—like a rooster crowing on a lousy farm a half mile away in a small town with a lousy plane buzzing off in the cold distance going nowhere. I didn't want to see a plane ever again.

I whispered. "L, Li, Lizzy? Baby. Knocking. Is. Someone knocking? Someone. Knocking. On. The door." Was that a sentence? It took so long to string the words together. My energy vanished. Why? Was I sinking into the floor?

The clock struck and I no longer heard Lizzy crying or the neighbor's dog barking. My mind opened up into an emptiness that wasn't painful and kept welcoming me as much as I'd fall into it. There was no bottom to hit, to hurt. Whoosh. I could feel a pressure against my legs. Whoosh. A pressure against my back, against my head, like a strong wind taking me away. Was it my breath? My lungs heaved air in and out . . . in and out . . . Why . . . Why? One, two, three, four, five.

Jim

Chapter 41

IT WAS LATE when I got home. The lights were on all over the house but there was no dinner saved for me. Charles was sleeping on the sofa. He woke up and said he made dinner—peanut butter sandwiches for himself and his sisters.

"Where's your mother? She didn't make dinner?"

"She locked herself in the room off the kitchen. There's something in the oven but it's not cooked."

I knocked on the door and asked Iola to open it. Not getting any answer, I yanked on the door. I knocked harder and yelled, "Open up, Iola. What's wrong with you?" Nothing stirred. Not a sound. My heart pounded, my hands shook. I banged on the door.

As fast as possible, I knocked the pins out of the door hinges and took off the door. She was lying on the floor, was warm to the touch, and breathing. After being nudged several times, she opened her eyes and said, "Go away. Buck died. Police told me."

"Come to bed. It's getting late. We'll talk in the morning. You can't lie on the floor. What's wrong with you?"

She curled up in a fetus position and mumbled something like fuck you.

I got a cot from the basement, opened it up, and managed to get her up on it. I covered her with a blanket, but she threw it off.

In the morning, Iola was in the same position. I told her it was time to get up; I had to go to work. Her body looked stiff and her head was bent to the side. The cot she was lying on was barely long enough for her. Her hands ran along the sides of the cot as if she was trying to feel what it was. She took a while getting up. With her hand against the wall, getting her balance, she stood. Her mouth agape, she stared at the door that was off the hinge.

"I took it off. You wouldn't unlock the door. I wanted to be sure you were okay."

The sun was shining through the curtainless window. She was still wearing the same pink dress she had on the night before. She whispered slowly, like she was talking to herself, "I almost walked away . . . last night . . . into the woods." She laughed and then cried. Her dress was full of wrinkles and dried perspiration. She looked stiff when she walked. I never heard her laugh and then cry before.

"Buck was killed in Arizona." Her voice was monotone.

"Yes, you told me. I'm sorry. You said fuck you. I never heard you say that."

"I don't remember."

"I'm glad you woke up. I was getting ready to take you to the hospital." I noticed that her dress was stuck in the crack of her butt. She walked like she didn't notice. I pulled it loose. She didn't seem to notice.

"I'm fine." She sat down, and stared off into space.

Starla helped me make eggs for everyone. She burned the toast and cried. I scraped the toast, smeared it with butter and grape jelly. "No problem." I took a bite. "It's good, sweetie."

Iola said she wasn't hungry, but she ate a few bites. "Thank you."

The way she looked—messy hair, her wrinkled dress, blank eyes, downturned mouth—was more than worrisome.

Starla asked, "What's wrong?"

"Everything, I've ever wanted, I've lost," Iola said.

"You have me." Starla looked like she was ready to cry. "You didn't lose me." Iola cried.

Lizzy's eyes widened, her mouth dropped open. "Don't cry, Mommy."

Charles, his eyes wide open too, kept looking at me.

Iola sat at the table doing nothing. I took her hand and pulled a little. I tried to get her to go to bed and rest, but she wouldn't move. I asked if she would like to take a ride in the country. Would she like to go to work? It was one of her workdays. I offered to call and let her boss know she would be late. Would she like to sit on the porch? Would she like to talk? What would she like? "Please tell me what's wrong." She laid her head on the table. I called her boss and said she was sick. I called my boss and said I had a family emergency and would be late. Norma was nice and babysat the kids.

"Don't leave, Daddy. Don't go," Lizzy cried out as I took Iola to the car and drove off to the hospital. Was my family falling apart?

Philadelphia, Pennsylvania
1955

Iola

Chapter 42

I WOKE UP with a muddled recollection of the day before, everything coming undone, my mind not working. There was a doctor with bad breath who had asked me questions, and two patients at the table with me in the dining room had argued with each other about something. The staff had to come over and separate them.

Being hungry, I looked forward to breakfast. The coffee and eggs were lukewarm. Afterward, a nurse came and took me to a room where six staff sat around a table and asked me questions.

"Do you know why you're here?"

"I wasn't doing well yesterday."

"Tell us more about how you were yesterday."

"Not well. Very tired. More than I've ever been."

"Tell us about that."

"Being tired?"

"Yes."

"I was too tired to move, to say a word. I had no energy."

"Are you thinking of hurting yourself?"

"Why would I do that?"

"You need to tell us. We're asking you."

"I need to tell you why I would hurt myself? I'm not going to hurt myself."

"Have you ever?"

"No. And I've never been asked that before."

"You were doing very poorly."

"I had a very bad day. Everyone has a bad day or two."

"Not like that. We're concerned you were catatonic."

The questions went on and some staff asked questions that had already been asked. Someone said I needed to stay in the hospital and meet with Dr. Athens for fifty minutes, five days a week. They assigned me to treatment activities without asking me what I might like.

After lunch, a tall skinny orderly with a pleasant face and voice led me to Dr. Athens's office. There was a technical-looking book on his desk. It was perhaps a half inch thick and had a gray cover. The title was *Diagnostic and Statistical Manual of MENTAL DISORDERS*. The two words in capital letters made it obvious what its main focus was.

Dr. Athens introduced himself and instructed me to lie down on the couch and "Speak any thoughts that come to you, as if no one is listening. Say whatever comes to mind."

I didn't know what to say and just lay there for a while thinking about the words in caps. I didn't talk and neither did he, but he seemed okay with the silence. I didn't wonder aloud why all my hard work had come to nothing. I thought of Peter Blythe who Jim had dragged home. Then Norma, then Oak Tree Road, my children, my hatred of Pilgrim, dead Buck, Zeke's murder, how good he was to me, reading me stories, drawing my picture. What sense did life make?

The hour was up. Dr. Athens smiled and said it was a good first session.

It was? How was that? I didn't ask.

I met more patients in the day activity room. Old and young, male and female. Some busybodies wanted to know my business. Did I have children? Had I tried to kill myself? Did my husband leave me? Did my children die? Did I hear voices? A young red-haired man drooled and didn't seem to be aware that his shirt looked a mess. There were two patients, each claiming to be Jesus. A small man made no sense at all when he talked. A well-dressed woman with blond bouffant hair said all she had now was her past, now that her mother died. She wrung her hands, and asked me, "Why are you here?" Her eyes blinked numerous times.

"Because everything about Amelia Earhart shriveled up into ugly," I said.

"She disappeared a long time ago. She's probably dead."

"I was talking about her influence."

"That doesn't make sense."

"Does to me."

"If you don't make sense you'll be in this crazy place for years." The woman giggled for way too long.

I didn't like being hospitalized but liked the lack of responsibilities. It was the closest I'd ever come to having servants. No cooking, cleaning, doing laundry. Ironic. In an odd way, the change of scenery seemed to give me some strength.

In the next session with Dr. Athens, I said little but he seemed okay with it. I slept for ten hours that night and awoke refreshed.

Next day, Dr. Julius Smith introduced himself. He said he was a psychologist and he needed to evaluate me. I had never been evaluated before, except for job interviews. We walked down a hall to a little room with no window. It had a long table, two gray metal chairs, a bookcase, and stark white walls.

"I'll be giving you a test that involves lots of little tests. Just try your best," he said. I had to put together some puzzles within time limits. It seemed easy as I quickly developed a strategy. The challenge helped me focus. I asked how I did, but he said he'd let me know afterward.

Dr. Smith asked me a series of questions such as how are a brother and a sister alike. They seemed easy to answer. Then it was naming all the animals I could in one minute. I named all the farm animals I could think of, then all the birds, all the big cats, snakes, African animals, all the ones around Pilgrim, some rodents, some fish. He wrote fast, and looked surprised. He asked me questions such as who was Louis Pasteur and where was Niagara Falls. I recognized most of the names. Next I was asked to define a list of words. They were all familiar except for *acclivity*. I knew *quotidian* means every day, daily. I figured it was a harder word to define. I had just read the word in a magazine in the day activity room and looked it up in a dictionary that was on a shelf. I didn't say it was pure luck.

After lunch, I met again with Dr. Athens. Since talking about something was expected, and it would probably help get me discharged, I talked about Charles, Starla, and Lizzy. I talked about Norma's bruised face and bruised legs and how I despised Ron—Norma's husband. "In fact, I hate him. I don't care if it's bad to hate." Buck and all his drinking, good carpentry, and playing guitar, and his fine tenor voice were next.

The weekend came and nothing significant happened except Jim visited and I told him I didn't like being with all the crazies. "It makes me feel worse."

"I called Dr. Athens yesterday. He said you need several months of treatment. Do you know you looked awful last Tuesday?" Jim asked.

"Really? I think I just needed a week of doing nothing. Do you know what it's like to feel completely exhausted? It's like being hit by a truck."

"I was worried you were going to die."

"Oh. I'm alive. No worry." I smiled and moved my hands to demonstrate.

ON MONDAY, DR. Smith gave me more tests. On one, I had to look at pictures and describe anything I saw in them. I saw foxes running and owls flying where there were splotches of color. I saw Buck in one but I said it looked like a man running with an animal. Some areas looked like clouds and planes and trilliums in the woods and the horizon of the earth. One little detail looked like a whippoorwill. Another like pawpaws. Another like a dead man. That bothered me but I managed to stuff it in my gnawed-up spot, which had shrunk in size. Mostly, I said whatever came to my mind. With another test, I had to look at some other pictures and tell a story about each of the pictures. In one picture, a man looked like he was in a city and was carrying something. I said the man had shot and killed someone years ago. That made me cry. When I was done crying, I apologized and said I was real tired and had enough. The doctor asked if I would talk about the man who was killed.

"What man?"

"The one you saw in the picture."

"I was just thinking of all the innocent people who don't get justice. Don't make too much of it."

"What about your tears?"

"I guess I was crying about my brother, Buck. He had talent . . . but his life. He died in a car accident. We were close." Buck's death allowed me to cry for Harry.

NEXT SESSION WITH Dr. Athens, I talked about cleaning Mrs. Atwater's house before I got married and how Mrs. Atwater had given me old dresses with seams coming apart, leftovers to eat, and meager pay. A few words were said about walking for a mile as a kid to visit cousin Alma, with the radio, how sweet she was to me. Jim and his cousin, Frank, got mentioned. I asked Dr. Athens if he thought there was something wrong with me, and he said, "How would it make you feel if I thought you had something wrong with you?"

"Relieved because I'd hate to be here otherwise." I smiled. Realizing I could be funny helped me feel better, and feeling better had to mean I was getting better. But I didn't share that, because Dr. Athens would probably disagree.

He said nothing, much less smile. Had he even thought it was funny? Had he hidden a smile? Something was wrong with him. Was he short on humor? Did I even like him? I asked if I had a mental problem, and if so, what was the name of it.

"The name doesn't matter."

"Every doctor I ever knew would tell a patient what illness they had."

"Well. Since you phrase it that way—depressive reaction and inadequate personality."

I said nothing but knew a response should be given. After a while, I said, "Ohh. That makes sense." One thing obvious, I was no wallflower and inadequate personalities don't fly planes and get in the WASP. He might've been believable if he said too much hard work all life long. In my thoughts, I gave myself my own diagnosis—grief over the death of the best man I ever loved in my life. Yes, it was grief. That put things in perspective; I wanted to get out of the hospital. I also didn't want to eat meals and do day activities with crazy people who talked nonsense, looked deranged, walked in circles with deadpan blank faces, laughed for no reason, and pulled out their hair. I didn't have the energy but I had the memory of a strong will, and the memory upped my strong will, which gave me some energy to force myself to move along.

Aunt Pleasant had once told me, "Sometimes, you have to just pretend you're happy and soon enough you'll get out of the doldrums." At the end of the session, I said, "Thank you, Dr. Athens. I understand things better." Buried under my breath, out of hearing distance, I diagnosed him—inadequate asshole. Yes, things were making sense.

Wednesday, Dr. Smith told me that the results of one of the tests indicated I was extremely smart and was in the top range of intelligence, meaning I was smarter than about ninety-eight percent of the population.

"What good does that do me?"

"What good do you think it might do you?"

"Darned if I know. That's why I asked." I was close to having a poor opinion of the doctor. When he was done talking to me, it couldn't have suited me better.

Out of sheer desperation, I decided to follow Aunt Pleasant's advice. I smiled even if I didn't feel like it. My mood improved a tad. Then I pretended for a whole minute that I was actually happy. Like kids getting into fantasy. I was happy to be alive, to see the tan, white and beige and pale blue colors in the room, to look out the window at the pretty tree with the fat squirrel running across a branch, to bend over and tie my white tennis shoe that had come untied. I tied a pretty bow. Such clever hands I had. Dogs can't tie shoelaces. Poor things. It helped if I pretended it was a game, or I was on stage. It worked, for all my worries seemed to melt away.

But they soon came back and I couldn't do it again, so I tried to do it for thirty seconds. No success but I was able to do it for ten seconds while looking out the window, which helped a bit, which then helped me do it for twenty seconds. It was like I was turning myself inside out, wringing out my grief inch by inch, spot by spot. I imagined my grief dropping away, and a bit of calm settled over me. I tried it for a few minutes, every so often. In between, I'd feel how much I missed Harry. But all in all it wasn't an awful day. Life moves forward. Dead things decay. Who doesn't have loss?

The next day, my grief resurrected strong as ever. But I knew that grief would only keep me in the hospital, and my priority was getting out. I imagined it dropping away again and sinking in a deep blue lake, making wide shiny ripples that went far away from me and got smaller and smaller and disappeared. I imagined letting go of everything—my grief for Harry, my blaming myself for his death and for Buck's death, my home, my family, all my dreams and wishes, even my exhaustion. A fear arose in me that I'd lose myself—my body, my heart, my brain, who I was—Iola Lewis, born as Boggs, grew up in ugly eensy Pilgrim. I talked to myself in my thoughts to find some courage to not resist if my heart, my brain, my body disappeared, if all of me disappeared. Why not give it a try? Soon a deep peace settled in and I was still alive. Iola—still here. Iola. Oh my, oh wow, so interesting. I got up and walked to the window. I had made myself better even though Harry, the best man I ever knew, was no more. Iola O, he had called me.

Emmeline, my roommate with the bleached hair and high-pitched voice, came in and said, "Ma'am." She called all the women ma'am, even the nurses. "You know why I went loco?" She didn't wait for an answer. "I came home unexpectedly and found my husband in my bed with another man. I could've handled a woman. But a man? Just the thought of me lying in bed with him, knowing where his you-know-what had been. Dirty. Too dirty for me. I couldn't handle that. I cried for two days, feeling like I'd been sleeping in feces. Couldn't stop crying. My sister brought me here. It tore me apart. Then it occurred to me—he never did seem interested in sex. When we did have it, it was over quick. What would you do if you found your husband in bed with a man? You have a husband. I saw him visit you. Would you kill him? After I stopped crying, I wanted to. Been married to a pervert. If I had remembered his rifle was in the garage, I would've killed him." She pretended she had a rifle in her hand and took aim at the wall. "Take this. Pow, pow." She narrowed her eyes. "Pow. Pow."

I didn't know what to say. "I'm sorry" served the moment. Zeke was killed because he was caught doing sex stuff with a man. He was good to me, talked nice to me, gave me some books, and a map of the United States, said I was smart. We were going to leave home together for Chicago.

Emmeline said talking about her husband made her tired, so she lay down on her bed and took a nap.

I left and walked to the day treatment area and saw the man who drooled, the two Jesus impersonators, the well-dressed hand-washer, the crybaby, and some other crazies. To myself I said, I loved Harry but he was gone and I had to go on with my life. I had no choice. It was better at home. My three children. Then I got a question I never had before—was Jim homosexual? I wasn't sure what to do. He never seemed much interested in sex either and he liked to primp like a woman does—in front of a mirror, making sure his hair was just right, and his eyebrows were combed, his tie perfect. And I couldn't remember him ever flirting with women. What would I do if he was? Why had I never thought about it? Maybe I had. Zeke was . . . and Uncle Edgar killed him right in front of me. Too many painful memories to deal with. I had shut them out. I'd never kill Jim, if only to make amends for Zeke. I had no need to kill him, nor plan, nor reason.

In my next session with Dr. Athens, I said my appetite was returning. I had more energy, felt more sociable, and looked forward to a visit from Jim. I didn't tell him about my letting-go-of-everything treatment that had given me a deep peace, or my questions about Jim.

At the end of the session, he said the results of some of the tests I'd been given by Dr. Smith indicated I had some deep troubles and I would benefit if I talked about them.

"What kind of troubles?"

"That's what we are here to find out."

Next time with Dr. Athens, I talked about Jim—that he rarely said anything good about me. I asked what the doctor thought about that and he asked me what Jim's lack of compliments meant to me.

Just to see if I could get a reaction from him, I said, "It means he doesn't compliment. Maybe I'll ask him."

Dr. Athens mostly listened. He finally said people hold back feelings for lots of reasons. "Didn't you say one time that Jim had a girlfriend before he met you, and she had left him? Might that have affected his relationship with you?"

"I suppose it might've. Do I love him?" I figured he might be wondering that. "No."

"What would you do if you left Jim? Do you think things would get better?"

"I wasn't thinking that. He's my children's father."

ON THE WEEKEND, Jim visited. We took a walk around the hospital. There were colorful flowers in the garden, and two blue jays squawking venom at each other. Jim gave me a watch—the first present in how long? I didn't tell him it was funny because I didn't need one at the hospital, as the nurses and orderlies were always announcing when it's time for whatever. Since I currently had no household chores, or job, I didn't have to look at any watch to know when to start dinner or take some dish out of the oven.

I said, "You used to give me lots of presents before we got married."

"Did I? I guess so. Isn't that the way things are done during courtship?"

"I suppose."

We sat down on a bench. "I want to see my children. I'm ready to go home."
Jim seemed surprised when I asked him if he would he get me out of there.

"How do I do that?"

"Drive me home. You drove me here. There was no reason for it. I would've
been fine if I had a week of doing nothing. Just plain nothing. Zero. I think I
just needed good sleep and nothing to do. I was exhausted. And then Buck's
death. I don't know why it affected me so."

"Well, shouldn't we first talk with your doctor?"

We sat awhile, saying nothing.

Jim broke the silence and said, "You got a phone call this morning from a
Mike Howard at the airport. He wanted to know if you might want to buy the
airport. He and another employee want to buy it and they thought you might
want to go in with them on it. I didn't tell him where you are. I said you were
on a trip and I'd give you his message. I wrote it down. But I forgot to bring it."

"Flying again doesn't interest me."

"He didn't ask that. He wanted to know if you'd like to go in on buying the
airport with them."

"I don't know why I would do that."

"What do you want me to say if he calls again?"

"Say no thank you . . . I guess. You have a better idea?"

He slid over right next to me—that had to have meant he missed me. It was
nice being missed.

"You know what helps me feel better? Not dwelling on problems," he said.
He stretched his legs out. His shoes were polished, like always.

"Yes. You're right, and it's when I do things even if I have to force myself.
Anything—walk around the hospital grounds; help my crazy roommate make
her bed. I sweep our room. It's going forward; otherwise you sink. And when I
look at the sky and squirrels and birds and feed them toast from breakfast. The
eggs here are awful, but I eat them."

It was unexpected when Jim suddenly asked me what I felt about death. It
was not something I expected. I sighed; he sighed and touched my hand.

"It's accepting loss, hard as it is. Nothing's permanent. Buck's death, it wasn't
expected."

He looked like he wanted to talk. Jim sighed again and then said, "It was
awful . . . when my sister died. I loved her. I didn't know what to do. First my
father, and then my sister within a month of each other. Her piano teacher had
predicted she would get a scholarship at the conservatory of music."

Jim looked nice with the sunlight shining on him. His dark wavy hair and
finely chiseled features. It's good to have a handsome husband. He said nothing

like it was my turn, like we were having our own little therapy session about death and grief. "My brother, Henry, was killed by his best friend in a hunting accident. And my sister, Starla, drowned in the river the following year. It was awful. And then Buck." Jim looked sympathetic. It was comforting that somehow I felt closer to him.

When I touched his hand, he shared more. "Some months after my sister passed, my mother and I were talking by the mulberry tree in the backyard. We had both looked at the fallen berries squished underfoot. It looked like splattered blood. We went back in the house. She got out her dust rag and I left and walked down the street and came back with two laborers who cut down the tree. They asked what I wanted done with the wood. I said, 'Take it.' I still remember it all. I hosed down the pathway of mulberry stains. I don't know how I . . ." He rubbed his hand across his mouth.

"How you got through it."

"But I managed—went to work. At home, every tool was oiled and sharpened; doors didn't squeak; windows opened smoothly."

"And your mother?"

"After she got somewhat better, every surface, every pane of glass was clean. The house was spotless, every day." Tension was all over his face, like he was trying to avoid tears. He looked toward the hospital and then the tree above us.

He quivered his leg. "Seems like a long summer. Can't live in the past. School will be starting."

Was he on the verge of tears? Not wanting to see him falling apart at the hospital, I said, "In Pilgrim, summers always stretched on until harvests were done and canning completed. Some years, school started a month late. Book learning was secondary. Reading, writing, and arithmetic was enough. We called it sums."

He gave a nod. Neither of us said anything for a while, but that's what you do in a successful therapy session—be accepting of silence.

He broke the silence. "Lizzy found a black wooly bear caterpillar. Ones with wide golden rings predict a long winter. You like cold weather?"

"Not really." Obviously, the therapy session was over.

"That's right. You like baking in heat." Jim soon went home, after kissing me on the lips.

IN MY NEXT session, I told Dr. Athens I was feeling fine. He agreed I was better.

"That's right. I'm feeling good. I sleep well. I want to go home. I can smile when something funny happens. My children need me."

G.M. Monks

"You're not ready to be discharged. You still have conflicts you need to understand."

"You know best." To myself, he was stupid. For him, I nodded my head.

France
Year Not Yet Known

Iola and Jim

Chapter 43

Jim

SINCE IT WAS warm and sunny, Iola suggested we walk outside on the hospital grounds. She pointed out a chattering squirrel up in a sycamore tree and a dove cooing on a windowsill. When we came to a well-manicured garden with flower-lined paths and benches, we sat down. A crumpled hanky lay on the ground near her foot. She said a new patient, who cried a lot and was always pulling hankies out of her pocket, likely dropped it. That didn't sound like something to talk about, so I mentioned Charles, Starla, and Lizzy and how they were getting along with each other because I told them it was extremely important. I said Norma didn't charge much for babysitting. "She sends you her best."

Iola offered me a cookie that she had saved for me. I broke it in two and gave her half. I missed her.

Iola

I WONDERED IF he was homosexual. If he was, that might explain everything.

"Things have definitely taken a different turn," Jim said. "You being here, you know . . . Sorry, that didn't come out the way I meant it."

"I understand. Did you know too much treatment can cause problems of its own? It's making me feel sad again. I want to go home and take care of my children. I'm tired of crazy people. I want to go home."

"Didn't your doctor say you're not ready?"

"He's ignorant and I said I'm going home. I'm in charge of Iola. I'll walk if I have to."

"What do you mean—you're in charge of Iola?"

"Means I'm walking home in a few minutes if you don't drive me."

"It would be real dark by the time you get there."

"I've walked in the dark."

He said nothing, like he was thinking. Suddenly we heard some screaming. We looked up at a window and saw a patient grabbing the bars on the window. "Time-out room," I said.

He touched my hand and said, "They shouldn't let the public see that. It's not a place I'd want to be. Do you want to get your things in your room?"

"I have what I need. We can leave now."

"What about the watch I gave you?"

I pulled it out of my pocket. He seemed amused when I pulled several pairs of underwear out of my other pocket and said, "I have what I need." I smiled and we got in our car and left.

"Are you going to be okay?" He looked concerned.

"I'll be okay. I wouldn't be if I stayed there another day." Halfway home, it seemed like a good time to ask. It required a tactful voice. Anything judgmental would be unproductive. "By the way, before we got married, you had two girlfriends and one died before you could marry her and the other . . . I think you said your mother didn't like her. Were you mean to me all these years because you were afraid I'd die on you too or leave in some way?" I said *mean* with intentional hesitation, and a softer voice. "You know, to protect your feelings. People do that sometimes. Self-preservation, I guess." I tried reading his face.

"I was mean to you?" He gave me a quick glance. "I did fear sometimes you might die. I guess so. I tried not to think about it. Maybe so." He nodded, looked at me again, wasn't smiling but wasn't frowning. His mouth wasn't turned down. Probably was thinking.

His comments struck me as sad. If I had known when we got married, maybe things would've been different. He could've told me, but he kept his fears hidden. Since he was open to my first question, I got courage to ask more. I waited until we got out of Philadelphia and headed toward Willowsburg. In my calmest, most benign voice, I said, "There was another patient in the hospital. Real talkative. Too much. She said her husband never had seemed interested in having sex with her. He never flirted with women. She had thought he was just well behaved. A gentleman. But she went berserk when she found him in bed, doing sex with a man. She lost her mind. I wouldn't lose my mind. Nope." I watched Jim while I was talking. He gripped the steering wheel real hard, making his knuckles turn white. He said nothing, and stared ahead. I stared ahead. There was an oncoming car, a pothole in the road, and another further down. He hit both potholes but avoided the oncoming car.

I wondered if I might regret my words, but I had to ask. "When I was a kid, Zeke, my brother, more favorite than Buck. Zeke was smart and good to me, but he didn't just up and disappear one day like I told you. You want to know what really happened?" I noticed Jim lean far back in his seat like he was bracing himself for disaster.

Jim

I SAID NOTHING and feared what Iola was going to do. She was going to pull my shame out and drown me in it. She was going to turn my life upside down. Most important, I didn't want to lose my kids. I felt sweaty, but my mouth felt dry.

She broke the threatening silence. "Truth is he was beaten up badly by Sledge Jr. and then shot and killed by a drunken uncle. Why—because Sledge caught him on the outskirts of another town doing sex with a man. I don't care he did sex stuff with a man. He was good and the best family I had. He loved me. I was wondering if maybe you were mean because you resented being married to a woman when you preferred men and felt you had to pretend all these years? I'd hate having to pretend I was something I wasn't. Especially something like that. Like a bull having to pretend it likes cows when it prefers bulls. It would certainly mess up an animal. Pardon the analogy. I mean I don't see us as a cow and bull."

Did she say what she just said? I didn't know what to think or what to say. I looked straight ahead like I was looking at confusion, knowing all these years, how I had to trance myself—what else was it? And thinking of all the dirty names for man parts, and thinking I was touching man parts, just to complete sex with her once a month, so no suspicion started. I rarely liked looking at her naked. There were a few times she stirred me.

"And I don't care if you do. I don't care if you go off and have some male date in the evening. I'm wondering now if that's what you did in the evenings when you went off or came home late from work. I don't care if you did it with Peter."

I almost missed a red light and stepped on the brake real quick. Iola hit the dashboard but wasn't hurt. The shock of it got to me and I pulled over to the side of the road and wept for not knowing what to do. Every feeling I ever had seemed to rise to the surface, faster than I could manage. I got concerned because I couldn't stop weeping. Was it my turn to get mental? After a few minutes, I stopped.

Iola

WE JUST SAT there for a while until I said, "It's okay if you had sex with Peter. The people that have been the best to me didn't fit the mold."

He let out a deep sigh. He still wasn't looking at me. Finally he said, "If you tell anyone I'll deny it. I won't hesitate. I'll claim you had sex with Harry. Sometimes, I wondered if you did."

"Are you asking?"

"I figured if you were having sex with Harry I wouldn't have the pressure of having to perform. You know. So I didn't care. Did you?"

"Yes. Me and Harry. You and Peter. Aren't we the couple. Certainly not average." In some way, I was making up for what happened to Zeke. It was taking me further away from Pilgrim. I was living my life like I wanted, making my own way.

Jim

MY GOD. IT was like a long-overdue baptism with the whole Atlantic Ocean sweeping over me like holy water. My wife—I never knew her—how good she was. The whole thing. All the years all caught up in my own shame, trying to be respectable. But here she was—accepting me. Certainly not the average couple. Average? I had craved average. The more I thought about it, the funnier it got. The more ludicrous. It hit me like a funny-boulder rolling right at me. I laughed until I could hardly breathe. The irony of it—I laughed until my eyes teared. She laughed. I started driving again but had to pull over to the side of the road because she kept laughing and I couldn't drive, laughing even more. It was pure. The two of us knew it.

The day was singular. It drained me. My whole life packed into one little hour. A battle had ended. I had won. Iola had.

Doubt soon set in. Was something bad going to happen? Was it crazy? "So what do we do?" It was a dilemma. Keep it secret? Share the same bed? "What about the kids?" I asked.

"What we have is called a marriage of convenience. We raise our kids. When they're all grown up, we can go separate ways. Think about it. Let's go home."

"It's not good if people know."

"Who knows? You can't keep a secret?" She shrugged. "How's Peter doing?"

"He's in Boston."

"Do you miss him?"

"I suppose. Well." I took a deep breath. "Of course."

"You know you can take a trip up there."

The rest of the ride home was quiet. I liked the quiet. I liked her. My God I did. She deserved respect.

When we pulled into our driveway, there was a letter in the mailbox from Frank. Iola read it aloud.

Dear Iola,

We hope you're doing well. We heard you witnessed a horrific accident and then later your brother, to whom you were closest, died. Sometimes everything falls apart. When Sarah was targeted by McCarthy and ended up getting fired from her job, we didn't know what to do. We feared I might be targeted next. But you already know this. I'm thinking of a friend we have. You met her when you came for a visit when our youngest was baptized. She wrote poetry and, if my memory is correct, she was about seventy. Her name was Josephina. She had lived in Poland before World War II started, but she had gone to Paris to be with her youngest sister who was ill and dying. While she was there, Germany invaded Poland and so she stayed in France. A cousin of hers had previously immigrated to the US and lived in New York. After her sister died, he suggested she come and live with him and his family. The Nazis killed all of her family still in Poland. She always talked about the need to move forward, to be flexible. We've kept in touch. If she could survive such a loss, Sarah and I figured we could deal with our setbacks and get our lives going again.

Then luck came our way when a friend introduced Sarah to someone who ended up offering her a teaching position in Paris. It helped that she kept fluent in French and has family here. You helped us so much when I had to sell my bookstore. It was always my dream to own one. The move was difficult. It's good now. I want to share something else. I was in a restaurant and in walks a notable author. He knew the person I was having lunch with. Introductions were made. I told him about my bookstore and the type of books I sell. He came to my store one time and said he'd tell his friends. Business has picked up.

We're happy. Something really good for us has come out of the ugly interruption in our lives. I know it doesn't always happen that way. Interruptions can spiral out of control and it has for some people and they never recover. Always stay open to the possibility

that something good will come out of it. We always liked you.
We know you'll get through these difficulties. Persistence is in your
blood. I knew it when I met you the first time in Philadelphia.
Sarah says to give you her love, as do the children. You and Jim
and your children are most welcome if you would like to visit us.
You'd love Paris. And not intending to be morbid, but we could
take you to the US cemetery in the north of France for the American
soldiers who died in the Normandy invasion. By the way, we were
driving through a town one day and there in the town center was
a statue honoring American soldiers who helped free France from
the Nazis. We'll take you to wherever you want to go.
Our warmest love to you, Jim, and the kids,
Frank and Sarah

"You're not going to go to France, are you?" Jim asked.

"No. I'm not, but I think Starla will go there."

"How do you know that?"

"She said so."

"She did?"

"You were there. You don't remember? The day you picked us up, after the second time I took care of their kids."

"Kids will say anything."

"They do . . . but sometimes they know. Believe me. She acted so sure about it. When Uncle Dillard took me on my first plane ride, I knew I wanted to learn to fly. I knew it would happen. Someway. Somehow. Sometimes things happen like that. Starla loved Frank and especially little Jeannette. When I helped Frank with his move, she was fascinated with things in his house—objects from China and France and England. He had music from countries all over the world. He taught her some French. She learned fast. He bought her French pastries and French bread. She didn't want them to move."

"You never told me."

"I never did? When she's twenty . . . maybe when she's eighteen, she'll go to France and I'll help her. I'll send her money when I can. I'll learn French if I have to. Bonjour. Au revoir."

"Are you going to keep flying?"

Iola

I FOLDED THE letter and put it back in the envelope. I repeated Jim's question and paused. "I have no desire to. Why would I?" But to myself, I wondered. Maybe I would. Just maybe. Just maybe I would. I went up to our bedroom and put things away that were lying about. In my dresser drawer was the scarf Harry had given me. I picked it up, kissed it, and then put it in a box in the bottom of the closet. I gently pushed the box to the back wall and tried my best to ignore my sorrow. In several months, I'd let myself feel it and maybe, maybe talk about it to Jim. Things needed to settle.

Out the window was a good view of degenerate Lester Causley's field. His wheat was golden under the late afternoon sun making rays through cotton-puff clouds. Like a painting in America where I had worked hard and respected hard workers all my life. Farmers and ditch diggers, physicians and teachers, and storeowners who opened their shops at seven in the morning and closed them seven at night with tired eyes and sore muscles, six days a week. I never stole a thing in my life except for vegetables and apples and a ribbon in someone's trash can and lost change buried in sofas while I sat in waiting rooms. Oh yes, I stole two hundred and forty dollars from Mr. Yalonsky. No one's perfect and he didn't need it. I had brought him good luck and let him flirt.

The children ran in the house when they realized I was home. The four of us squealed. Love you's, love you's flew back and forth.

"It's good to be home," I said. When we all calmed down, I walked into the kitchen, and noticed lying on the countertop, a note in Jim's handwriting, saying, *a Mike Howard called. He wanted to know if you'd be interested in buying the airport with him and someone else.* I folded it and slipped it in my pocket. After a second or two, I took it out, opened a drawer near the phone, put it inside a small box with my address book, and started dinner. Starla set the table.

I said, "*Merci beaucoup.*"

Starla brightened with her widest smile.

Lizzy looked so pretty. She was quiet like usual.

I said, "Very pretty."

Starla said, "*Très jolie.*"

Charles lowered his head and said grace at the dinner table.

I put my head down and said nothing but moved my lips. I wondered why my son had become so religious and hoped he didn't become an alcoholic like his uncle.

Jim said the dinner was very good and he was glad I was home.

At the end of dinner, Starla asked, "Is Cousin Frank ever going to visit us again? I want to see Jeannette."

"Probably not for a long time but he wrote a letter. I'll read it to you," I said

"She won't understand what he wrote," Jim said.

"Sure she will."

"Is she old enough?"

"Of course." I got the letter and read it.

Starla listened to every word and then announced, "I'm going to France when I grow up and you're going to fly me." She twirled in a circle with her arms held high.

I picked her up and held her, looked at her. She smiled. I did. She nodded her head and so did I. And another reciprocal gesture. And another. A two-person drama, a two-person audience. Unspoken plans were made that day.

G. M. Monks grew up in California and lives in the San Francisco Bay Area with her husband. Besides writing short stories, poems, a novel, and creative nonfiction, she loves to travel. She has visited Canada, Australia, Mexico, and many countries in Europe and many states in the US. One of her favorite places is Yosemite. A few of favorite authors include: Alice Munro, Toni Morrison, Ernest Hemingway, Sandra Cisneros, Augusten Burroughs, and Arundhati Roy. Her favorite artists are Georgia O'Keefe and Vincent van Gogh. She is over half fluent in French.

Her work has appeared in: *The Hunger, Vine Leaves Literary Journal, The RavensPerch, Embodied Effigies, Kaaterskill Basin Literary Journal, GFT Press, Kansas City Voices, Picayune, Alehouse*, and elsewhere. She was the runner-up (with publication) in the Big Wonderful Press Funny Poem contest and received an honorable mention in the 2016 New Millennium Writings Award competition. If you want to read more about her, please visit gmmonks.blog.